SING THE MICE

J. Daneway

Library of Congress Control Number: 2021905012

First paperback edition April 2021

Cover design by Todd Klebenow
Interior by KUHN Design Group

ISBN 978-1-7368484-1-8 (print)
ISBN 978-1-7368484-0-1 (ebook)
ISBN 978-1-7368484-6-3 (EPUB)

www.jdaneway.com

For Aunt Bobby, as promised.
And for my husband, for too many reasons.

CHAPTER 1

1982 *Tenuem umbilicus*

"Where have you been, Aline?" my mother asked. She shook my shoulders with fury.

"School?" I wasn't sure how she expected me to answer.

Our extended family lived in Southern Oregon, in a town, if one could call it a town, of a few hundred rural families. The Chaparral climate supported biodiversity consisting of nature, weirdos, weirdos hiding in nature, and pot plants hiding with weirdos in nature. Aside from living in harmony with nature and weirdos, we didn't fit in.

"Don't be smart with me." She pinched the back of my arm.

"What did I do?" I scowled and rubbed the welt forming on my arm.

"School got out at three. Where have you been since? You're supposed to come straight home from the bus stop." She awaited my answer with her hands on her hips.

The school bus dropped me on Lakeshore Drive next to the mailboxes at 3:30. We lived precisely one mile from the stop. One mile equated to a six-minute-and-thirty-second adrenaline-fueled run down an unnamed dirt road that paralleled an unnamed seasonal creek.

"I did come straight home," I said, taking a defensive tone. I took my backpack off and dropped it on a dining chair. A pot simmered on the stove behind Mother—rabbit in wild mustard and Uncle George's experimental wine. I recognized the smell. I'd heard Mother tell Uncle George once that his wine paired well with rabbit. The pantry was full of his wine. She'd not let it go to waste; she'd say until Uncle George perfected his craft, his wine's highest and best use was in a pot blended with other, more palatable offerings. As far as I was concerned, neither the rabbits nor the wine had become more palatable. I cared for the rabbits, gave them names, cleaned their cages, fed them, and I resented that we ate them.

"And what happened to your tights?" She grabbed my arm and turned me around to inspect my previously white tights. "Is that what you've been doing for the last two and a half hours—jumping in puddles?" She shook her head with disapproval. "Aline, we talked about this. You come straight home from the bus stop. Otherwise, how will I know if you even got on the bus?"

"I did come home," I whined.

She cocked her head to the side. "Are you saying you weren't playing in puddles? Your tights got muddy by themselves?"

"It was an accident. I ran home. Please believe me?" I had stepped in puddles, but I hadn't been playing. I'd been running the puddle-pocked dirt road as fast as my legs would carry me. But no matter how hard I tried, I could never have kept the tights clean, with or without puddles. The tights were Mother's special booby trap. I knew as soon as she pulled them out in the morning that I'd have a lecture coming.

"Maybe you *aren't* old enough to be in school," she said and narrowed her gaze on me.

It was a false threat, pulling me from school. I had entered the public school system with considerable hassle on her part and personal embarrassment on mine. With my youthful appearance and much smaller-than-average height, the administrators had accused my parents of forging my birth records to enroll me in elementary school before the allowed age. Apparently, people perpetrated such scams to save money on daycare.

Mother had cleared my enrollment by providing my birth records and an attestation from the family doctor, but suspicious minds still made comments. "Are you sure you're old enough to be in the first grade, baby?" my teacher had asked me a few days before, probing to uncover deception. Mrs.

Breen, like the stuff inside a whale's gullet, had gnat-catcher hair and indiscernible eyes under the cataract of grease that smeared her magnifying-glass spectacles. "I'm not a baby. I'm seven," I had yelled at her, earning a seat in the corner, where I cried and hyperventilated until I passed out. She sent me home early that day. Mother had sided with Mrs. Breen. Mother never believed me.

"It's almost dinner time," Mother said. She turned her back to me and walked to the stove. "Go get those muddy clothes off. We'll discuss this with your father. He's out doing *your* chores right now," she chided. We grew our own vegetables and kept chickens and rabbits to supplement the limited food available from the local convenience market. It was my job to feed the animals and pull weeds after school, but today I was delayed.

Without hesitation, I ran to the laundry room to remove my clothes. Careful not to make a mess on the floor, I rolled my tights down and thought of the cause of my tardiness. More than once, I'd encountered the green-skinned-serpent creature standing in the bushes next to the road. It waited for me after school. Without moving or speaking, its eyes would follow me with what I perceived as predatory intent. The expression it wore, on its serpentine-featured face, struck me as anger, hunger, or both. And its human-like muscled arms, chest, and neck punctuated the intimidating presence.

Each time I'd discovered the creature waiting in the bushes, my heart raced, and terror propelled my legs to run the road home. Yet with each encounter, the road home took at least an hour longer than it should have. I ran the mile in six minutes and thirty seconds. This I knew because I'd won the mile race at my school's track meet. Despite my small size and seven years of age, competing in a field of sixth-grade boys, ankle-biting Yellow Star Thistle, and a minefield of gopher holes, I'd won the mile race. Six-minutes-and-thirty-seconds it took me, not hours.

I'd told my parents about the serpent man the first time I'd come home late. At first, they were angry and accused me of making up lies to explain my tardiness, and then they thought it was my imagination or that I must have seen it in a movie. So, I stopped trying to explain why I was late. I didn't use the serpent man as an excuse again, and they didn't ask me about him.

Those times I'd seen the creature, I had no memory of going anywhere, only the memory of running on the road as if pursued by a mountain lion.

Whether I'd sighted the serpent man or not, each day I'd run the whole mile as fast as I could. Keep your eyes on the ground, I told myself; he's not real, my parents had told me. But the fear persisted.

In a catatonic state, I sat at the dining table. I could hear, but I couldn't speak or move. My parents had called nearby relatives to help look for me when they'd discovered I wasn't in my bed. Now, the whole clan stood gathered around the table shouting.

"That's the way I found her," Uncle George said, waving his hand in front of my face. George had picked me up out of the dirt and brought me home. "I saw her hair in my headlights from the road," he motioned in the general direction of the road, "... in Dutch's field curled up in the dirt." My blonde hair was so pale, it reflected light at night.

"Where did you go, Aline?" my aunt asked.

"*Why* did you go?" my uncle clarified.

The only thing I could remember were lights and sitting in a plowed dirt field, but I couldn't speak. They resumed their discussion as though I wasn't there. My dead-tired eyes stared at my own reflection in the glass of the oven door. The orange linoleum also reflected in the glass, giving the impression my face was afire. Thick cigarette smoke added to the illusion.

"Maybe she sleepwalked there," my father said.

My grandmother suggested, "Maybe Dutch kidnapped her." Dutch owned the neighbor farm where my uncle had found me. "Maybe he did something to her," she added, pacing behind my uncle.

"I don't think so, Claire," Uncle George responded. "I found her in the dirt near the road, not near Dutch's house. And besides, when I found her, Dutch came out of his house to see what all the lights were about. He was surprised."

Lights–I remembered lights. Dutch hadn't taken me, but I couldn't tell them. I didn't know why I was in his field, but I knew it wasn't his fault. My mother and grandmother glanced at each other, troubled understanding clear on their faces.

"Lucky I didn't get shot." George made a nervous grunt-laugh.

"Well, if nothing happened to her," my aunt asked, "why is her night-gown on backwards?" Silence followed. "Maybe we should call the sheriff," she proposed.

"Why? He won't come," my dad reasoned. "Or else he'll come three days from now. He's the only sheriff for the whole county, and he's an hour up the highway."

"Ben's right." My uncle nodded in agreement.

"Calling the sheriff will just piss off the neighbors. They grow weed, you know." My dad continued. "Besides, there doesn't seem to be anything wrong with her." He leaned in for closer inspection and tugged at my ear to get my attention.

"Maybe when you feel better, Aline, honey, you'll tell us what happened?" my grandmother asked. But I still couldn't respond. "I'm just happy she didn't get run over crossing the road. No one would have seen her, poor little thing." She ran her fingers through my knotted hair.

Until this moment, Mother had been chain-smoking cigarettes in the corner, one hand feeding her habit and the other rubbing her forehead. She smashed the butt and rushed to me in three fluid steps. Kneeling before my chair, she squeezed my rigid body, and tears rolled down her face.

"Let's put her to bed, June," my grandmother said to my mother. Mother scooped me up, and we left the kitchen. My toes inched into her high-waist jeans pockets, and my head curled into her neck. Grandmother followed, but not before shooting my dad a disquieting glance.

"Must have been sleepwalking," I heard him mutter behind me.

That night I slept so hard; by morning, I'd almost forgotten about my experience the night before. The sound of driveway gravel crunching under Dad's truck tires woke me, and I bumbled down the hallway, stomach howling for breakfast. Where would he have gone in the morning, I wondered. Grandmother's voice made me stop in the hall. Why was she still here? Had they stayed up all night talking?

Hidden in the hall, I scratched my head, trying to decide if I should go back to bed. Grandmother and Mother conversed in hushed tones until Dad walked in the door.

"Morning, Claire," Dad greeted my grandmother.

"Did you get the milk?" Mother asked him.

"Sure did."

"And?" Grandmother asked him, expectation in her voice.

"And … the manager over at Ray's said some people came in the store last night saying they saw lights over on Onion Mountain, up by Grants Pass. And George asked around too. A firefighter from Cave Junction told him some people called in a possible fire. Orange glow in the Klamath Mountains. But it turned out it was on the California side over by Happy Camp, so CalFire investigated, and they didn't find anything."

"Shoot," Grandmother said, "I thought we'd moved far enough away from all that. They won't tell you anything, even if they know. The last time I saw one of those *things*, it was flying over the car on 101. It was night, but *on 101—* lots of people had to have seen it. I called it in, and they told me Vandenberg was testing rockets. A rocket that flies horizontal—can you believe that!" She sounded incensed. "I never saw a rocket like that. Well, I won't move again. We'll just have to live with it. Poor kid. She'll get used to it. Or we will."

Mother mumbled a response, and then they said their goodbyes, and Grandmother went home. I ate three bowls of corn flakes with a spoonful of sugar on each, and Mother didn't stop me. No one brought the incident up again.

Within a week, my middle finger had swelled with a black sliver embedded deep in the flesh. "That's got to come out," Dad said, removing his pocket knife from its leather holster. His right hand gripped mine, and his other hand performed surgery while he pinched my squirming torso between his thighs. "You have to hold still, or I can't get it," he said with an exasperated tone as the object continued to elude him.

Flayed to the bone, my fingertip streamed blood. I screamed and sweat, but he prevailed and removed the object, a thin piece of metal like a broken needle tip, only black. As soon as he released me, I ran from him like a feral animal.

"Don't you want to see it?" he called after me, displaying the black bit on his fingertip.

"I hate you. I never want to see you again." I continued to run, pinching my bleeding finger.

He yelled, "It had to come out, Aline."

I climbed the nearest bay tree and spied him from a safe distance. He dropped the bloody sliver on the ground and then stomped and twisted it under his boot, as one would a yellow jacket that might spring back to life. He bent to inspect it, stood, and then ground it again under his heel.

After my experience of being found in the neighbor's field, for reasons unknown to me, I had a powerful urge to stargaze. For this purpose, I grew a grass patch in the middle of our own vegetable field. I raked the soil smooth, seeded, and watered the patch until the blades grew to a finger's depth. At dusk, I'd skip barefoot over the forest scorpions' dens on the worn dirt path to reach my bed of green. There I'd fall asleep to mewling Myotis bats as they swooped for Sphingidae moths against a backdrop of shooting stars. Mother would sit vigil, watching from the kitchen window. When I fell asleep, she'd collect me and place me securely in my bed, where I would find myself in the morning. On these starlit nights, I knew how I ended up in my bed and where my time had gone.

Life returned to normal. I went to school, learned to read well on my own, no thanks to the unconvinced Mrs. Breen, who had tried to hold me back a year because she didn't think I was ready to move on with the "older" children. But Dad talked sense into her.

I didn't have any more trouble at school until the third grade when they administered what they told the students was a "career aptitude test." On my score sheet, next to some numbers that had no meaning to me, the suggested career column read: lumberjack. I asked the teacher why the test thought I should be a lumberjack. He responded, "Well, it says here you have an interest in nature, and the test takes into account where you live. Lumberjack is a fine career for an Oregonian. Don't you want to be a lumberjack?" He laughed, and I understood he wasn't serious.

Never mind that I had grown to only two-thirds the size of my peers, the visage of my wisp of a body wielding a chainsaw almost made me want to be a lumberjack. My parents found my test result disconcerting.

When I got home from school that day, I rushed through my chores. Mother found me in the garden hanging a spent sunflower stalk from a tree branch, root ball attached, to create a pendulum. I climbed down from the tree.

"Aline, I talked to your teacher today," she said, as though it was a regular occurrence. "He says you don't play with the other kids at recess."

I had thought she'd bring up the lumberjack thing. "I play," I said with a defensive tone and then swung the sunflower stalk and root. I took her hand and led her out of its orbit.

"Do you have any friends at school?"

"I don't know. Sure." I watched my makeshift pendulum complete a few circuits and then groaned.

"What's the problem?" Mother asked.

"It's not right."

"Looks pretty good to me," she frowned. "What is it?"

"I want it to move like …" I couldn't describe what I wanted it to move like. "Like up there." I pointed to the sky, to the location of the mashup of stars I regularly viewed at night from my grass patch.

"What do you play with your friends?" she asked, changing the subject. Her eyes took on a glassy look as if tears might spring forth if I answered incorrectly.

I faced her and answered straight. "Monkey bars and hula hoop. They aren't very good at it, though."

"The teacher says you go sit under a tree far from the playground."

"Sometimes." I talked to that tree but thought it best not to disclose the fact to Mother.

"Don't you want to play with the other kids?"

"Well, I tried jump rope with them, but they don't do it right."

"Do they trip on the rope? What makes it not right?"

"They just want to sing; they don't count right."

"What are you trying to count? How many times you jumped?"

"So, one song goes three, six, nine, the goose drank wine. So, I said we should do four, eight, twelve. They can't even do fives. Five, ten, fifteen, twenty, twenty-five, thirty ..."

"That's good, Aline. I get it, but you should have friends."

"I have friends," I said, determined to get one of her questions right. "I'll show you."

An odd hobby for a child my age, but I took it seriously, collecting, preserving, and identifying bugs and plants. I had nets, loops, a microscope, bug mounting, and plant pressing equipment, and the county librarian helped me locate the books needed to identify my specimens. She'd tell me to keep them as long as I wanted, if nobody else had reserved them.

I took Mother's hand and led her to the shed where I kept my collection organized and out of the sun. Discarded mayonnaise jars, jam jars, and peanut butter jars lined the shelves. Each jar contained a specimen, some dry grass, a twig or perch of some kind, and air holes driven into the lids by nail. Two large jars at the end of the shelves contained food, seeds, and leaves. Grasshoppers flicked and pinged at the glass of one jar.

"These are fine, Aline, but you can't keep friends in jars—Is that a rattlesnake?" It coiled, poised to strike. Mother jumped back and then ushered us out of the shed.

"It's just a baby, Mother. It can't hurt you. It's in the jar."

"We'll have to talk to your father about that. Did I see a black widow in there too?" She marched me to the house by the arm.

I regretted sharing my collection with her. Dad knew I collected these things; why was she so surprised? "Let go, Mother." I tried to pull my arm from her grip. "I have to feed them, or they'll die."

She released my arm, and a horrified look crossed her face, a look that made me feel far away from her. "No more poisonous things ... after today. I mean it," she snapped.

I'd disappointed her again. I stalked off and prepared to release the snake and the spiders— no sense feeding them if I had to let them go anyway.

She and Dad had an argument inside the house not long after. The screen door and kitchen window were open, and I could hear them. "She's not like the other kids, Ben. What are we going to do with her?"

"So? You don't really want her to be like them, do you? Look at her, June," he said from the kitchen.

I pretended to be distracted by a hatching chrysalis. It dangled precariously within in its spiral sac, connected by a stem to its milkweed nourishment source, unaware of the world that awaited. I tried not to look at Mother's disappointed face in the kitchen window. To block the view of her, I raised the wriggling sac to my eye until it became a black slit against the blinding sun.

"She's just smarter than they are," Dad said.

"The teacher said she's not even trying," Mother said, sounding unconvinced.

"Screw them! It's not like they have private schools way out here. You're the one who wanted to move here."

Mother said something I couldn't hear.

"She's fine, June. She's just like you," Dad barked, and a door slammed in the house.

That was the end of their argument about me. I continued on schedule in school with the other kids my age. Mother let me keep my non-venomous specimens, and to pacify her, I followed the teachers' directions more often and paid attention in class. And when I'd gotten myself invited to two birthday parties, she beamed with pride.

CHAPTER 2

1987 NIGREDO

Behind the house, I climbed to the pliable top limbs of an incense cedar. A storm threatened, and I intended to take a front-row seat to spectate and sway in the wind. I had done it before, climbed to the top when my parents were at work, and I could get away with it.

Like the tide, clouds surged over the Siskiyou Mountains, filling the volume of the valley. From my perch of at least fifty feet above ground, I could see the next county.

Lightning flashed; a boom followed. "Zeus," I yelled, shaking one fist in the air while gripping the axis branch with the other hand. Unlike my friends who read comics, I read Greek Mythology. Zeus, I knew, threw lightning bolts.

I sat atop a thin limb, too thin to support my weight. It wouldn't snap, I thought; it was green and pliable. As the wind picked up, I kept both feet resting on a branch below, and my arm hooked around the tree's axis.

Bears ate cedar flowers, I remembered, as I swayed with the force of the wind and recoil. I'd found it in their scat. I plucked a fragrant cedar flower, popped it in my mouth, and sucked; the bitter and menthol heightened my senses. I counted until the next bolt struck, and the next. The time between strikes reduced as the storm approached. Wet wind stung my cheeks, wet strands of hair stuck to my eyes and mouth, and my teeth chattered, but I endured–fueled by exhilaration.

A gust bent my perch too far, and my legs flailed. In search of lower-sturdier branches, I hooked my knees around a thicker offshoot and let go my arm. The axis sprung upright, flinging water droplets and needles. I started to fall backwards over my knees but caught the righted branch with my arm just in time.

Crack. Flash.

Raindrops scintillated in the surrounding air. The treetop snapped, and I slipped a few feet. My abdomen landed square on a green branch, which bent under my weight, releasing me to the next branch. Vision blurred and focused, blurred and focused. I gasped for air but crashed on another branch before my lungs filled. Crack. That was my ribs. Pain prevented breathing. I straddled the next branch, and new pain ripped my groin. My arms flailed and grabbed at air. When I did catch a branch, my hands filled with needles ripped from its length, but my descent did not slow.

Time trills and skips with heartbeats in the moments before death. I plummeted at an impossible rate, much faster than the force of gravity would dictate, but each crack of pain slowed time, focused me to think, to respond, and to survive.

About three meters from the ground, my body draped over a fat branch, and descent halted. Balanced on my abdomen and unable to move or breathe, I hung, awaiting the inescapable Earth's invitation. Then I met the remaining distance to land flat on my back in a bed of accumulated tree mulch.

CHAPTER 3

1987 SATURN BINAH

A tanned man, with the curled horns of a ram and shag-haired-satyr legs, sat on a stepped gold altar before me. Eyes closed, he appeared to be meditating. I chose not to interrupt and instead studied my strange surroundings. At first, I thought the room was dark, but once my eyes adjusted to the dim light, I discovered we were not in a room but a vast expanse. Except for the faint light behind the horned man, darkness reigned in six directions. Golden firelight penetrated a symbol behind his altar. The dim illumination outlined an inverted triangle surrounded by a circle. The point of the triangle disappeared behind the altar, and the circle arched over him like a halo.

"Am I dead?" I asked.

His eyes opened and visually appraised me as if he evaluated an acolyte. I bristled under his judgment; it reminded me of Mrs. Breen.

"You are ugly," I said. My hand flew to cover my mouth. Where had that rude outburst come from, I wondered. "Sorry." I winced. Though only twelve, I had manners most of the time.

I pulled at the hooded robe I wore and thought it, too, was ugly. Not something I'd ever wear. Not that I was fashion conscious, but neither the expansive black décor nor the meditating ram-man were inspiring to my twelve-year-old self. Where was this place, I wondered. I'd fallen out of the tree, I remembered. I touched my cracked ribs but found no pain.

"You should not concern yourself with my appearance," he said, fixing his eyes upon me in condemnation.

Ashamed, I lowered my gaze to the floor.

"Your color is black," he announced with a finality in his tone.

"I don't want to be black. I don't like black." Again, I gave a horrified glare at the hooded robe I wore and assumed he meant me to wear it in public. I *would* rather be dead than wear the robe to school, I thought.

"Everyone starts at black," he said with a dismissive tone.

"Can't I be pink instead?" I was a girl. Pink was more fitting, I'd decided, and pink would not result in a permanent mark on my reputation. Mother would never agree to black, anyway.

"You will come to understand creation through nature," he answered, ignoring my question as if philosophy was an acceptable substitute for fashion.

I narrowed my eyes and twisted my expression to reflect consternation and defiance.

Without warning or an opportunity to argue, consciousness returned to my body under the tree. My skull burned, my ribs burned, and my abdominal area felt pulverized. Lashes and abrasions stung my arms. I moaned and opened my eyes but couldn't see. Everything appeared white-hot. On my knees, I crawled, groping my way toward the house. Once inside the sliding glass door, I slumped and caught my breath, then ran my hand along the wall to my bedroom. My hand searched the back of the bedroom door for my jacket, and I put it on to hide my lacerated arms, then climbed into bed. Sleep grabbed me in a snap-jawed, death vice.

"She's awake. Get the doctor," I heard Mother say. "Aline, stay awake, honey. Aline ..."

I didn't want to be awake. My eyes closed until a sharp pain on my chest startled me awake.

"Ouch!" I yelled. "What are you doing?" I swatted at the source of the pain. The doctor had pinched the skin on my chest to wake me. His face came into focus. He ignored my question.

Mother sat next to the bed, weeping. The doctor ignored that too. He said, "We'll keep her overnight one more night. If everything goes well, she can go home tomorrow." He held my eyelids open between two fingers while shining a penlight in each eye. "Follow my finger," he said, "push your feet against my hands, now pull. Now make a fist." He conducted the neurological examination with efficiency.

"Mother." I choked on a cough. My fingers palpated my ribs.

The doctor said, "You've broken your ribs and your head, young lady." He clicked his tongue and made a motion like door-knocking at my head. "Mind telling us how that happened?"

My fingers traced a bandage on my head. I caught Mother's eyes and hesitated from shame.

"Would you mind leaving the room," the doctor said to Mother.

"But she's just woken up," she gasped with a pleading look on her face.

"Just for a moment while I do my job." He nodded at the door.

She stood. "I'll be right back, Aline." She squeezed her hands at me as she backed out the door.

"Why didn't you answer my question?" he asked. "Were you afraid to say it in front of your mother?"

Why didn't you answer mine, I thought irritably. But I could only think of the consequences of this incident. "I'm going to be so grounded."

"That should not worry you right now. Besides, I'm grounding you ... to bed rest. So, out with it," he said, curling his fingers in a coaxing motion.

"I fell out of a big tree behind the house."

"Are you sure that's what happened?" he asked. "You're not afraid of angering your parents?"

I hesitated again, remembering the horned man. What all *had* happened, I wasn't sure, but I was certain I fell out of the tree. "I fell on a bunch of branches on the way down and scratched my arms up. I just wanted to watch the lightning."

"You're a very lucky girl," he said and patted me on my knee. "I think your tree-climbing days are over, though. Promise me you won't climb any more trees?"

I considered it a moment.

"Promise me," he repeated.

"Promise." But I didn't really need convincing. My throbbing head had done that for me.

He stuck his head out the door and called for my mother. "All done here. You can come take her home in the morning."

She entered the room and draped my body in her curly auburn hair and cigarette-soaked sobs.

"Mother, it hurts." I coughed and pushed at her head.

"You were out for three days, Aline. Three days I've been here watching you. I thought you weren't coming back to us."

Dad walked in with coffee and a white paper bag of something he dropped on the floor. He rushed over and draped himself dogpile-style over my mother.

"Please," I croaked, "get off of me."

"Sorry, hun. Sorry," Dad said, springing back as though I'd bite him.

They retreated to metal and pleather office chairs on either side of my bed. Each took one of my hands and cried. I'd have time enough to confess I'd climbed the tree later.

With much fussing by my parents over the safety of my activities and whether I was old enough to be home alone after school, I recovered from my injuries and attempted to be less *wild*. Instead, as I aged, I turned my energies into my books. I learned. I never encountered the green serpent-man again. What his purpose had been in stalking me and where I'd gone that night Uncle George found me in the dirt field were questions I never answered. Aside from that, I never again disappeared in the night or failed to arrive home in time for my chores. My experience with the horned man, likewise, yielded no answers. But life provides more questions than answers. Memories of the events faded with years. The earth spun, the sun rose and set, and I ran the dirt mile home.

CHAPTER 4

1994 *Umbilicus repostus*

As fortune had it, I was not forced by default of locale to pursue a career as a lumberjack. There existed places other than Southern Oregon for those interested in life science, and in 1993 I was accepted to Emerald City University to study molecular biology. My sophomore year, 1994, I met my future husband, Jeff, on a ski trip with friends and friends of friends. Jeff had made eyes at me in the van on the way to the resort. But once we hit the slopes, I only had eyes for the skis on my feet. My first time skiing, I'd focused so hard on my skis making pizzas and french fries that I forgot to look up and turned right in front of Jeff, causing an explosion of gloves, skis, hats, and poles. While I survived unscathed, I'd busted his bindings, scratched his skis, and torn his jacket. He'd taken the coat off to inspect the damage, and I blurted in a forward manner, "Is it that easy to get you to take your clothes off?" He'd replied, "Oh? You'd like to see more, would you?" I'd had to stop him from disrobing. The accident had been my fault, but Jeff insisted on taking me to dinner in the lodge to apologize. We eloped six months later.

A couple months after our nuptials, Dad called to wish me a happy birthday. When he finished well-wishing, he asked, "Will you and Jeff come home for Christmas?"

My new life held promise; I was happy with myself and in control. I could almost see Mother in the background, smell her smoke, drying herself out from the inside, judging me from there. She didn't come to the phone; she didn't ask me to come home for Christmas—sour grapes. She'd given up her career and ambitions to move to Southern Oregon with Grandmother and the rest of the clan. I hadn't made her choices.

"No, Dad. We promised Jeff's parents this time," I lied. "Sorry."

Silence.

"Jeff's dying to meet you guys, though," I added in a conciliatory tone.

"Well, maybe we'll come up there for a visit."

"You should," I said but didn't mean it. I almost said, say hi to Grandmother, but then I remembered she'd died a few years ago. It wasn't that I didn't care; I just tried to put unpleasant realities somewhere else as if they'd never happened.

"Your mother would like to see you."

I doubted it but made nice. "I miss you guys too." Mother didn't deserve that I pushed her to the side, and guilt caused me to hold my breath. In one breath, I released the disingenuous question: "So, how is Mother?"

"She's not well, Aline. She's sick."

In that moment, I thought only of myself. Would I have to withdraw from classes, quit my job ... go home? "What's wrong with her?"

"I'm afraid it's not good. Lung cancer."

"Oh," I said. My voice turned faint, and I braced myself against the counter. "How long?" I asked, but I knew. She'd have six months at the max. I'd grown small-cell lung cancer cells in class and knew the disease course.

"The doctors are hopeful that with treatment—"

I cut him off, "Should I come home now?"

Mother muttered something in the background. Her voice was tight, and her nose sounded congested.

"She'll let you know when to come."

"I could come now. I mean, I'd have to withdraw from classes, but I can come."

"Let's just see how it goes for now."

She wouldn't tell me when to come. She'd tell Dad not to bother me.

Now I'd have to call there to find out, pull it out of Dad, like extracting a sliver from the flesh. My insides rebelled against calling home. Calling an eventuality, calling somewhere I never wanted to see, feel, or hear. My parents cared for me, I told myself. My reticence was unfair to them, but the situation felt like a trap. My parents weren't life hinderers, but I feared I'd get stuck there if I went back.

"Well, I'll call again soon then," I said. "I'll find out about taking time off from school. I love you guys. Hang in there." It wasn't enough, but I didn't know what else to say.

CHAPTER 5

1998 BECOMING

*They sing a new song before the throne, and before the four living creatures
and the elders. No one could learn the song except the one hundred
forty-four thousand, those who had been redeemed out of the earth.*

(Revelation 14:3 World English Bible) Public Domain

Where was he? Tardiness was atypical for my husband, Jeff. I paced the atrium in my too large, white lab coat. I'd asked him to come see where I worked. After all, I'd seen where he worked and thought it only fair. This Lab Tech job was my first real job after graduating. In spite of the fact the laboratory, referred to as The Dungeon, lay hidden in the basement of the Health Sciences Building, I was proud. I worked for a famous geneticist creating transgenic mice and synthetic DNA. Far from the bug-collecting-country girl who had fallen out of a tree, my twenty-three-year-old feet had carried me a long-distance-dirt run to this achievement. I had come farther than anyone else had assumed I was capable of, and I wanted acknowledgment.

I positioned myself in a different spot in the atrium in case I'd failed to see Jeff walk in. When he still did not appear, I decided he must be lost, so I stepped outside the bank of front doors to hunt for him. Medical students flanked the stairs, armored and invincible in white lab coats. Jeff stood at the bottom step, one foot still on the sidewalk, waiting patiently as a student with a clipboard and a vial spoke to him. Must be a survey, I thought, as I descended the steps.

Jeff noted my approach with a relieved expression, waved at me, then excused himself from the conversation and started up the steps to meet me. The med student next to me stopped a young man carrying a backpack. I overheard the med student say, "We're doing an HIV study. Are you interested in a free HIV vaccine?"

"Sure," the young man said and pulled his sleeve up. The med student drew liquid from a vial and injected it to his fellow student on the stairs in front of the Health Sciences Building as if this was the normal procedure for receiving medical care.

"What are you doing?" I asked the med student in the lab coat. "There is no HIV vaccine."

"It's just saline," he replied. "A placebo. We're doing a study to see how willing people are to get vaccines."

Jeff reached the step below me and stopped, just in time for my tirade. I turned back to the med student. "You can't do that. You're supposed to get consent. Who gave you approval to do this?"

"I asked him, he said yes." The student referred to the young man he'd injected.

"And what if he goes out and has unprotected sex and gets HIV thinking he has just had an HIV vaccine that was really a placebo? I was standing right here. You didn't hand him an information sheet or tell him it was a placebo."

"Well, I hadn't thought of it that way."

"I bet not. You guys get off these stairs right now, or I'm calling campus police." I yelled down the stairs to the other med students before they could inject anyone else.

"It's a study. We're doing it for our class," one of the students said.

"You have to get approval to do research on people," I said.

"It's not like that. It's a placebo."

"I mean it," I yelled down the stairs. "I'm calling campus police."

Jeff interrupted, "I'll just wait for you inside." He pointed to the atrium as he ascended the stairs away from the hubbub. His expression sagged as if I'd dragged him into battle against his will, and he couldn't retreat fast enough.

The students dispersed, glaring at me on their way into the building. I didn't call campus police, mostly because I didn't know the number, and Jeff was waiting for me. Instead, I hoped I'd scared them enough to go back to their professor for clarification.

I entered the atrium and found Jeff at a table far from the doors. "Jeff, I'm sorry. They didn't touch you, did they?" I grabbed his arm and prepared to lift his sleeve for inspection.

"No. I wouldn't let them." He pulled his arm away and smoothed his sleeve. "You know how I hate needles. Plus, I don't think they're actually doctors."

"Not yet. They will be, though. They will be released upon the world, like a plague of Dr. Frankensteins."

"That's not concerning," he said with an indignant tone.

Performing my best impression of Frankenstein's assistant, I hunched my back. With a deep lurching voice, I said, "Follow me." Jeff was tall and had to duck under ventilation pipes as we wound through the maze of halls. "Heads," I called behind me and then slowed to let him catch up. The smell of urine-soaked straw indicated proximity to the animal facilities.

"Don't step on the mousetraps," I warned. "They're there to catch escapees."

He side-stepped with a grimace.

"The traps are necessary, Jeff. Transgenic mice with human DNA cannot be allowed to escape and pollute the wild mouse population, but they do try." Clever pickles, I thought. If they escaped, they'd breed like, well ... mice. My mice had been altered to carry specific human genes or remove specific genes (knockouts). They weren't exactly growing human digits from their spines or anything as wild as what people see in the news. Nonetheless, introduction of mutations into wild mouse populations would adversely impact the survival of wild mice and their offspring, their evolution, not to mention the environment. Preservation of the natural order was a mandate. I said, "Mice are an important part of the ecosystem. We need to keep them pure." Jeff nodded but kept his eyes to the floor, looking for additional traps.

We arrived at the lab. "Meet my coworkers," I said, waving my arm at shelves of pickled mice, floating at odd angles in jars of formaldehyde.

Jeff swayed and placed a hand on the benchtop to steady himself, then removed his hand and wiped it down his pants. "I can't believe you work in such—" His eyes took in the library of mice as he searched for a word, "—such macabre conditions. This is disgusting, Aline." He took a breath and held it.

"It's sterile, I assure you," I said. A shoebox with a taped-on lid shifted on the counter beside me; scratching noises emanated from within it.

"What is that?" he asked, motioning to the moving box.

He sounded incredulous, I thought. "They're just mice, Jeff. They can't hurt you. These ones, unfortunately, have been selected for euthanasia." Restlessly, they scampered the interior perimeter of the box as if they under-stood their fate. "One was found with his hind leg in a trap, poor thing." I rubbed my hand over the top of the box to calm them. "Shush, pickles," I said with affection. I called them pickles, the dead mice and the live mice—all pickles—for their fates were predetermined. Each ended up pickled in jars of formaldehyde, holes from tissue samples punched through their ears, and vital organs removed and frozen for future study.

"They're in there waiting to die?" Jeff asked. The mice seemed to sense his angst and scratched wildly at the lid. "This is inhumane."

"Don't worry," I said, holding a finger up for him to wait. "Watch," I instructed. I sang a single tone for a stretch, as long as I could on a breath, and they stilled. "They like B flat. It calms them," I explained. I always sang to those I euthanized. I had empathy for the mice, perhaps more so, at times, than for people.

He gave me a look of skepticism, or disapproval, or both. I wasn't sure.

"What?" I asked with a defensive tone. "I'd pet them, but they bite."

He let his breath out slowly between pursed lips. "I need to leave. Now," he said, looking at me as though I was a stranger who might euthanize him and place him in a jar on a shelf someday. Without another word, he turned to leave but halted when confronted with the hallway maze.

He chose the passageway to the left. He'd selected left, I thought, as though he didn't care if he got lost. I shook my head in disappointment. Males often chose left first, a conditioned behavior learned from the placement of restrooms in buildings. Men's rooms on the left—relief follows.

I let him walk alone a minute then went to rescue him. "You're going the wrong way." I walked up behind him.

A mousetrap snapped next to his foot, and he jumped. "Dammit! I want out." On stiff legs, he continued walking in the wrong direction.

"It's back this way." I took his arm, leading him on the shortest path to the exit.

"Why do you work here?" he huffed.

"It's important work." My tone was defensive. It wasn't the most menial entry-level job. I didn't even have to clean cages or feed the mice. "I'm sorry I brought you here. I hope you won't hold it against me?"

He glared his disapproval.

Within a month, I quit and landed a job with a more glamorous molecular biology laboratory, studying cell structures. The cells arrived in frozen tubes, sampled from animals and people somewhere else, with existences far removed from my own. There were no human mazes, traps, or unsanitary smells associated with my new lab. Still, the mice from my previous job haunted me. My pickles. What if people had novel exogenous, non-human-viral, animal, or other DNA sequences incorporated into their genomes, accidentally or purposefully? What if someone knocked out genes? What manner of traps might be laid out to catch escapees in that maze? If even one escaped, it would be too late, as humans breed like, well … mice. They'd pollute the wild types.

Who will sing to them when they're caught?

CHAPTER 6

1999 BLACK SUN, MINKOWSKI SPACE, AND THE VESSEL

"Kwang-ȝze [Chuang Tzǔ] had dreamt that he was a butterfly.
When he awoke, and was himself again, he did not know whether he,
Kwang Kâu, had been dreaming that he was a butterfly,
or was now a butterfly dreaming that it was Kwang Kâu."

JAMES LEGGE (1891), *THE TEXTS OF TAOISM, IN SACRED BOOKS OF THE EAST*, VOL. XXXIX,
OXFORD: AT THE CLARENDON PRESS PRESS, P. 130. (PUBLIC DOMAIN)

Did I smell cigarette smoke? I'm dreaming, I told myself and pulled the covers tight under my chin. An iridescent field, a window of sorts, appeared before the closet door. On the other side of the field sat a wailing child in a nappy. The child's hair was as white blonde as mine had been at the same age, only, the child's hair had ringlets. My fingers felt the tips of my now auburn hair at my shoulder, the same color Mother's hair had been when she was my mother. *Not* red, *not* blonde, *not* brown, she used to say, but always in a *knot*. The child looked familiar.

"Mother, is that you?" I asked. A few years before, Mother had succumbed to lung cancer. I had seen ghosts before; I'd seen Mother's ghost before (often preceded by the scent of cigarette smoke), but she had never presented in an unfamiliar form until now.

"Stop crying," I ordered. I had no patience for children. Mother had behaved immaturely her whole life. She'd often cried, blubbering tears over slights or scenarios of little consequence; this baby proved no different. I felt the toddler was my mother, but why appear to me in this form?

"I'm sorry. I'm sorry." She sobbed through a stuffed nose. Her tiny fists clenched the tousled bed sheets, and she drew in a gulp of air, inflating her lungs for a fresh round of wailing. "I should have been there for you, Aline."

"You did your best." I'd had trouble forgiving her distant attitude until her last months when I'd never felt closer to her. There were no deathbed revelations, but somehow, it was as if barriers between us had dropped away—reasons *why* no longer mattered. Besides, I figured, I couldn't keep judging her when she wasn't present to defend herself.

"Why are you here as a child?" I asked.

Between gasps for air, she answered in unintelligible words. The field blocked the sound transmission.

"Mother, I can't hear you. I can't understand what you're saying. Slow down. Take a deep breath."

She nodded her head but then raised her balled fists to cover her eyes. I wondered if her diaper was wet and the cause for the tears. I'd go to her to comfort her, I thought. She was, after all, just a baby. In response to my touch, the iridescent window flexed and reflected a bright light, obscuring Mother on the bed.

Rather than with words, she spoke to me in my mind. "You can't come here. You can't come to this time because you don't exist here," she explained in a tone too rational for her age and emotional state.

Hypocritical, I thought. She appeared in my present when she didn't exist. I comprehended her reasoning but couldn't comprehend how she could know who I was or speak to me as an adult in a child's body.

On the other side of the window field, she sat in a bedroom I recognized. Beyond her bedroom, intense sunlight illuminated the hallway. It was the house four generations of our family had lived in, on 22nd Avenue, in San Francisco. Grandmother always said the San Francisco house had too many uninvited ghosts and gobbledies. So, she moved the whole family, a multi-generational litter of co-dependent strays, to Oregon. That was long ago, before I'd dislodged myself from the family to go to school and live in Seattle with Jeff. I now stood in *my* house, in Seattle, not San Francisco, where a scene from my mother's past played out before me.

"How can you be here now and in your past at the same time? How is this possible?" I asked.

She attempted to answer telepathically, but the field between us filtered the transmission. It came through muffled.

"I can't hear you. Speak slowly." I vocalized the words as she continued on in my head.

I tried to pay attention to everything she said, but I allowed myself to become distracted, tapping at the window field, trying to figure out what it was and how I might fix the transmission issue. Bits and fragments of apologies and odd words that made little sense escaped the barrier.

"Minkley. There will be diamonds," she said.

"Minkley?" I asked. Mother had lived in Alaska once before I was born. Surely, if she meant McKinley, she'd say McKinley.

"Minkskvy." It came through nonverbally. "Min … kli."

Why wasn't it coming through right? What was she trying to say? My brain received quantum physics information that I didn't understand, but it was the answer to my question.

"All time is simultaneous," she said. These words came through as crisp as if she'd etched them in glass.

"I can see that," I said with a snort. Time was all mixed up for sure. I had not been present when she was a child, she did not have her adult mind as a child, and recently deceased, she no longer existed in my present. These three states had never existed simultaneously, in my experience. Again, I wondered if this was Mother or someone else using her life's memories to speak to me. And why did she tell me of quantum physics? She'd been a genius, true, but she'd studied geochemistry in college, not physics.

"You can't come here," she repeated.

"I'm fine with that," I said, bemused. I had no desire to rescue my toddler mother from her wet nappy and runny nose. I was clean, comfortable, and appropriately time-oriented.

An image of a place I'd visited in an out-of-body experience entered my consciousness. A grayscale world with hurricane-force winds; I visited there as a blackbird, not a human. Every stone, leaf, cloud, and speck were black, white, or shades thereof. An anti-sun loomed full and black, high in the white sky. Its corona, or accretion disk, radiated from behind. In the grayscale world, I searched for people I knew to try to lead them out, but when I encountered familiar people there, they wouldn't respond to me. Those I encountered were dead, but not yet dead in my time; their deaths hadn't happened yet from the time point I usually occupied. Their sightless eyes reflected the black sun, and they moved in one direction as if in the throes of an unseen force, unhindered on their intended paths while I labored against the wind.

Once I located a relative in the grayscale world. I swooped and flapped my wings in her face, begging her to follow me, to let me show her the way out, the path to the light. But her path was fixed, and she would not be dissuaded. Leaving the grayscale world required every ounce of my strength. I flew in long arcing swoops against the resisting force of the wind. When I landed in a dead oak tree for a rest, the branch broke, and a swirl of dead leaves caught me in its spiral, floating me farther and farther away until I left the world of the blind and lost.

I'd been to the grayscale world twice. Each time, I failed to convince the future dead to leave. If all time was simultaneous, I wondered, had their deaths already happened? Was the future fixed?

"You are not allowed to go there," Mother said, referring to the grayscale world.

Let me guess, because I don't exist there, I thought she'd say. If she'd wanted to convince me, why had she come as my departed child-mother? Children lacked credibility. Besides, she'd never believed *me* when I was a child.

She resumed crying. "You'll get stuck. Don't go there," she told me in warning.

My memory flashed to when Mother died. She'd writhed around in a morphine delirium and said, I can't open the door, it won't open; it's black

… the sun is black … it's a trick. And then a haunted acceptance crossed her face, and she smiled with a disturbing satisfaction, unlike any smile I'd ever seen on her face. The priest who'd taken her last rites told me he'd given rites to other terminal patients who'd described the same ominous sun. He'd seemed resigned as if the black sun had determined her fate. I thought Dad would hit the man, but he controlled his voice. June was a good Catholic, he'd warned the priest.

My awareness snapped back to Mother on the bed before me now. A motion appeared in the illuminated hall behind her. Someone had finally come to change her diaper. She turned and held her arms out to be picked up.

Without transition, she wasn't there anymore. The field blinked off with a zap, and I found myself in bed, under the covers. Jeff snored next to me, and the room was pitch black. Had it been a dream? It seemed so real. Did I still smell cigarette smoke? Yuck. I sniffed at the air. What did it mean? Worry filled me, worry for the fate of Mother's soul and for my own. Did I even believe in souls, I asked myself? As a syncretist, I picked pieces of various religions that fit. Still, prudence dictated that I follow Mother's advice; otherwise, my eternal soul could be in jeopardy. But how could I prevent myself from going to the grayscale world when I hadn't sought it out in the first place?

The vacuum tank smashed the corner of the wall behind me, denting the plaster and leaving a white pile of dust on the floor I'd just cleaned. "Shit, Jeff, couldn't you give me more warning?" He'd invited a new couple over for dinner. I wasn't clear whether he'd met one of them at work or how he'd met them, but I panicked. I had no dinner plan, and the house hadn't been cleaned all week. "Get the broom if you want to help," I snapped. Not that he'd offered to help.

"They're laid back. You don't have to impress them. The house looks good enough."

I rolled my eyes and snatched the bathroom caddy of cleaning supplies from his hand. "*You* are going to get takeout after you clean that up." I pointed to the pile of white dust I'd caused. "We don't have anything suitable unless you want popcorn tacos."

"I'm sure they'd be fine with that." He made no move to retrieve the dustpan.

"I'm not fine entertaining willy-nilly." I shot him a glare and smacked the toilet scrubber on the rim of the toilet with force. "Get wine, too, while you're out."

"We have beer in the fridge."

"Two bottles of wine." Keep talking, and I'll make the list longer, I thought, with my eyes shut. Jeff had a way of inviting people over on impulse after having hyped my cooking skills. I held my own in the kitchen, but I still had to plan ingredients and go shopping. Jeff lumbered off with a sullen expression, and I stomped into the bedroom and dropped to my knees to collect his dirty socks from the floor.

After hiding unopened mail under the sheets and shoving the stinking kitchen garbage can outside, I ran to the bathroom to brush my hair and reapply deodorant. Did I smell like the tissue cultures I'd been splitting in the lab? I thought I could smell the animal sera in my nostrils, but it had to be my imagination. Dark circles betrayed my lack of sleep after seeing my dead mother in child form last night. I ran a finger under my eye and then rummaged the drawers for concealer.

Poor Jeff. I'd been too harsh with him this evening. We'd found it hard to make friends in Seattle. I appreciated that he'd found a couple for us to socialize with, I really did, but I didn't understand why we couldn't have met them at the pub. Maybe because most people our age had kids, commutes, and went to bed early. They didn't want to spend money going out for drinks and dinner. I hoped this couple could stay up past eight. Or maybe I didn't, I thought, leaning into the mirror, noting the concealer hid nothing.

The doorbell rang.

Where was Jeff? He should be back already. I huffed my way to the door and threw it open with a forced smile and an outstretched hand. "I'm Aline. Jeff will be home shortly. Come on in."

"Keith and Becca." They introduced themselves. We shook hands, and Keith handed me a bottle of wine. That would piss Jeff off, I thought, that I'd sent him for wine unnecessarily. We walked into the kitchen and exchanged the scripted lines of meeting new people: This is a great place … how long have you been here, etc.

Tired of small talk already, I scrutinized the wine label. "This looks good. Shall I open it?" I asked.

Becca nodded. I poured four glasses, assuming Jeff would arrive before we finished.

"So, how did you meet Jeff?"

"Just walking in the neighborhood," Keith said, pointing vaguely in the direction of the street.

That sounded like Jeff, meeting random strangers on a walk. "Oh, so you live in the neighborhood?"

"No, we're looking here, though," Keith said.

Becca gave him a questioning look, and he patted her leg.

"Well, it's a great neighborhood. Where do you work?" I asked. Most Seattleites first asked where one worked, followed by where one completed their postdoc.

"I'm a defense contractor at the airfield," Keith said. Again, Becca gave him a surprised glance as though she didn't know him.

"Really? It's a very long commute to Everett from here, but it is a nice place to live, and nice people live here." I pointed to myself haughtily. I couldn't imagine anyone commuting to Everett on a daily basis from this end of Seattle. They'd be the early-to-bed types, I concluded regretfully. "So, Becca, have you guys lived in the area long?"

Arms full of food and grocery bags, Jeff walked in before she could answer.

"Jeff, man." Keith sprung from his seat. "Can I help you with that?" He took a bag from Jeff, and they deposited them both on the counter.

I handed Jeff his glass of wine and ushered everyone into the living room to talk, so I could serve the takeout. My mouth watered over the aroma of duck with pineapple, curry, and coconut. I knew Jeff would remember to ask them to omit the fish sauce for my allergy. He carried a handwritten

card, requesting the omission in the Thai language. We'd had it made for
our trip to Thailand, but we had used the card more often in the U.S. In
Thailand, I'd resorted to requesting the monk's preparation of vegetarian
green curry dishes. Allergies weren't common there, and I often had the
impression no meant yes and vice versa, but they took the Buddhist requirement very seriously not to harm a living animal if you specifically requested
a monk's preparation. Otherwise, every single dish had their version of fish
sauce in it.

It didn't pair with the meal, but I opened another bottle of red wine. The
house was clean-ish, we had food, and relaxation and conversation beckoned. I had Jeff to thank for all of it. He deserved an apology, which I'd grant
after our guests left.

"I hope you like Thai food. Dinner is served."

They filed into the dining room, and I refilled wine glasses as they sat at
the table. I reached for Jeff's hand under the table and smiled at him gra-
ciously, hoping it conveyed my contrition for bossing him earlier.

"Becca, I was about to ask if you have lived in the area long," I repeated
my earlier question.

"No, actually, Keith just transferred from Maryland last month. We've
just unpacked."

So that was why she'd looked at him so funny when he'd said they would
move to this neighborhood—they'd just finished a move. I passed the appe-
tizers around the table. "What do you do for work, Becca?" I glanced at Jeff,
hoping he'd carry some of the conversation soon.

"I've scheduled some interviews at the Cascade Lab and Brany Institute ..."

I interrupted, "But that's where I work, Brany! We could be lab mates!"

"Really?" She looked to Keith, who encouraged her to continue. "But
unfortunately, I've already accepted a position at the Hatch." She shot Keith
a look that said she challenged him to contradict her.

"That's a great place to work. Highly competitive. You must be a high flier."
It was impressive to get that many interviews at top Seattle research institutions. I supposed it was possible to get in by who you knew, but connections
wouldn't do your job for you. Becca had to be smart.

Becca squirmed a little at my compliment, and Keith interjected. "Bec is much smarter than I am. And better looking." He squeezed the back of her arm, and she stiffened. I thought it an odd response, but we'd only just met them.

Jeff talked about his work, relieving Keith of having to talk about his. Keith struck me as secret service or at least working on a classified project. Those types couldn't talk about their work, and if they did, they had to report you as someone who knew they worked for the government. I didn't press. We'd met a few potential friends who worked on classified government grants at the university. They could never talk about their work either. I didn't take offense. In fact, if scientific topics came up during conversation, they would usually steer the conversation back to Jeff or me, or they'd quiz us like professors to see how much *we* knew. Textbook early-to-bed types.

I choked on a bite of pineapple and took a gulp of wine.

"Slow down there, babe," Jeff said.

I hated when he called me that. Jeff meant it as an endearment, but it reminded me of Ms. Breen. I choked some more and excused myself to get water in the kitchen. After a few sips of water, I continued to cough. My tongue felt thick and … itchy.

"Jeff," I said, keeping my voice calm.

He kept talking to Keith.

"Jeff!" I put my hand to my throat.

He glanced at me, and his smile faded to an expression of fear. "Where's the epinephrine pen?" He shot up from the table.

I pointed to the bedroom, but already my throat had started to close. I croaked, "The top drawer."

He ran to the bedroom, and I grabbed my phone in shaking hands and tried to call 911.

"I can't find it," Jeff yelled from the bedroom.

Keith stood and grabbed my phone from me. "Becca, you call 911." He thrust my phone into her hands. "I'm going to get ours from the car."

Becca took the phone and crouched beside me where I sat on the floor with my back to the kitchen cabinets, trying to take slow breaths through my nose and out my mouth.

"Oops, disconnected," Becca shook my phone as if it had bugs. Then she retrieved her own phone from the countertop and dialed.

"I can't find it," Jeff yelled again, his voice frantic. I heard him dumping the contents of dresser drawers on the floor, and then he started tossing the bathroom.

Becca handled the emergency operator with the calm of an expert. She even knew our address without having to ask me. It seemed like hours since Jeff and Keith had left the room. Where was Keith, I wondered? Maybe he didn't have epinephrine in his car after all. Just my luck, Thai food, and no epinephrine. I closed my eyes, tired from struggling to breathe. I wanted Jeff to come sit with me.

"Stay with me," Becca said, poking me in the shoulder with her index finger as if I was dirty and she'd rather not touch me.

I frowned and focused on slowing my heart rate by counting the beats slower than they thumped.

Keith burst in the door and yelled to Jeff, "I have it, Jeff."

"Next time, don't park two blocks away," Becca snapped at Keith.

"Just following protocol, hun."

"It's your hide, not mine."

The interchange struck me as peculiar, but I didn't have the energy to think about it.

Jeff grabbed the kit from Keith and burst its contents open on the floor next to me. He started to inject me with the practice syringe, but I stopped him, took the one with medicine in it, and plugged it into my thigh. I took his hand to depress the plunger, reluctant to do that part myself.

The ambulance pulled up. Keith met them at the door and handed them what looked like a business card as they walked in, but I couldn't care less. Everything about this evening had been odd; what mattered about another interchange that didn't click?

With apologies, Jeff left Keith and Becca at our house to accompany me to the hospital. I hoped they'd lock the door when they left.

In the ambulance, an EMT gave me a second epinephrine injection. "You're lucky your friend had a kit, or you might have died," he said. "One isn't always enough for some people."

I had a kit somewhere in the bedroom; I was sure of it. Maybe it expired, and I'd thrown it out. The EMTs were right; I owed our new friends my life. Next time, I'd make them a fabulous dinner—no Thai takeout.

The epinephrine didn't help my racing heart, but Jeff held my trembling hand, and I felt myself calm as soon as I could take a half breath.

"I'm sorry, Aline." Jeff had tears in his eyes. "I gave them the card with your allergy."

"I know you did, Jeff. It's not your fault." I patted his hand and wondered at the timing of the experience. Had Mother … the child apparition of Mother, known this would happen? She hadn't warned me, or had she? I might have died; the EMT said so. Mother had warned me not to go to the grayscale world. Was that where I'd have ended up if I died?

For years Keith and Becca remained fixed at our sides. After they moved to our neighborhood, we saw them almost weekly and even took vacations with them until their kids were born. Becca and I never talked about her lab, and I'd never met anyone with whom she had worked at the Hatch. I suspected she'd made it up to impress me, but I didn't know why. Seattle was cruel that way. Maybe Keith had wanted Becca to impress me. Becca only expressed opinions supplied by Keith, and we did not share the same interests, but she was present and a good listener.

A mystery egg, she was the kind you weren't sure had been hard-boiled or was still viable, the kind that wouldn't do you the courtesy by labeling itself hard-boiled. And if you cracked the shell to have a look, you risked a mess on your hands.

Once their kids were born, Becca quit her job, and all conversations turned to breastfeeding and potty training, which held no interest to me, but she opened up more than she had before the kids. Outside of our friendship, she had a whole group of friends with interests similar to hers. *They* shopped at malls and had day-long events at salons anesthetizing themselves with champagne, nail polish fumes, and hair chemicals while someone else watched their kids. Becca's other friends often accompanied her on *our* social outings and to my dinner parties. With them in tow, her shell came off; she could be herself. We both felt more comfortable when she could be herself.

Keith clung to his hypervigilant ways, and his politics were incongruous with our own. In silence, I wondered why they remained our friends, but I never questioned. Jeff and Keith spent enough time together to call each other brothers. Keith had an uncanny ability to phone and ask if we had plans for the day or weekend, the moment Jeff and I had decided to go anywhere, like on a hike, to the movies, or on a trip to visit family. When Jeff and I planned trips far from home, Jeff had become accustomed to inviting Keith and Becca. If he didn't invite them, we'd discover one of them had a layover, business trip in the area, wedding, or just happened to be passing through on their way to BFE, and we'd see them anyway. If Keith acted overly nosy or interested in our comings, goings, dietary habits, reading preferences, sleep habits, or other activities of daily living, I let it go. It was just his personality, I told myself, that, or his work formulated his behavior. I owed my life to Keith and Becca. Jeff and I would never turn them away.

CHAPTER 7

DAY 0, 2020

Centers for Infectious Disease (CID) physicians escorted by armed military guards went door to door in neighborhoods where they'd identified "outbreaks" of cases. They administered the Clinical Features Scoring System (CFSS) to identify cases for quarantine. Any person in a defined outbreak zone with a score of four or higher was sent to a quarantine detention center. Each person in our neighborhood scored an automatic point just for living in an identified outbreak zone. That was my fault.

I'll never forget the look on Jeff's face as the CID physician read my thermometer's temperature at 103. Fevers scored two points. I don't get fevers because of my condition. I've never had a fever … ever … even when sick. My husband, Jeff, knew this.

Last week the news stated that an emerging, infectious hemorrhagic disease had been discovered in Florida. This was it, what I'd been waiting for. That evening I cornered Jeff outside the house for a serious discussion. I explained everything that would happen, that they were coming to take me and others, not because there was a pandemic, but because we carried genes they didn't like. I reminded him where I'd stored my journal and the disk drives with the information that might someday be useful.

"I quit my job," I had told him as an afterthought. "I need to pack." I went into the house to make a list. "And, oh, my Dad will probably be coming to see you soon," I had warned him. I'd avoided Dad after Mother died. It wasn't fair, but he was as lost as a grayscale zombie. He'd stare at me, eyes glazed over, and say, "So much like your mother."

Jeff hadn't taken me seriously; he hadn't believed me, especially when I told him not to trust Keith or Becca. "Our best friends, Aline?" he'd asked in a disbelieving tone. While I packed my bag, Jeff had protested and tried to remove my clothes from the suitcase. I told him I loved him and that I could never have hoped for a better husband. His face had turned remorseful and confused as if he'd lost me to the grips of paranoia. Within a few days, the contagion had expanded to an epidemic, and in less than a week, they advanced to declare a pandemic. I didn't discuss it further with Jeff; I'd never convince him. On the night of the pandemic declaration, I spooned Jeff all night, savoring his snores and marveling that he could keep so still while sleeping. The CID arrived the following morning.

Events unfolded exactly as I'd warned Jeff, but he now sat on the couch paralyzed in shock. If he *had* listened, things would have turned out the same. Still, I wish he'd believed me.

My supposed fever (two points for me), Jeff's close contact with me—a symptomatic suspect (two points for him), plus each of our points for living in an outbreak zone, put us each at three. The CFSS included other measures such as low blood pressure, dizziness, eye redness, petechia, and vomiting, but the physician didn't examine us for other symptoms. I didn't point it out. It didn't matter. They were here to take me; the score was for show; testing the neighborhood was for show.

Jeff's shocked expression turned pained when the physician pricked my finger and squeezed a drop into a plastic micro-tube. Blood smeared the exterior of the tube, and the physician repeated the sample in a new tube. He left the defective sample on the kitchen table and popped the second, clean sample into a handheld device that read Mtag PCR on its cover. After a few moments, the physician tapped the display on the device and informed me I was positive. Points didn't matter. With a positive hit, I'd go straight to quarantine. Jeff finally understood.

"Aline Orr," the physician said, in a curt tone while writing my test results on his clipboard, "you'll have fifteen minutes to gather your belongings."

"You forgot to test my husband," I said, challenging his charade. They'd come only for me. Not because they thought I had viral hemorrhagic fever.

The physician paused writing but kept his eyes on the clipboard. "Yes … well, we'll get to that while you're packing." He wore gloves and a white lab coat but no protective suit or mask, and neither of the two armed guards wore masks, actions inconsistent with the handling of a Biosafety Level 4 contagion. The badge on his lanyard displayed his photo and the Centers for Infectious Disease (CID) emblem, but no name or title. He probably wasn't a physician, I thought. He was young and appeared unsure of himself. I wondered if insecurity caused his harsh manner. Maybe he was an officer, used to giving orders. Or, perhaps he was harsh because he felt I was not worthy of empathy, less than human.

The Central Division of Defense (CDOD) had compiled our sequenced genomes, along with every Americans', in a secret database, a database I had reviewed at work. The CID physician's job was to genotype me and compare my sample to the one they'd pre-identified in the database. Positive didn't mean I had viral hemorrhagic fever (VHF); positive meant my genotype matched those they'd pre-identified in their database—the ones they were rounding up now.

With my bag in tow, I met Jeff in the living room. "Did you test negative?" He nodded. I didn't have to say, I told you so. Jeff's face said it for me. The doctor and the guards joined us in the living room.

"Time to go," the doctor said. He motioned to one of the guards. Jeff and I tried to hug, but the guard pushed us apart, depriving Jeff of the opportunity to say goodbye on his terms. So we waved and threw kisses in the presence of impostors.

One guard escorted me by the elbow out of the house, while the other marked the outside of our door in red wax pen with the letter X, a number two written above counting the number of occupants, a one below for the number taken to quarantine, and the date. The mark was intended to cause fear and avoidance, stigma and warning, to set us apart. The mark divided people into *us* and *them*. No one would knock on our door, no matter how curious.

CHAPTER 8

2008 A NOBLE TRUTH

For five years, I'd worked as a Medical Research Ethicist at a national Health Maintenance Organization (HMO), after my work in genetics labs and at pharmaceutical companies. But why had I taken *this* job? I tried to remember, as I sat at my desk reviewing the latest research proposal, a stream-of-consciousness spewing, ethical enigma. Oh yes, I recalled—to absolve myself of my previous participation in the corporate-pharmaceutical cesspool. "Ethicist" sounded impressive when introducing myself at parties, but I didn't believe it was an impressive job, so it never sounded convincing to me.

In this ethics position, I reflected while turning the page on the research proposal, I'd hoped to turn the pharmaceutical paradigm against itself by using what I'd learned to prevent the uninitiated from unwittingly sacrificing themselves for the enrichment of corporations. I'd been told to apply the knowledge gained during my tenure in the pharmaceutical industry, to use it on behalf of the HMO, its research studies, and its patient population, hundreds of thousands naïve.

Were mice in a maze so deceived? Did they envision a beneficent puppet master controlling their reality? Did they have free will, or were they subjects observed performing to an expected outcome? Had I been naïve in succumbing to an ideal, believing that *I* could influence an outcome, introduce variability or instability in the systems orchestrated by my puppet masters? Or, was I deluded, unaware that I'd placed myself in a new maze, and instead of introducing variability, had I mistaken my free will to change careers for performing to an expected outcome in another system?

Just as I tilted my latte back for the last drops in the cup, a knock sounded at the door, and I dropped the cup in my lap with a start. An unapologetic researcher walked into my office without invitation.

"Did I do that?" she asked, pointing to the cup in my lap.

"It's OK, Gerry," I said, tossing it in the trash. "It was empty anyway."

"Oh, good." Without further concern, she launched into her complaint. "So, I can't put your changes in the consent form. The dizziness and risk of bipolar relapse; they're rare. It's just not necessary to warn people of every rare thing. And besides, this drug is already approved. It's a post-marketing study."

"I am aware," I said and waited to see if she could come up with a better reason not to inform her patients. She lifted her brows in challenge. "Well," I went on, "your post-marketing study has revealed two new adverse events that weren't apparent during the clinical trials." Actually, I had revealed them, doing her job for her. As a condition to conducting a post-marketing study (a.k.a. a marketing gimmick on the part of the pharmaceutical company to get our doctors to prescribe their drug) I had a rare win and influenced our committee to require Gerry to report adverse events to both me and the Federal Drug Agency (FDA) as though the drug weren't already approved. I ran the numbers on a few that kept coming up and found the rates were greater than what had been disclosed on the product label. So, I told Gerry she had to report the events to FDA and add them to the consent form.

"No," she huffed. "I'm not required to do this. The drug is already approved. I'll never get funding again, and this research is too important."

It could hardly be called research. It was a marketing campaign in which the pharma paid her to use her influence with our doctors, but I could see how it was important to her bank account. "Patients died, Gerry. Dead."

"Don't tell me that," she spat, "like I'm not taking it seriously. I didn't kill them, and neither did this drug. This drug is doing more good for people than the few rare instances—"

"More than a few of the patients felt it worrisome enough to report that they were experiencing dizziness to their doctors."

"It wasn't the drug. It could be an underlying disease." She scowled. "You're an obstructionist; that's what your problem is."

I rolled my eyes. "Fine, it could be an underlying disease, or it could be the drug. They just need to be told in case any more of them happen to work at a marshmallow factory, get dizzy, and fall into a giant blender to drown in white goo. Or—I don't know—*drive* to work," I said sarcastically. One of the dizzy patients had died in a motorcycle accident. "*Take care when driving or operating heavy machinery* is hardly going to kill your career."

"They don't want it." She meant the pharmaceutical company.

"It doesn't cost them anything to put it in."

"The other one," she said flatly.

Now we were getting to the real issue. "Like you said, it's rare, so what's the problem." A couple patients had relapsed in their bipolar disorder after decades of quiet control.

"They won't let me change the consent."

"It's not up to them."

"I'm serious. If I move forward with this, they have let me know, they will never contract me again."

I'm fine with that, I thought. That pharma was full of liars, and I knew it. "Well, send it to FDA anyway. You don't even have to tell your benefactors you're sending it. If FDA says they don't need to change the label or the consent, then fine. I'll put a note in the file, and we'll call it done. Fair?"

"I'll think about it." She stood to go, but not before Karla, my boss, poked her head in my office to say good morning.

"Oh, just who I wanted to see," Gerry said in a wry tone. She took Karla by the shoulder, and the two of them walked to Karla's office. I prepared a record of our conversation to place in the study file, where Karla would stumble upon it and throw it away. Then I returned to the study I was reviewing and my thoughts on why I had taken this job.

In this system, some HMO physicians conducted studies of drugs and medical devices on their patients. Either the government or the pharmaceutical companies paid the physicians and supplied the drugs. The patients did not take part in studies without first signing a legal document claiming they understood and agreed to enter a research study, that the study carried risks, that research wasn't the same as medical treatment, and that they, the patients, could choose not to take part in the study. The patients received the *required* level of consent … unless it was inconvenient for the physician. Research physicians lack the incentive to reschedule declining patients for regular care or to even suggest regular care as a possibility. High research participant numbers support an expected outcome.

A patient could wait three months to see a doctor, only to arrive at the doctor's office to discover the scheduled visit entailed research and not medical treatment. Would the patient refuse to be part of a study or wait three additional months for a rescheduled appointment to see a physician for regular medical care? Most likely, not. They'd take whatever came with the research. Medical research in a healthcare setting proved corporate familiar. I learned what should have happened by witnessing what did not happen.

Two months earlier, Karla warned me to expect this research proposal on my desk. Two months earlier, precursor research proposals were approved. A multi-institutional, national database of vaccine safety information and a prototype software that scanned medical records en masse for keywords to target individuals for research, both less concerning at the time than the proposal I read now. Future profits, and the birth of future systems, depended upon the massive accumulation of information data.

The government proposal before me sought approval for the nation's research centers and universities to turn over their patients' genetic data for incorporation into a national database. The database, according to the proposal, was accessible only to researchers, including "government researchers." Karla had assigned it to me for an unofficial prereview, to scan it for show stoppers. The Director of Research had primed the full committee to approve it. There was no point in even trying to argue with our committee. Should I finish reading this horseshit, I wondered.

Our research physicians clamored at the prospect of open access to a searchable database of hundreds of thousands of patients' genetic information. They had only to contribute—or sellout, depending on one's perspective—our own patients' genetic information. No one at our institution would know but our researchers, and me, as our patients never even knew they had agreed to share their genetic data with anyone and everyone. Or, if a patient had knowingly agreed to give their DNA to a particular researcher, they didn't realize that the researcher might then share it with the government or anyone else they chose.

It begins when a patient stands in line waiting to see the doctor, and the receptionist prompts them to sign a screen acknowledging that they consent to the privacy practices. The patient chooses not to hold up the queue to read the small-font, verbose-copy of the privacy practice and instead signs the nebulous black box with the attached pen (to prevent theft) and then takes a seat in the lobby. No one would choose to torture themselves with such tiny font. Well, had the patient read and understood—a highly unlikely scenario—they might have discovered that blood, tissue, biological samples, data and measurements, images, and test results in their medical records are fair game for re-use and analysis. This includes gene sequencing for future "research" purposes. While the forms don't explicitly say the HMO can *sell* your data, they say that the patient will not be compensated for the use of their data, nor will patients receive compensation for any developments or patents that arise from using patient data, implying they will sell your data. And the patient agreed by implication.

That's how the government compiled a genetic database of almost every individual in the country.

Conflicts of interest placed to the side, our researchers had everything to gain and nothing to lose. As long as they didn't sequence the *entire* genomes of our patients, the researchers decided that smaller sets of sequences posed an unlikely risk of identifying a patient from the database. I provided our committee (comprised of researchers disclosing no conflicts of interest) with journal articles proving otherwise, proving that independent researchers had identified people by multiple tiny fragments of genetic data in a pool of other genetic data. The committee thought it unlikely anyone would ever make the effort to identify someone in a database. They had trouble envisioning misuse of the genetic database by employers, insurers, or our benevolent government.

I'd argued that, in the interest of full disclosure, our institution should ask for the patients' consent again before sending the information to a government database. The committee decided it wouldn't be workable to ask everyone's permission. Too cumbersome and costly, they said. They argued that States' public health departments had taken part by sending genetic samples on every infant born—the heel stick. They had captured an entire generation starting at birth. This was no different. They'd get the sequences one way or another.

Study approved, data sent.

This was my last battle, I decided. With zero victories and no rewards, I worried perhaps I wasn't any good at this. People—people who didn't read privacy statements and who could blame them—deserved better than just me. They deserved someone of stature—someone convincing—someone with a reason to continue responding—a victorious someone. They deserved an army of someones fighting on their behalf.

While hunched over the proposal, I took even bites off my cheese and mustard sandwich with one hand and turned pages with the free hand. Each morning I made a sandwich that could be eaten with one hand, frugal sandwiches without messy things, like lettuce, that might fall out. Instead of taking care of myself or even enjoying myself with a little meat and lettuce in my lunch, I spent my time waging futile battles against unseen and poorly defined foes, such as "The Government" or "Big Pharma." I had no expectation of reward. Patients didn't know these battles were waged on their behalf, but still, I completed the maze and received paltry paychecks and system-generated shocks in no implied order of importance. Why did I continue to participate without rewards? Was it altruism, a true give response, or absolution? Why had I waged unwinnable battles continuously for the last five years? A mouse wouldn't keep dancing this tune for Muenster. My commitment to continued response sat in limbo land, in jeopardy of rapid extinguishment.

Disgusted, I dropped my sandwich on the proposal and left to go purchase a triple-shot latte from the coffee kiosk.

The barista asked the same questions, despite recognizing me and knowing how I'd respond. "Whole milk or skim?" she asked. Followed by, "flavors and size?"

To which I replied, "Any milk, no flavors, small," refusing to comply with the prescribed size-naming convention.

"Short," she corrected.

"Eight ounces."

"Short," she repeated.

"Yes, I am short."

She held up the eight-ounce cup, and I nodded affirmative, hatching a plan to try milliliters on her next time. We repeated this daily exchange without humor for at least the last three years. Why did she do it? Why did I expect a different response?

I finished the latte by the time I returned to my desk. With caffeine-induced anxiety, I burned up the search engines, hunting for legal protections covering genetic information. My research led me to discover an unpassed bill called the Genetic Information Non-Discrimination Act (GINA). It seemed pharmaceutical interests had won over a few politicians to ensure it didn't pass.

I phoned my representative from my desk phone. "Yes, I am a voter in your district, and I would like to request to speak with my *representative*," I said to the aid on the line, taking care not to refer to him by his nickname, Doormat.

"Can I ask what it is regarding and who is calling?" she asked with efficiency.

I heard the line ringing on her end with calls stacking up behind me. "I'm calling to ask if they can revive the Genetic Information Non-Discrimination Act. My name is Aline Orr, and I'm a voter. My mother had the breast cancer gene, and I'm afraid I won't be able to get insurance if they don't pass this," I said, in rapid-fire, trying not to sound spun-out on caffeine.

"Oh, I'm sorry to hear that," she responded. Before I could sink my fangs in and appeal to her emotions, she added, "The Congressman is on the other line, but I am happy to pass a message on to him."

"OK."

Silence.

"Well, that was the message. Can they revive the Act?" I asked.

"We will certainly look into that. Is there anything else I can help you with today?"

"That was it."

"Thank you for calling."

"Don't you want my number?"

"Oh yes, certainly," she responded as though she'd write it down, pass it on, and I'd receive a return call.

I rattled my number off and said I'd look forward to hearing from him.

This dialogue repeated with my State's Senators' aids until I realized they required an economic argument. I might have better luck arguing with my barista, I decided. Reason is futile; money always wins.

I continued calling up my list of politicians until I reached the Senate Majority Leader's office and got a bite.

I argued, "Research participation for both government-funded and pharmaceutical industry-sponsored studies will decline if patients have no assurance that their medical information won't be used to deny them insurance or used by their employers to fire them. That will waste tax dollars. I mean, will anyone identified in this new government GWAL database," I mentioned the database by name, the one I'd reviewed at work, "even be able to get life insurance if some life insurance company finds out they have a gene for high cholesterol?"

"I can see the importance," she said, but her tone lacked sentiment.

"Well, there's already draft legislation written; can't they just bring it back for another vote? It *is* an election year." The election-year incentive should have done it but hadn't worked on the other calls either. "Looks good. It's newsworthy," I said, cringing at the fact that I'd used one of Karla's compromised arguments.

"Can you please hold a moment?"

"Sure." I hoped she wasn't placing me on hold to count how long before I hung up. The receiver clicked, but no music played. She'd accidentally failed to place me on hold.

"I have a caller who is bringing up that database that came up in the Select Committee on Intelligence meetings," she said to an unidentified person.

A man's voice responded to her in the background, the words jumbled.

She repeated what I'd said to her. "Well, she's saying people won't agree to have their genetic data uploaded to the database unless there's some assurance they can still get health insurance. How important is the database?"

Mumblings ensued, and the receiver clattered. She pressed the hold button again, and patriotic marching tunes sounded.

She returned to the line. "Yes, the Senator agrees. This is an important issue. We will look into it."

We finished the call. She didn't ask for my number. I desperately wanted to ask why the database might be the subject of an intelligence meeting, but I shouldn't have heard that part. I'd take my breaks where I got them, I thought, reviewing the call in my head. The Senator had responded because getting people into the database was important to Select Intelligence, whatever that was, not because of an election year, newsworthiness, or to benefit people involuntarily donating their DNA.

Within a week, they'd credited a retiring Senator with the Genetic Information Non-Discrimination Act. "A very important piece of civil rights legislation," they'd touted on its passing just before the presidential elections.

I'd lobbied for GINA to give a voice to those who didn't realize their doctors had sold them out again. GINA provided them protection, or so I thought. I didn't inform my work that I'd lobbied for the legislation. I hadn't used their name and didn't feel obliged to tell them. Had I used the HMO's name, I might have had an easier time. Someone might have listened, thinking I'd had the backing of a large HMO. But the HMO would have fired me if I'd used their name. So, I shouldered the important work on my own, the hard way, without support.

CHAPTER 9

DAY 3, 2020

Journal of Aline Orr: We do to each other what has been done to us. The oppressed become the oppressors in an inescapable, undulating paradox. Momentum is conserved; history is repeated.

I know the way out.

Upon my observation, I collapse the wave. I define the Now; I create the Now. Your suffering is mine. I choose the path and steal your freedom; yet, I am your liberator.

I skirted the edges of the quarantine detention center, observing the others, hunting for signs of trustworthiness, but soon gave up. I needed allies for safety. If I made a mistake and trusted the wrong person …. Outward appearances provided no indication. I knew better than to judge.

Eight red dots of fabric poked out of the holes in my garbage bag of belongings where my fingernails had punctured the bag, creating an image I interpreted as a frowning clown face. If I left the bag on my cot in the gym, someone would steal it, like they'd stolen my suitcase. So, I lugged the clown bag and wedged my blanket roll under my arm. I scanned the floors for the suitcase, though I wouldn't challenge whoever had it. A consolation, I supposed, they'd emptied my belongings out of the suitcase before stealing it.

Still, if I found the jerk who'd stolen it, I'd take satisfaction in crossing them off my list of potential allies.

People congregated for lunch in the cafeteria as if eating lunch at lunchtime meant there was no crisis, that it would all pass soon enough. Steam from canned green beans and body odor wafted from the buffet line. A bent old man shuffled his feet up to a table and clapped his green-plastic-food tray down, launching a volley of peas that skittered and hid under neighboring tables. He sat to eat, oblivious he'd lost his vegetable group.

"This is our table, man. Get your own," yelled a rugby-sized man with a topknot. He slammed his fist on the table, knocking over his son's milk. The room fell silent, and the silence consumed the structure of normalcy created by observing the lunch routine.

"James, lower your voice," his wife scolded him and mopped up the spilled milk as their son rocked back and forth, upset by his father's outburst. Their super-sized family of six claimed a table meant for twelve. There weren't enough tables and chairs for everyone to sit and eat at once; even so, people kept their distance.

The old man shuffled off to another table. James' wife approached the old man and apologized. Once the excitement passed, the din of voices grew, and the people resumed their mechanical movements, wheels and cogs, conditioned routines.

Despite my "positive" test result, they had not placed me in isolation, as one would expect with a communicable disease. In fact, I noticed no sections of the school reserved for isolation cases. They had not separated those quarantined based only upon symptoms from those who tested positive. Territorial claims on dining tables and cots appeared to be the only reserved sections in the commandeered high school. Had everyone tested "positive" by genotype? If so, the number of potential allies just increased.

The cafeteria television blared nonstop news segments. Dramatic music clips and evocative images flashed, punctuating somber anchors, exploiting fear, and dividing emotions into bipolar swings. The networks recycled a photo of our front door with its red x as the background image behind the news anchors. I was grateful they hadn't used a photo of Jeff or me. In hopes of a smaller crowd at the showers, I left the cafeteria while people ate.

Only three women stood in line at the locker room. I plopped my bag of belongings, which I had named BOB (short for Bag Of Belongings), on the ground and sat on the rolled blanket. I fished the depths of BOB for shampoo. The woman ahead of me shifted on her feet.

"They should have time limits on the showers," the woman commented to no one in particular.

I found my shampoo and set it to the side. A poster on the wall at the locker-room entrance read: 2020 Everett High Senior Prom King and Queen Nominations Due Friday—Homeroom. Someone had written in permanent marker: Vote Rick and Adrian for Queen and Queen. Poor kids, prom canceled. Lucky for Rick and Adrian, I thought; it sounded like someone had it out for them. High school evoked feelings of penal servitude, yet here I was once again, twenty-seven years later, in detention … quarantine detention. I laughed out loud. The women in front of me didn't pay notice, and I didn't engage them. Not that I didn't want to talk to the other cases, but I couldn't risk it. If I asked questions, I'd be obliged to answer questions.

I'd been bussed here with seventy-one other cases. Except for me, most of the other cases on my bus had come from Oregon. By my estimate, there were twelve-hundred quarantined at this site. CID maintained multiple quarantine locations around the country, none large enough to hold the number of cases; they weren't built to handle pandemics. They'd moved the Port of Seattle quarantine detention center here to the Everett High School. The location met quarantine requirements: room for twelve-hundred people, close to a port (should off-land quarantine be required), and the Central Division of Defense guards could maintain a large perimeter around the structures. The guards hadn't killed us yet. Why did they wait, I wondered, when no cases had arrived for three days?

A maternal voice sounded over the intercom. "A vaccine for VHF is now available." Cheers erupted from the cafeteria. "Anyone who chooses to receive the VHF vaccine will be relocated to temporary quarantine in the south building and released after four days free of fever." She made it sound like a transfer to HomeEc or somewhere they served pancakes with lessons on top. "Please bring your belongings and proceed to the rear parking lot to receive the vaccine and transfer to the south building. Remember, once you enter temporary quarantine, you will not be permitted to return to the quarantine detention center, even if you are separated from your family members." The intercom clicked off with a short beep.

"BOB," I said, in a fake accent to my bag of belongings, "That just don't make sense. Everyone here is supposed to be symptomatic or positive, according to the CFSS. And, everyone knows once you've got it, the vaccine won't do you no good." Or, did they know, I wondered.

The woman ahead of me turned around. "Are you a doctor?" she asked, her tone irritated.

"No." I looked down at my crossed legs and the blanket roll I sat on.

"Well, if you're not a doctor, maybe you should keep your opinions to yourself." She stepped forward, shaking her head.

The line progressed by one, as a woman rushed past us, drying her hair with one hand and buttoning her pants with the other. She must be going to get vaccinated and get out of detention, I thought.

I scooched BOB and my blanket forward, but not too close to the woman ahead of me. She wore her hair short in a buzz cut, except for a stretch of bangs dyed red that obscured half her face. A tarnished metal plug protruded from a hole in her cheek, and she sported a barcode tattoo on her neck. Thick eyeliner complemented black lipstick and camo pants—Seattle cliché. I couldn't understand why the grunge thing was still going twenty years later, but the style hung on to Seattle like a case of herpes. I'm one to judge, I thought; I'm wearing the same day-jammies they took me away in three days ago. I'd known they were coming. Why hadn't I put real pants on, like most people? Or at least something I'd wear with pride to my cremation.

The woman turned back to me. "So, why did you say that, anyway? I mean, there has to be a cure." She clenched her hands together in front of her. Poor twenty-something, I thought, vaccines are not therapeutic, they don't treat viruses, they are viruses.

The networks aired footage of supposed cases at supposed detention centers. CID provided the footage of people in hospital beds bleeding from orifices, blood-soaked sheets, faces blurred to protect privacy, and attended by faceless doctors in hazmat suits. Simulations.

"Do you see anyone sick here?" I asked, waving my arm in the cafeteria's direction. "I mean anyone with even so much as a cough? Do you see anyone here bleeding like what they're showing on TV?"

"Well, they said it has a nine-day incubation period."

CID instructed those not quarantined to stay at home–shelter in place. Scaring people into hiding meant fewer questions.

"So, you think not one person here has had it for more than nine days?" I asked. "Not one person …? We've been here three days, and now they're saying you can go home after four more days without fever. You do know that adds up to seven and not nine, right?"

"What are you saying?"

I shrugged. I couldn't convince her; she had to put it together on her own. My appearance, short and younger looking than my forty-five years, made it difficult to convince anyone of anything. My day-jammies didn't help.

"You think we're not sick?" she asked.

"Do you see any doctors?"

"We're contagious. They're probably staying out until we need them." She nodded her head in the affirmative as if convincing herself.

I shrugged again. They were staying away, but not because we were contagious. They didn't want to answer questions. Even the food was self-serve. After our "keepers" prepared the food and left, the cafeteria doors opened for specified hours. So far, people remained civil, a condition contingent upon many variables, food being one of them.

She rolled her eyes. "If we're not sick, why are they keeping us here?"

"Why indeed?" I paused and stood up. "What's that tattoo for—on the back of your neck?" I looked her in the eye to gauge her response.

She gulped and placed her hand over the barcode tattoo. "It's nothing."

I focused on her eyes. "It's symbolic then, is it?" I asked, challenging her to respond otherwise.

"I have to go," she said, turning to walk away.

I caught her arm and pointed to the showers. "Wait. It's your turn. The line's moved ahead."

"Later. I'll shower later. You go ahead." She pulled her arm free and hurried away, rubbing her forehead.

CHAPTER 10

2009 GOLDEN STANDARD

*Note to File Regarding Correspondence on June 5, 2009,
11:09 a.m.:*

Spoke with Mr. Gearhart at Gearhart, Blackburn, and Cline regarding filing a whistleblower complaint for misuse of federal funds. He had researched my issue prior to the call. I explained again the misuse of tax-payer funded research monies for personal gain (investing and keeping the interest). I also explained the defrauding of the Federal Government by claiming to work on others' research studies to boost the chances of winning an application for research funding award. Mr. Gearhart informed me that since I did not have access to the grants system to document the investment claim, and that it was only hearsay, my having overheard conversations from the office next door. He said that I could not file the complaint. He also suggested that should I obtain documented evidence and turn the information over to the institution to allow them time to take corrective actions, and that if the institution corrected their actions, no suit would be filed and whistleblower protections would not apply. He suggested that were I to press the issue and get fired, finding another job in my field could be difficult. He agreed, the Director's practices were wrong, but they were common practice and occurred at many institutions, and for that reason, his firm would not represent me.

Karla, I have a big problem with this study," I said, walking into her office unannounced and taking a seat. "They can't just skip Phase I, intro to humans. Sheesh, they skipped Phase II too." I flipped to the page in the pandemic H1N1 vaccine protocol to show her the phases. "I read the Bioterrorism Act, and the requirements aren't met here. I don't care if the CDOD says the rules don't apply to them. Just because the government makes the rules doesn't mean they're exempt from the rules." They had proven me wrong on that topic many times over, but I still believed it.

When my excitable voice attracted the front-desk receptionist to come ask if we were OK, Karla asked him to close her office door.

She leaned into her computer screen as though engrossed in an important email that required all of her attention. I'd seen the tactic. She hoped I'd stop talking and leave her alone if she looked busy. But I continued badgering her, desperate to beat morals into the situation.

"Since when is it OK to take a new vaccine and test it in nine Russian ferrets and then go straight to injecting the entire human population? No one does that." I said while twisting my papers into a roll and whacking the improvised bat on my leg. Someone who didn't know me might assume it an aggressive act, but my short stature prevented me from ever pulling off a threatening demeanor.

Karla had chosen me for the position because she viewed me as weak. Today she wore gray, red, orange, and green striped tights of some synthetic material and earring hoops that stretched her lobes to improbable lengths, but she was the boss.

At four-foot-nine and twenty years her junior, my clothes matched, but I lacked her authority. I was smart enough to understand the material but too small for anyone to take seriously. When I challenged people, they issued dismissive remarks such as, "Big thoughts, for such a small person."

Karla had admitted to stacking the decks, in not so many words, when she told me she'd appointed the ethics committee members based not upon qualifications but by whom she judged might ask the fewest questions. More questions meant more work, she told me. But she'd misjudged me. I knew she regretted hiring me, but she needed me. I had memorized the laws governing research. While she considered obeying the laws optional, applicable at her discretion, she still wanted to be told what the laws were before breaking them.

She said, "Actually, they alter the influenza vaccine every year and give it directly to the population without testing because they already tested virtually the same thing last year."

"This is not the regular flu vaccine, and you know it. This swine flu is entirely new," I said and held up my hand to stop her. I knew where she'd go. "It's not the same virus as the 1976 flu, and they've included recombinant DNA technology in creating this version of this vaccine. It's totally untested."

"But they did have a swine flu vaccine in 1976," she said as if she'd won the debate.

"Yes, but they stopped giving it because it caused serious neurological adverse events in too many people."

"So, what do you want me to do," she asked, placing her palms together on her desk, "take you off the study?" She meant it to be a threat of punishment—as in, if I kept hounding her, she would reassign me. Her gaze returned to the computer—something else merited more attention. Perhaps an email from her weasely, thirty-something son, asking for more money to pay for a bigger apartment and informing her that his tuition was due. She loved telling people how much money she spent on weasel boy's medical degree.

Karla had the authority to remove me from the project. She was my boss, and, like it or not, everyone answers to someone, even if that *someone* wore clown-striped tights. "No. I'll finish it. It's my job," I said. "Just don't blame me if this comes back to bite you in an audit. I am documenting everything they refuse to do."

"That's fine. Good," she said with mock enthusiasm and grabbed her purse as if she had somewhere to go. "I'm going to retire soon anyway. If they find anything, I'll be long gone."

The same game; I deflated. We'd done this two-step repeatedly. She only wanted to make it to retirement without rocking the boat or causing more work. I asked for xyz changes to the protocol, physicians complained, and then Karla stepped in as a savior, and—as if by magic—the final versions of the reports contained none of my requirements. I even tried to get our lame-duck committee to ask for my requirements. The committee meetings were recorded, which, I thought, would incentivize honesty. The few times the committee did as I suggested, Karla later edited the requirements out. One spineless committee member said, "I agree with everything she said," pointing at me, as if I'd made him follow the rules. Karla appointed his replacement within a month.

"Oh, and you know they can't do that autism/MMR study, right? I mean, the regulations clearly say funding cannot be contingent upon results, and there can be not even the slightest appearance of a conflict of interest. It's not open to interpretation," I said, reinforcing my position. The CID and CDOD had requested our researcher pull MMR and autism data before proceeding with the H1N1 study.

"Well, the lawyers think otherwise. They've said it's not legally a problem," she said as if the lawyers were the last word, "because the MMR autism study is being done for free, so results of the separate pandemic vaccines are not contingent on that study."

The lawyers were not our overseers; they represented the HMO, not the patients' rights. I suspected CID and CDOD weren't paying our researcher for the MMR autism data, because if it didn't get federal funding and someone snooped, CID and CDOD would have deniability. If subpoenaed, it would be hard to find a commissioned study that never received any money. One would have to know to ask for unfunded data requests. What study, they'd say; we never funded any such MMR autism study—and technically, that wouldn't be a lie.

"Besides, we all know vaccines are safe; it's been proven *over and over* again," she added with a tone that implied monotony.

It was as if she had not been present for the discussion. I pressed onward. "Why are CID and CDOD dangling the twenty-five-million-dollar carrot in front of him *until* he says MMR doesn't cause autism? If there's no need to lie, why the coercion?"

"Do you think he'd lie?" Karla diverted.

The physician-researcher in question had impeccable credentials. No one questioned him, so I framed my questions around the CDOD and CID, who were telling our researcher to dig up some data saying the MMR vaccine doesn't cause autism; otherwise NIHR won't grant him any money. There were other aspects to the MMR study that gave me pause. The researcher was not using data taken from the new national vaccine safety database they'd just created, rather, only data from our HMO medical records. Was he trying to prevent someone from checking his data, I wondered. Why not use the larger data set?

"It looks bad, Karla."

It wasn't the first ugly study this impeccable researcher had proposed. Last month he'd completed a data-pull of spontaneous abortion after influenza vaccine in pregnant women. He'd claimed it was a "retrospective data study," as he didn't administer the vaccines. The public health department gave the vaccine—so for our researcher, it was an arm's length transaction. The committee never reviewed the study; instead, Karla's handpicked expedited reviewer approved it—fewer questions.

Out of curiosity, earlier in the week, I had asked his project manager about the study and received a rousing dose of disapproval that I'd dare question our morally infallible researcher. Our saint had recruited specific patients from an abortion clinic and told them to make the loss mean something for society by having the vaccine, and if that didn't cause a spontaneous abortion, they could still have the abortion paid for, as long as they donated the fetus. They were going to abort anyway, she'd explained. He had not sequenced the DNA to rule out chromosomal causes for spontaneous abortion, and he hadn't described his recruitment procedures in the protocol. Not much to say or do about that study; Karla hadn't assigned it to me for a reason. If you want answers, ask questions. If you don't want answers, don't ask questions.

"It's for the greater good," Karla said, referring to the MMR autism study, pulling me back to the present.

It took practiced effort for me not to roll my eyes. Karla often used the greater good argument inappropriately. For "the greater good" does not mean at the expense of others. Besides, our ethical guidelines banned us from justifying research based upon greater good arguments alone. Our guidelines mandated we consider the individual's rights over the many.

"Not to sound like a broken record," I said, attempting to keep the sarcasm out of my tone, "but the Helsinki Declaration, you know … one of our ethical mandates … says we need to consider the rights and welfare of each individual subject *before* the greater good." It killed me when she pulled the utilitarian, greater-good argument from her toolbox of irrational thinking. She was incapable of comprehending that the ends don't always justify the means. If they did, we'd be living under a dictatorship. The Nazis had justified research on Jews, rationalizing that the benefits to society at large outweighed the horrors experienced at the expense of a few imprisoned Jewish research subjects. They placed little value on the suffering of individuals and great value on the benefits to themselves; they defined themselves as the recipients of the greater good. The basis for the Nuremberg Code, the historical lessons informed our legal and ethical research practices. At least, they were supposed to have, but people have short memories.

"Besides," Karla said, waving a hand dismissively, "the doctors take an oath to do no harm."

Another from her toolbox. I screamed in my head. The oath to first do no harm appeared to me to be corrupted by the promise of millions of dollars. And the oath was only as good as the person giving it. I thought of the many HMO research physicians at our HMO motivated by money, status, ego, or all three. To be fair, the physicians' oath contained a promise to do the greatest good for the greatest number when providing *medical care.* Their oath contradicted ethical mandates to prioritize the rights of the individual when providing *untested and unproven research treatment.* I doubted any of them had considered the conflict. I knew the patients didn't see the difference. This was too important to have her altering the report and declaring it "case closed." I tired of wasting mental energy on rehashing old arguments with her and switched tactics.

"If I were you, I would send this autism/MMR issue up the ladder," I said, thumbing in the direction of the Director's office.

Karla's squinty conniving eyes told me she mulled passing the mess on to her boss, and then her face contorted as if she'd laid an egg. "I like it!" she exclaimed, raising her hands. This motion caused a disordered jangling of her earring hoops, and I worried something would tear.

Karla's boss, the Director of Research, was a man of stature with a weak moral spine. The pair of them amounted to less than one. His height lent convincibility, which people equated with credibility. The man took every opportunity to stand up for himself or stand on the necks of those below him. He added fees for "advisory services" to every research grant at the HMO and often lent his name to studies for money. No one saw the harm. To have the Director of Research's name on their study, as if the Director performed work on the study, gave the younger researchers better chances of winning grant money. A win-win, so I'd been told. He also invested the federal grant monies for every study awarded at the HMO, and he kept the interest at the end of the year.

The grants manager, a woman who sat in the cube next to my office, managed the interest-bearing-investment turd. Once, she admitted to me that she didn't agree with the practice, but she'd had difficulties getting her medical leave approved and couldn't afford to get fired. Her department doled money out to researchers as needed, but never all at once. The undistributed money earned interest—no one questioned.

A certainty, the Director would take his slice of the new tax-payer funded, multi-million-dollar vaccine study, and the interest too, just for gracing us with his presence. Five percent on twenty-five million, plus a percentage of the other invested grant monies, is more than enough for retirement.

"And," Karla added, as if she'd been mulling the implications of throwing her boss under the bus from a lonely perch, "it won't affect our budget because I won't be the one in his way!"

By law, our ethics department was supposed to be independent of such budgetary persuasions, but everyone answers to someone. The Director held the purse strings to our departmental annual budget, the surplus from which Karla had efficiently applied to her own salary and quickly redistributed to weasel-boy's tuition.

I nodded from my lonely soapbox in awe of her self-serving behavior. "Whether or not you're retired, this study is one that could come back to bite you," I said, goading her desire to keep controversies well hidden. "It's newsworthy," I finished, feeding her one from her own toolbox. Rather than assessing studies according to risks to the research subjects, she often encouraged reviewers to consider whether the research posed controversy or could cause unflattering news as a barometer for her personal risk. I walked out ahead of her to return to my office.

"It won't bite me!" Karla said. Her voice took on a yodeling quality, and she shook her finger in defiance, causing the hoops to tug again in a painful display of earlobe gymnastics. "Not if it was *his* decision to move forward," she said, summing it up into a tidy buck passed. "The committee can approve the rest of the study—conscience clean."

Karla's kind were capable of justifying discrepancies in cooked books, and she buried controversies like a gravedigger working the night shift. Motivated by the golden standard, it was lucrative for her to herd every study to approval and ensure the bucks didn't stop flowing because of a hold-up in her department. Money flows, and the world spins. If the world only knew how their very future depended upon seemingly insignificant decisions made by a few spineless and greedy individuals. The greater goodness … they had applied it to themselves like tanning oil.

CHAPTER 11

DAY 3, 2020 CONTINUED, BARCODE

Journal of Aline Orr: What is evolution? We harbor a notion that need, circumstance, conditions, or the maze influence evolution. Evolution is less elegant. Picture a teenage gamer. Evolution wears the dirty shirt from the laundry pile and has faith the wrinkles will work themselves out with time.

When fewer than six hundred people have traveled to space, why are humans evolving and adapting to life in space? The mutations characterized by my type, most of which are present on Chromosome 6, provide me with: lower body temperature, resistance to atherosclerosis, increased ability to process radiation via metallothionein upregulation, physical traits that allow for upward movement of the brain within the skull, lower starting intracranial pressure, pressure suit compensated proprioception differences, not to mention the small body phenotype requiring less physical space and fewer resources. None of these traits are necessary on Earth. How can I possess physical adaptations specific to living in space? For virtually all the negative side effects of spending time in space experienced by astronauts, I was born with adaptations. I carry genes that will allow people to live in space, and I'm not the only one.

How?

Researchers and physicians have given it a name, a mark, a stigma that sets me apart from the rest of humanity, somewhere side-lined on a bell curve of their definition of normal. They call it a genetic defect, that is, what they think is wrong with me and why they think I don't deserve to live. I'm not saying there aren't downsides. Some with the mutations suffer more than others. They're evolution's wrinkles. But I will label myself, thank you. I am of the Chromotype 6 evolution. Across the globe, roughly one in five thousand people have my collagen disorder, and there are others of us with different sets of evolutionary mutations, other chromotypes, who remain yet unnamed or unidentified. For my chromotype, the rate of identified collagen disorders is identical from country to country.

How is it possible that this particular set of mutations could be fixed equally across the entire globe, unaffected by race, ethnicity, or environment? These adaptations should not be present in these numbers until people live in space and are exposed to environmental conditions that influence their evolution through natural selection.

In the locker room, I took my time savoring the hot water and privacy. I'd never get another shower alone. All the other women had left to get vaccinated. If only I could sleep alone, I wished, without the restless sounds of the others sighing and tossing on their cots. A few cried. Theirs were the sounds of boxed people waiting to die.

I took mental inventory of the quarantine population once more, creating a shortlist of potential allies. Red bangs with the barcode ranked first on the list. She'd come around. Though the Pacific Islander family struck me as hostile, their autistic son showed signs of having the Chromosome 1 anomaly. And he was smaller than the rest of his family. Small like me.

I'd noticed a teenage boy who appeared to be alone. He had thin arms and legs. His forehead was broad, like mine. Could he be a Chromotype 15, with a mutation on Chromosome 15, I wondered; it was the rarest type. Could I trust a teenager? There was the woman leading yoga and meditation sessions in the corner of the cafeteria. By showing off her yoga flexibility, I identified her as a potential Chromotype 9. Too many followers, I decided. None of the people here knew they harbored exotic genes, but they might understand they were different. I'd never convince them. Without that knowledge, did they have a motive to escape?

Meditation sounded like release, I thought, as I walked to my clean clothes awaiting where I'd left them folded on a bench. But focusing long enough to clear my mind sounded impossible. Perhaps before bed. I hadn't packed a towel, so I dried off with the dirty t-shirt I'd been wearing and then got dressed. At the sink, I washed my dirty garments with shampoo, wrung them, and held them under the hand driers. The process felt homeless.

"Excuse me," someone yelled behind me over the dryer noise.

I jumped, startled. "Oh, sorry," I apologized and stepped to the side. I'd hogged both driers. Red bangs, barcode-girl stood waiting as I bundled my damp clothes in my arms.

Raising her voice, she said, "Don't stop on my account." Then she sat on the nearest bench. One dryer timed off. I reached to turn it back on, and she said, "Actually, I wanted to talk to you."

"OK." I stopped drying my clothes and walked over to a bench. "Shoot."

"So, why do you think we're here?" She bunched her hands in her shirt sleeves.

"Not until you tell me about the tattoo." I'd not risk having her as an ally if I was wrong. "But first, let's move somewhere quiet, just in case." I pointed at the intercom on the wall nearby as I ran to the dryers and pushed the on buttons. I grabbed my stuff and motioned for her to follow me to benches between rows of lockers. We sat an arm's length apart. "OK, I'm ready to hear about your tattoo."

"I think you know what it means already."

"So, say it. Are you ashamed?" I leaned forward to catch her eye.

"I'm not crazy. OK?"

"I'm not judging. Besides, I already know, right? I just want to hear you say it first."

"Yes, I'm an abductee. I had the tattoo put there when I had a tracking device removed, as a reminder." She pulled her hands out of her shirtsleeves. "Happy?"

"Thank you for sharing," I joked, "Welcome to Abductees Anonymous! Keep coming back." I patted her on the back, and we both laughed a sleep-deprived-nervous laugh.

"So, what does that have to do with VHF?" she asked.

"There is no VHF. The government invented it to get us all in one place—quarantined together."

"But why?" A perplexed expression crossed her face. "I mean, they already know about us, and I'm pretty sure they've been keeping tabs on who's been abducted anyway." She shook her head and put her hand out, "So rude, sorry. I'm Robin, by the way."

"Red Robin," I said, noting her dyed bangs, "easy to remember." I shook her hand. "I'm Aline. Nice to meet you." I moved to the opposite bench to face her. "So, I think … I mean, I know …" I said, placing my palms together in front of me, "… they mean to kill us. The vaccine will kill us. I'm pretty sure."

"No," she said, waving a dismissive hand. "What for; we're no threat? I just don't believe that."

I slumped. I'd have trouble convincing a dog that it has a tail. I straightened my back and attempted again. "Did they ever tell you that you were special, or different, or chosen, or that you have a special purpose? The aliens, I mean."

"They tell everyone that crap."

"They tell *abductees* that." Aliens had introduced transgenes into our genomes, genes that coded for survival traits, but I didn't try to explain that to Robin.

"I work night shift in a psych ward, for minimum wage. Not special," she said, pointing to herself. "Nobody is special."

Everyone is special, I thought but understood how life led some to conclude otherwise. "We're different because we have different genes. We're—" I struggled to explain. I wanted to say we weren't Homo sapiens sapiens. "More evolved. I mean, in the future, more people will be like us. I'm not saying it makes us better now, but we are different."

She looked at me with a flat expression. "We are nothing alike. You are super short—I mean, really."

I sighed. Hadn't anyone ever watched gymnasts, I wondered. Tons of gymnasts are Chromotype 6, with obvious superhuman abilities. It takes more than hard work to bend around and fly through the air—it takes a genetic profile. No amount of hard work would turn me into a basketball star, and no basketball player could ever be a gymnast. At forty-five, I wondered if I could still do a backflip. To convince Robin, I might have tried. Small body types maximized efficiency, output per resource-unit input. Simply put, smaller people require fewer resources. The effort wasn't worth it. Robin would remain unconvinced, just as the brainwashed majority believe bigger is better. But bigger is only better if there is no technology to replace physical strength. Bigger is not better with population explosions, finite resources, higher planetary temperatures, and atmospheric pressure, or limited habitable space.

"I mean no offense, but …," she attempted to explain, placing her hand horizontally mid-chest.

"Stop," I said. My differences were too great to conceive of a future of people like me. Lilliputians overrunning the planet? Laughable.

"It doesn't matter." I got up to go but left her with something to mull. "It's evolution, Robin; it's not instantaneous. When the differences become apparent, one evolutionary branch fights for supremacy. They'll kill us because we're different. It's called genocide." Our beneficent government called it a new, less stigmatized name, "Genetic Remediation." They defined it as the removal of unwanted-introduced genes from the population to restore the baseline.

I jammed my clothes and shampoo in BOB, grabbed the blanket, and walked away. "Hell, they kill each other over meaningless differences—ethnic cleansing," I said over my shoulder. The homo-type species don't support coexistence, I thought; they value sameness.

She said to my back as I left, "But the news shows bloody, sick people. I'm not going to end up like them."

Then you're as good as dead, I thought, but withheld the snide comment. "Good luck with that." I'd find other allies and a fresh approach.

CHAPTER 12

2009 CLOSED SYSTEM

Journal of Aline Orr: The government-pharmaceutical-industry complex is the new war economy.

Memo
From: Legal

The HMO has been subpoenaed to divulge the address and contact information of one of our patients, Medical Record Number 156 07 39. Mr. M is receiving prostate cancer treatment from one of our hospitals. He is not a citizen or permanent resident of the United States. The National Institutes of Health and Research (NIHR), at the direction of the National Intelligence Administration (NIA), used a biological sample to locate Mr. M in the GWAL database and tracked the source of the genetic information to our institution. Our department has been ordered to turn over his medical and contact information. This is a matter of national security. Should your department receive any inquiries regarding this order, do not divulge any information. Immediately forward all inquiries to Chief Legal at extension 2-203. This memo contains protected health information. Place in the secure shredding receptacle after reading.

May I please speak to the authorized representative on this study of the novel H1N1 influenza vaccine?" I asked, tapping the input field of the protocol listing the sponsor's contact information. Why was the Central Division of Defense listed as the sponsor and not the pharmaceutical company that manufactured the drug? After being transferred to a General, I introduced myself and provided the reason for the call.

"How did you get my number?" the General asked.

"It's inside the protocol cover—the sponsor's here." I flipped to the page. "Director, United States Military Medical Research Institute. Is that you? Am I misdirected?"

"Yes. The materials should be self-explanatory."

"Actually, I just need to check off a few regulatory hurdles to be able to advance the study for ethics committee review."

"Sure."

"Did the Federal Drug Agency issue a protocol number for this investigational vaccine? It's usually on the protocol cover page, but I can't find it anywhere. Can you give me the protocol number? I just need to verify that FDA has reviewed the study." New drugs and vaccines, are issued protocol numbers when FDA permits them to start clinical trials.

"The Central Division of Defense is not required to have its studies reviewed by the FDA."

"Well, actually, this is a study in the civilian population, so, as far as I can tell, it does have to go through FDA."

"The study is being done under the Bioterrorism Act."

"Yes, I'm aware. The Bioterrorism Act requires a protocol number, a statement of approval by the Secretary of Health, and public notification. Which leads me to my next questions: Can you send me a copy of the documentation of approval by the Secretary of Health? And can you let me know where I might find the news articles giving public notification of this study in civilians?"

"No one else has asked for these documents; I'm afraid you must be mistaken. I suggest you contact the Principal Investigator."

"I did that. I'm sorry, General, do you have an ... assistant who can help me? I'm just doing my job, and the law says I have to document these things before we experiment on our patients. I also need the preclinical studies, and the Biosafety Committee Review, and manufacturing information, and—"

"Who do you think you are, asking these questions?" he said, with disdain in his voice. "Actually ... I don't care who you are; I don't have time for this. The Central Division of Defense is not required to provide *you* with anything. The information in the protocol and Investigator's Brochure is all that you need to know. Do *not* call me again. Do you understand?"

"I can't forward this study on for review until I have the required documentation." Hearing the words of an obstacle-course bureaucrat come out of my own mouth made me cringe, but the requirements protected people, I reminded myself, and it was my job.

"DO YOU UNDERSTAND?"

"Yes. Thank you for your time." I hung up. The Principal Investigator had blown me off with less condescension than the General, but still, the General had issued a definitive bugger off. No choice remained *but* to call FDA, I conceded with dread and surrender. At times, calling FDA was like calling outer space. If you were lucky and reached a human after an hour of touch-tone hide-and-seek, they reserved the right to forward your message to a black hole in the next galaxy. My email inbox dinged as I reached for the phone receiver.

Subject: *Fill out your Wellness survey to receive your monthly premium discount.*

Hell, yes! I am in the mood to take out some frustration.

Did you complete your fitness challenge for the week, yes or no?

What fitness challenge? No.

Did you get a doctor's note excusing you from exercise?

No.

I'm sorry. You don't qualify for the premium discount this month. Please complete the weekly fitness challenge to receive next month's discount.

Back <, back <.

Yes, I completed the fitness challenge this week.

How many times did you take the stairs?

3.

I didn't have time to put lettuce in my sandwich or walk down the stairs to eat in the lunchroom. This survey was such a joke. I only filled it out to get to the explanation boxes.

I answered the other questions about the number of servings of alcohol, illicit drug use, no cigarettes, no desserts, etc. Did anyone take these surveys seriously? Was it legal to ask about my menstrual flows? Did they use it to link responses to postmenopausal employees? A promising question finally came up.

Do you socialize with coworkers outside of work?

No.

Having one or more friends at work is associated with workplace satisfaction. You should consider making a friend at work.

That is *definitely* the reason I don't like working here—nothing to do with corruption or egos. Not to mention that I *audit* my coworkers. Last time I checked, friends don't usually like it when you find everything wrong with their work.

What do you consider your sexual orientation, heterosexual, homosexual, other?

Other.

This is going to be good, Madlibs for the disgruntled.

Explain.

I trembled with excitement. They fired people in Washington State based on sexual orientation. This was worth getting fired for. They were assholes. I typed in the explanation box:

Animals.

Do you use protection?

Yes.

Explain.

Muzzle.

Did it pause? Was it calculating a response?

Have you discussed this with your doctor?

Yes. The response had to be yes because they'd never call the doctor to ask and because I wouldn't get my blessed discount if I said no. I prayed for another explanation box.

Please review your responses and press submit.

Shoot. I'd hoped to say: I wear a muzzle because I bite and because I'm trying to make close friends at work.

Why were they so nosy? People work here; they don't fornicate here. God, I so needed a leash and collar to hang on my coat hook. Props.

Submit.

I beamed with the satisfaction of a juvenile delinquent for a moment until I realized they'd throw my response out as a statistical outlier. The surveys claimed anonymity, but I doubted the truth of it. How would the HR lady respond? I envisioned a middle-management delegator saying, "Ahem. Freda, we're going to need you to have a talk with this employee." Time to quit daydreaming about how to respond to the HR lady. Heading for the stairs, I left my work to torment the barista with the afternoon caffeine routine.

On returning to my desk, the FDA phone number glared at me from a sticky note. Resolved to get it over with, I sighed and dialed the number. Within an hour, I had reached a human.

"I'm just trying to verify a protocol number has been issued for this CDOD study. It's your requirement! *Your* laws require that I verify the study has a protocol number!" Aggression was not an effective interrogation tactic, I told myself, but my patience had dwindled, and I was ready to start waterboarding.

"As I told you already," said the Federal Drug Agency representative, "we cannot give out protocol numbers or verify that kind of information to anyone but the study sponsor."

"Then why require that I verify it at all?" He was wrong. I had worked for pharmaceutical companies. The FDA was restricted from giving out the information to anyone who might be a journalist or corporate raider. Companies wanted control over information affecting stock prices, but this was a Central Division of Defense (CDOD)-sponsored study. If CDOD manufactured the vaccine, I couldn't discern because they hadn't provided manufacturing information. Either way, CDOD was not a publicly traded entity. Telling me whether there was a protocol number, in my capacity as a federally-regulated and confidentially-bound ethics reviewer, did not pose an insider trading or privacy risk to anyone. Health Research Services had my name on file as an authorized reviewer for our HMO, and CDOD had the ability to verify my identity.

"OK, I can't forward this study for review without an FDA-issued protocol number. So, I guess you'll be getting a call from the CDOD."

"As I said, I will pass your concern on to my supervisor."

I'd hoped for a checkmate but got the black hole. In case I didn't hear back, I took down the rep's name and direct number and the name of his supervisor. After three days, I called again, left a message, called for two more days, and then resorted to touch-tone madness to try a different department. I repeated the request to verify the protocol number with a second FDA representative and received the same scripted response and no returned calls.

Despondent, I stood in the office of my unsupportive boss. "Karla, this is a clinical trial. A *big* one. It's not like that psychobabble trial evaluating how tennis shoes improve mood. There are real risks here, and there's no documentation this vaccine went through FDA. Even the individual emergency use approvals for dying people get a protocol number issued by FDA overnight. I can't move the study on for committee review without something, anything from FDA saying it's OK to do a clinical trial of this novel vaccine—*anything* on their end showing CDOD jumped the hoops."

I just knew FDA had refused to talk to me because somebody broke the rules. They knew it, and they wouldn't put their names on this study or give it the green light. But why had no one else asked for the protocol number? Had the General scared inquiries off? Who are you to ask, he'd said. Humph. Who was the General to be doing clinical trials? Really, was he a one-man band? Was the vaccine manufactured in the commissary sink?

"Well, Jet City U already approved it, and so did UC."

Though suitable only for schoolyards, Karla used the—*they did it, so why don't we*—argument often. I tried not to smirk. "Great, I'll call them and see if they have a protocol with the number on it." They wouldn't have the protocol number either, but Karla seemed appeased. "And there's another thing."

"Yes?" She struggled to remove the tennis shoes she wore under her desk without my noticing. I bent and picked up the cork-soled-rectangular sandals that hid under the table I stood next to and handed them to her. Caught, she sighed and gave up on removing the tennis shoes while I stood a little taller in my kick-ass, knee-high boots. As if she needed to leave, she reached for her purse. Last week she'd had the same avoidant response to my questions.

I positioned myself in front of her door. "The World Health Organization has changed the definition of a pandemic. It has the appearance of a conflict of interest, that they changed the definition so that this H1N1 outbreak could be elevated to a pandemic level and trigger the implementation of the Bioterrorism Act and the countermeasures procedures."

"I don't see the conflict? Maybe the definition needed changing."

"The members of the pandemic committee who changed the definition are also representatives of pharmaceutical companies contracted to make the vaccine." They'd since announced manufacturing contracts in the news, but they had yet to provide me with any details regarding the manufacturing.

Karla blinked her eyelashes enduringly. "We have no jurisdiction over the World Health Organization. I'm sure they have their own procedures for reviewing conflicts of interest. The study is scheduled for Wednesday's committee," she said, indicating that I needed my questions answered by then.

"OK, I'll call JCU now." She was right, I thought. The World Health Organization (WHO) had to address their own conflicts of interest, but I'd warned her; it was newsworthy. I left her office and returned to my desk.

JCU did not have the protocol number, so I called UC. "So, did you guys get the protocol number," I asked, Ravi, my contemporary at UC, "or Biosafety Committee review, or manufacturing, or preclinical, or anything other than this half-assed protocol?"

He went through his file while I waited. We'd collaborated on other studies, so I trusted he'd cooperate with me.

"No .... What's Biosafety Committee Review?"

"I hadn't heard of it either before this because we've never approved a study involving injecting recombinant DNA into people. The Biosafety Committee thing is in the CHS [Citizen's Health Service] regulations. It says federally funded studies that involve recombinant DNA technology have to get Biosafety Committee Review. And you know, Ravi, it sounds like a good thing to me because they didn't exactly explain what part of the vaccine involved recombinant DNA. They didn't give us any manufacturing info." Experience in molecular biology labs and study of genetics meant I had the qualifications to understand the material—or lack thereof, in this case.

"Well, I admit, I didn't read the CHS regulations."

"Don't feel bad. I'm weird like that," I said, keeping judgment out of my voice. Nobody, where I worked read the regulations either–except the lawyer and me. If I stayed in this job long enough, I'd earn a set of lawyer hemorrhoids, too—a retirement gift.

"We've already spent money," Ravi said, "and I think they've started identifying subjects, so we're pregnant—no going back now. Shit. I hope I don't get fired."

"You won't, Ravi. Jet City approved it too."

"That doesn't make me feel better. If you get the number, will you send me a copy?"

"Sure. You do the same." It was a checkbox item. A big checkbox, but still a checkbox. He couldn't stuff a copy of the other missing items in his files surreptitiously as though his committee had reviewed them. Odds were low that I'd get any of the missing documentation before the review.

I tried phoning FDA one last time, but they'd stopped answering my calls. Had they blocked my number? Impossible, I thought. The FDA worked for taxpayers to protect the people. We were on the same team, weren't we? Had I been too naïve to realize that perhaps I had created the "Team good guys" label? How many FDA employees thought they worked for the good guys versus those biding time until selling out for big salaries at pharmaceutical companies? They made connections and brought those connections to the corporate world to help develop drugs that helped people. I'd have fallen for it. I did fall for it. I worked here at the HMO, thinking I'd brought my pharma experience here to help people. Does everyone start out meaning well, only to end up compromised or enablers?

Karla would push the study along without the manufacturing and pre-clinical materials. If you don't know it's missing, you don't know to ask for it. The physician's resume was never missing from any research proposal, a chance to grandstand. Familiar with the physician by reputation, the committee would review his resume highlighting his infectious disease experience at CID, see the twenty-five million dollar budget, and give rubber-stamp approval to the study. Why not? The government trusted him with the money, a man of stature doing important work. Physicians know best. And, if the committee didn't cooperate, Karla would replace the members. Advancement of the study was inevitable.

I wrote up a letter to include with the committee members' review packets. It addressed the WHO conflict and the missing information. No need to tell Karla my plan; she'd never allow it. On Wednesday, I'd hand the letter to the committee members as a last-minute addendum to the agenda, the official record of what the committee reviewed. Karla could edit the meat out of the final report, but she couldn't play ignorant.

CHAPTER 13

DAY 3, 2020 CONTINUED, RECRUITS

With the blanket roll under my arm, I overheated, and sweat formed on my neck as I lumbered into the cafeteria. The Pacific Islanders' table sat empty, I noted. Cafeteria hours were almost over. I placed BOB on a table near the buffet and took some fruit and a bag of chips from the self-serve for later. In the few moments I'd turned to get food, someone had spotted my unattended belongings.

"Hey," I said, dashing towards the young man who stood over my belongings with his back turned to me. "That's my stuff."

"Uh, yeah," he muttered and lunged a gigantic step to the side. "I don't want your stuff. Sorry, can I sit at this table?" he asked, turning to face me just as I reached the table.

"You!" The teenager was third on my list. "Sure, you can sit here. What's your name?" I tried not to sound too anxious and took a seat after squeezing BOB out of the way under the table.

"Scott." He didn't ask mine but sat and clicked on his phone. "Shit," he said, setting the phone on the table.

"Does it work?" I asked. The guards had confiscated cell phones on arrival, but he must have hidden his well. By accident, I opened the bag of chips I'd meant to save for later.

"No. There's no Wi-Fi either. I keep trying to poach one of the guards' signals, but they must not be carrying phones, or someone's jammed the cell signals."

Young people are too trusting, I thought. They shared too much. "Here by yourself? They didn't bring your parents in with you?"

"They weren't positive, so I told them to stay home." A picture of his parents on a sailboat called Sounding Off blipped onto his phone, and he flashed it in my direction. "Battery's almost out." He turned it off and put it back in his pocket.

"They look like nice people." Based on the name of his parents' boat, I determined he lived somewhere nearby. The Puget Sound, an inlet of the Pacific Ocean, extended south to Seattle and ended at Olympia. The quarantine, where we were in Everett, Washington, was also a port city on the Sound.

With a long-slender-index finger, he probed a scar on the formica table, and his features took on a dissociated, abstract look.

"I'm sure they're frantic that they can't talk to you," I added, attempting to comfort him.

He placed his forearms on his thighs and leaned forward, head down.

"Not going to get the vaccine, I take it?" I asked him.

"They told me not to trust them," he said, head still hanging.

"Who?"

"My parents told me not to trust the CID." He sat upright and tapped his heel on the ground. "But now CID's saying we might be able to go home."

"Your parents are smart. If there really is nothing wrong going on here, we'd be allowed to speak to our families. You'd be allowed to ask your parents' advice."

"That's what I thought."

"I'm not getting the vaccine either."

His eyebrows shot up.

"Be careful what you tell the others," I warned. "That woman on the intercom is giving us a choice to get the vaccine now, but soon I don't think she'll be asking for volunteers if you know what I mean?"

He nodded.

The ever-present television blared in the background. A ticker blurb ran across the bottom of the screen. It read: Citing security concerns, U.S. military denies applicants who have undergone gene sequencing through public or private companies such as X and You.

Security concerns. Hah. The military didn't want evidence that service members were genetically altered *after* joining. I turned my chair away from the T.V. It hadn't helped to know their agenda; it only fueled my helpless frustration.

"I could show you something if you want to see."

"What's that?" I finished the last chip in the bag. Only stress could cause me to eat this crap, I thought, wadding the empty wrapper into a ball.

"A bunch of trucks behind the other building. And you can see inside in a few spots."

"Let's go see." I tried not to sound too enthusiastic as I got up to throw away my wrapper. The garbage cans overflowed. Despite the degradation, I placed the wrapper on the ground next to the can. The dirty conditions only served to highlight that they didn't care what happened to us in this holding pen. Caged animals must crap in the cage.

As Scott walked out of the cafeteria, I followed him with BOB and blanket in tow.

Beyond the gym, we entered a set of double doors marked emergency fire exit only. Teachers' offices lined the hallway around the first corner. The empty hallway was like a dare, egging me to run, I thought, as I skipped after him.

"The door didn't trigger the fire alarm," I said, pointing in the door's direction.

"I disabled that one."

"Wow. Skills!" Scott had tried to hack a cell signal while I couldn't remember my own passwords. Where did kids learn these things, I wondered. I needed him for my escape plan. "Will we come back this way?"

"Yes."

"Good. I'll leave my stuff here then." Pleased to be unencumbered, I

ditched my belongings and shook out my squished fingers. "Can you disable door alarms too? Can we get out of here?"

"*Should* we get out of here?" He looked at me with a serious expression.
"The guards will shoot us," he said. "This way."

Scott opened the door to a single-occupant office containing a desk littered with papers and two shelves of books on the wall. The top shelf held
dusty reference materials dedicated to principles of teaching for educators,
and the lower shelf, old but dust-free classics. At least Scott didn't object to
our escape on the basis we might infect people, I thought. And he'd considered escape before I found him. Promising. Top of the list. My finger traced
Shakespeare's spine. I dislodged the Shelley from the shelf and then dropped
it on the desk. Everyone dies in the end, I thought, even Frankenstein and
his creation.

Dark window tint covered the west-facing office window with a view to
the rear of the south building. Four camouflaged cargo trucks, parked side
by side, sat empty and ready for loading. Ramps led from the truck beds to
the back of the building. I could make out a white diamond, HAZMAT Bio-
hazard placard for transporting hazardous waste on the nearest truck. Why
did they need four trucks for disposing of vaccine needles, I wondered. The
"sick" people were in our building, not the south building. A man in a lab
coat came around the end of the truck, and we ducked below the window.

"Privacy tint," I whispered, pointing up to the window, "but we shouldn't
chance being seen."

"I don't think he can hear us," Scott whispered back and used fake sign
language.

"Oh, yeah. Guess I don't need to whisper." I inched my head above the
edge of the window and saw the man smoking a cigarette fifty meters away.
"He's smoking. Have to wait."

Waiting for the smoker to finish, we sat below the window with our legs
outstretched, feet resting on the desk's drawer pulls. How to justify escape, I
wondered. The truth hadn't worked with Red Robin.

Scott tapped his finger on the floor with impatience. "You want to see
the next spot—into the building?"

"In a minute." Putting on a serious expression, I changed the subject. "Scott?"

"Ya?" He stopped tapping his finger.

"I think we should try to escape," I squeezed my face in anticipation of rejection.

With an excited tone, he said, "Let's say we make it out of the building. How do we get past the guards? They have guns, and there's razor wire out there in the road."

He'd collected a shocking amount of surveillance, and I wondered if Chromotype 15 included enhanced observational abilities. "Don't you want to know *why* I think we should escape?"

"Well, those trucks," he answered as if I'd called on him in a classroom, "they didn't bring people or guards here. Yesterday, they unloaded boxes from one truck, but I couldn't tell what was in the boxes."

"You're smart." I tugged his sleeve. "Your parents would be proud."

"And they won't let us speak to anyone outside," he said. He considered a moment and went on, "The vaccine thing is weird. If there's a vaccine, why isn't it on the news? Why aren't they vaccinating the public?"

I grinned. He was better than genius smart; he was useful-information smart. His Chromotype 15 traits appeared more useful than mine. "Good! We're on the same page."

"There's more," he said with hesitation in his voice. "I've met you before." Now he winced. "On the ... spaceship." He choked the last word.

Was he embarrassed, I wondered? "Well, happy to meet you again. I'm Aline."

"I know your name."

"But I don't remember having made your acquaintance, Sir." I put my hand out for him to shake.

Eyes widening, he ran his hand through shaggy-black-teen hair. "But ... they put you in charge. You really don't remember?"

"Not a thing," I lied. "Memory wiped." Guilt hit me, and I dropped my outstretched hand; he'd been so truthful. I didn't remember him, but I remembered more than I'd admit now because my memory was plagued with uncertainty. For instance, I wasn't sure it had been a spaceship, and I wasn't sure *they* were aliens. Bright lights had appeared above me more than once, but I didn't remember seeing a craft from the ground. *They* were foreign to us, but were they alien to earth? Were we indigenous? The aliens, for lack of a better word, hadn't put me "in charge" as Scott put it. In fact, I could interpret the cryptic message they'd given me as many ways as there were to tie mental knots from theoretical string. Instructions would come to me at the right time, they'd said, but I didn't have a clue what to do next. None of what I recalled involved this quarantine debacle. Besides, if I didn't survive this, I wouldn't be in charge of anything.

I peeked over the windowsill again. The smoking guard had gone, so I stood.

Scott hopped to his feet, exhibiting unusual agility for such a gangly figure. Agility, an unremarkable difference I recognized because I knew everyone here had genes that conferred traits beneficial to survival—genes that coded for advantageous traits under microgravity conditions, ability to survive constant low levels of radiation, ability to tolerate toxins, and even physiological differences to accommodate variable atmospheric and temperature differences. The collection of specimens in quarantine simply put a magnifying glass to the traits. The traits were apparent when viewed en masse.

"Let's go take in your other view." I gestured for him to lead.

CHAPTER 14

2009 CAUDA PAVONIS

An interview of a new age, self-helper streamed on my phone hours after I'd fallen asleep. Her words replayed in my head, storing themselves in packets of information for later retrieval. I didn't need a clock, didn't even have one in the bedroom; I woke at the usual time. 3:22 a.m., a coordinate, a time and place. Had sleep come to me easily, I might have gotten out of bed to pee; instead, I overrode the urge and squeezed my eyes shut in defiance. The urge remained, so I opened my eyes to assess how close we were to sunrise, a length of time proportional to how long I could hold out with a full bladder.

Waning moonlight illuminated a grim reaper of sorts, standing in the doorway beyond the foot of my bed. I didn't bother to reach for my glasses on the nightstand. Instead, I retrieved the words from the radio program and repeated them in my head in a mantra-like fashion: Release all fear; open your heart to new experiences. Then I told myself, you don't have to pee; go back to sleep.

The ominous figure shifted. Hooded in a black monk's robe, it stood holding a staff just taller than its bearer's height. Had my myopic vision changed for the worse? Was I dreaming and thought I was awake, or had my mind created the figure from the shadows. Neither my husband nor the dog stirred. In anticipation the figure would disperse or I'd wake, I repeated the mantra in my head without moving or breathing.

It was still there. My hand fumbled the nightstand for my glasses, but the figure approached my bedside and leaned over my face. I was fearless. I had my mantra and had faith in it. But a part of my fearlessness resided in my brain's comprehension that I might be dreaming. White specks of light reflected in its hood where a face should have been, set as if stars in a black sky. I searched for a face, but none appeared. Then the stars in its hood stretched from specks to infinite white lines. Immense sensations of endless continuity dragged at the edge of my consciousness, leaving my physical, fixed-point self a distant memory.

Barefoot and confused, I stood in my backyard wearing my husband's white cotton undershirt. To steady myself, I placed a hand on the brick exterior wall that separated my bedroom from the great outdoors and wondered if I'd left my body lying in bed next to my husband on the other side of the wall. Were we still sleeping on the other side? Open my heart to new experiences, I told myself.

I turned and faced the hooded being, who stood waiting for me to orient. It communicated wordless instructions, directing me to float up into the light above us.

I raised my eyes skyward. Above the power lines, an aperture radiated with such brilliance that nothing outside of the shaft of light that encompassed us was visible. A single beam, like an I-beam used to build a skyscraper or bridge, spun silently within the diameter of the blue aperture. Anxiety and skepticism raised my hair as I envisioned navigating directly into the power lines or the spinning beam.

The hooded figure, whom I call a "he," provided mental reassurance that I'd float through the wires and beam safely. As if to demonstrate, he ascended above me, staff in hand, in complete disregard of dangerous obstacles.

Curiosity overrode decency as I observed his feet and legs under his robe. The legs, covered in thin fuzz, glowed a pale blueish white and bent backward at the knees. Toes, two or three, bent sharply at the phalanges, like a cat's or a rabbit's foot without a heel. He seemed to sense my voyeurism because his feet and legs changed. They morphed to appear as goat hooves and legs. But I had seen other legs. Where he grasped his staff, I searched for hands, but my eyes perceived none. He disappeared into the blue aperture above, and I followed, bypassing power lines and the metal beam in safety as he'd promised.

Awareness blanked out for a time. When it returned, I stood before a window that served as a display screen. My mind expected stars, planets, and the beauty of space beyond the screen. I thought I'd seen planets, but at once, their memory faded. There were beings behind me, and I understood telepathically that they didn't want me to turn around to look at them. They compelled me to face the screen.

Without a frame of reference, no times, no locations, no dates, the screen displayed images of destruction: earthquakes, tsunamis, fires, war, and dead people. I didn't know if I'd just witnessed real-time events or future events. In one moment, I thought the beings behind me were responsible for the destruction, but they clarified that they wanted to observe my reaction to the scenes presented. As with my hooded guide, communications took place telepathically.

"They deserve it," I said wordlessly. Tears streamed down my face in resignation.

Behind me, the unseen beings collectively gasped in astonishment.

Ashamed by my callous response, I revised my statement. "*We* deserve it." Unsure of who I meant by *we*, I wondered if *I* was speaking at all. Knowledge existed within me but outside of my grasp, and I said things not of my own volition, in a manner less restrained than typical.

The beings' disapproval hit me as an emotional burst, and I responded defensively. "We've ruined the planet. We deserve to die." I blurted, "Mining ruins the planet too. Black rock." Where had that come from? Did I have knowledge they mined the planet, or was I making things up as I went? Their silence hinted at culpability.

They repeated that the events hadn't yet happened, and that their kind were not responsible for the catastrophes.

As if dropped into the middle of a conversation, I fretted over why I was there and why they had shown me scenes of destruction. The packets of stored information eluded recall. I'd studied something, saved it in my mental cloud, but the folder read empty.

"Have I been chosen to survive?" I asked.

No response.

"But I've seen the creator; I've seen my past lives; I've even seen bits of the future." I ticked the reasons off on my fingers. "I can tolerate warmer climates; I require fewer resources because I'm small; my genotype is acceptable for space travel and living under high-pressure environments." Where had these rationales come from? As if someone else stood there making the argument for me, I communicated with the beings, and yet, I had the knowledge that I possessed a few of the qualifications I'd listed and only vague awareness of others.

I sensed they thought I lied about seeing the creator, so I showed them the experience, the great golden light, telepathically. How I came to define this experience as visiting "The Creator," I don't know.

Some months before, I had gone to the light to heal my sick friend. I picked her up, in my out-of-body state, and carried her into the light. Not deliberately, I'd done it out of instinct. At first, the light tickled as though every particle of my being had merged into the glittering warmth, but it soon overwhelmed me. After a short time, the experience became less golden glitter and more like I'd dematerialized in a bolt of lightning. The next day, unsolicited, my sick friend related her unusual dream of being in the good light and claimed her symptoms had improved. I conveyed this to the beings behind me. Yet again, they did not respond.

Desperate and selfish to save myself from the death and destruction they'd shown me on the screen, I scrambled to show them my past lives and how I viewed the past and future. But I am not a selfish person, and I care deeply about humanity. Although I believe mankind deserves to die for what we've done to the planet, I would never, in my right waking mind, advocate for its destruction while trying to save only myself. Again, it was as if someone else controlled my impulses, or I operated under a different user's manual.

After private deliberation amongst themselves, they offered me a choice. Go with them, or join infinity.

"What do you mean, join infinity?" I asked, incredulous as if I had rights and could call the American Civil Liberties Union. My questions demanded answers. *Where* would they go if I went with them? But I didn't get a chance to ask. Yanked from the screen, they placed my consciousness into what I perceived as outer space. My consciousness hovered above an infinite stream of light, a rainbow-colored ribbon that bent through space as if flowing on the wind. They instructed me to enter the stream and experience infinity before I made my choice.

Within the ribbon, every moment in time was accessible, and the moments and light blended in a prism of color. As instructed, I attempted to enter the stream of light but had the same dragging sensation I'd had when my hooded guide pulled me through the brick wall of my bedroom. Only this time, the sensation magnified, like walking into a hurricane-force wind or against a tidal wave. The thoughts and experiences of every consciousness everywhere resided within the light stream. Immense and incomprehensible, I was incapable of dissociating *myself* from the totality of information in the light. If I had let go of my identity, I think I would have integrated into the infinity stream. But I was afraid I wouldn't be able to return to myself if I let go. Fear comes and goes for me. Sometimes it creeps in, like irrationality or hypocrisy. I feared entering the stream, feared it meant certain physical death. And I didn't trust the beings, suspicious they'd trick me into choosing death. So much for my mantra of releasing fear and approaching every new situation with an open heart.

I reappeared in front of the screen and sneaked a forbidden glance at the beings behind me before they compelled me to look back at the screen. From instinct, I knew not to make eye contact with them. My peripheral vision caught spindly, tan, insectoidal arms and legs. They sat in angular, throne-like seats with the appearance of stone or some other highly polished construct, hard and uncomfortable. Had I seen claws? I thought I'd seen claws. Why were hands and feet so difficult to observe and recall, I wondered in annoyance. Against my will, my gaze returned to the screen before me.

They asked me again if I wanted to join infinity.

"No. I don't understand it; I can't integrate into it."

They did not offer further explanation or instruction.

"Can I bring my husband and my dog if I go with you?" I asked.

They declined, and I sensed they considered me … petulant.

"Fine, I love my husband and the planet. I'd rather die there with them." In self-defense, I showed them my love telepathically. Perhaps it was a childish and selfish request to expect the insects to allow my husband and my dog to ride shotgun in their spaceship, but they had reserved too many details for me to take them entirely seriously. Under every scenario, with or without insects and outer space, I would rather end it all in a fiery inferno on earth with Jeff and the dog roasting alongside me. Perhaps I am naïve. One might conclude the infinite stream meant immortality, but I worried the lack of detail or explanation meant it represented reincarnation. Even in my right-waking mind, I was certain I didn't want to keep doing this *life* thing anymore. I've earned the right to say the human existence exercise is barbarian, and I don't want it. My interaction with the insects ended without pause to reconsider.

With no recollection of how we'd arrived or how much time had elapsed, I followed the hooded being through an underground maze of dark and humid tunnels. Crystalline blue freckles reflected on the black stone walls of the tunnels, marking the way. Overhead, blue light wells glowed like aquariums framed in the stone. The dichromatic color scheme had not escaped me. Unlike with the insect beings, everything in the tunnel realm appeared black, blue, or shades thereof. I wondered if everything really existed in black and blue or if my eyes contained receptors capable of perceiving only those two colors here. I wondered, too, about the grayscale world and if it was truly monochromatic. If my experience was incorporeal, my eye receptor theory was invalid. Consciousness does not require eye receptors. And that led my mind to distraction over whether I needed my eyes or brain to experience this consciousness event at all.

The hooded being turned and touched his staff to my abdomen, and energy coursed up through my body. The staff held a blue rock at its head. Or was it black? The color eluded me, as had the recognition of hands and feet, but surely the stone was blue or black. The rock in the staff contained orgasmic energy so pleasurable as to be temporarily disabling. Could I resist it, I wondered. Did it make me compliant and dependent? Was it meant to be addictive? I cringed at the thought.

"Don't have fear," he told me. "Don't feel any fear," he emphasized. "Human fear makes my kind angry. We absorb your fear, and the sensation causes us to behave with anger and aggression. We don't enjoy the feelings of anger or violence. If you control your fear, my kind will not have to endure the unwanted sensations."

I thought of aggressive dogs and not running, but walking in a calm and deliberate manner in the opposite direction to prevent an attack. He agreed with this thought.

We passed other hooded beings. Like him, they had no faces.

"Some of them," he explained, "don't want you here because you are human."

I felt the void of their stares and their displeasure with my guide, so I worked to control my emotions.

"Where are we going?"

"To meet someone," he said. "You must show that you are not afraid as you did when I met you in your bedroom; it is a test."

"Where do the caves go?"

"Stay close to me," he evaded my question. "If you get separated from me, the others will hurt you." He impressed the importance upon me telepathically.

We entered an enclosed cavern. At the opposite end of the cavern, a blue, glowing creature stood manacled and chained to the cavern wall. He had an ant's head with black, almond-shaped eyes and crab-shaped claws for hands. Two glowing antennae with round feelers on the ends whipped atop his head as if they sensed or probed independently of thought. Other faceless-hooded beings stood behind him at a console. They compelled me to stop looking at his chains.

"Why is he chained?" I asked.

No response.

"Why have you brought her here?" The ant asked, in a booming voice tinged with disappointment and a hint of betrayal.

"She is different," my guide said. The ant and my guide had a private tele-pathic conversation.

"Show no fear," my guide repeated the instruction—my test.

The ant waved clawed arms and roared with a maddening wail. Frozen, I stood next to my guide and looked at the floor.

"Take only what you need. Take only what you need," the ant screamed repeatedly.

I perceived his pain. "Is he talking to me?" I asked my guide, unable to tell if the ant was yelling at me, at my guide, or at both of us.

My guide didn't answer; he stood motionless. It was my test; I was on my own.

Defiant of the compulsion, my gaze returned to the ant, and I stood transfixed. The hooded entities behind worked a machine extracting body fluid from the ant. Glowing blue blood, the same glowing color that showed through the light wells in the ceiling, like Cherenkov radiation, flowed through tubes to a receptacle out of view. I looked away and tried to iden-tify my emotions. Was I ashamed? I had no fear. They'd compelled me not to watch the extraction, I sensed.

I grasped for communication mentally. Did the ant mean for my peo-ple to take only what we need from the planet, or did he ask my guide to take only the number of people he needed? I sensed he told the other beings to extract only the amount of fluid they needed. Without communication, doubt crept into my thoughts, and doubt lived not far from fear.

My guide told me to not be afraid once again, but the ant thrashed his arms and knocked a table over. I wondered if he got loose from his chains, did he intend to hurt us?

The ant's claw swiped within inches of my face. I turned my head and told myself I did not fear being hurt, that I had only a natural sense of self-preservation, then I ducked behind my guide and stilled my emotions.

"You brought me here; you protect me," I said.

I didn't want to be part of whatever they were extracting from the ant. Was he a prisoner or a leader? Had he done something to deserve chains? The only certainty was that the ant wasn't pleased they'd extracted his body fluid.

"I don't want to be the cause of his suffering," I said to my guide.

"What is your will?" my guide asked.

As with much he'd said to this point, I sensed a double meaning. I sensed he meant to ask me what outcome had I expected, but I also sensed he wanted me to exert my wishes upon the situation. How could I have expected an outcome if I didn't know what to expect? My mind raced with confusion.

As if a contestant on a game show, an answer popped into my head. "I hope you will free the ant." I sent the thought to both my guide and the ant. My desire to free the ant from captivity outweighed fear, even if it meant he'd kill us. I wouldn't partake in torture, especially not in a scenario contrived to test me. Still, I am motivated to take things seriously when first informed of the consequences. Losing patience, I formulated a devious desire to wish they'd turn into puppies or butterflies.

"We have to go quickly. Follow me," my guide interrupted. He turned and pushed me to the exit, his robes flaring behind him. The ant threw the table across the room, crashing it into the hooded beings at the console.

We rushed through the tunnels. Between poor visibility and distracted by my curiosity, I almost lost my guide twice. Humming, like a swarm of bees, approached us from farther down the tunnels. Other hooded beings flooded side corridors, projecting menacing anger that my guide had brought me to their home. My own emotions rated a stifled ambivalent, and I was pleased I hadn't caused their anger.

With haste, my guide floated up through a blue light well. I followed, grabbing hold of the end of his robe. Once safely through the well, I lost awareness.

CHAPTER 15

2009 JIMSUN - DEOSIL - WIDDERSHINS

My guide and I stood in the backyard outside my bedroom. We'd been having a conversation, but I couldn't remember the details except that I'd said something humorous and disappointed him. Sarcasm was completely lost on him, I'd noticed.

"How did you find me?" I asked, but the question seemed to come from another life, as though I'd known him in the past and lost contact or that I'd hidden from him.

"Your garden." He motioned to my plants and bent to inspect one in particular.

"It's a Jimson Weed," I explained of the plant. "But it's not a weed, actually. It prefers a drier climate, but—" I stepped forward to intervene just as he reached to touch the white trumpet flowers. "It's quite poisonous! And hallucinogenic, but I wouldn't try it. It can damage your liver and cause paralysis from the Atropine and Scopolamine in it." Risking disapproval, my derisive self wondered if he even had a liver.

He stood politely, letting me ramble on about the drought-tolerant characteristics and medicinal uses of my plants. When I'd finished, he communicated that he'd been collecting plant specimens in my yard and that he already had knowledge of my Jimson Weed and its hallucinogenic and anesthetic properties. To his kind and some other species, he impressed upon me, the plant glowed like luminescent diatoms in the ocean. It absorbed light in such a way that the rotation of its molecules were equally opposite, canceling each other, so the light passing through ...

My mind fizzed, trying to understand. I'd taken chemistry, lots of it, but couldn't recall the difference between achiral molecules and racemic enantiomers? Why would this plant appear to glow to his eyes but not mine?

A stunning array of information passed from him to me. The passage of light through certain molecules, he tied to quantum theory and time. And he attempted to explain handedness and how some particles appeared left-handed or right-handed, not identical, but I couldn't understand what this had to do with light appearing different to him. A molecule that spins clockwise, he showed my mind as if teaching a child, moves in a way compatible with the direction of a clockwise spin. Like falling down a corkscrew, the ball only rolls in one direction.

My head ached with too much information. It seemed my hallucinogenic plant could spawn an entire field of scientific inquiry beyond my abilities. I gazed at the white trumpet flowers, trying to see them as he had described. The petals, to a lesser degree, glowed a faint blue, the same as his fuzzy legs. Or was that moonlight?

With some vague sense of unease, I no longer wanted to know why he was collecting plants from my garden, and I changed the subject. "That tree is self-aware." I motioned some distance to the right, to a Golden Rain Tree. "I talk to it regularly." Embarrassed, I looked down. "It's not native," I said, rambling again.

I sensed his amusement. He didn't appear to have an interest in what was or was not native to the area, but the fact that I talked to my trees amused him. Sarcasm was not acceptable, but self-deprecation was.

"The apple tree is not self-aware, though," I said, wrinkling my nose.

As if to console me, he reached his staff to my abdomen, and my knees buckled from orgasmic energy.

"You should reproduce," he suggested, reaching the staff towards me again, but I backed away.

"I can't. I have a genetic condition, and I don't want to pass it on." In truth, I'd never wanted children. Diapers and shoe tying tried my patience.

"That's the point," he explained cryptically, "to pass the genes on." In a placating voice, he said, "You are special."

Special ... I'd heard that before, but when? I didn't take it as a compliment, and it didn't placate me. Dread welled in my stomach. Special ... as if I was a mouse selected to reproduce and eventually end up pickled and numbered on a shelf.

"Why would I have a child if the world is about to be destroyed?" I asked, squinting one eye at him.

He didn't answer. His disapproval of my defiance was obvious. As if to pacify an unruly child, he leaned his staff in my direction yet again.

"No," I insisted and took a step backward. "I only want to feel that way with my husband." With an uncertain pause, I looked at the ground. When I recognized I'd been accommodating him to a level out of character, any shame or remorse I'd felt vanished, and I raised my head high. "How does it work?" I pointed to his staff, determined to wrest back some control over the conversation.

He straightened and communicated astonishment that I didn't understand how to elicit such a sensation myself.

"Anyone can take this energy from the ground and up through the body." He demonstrated, tapping his staff on the ground, and the stone at the top glowed brighter.

Was the stone blue? Again, I tried, but the color defied recognition. I felt a pinky finger of guilt. If he'd been trying to control me, he hadn't done anything to me he didn't think I could do myself.

"Can you tell me what my purpose is, one more time?" How had I come up with that question, I wondered.

He cocked his head to the side, observing me from another angle, and I wondered if my molecules spun in a different direction. Again, he seemed surprised as if we'd been over my purpose, and I should remember. My consciousness must split, I thought; I remembered some things but not others.

"You will teach people to survive," he said, matter-of-factly.

For balance, I placed my hand against the wall while mentally reviewing the scenes of destruction shown to me by the insects.

"What does that mean exactly, teach people to survive?" I should remember, I thought, shaking my head. "Will I survive and teach the remaining people how to survive?"

He didn't answer.

I could camp if necessary. From my interest in plants, I knew how to forage. But to become a prepper? Me? No. Besides, teaching under unspecified conditions was highly inefficient. The fiery scenes they'd shown me were nuanced at best. I'd have no idea what kind of destruction awaited.

An unsettling realization caused me goosebumps. "Or will you use my genes to help future people survive?"

"You will learn to understand creation through nature." He redirected with a paternalistic tone.

Losing patience, I huffed. "Can you stay on topic?" My husband plays those games too, I thought. Changing the subject or pretending he didn't hear my question ... I'm an expert at recognizing those kinds of diversions.

"When the time comes, you will know your purpose."

That's all I'd get out of him—creation and nature. Where had I heard that before?

He changed the subject and his tone turned serious. "Never return to my home, or you will be punished."

How would I get there, I wondered. It's not like I had a spaceship in the garage.

"If you come, you'll be followed by others who would destroy us," he went on.

I nodded as if I understood, but I was completely baffled.

"You cannot tell anyone what you've learned or what we've shown you."

As if they'd believe me, I thought.

He handed me a glowing blue drink in a beaker-like container, with hands I still couldn't perceive. I hadn't seen him carrying the beaker before this moment. It simply materialized.

"What is this for?" I took it from him and inspected the turbid fluid.

"It will ... protect you," he said with a hint of omission.

"Protect me from what?" But the other part of my consciousness, the one that seemed to know what was going on, ignored my doubts. I drank the fluid greedily as if it was a reward better than chocolate milk. The half of my mind under my control wondered what I'd just done by accepting a mystery substance from a weirdo I suspected of collecting date-rape drugs in my yard, but the other half kept chugging. I squeezed my eyes shut in a slight panic upon realizing the drink was the same color as the ant's blood. The flavor and smell of the substance eluded me, as had hands, feet, and the color of the rock. I finished the last gulp and handed the container back to him.

The other half of my consciousness said, "Don't let the radiation from your ship damage my plants on your way out."

Maybe my other half was like my grandmother, I thought. She used to yell at me not to ride my bike on the lawn, accepted drinks from strangers at the local tavern, and thought she always knew what was best for my mother.

I woke in my bed the next morning, filled to distraction with an abnormal sense of well-being. With my arm draped around my husband, I pushed the dog out of the way with my knees and snuggled deeper. A vague recollection that something strange had happened the night before tickled at the back of my mind, but I couldn't quite put my finger on it. Maybe after coffee. There's something I'm supposed to do, I thought; I just can't remember what it is.

CHAPTER 16

2009 BLACKLISTED

I pulled four more glasses down from the cabinet and opened three more bottles of red. Someone handed me a bottle of barrel-aged whiskey for the offerings, so I added more ice to the bucket and water to the pitcher. I'd outdone myself, I thought, both for my own enjoyment and to keep my enemies close. Tonight, I served stuffed cuttlefish baked in homemade tomato coulis over ink-black pasta, blanched broccoli with pine-nut salad, and baked pimiento peppers stuffed with walnut, pomegranate, goat cheese, and orange zest. The sink heaped with dishes from dinner, so I placed a towel over the mess to hide it from view. Dishes could wait until after the party, and people could use the bar sink if they needed to wash their hands. I had begun not to care what these people thought of me. I hadn't even vacuumed the floor before the party.

Over the years, Keith had introduced us to his other *friends*, people he knew from work, excellent conversationalists who enjoyed my cooking and had the same tastes in wines, whiskey, and travel. They were people Jeff and I were meant to have things in common with. Many of Keith's invites were here at tonight's weekly potluck, the kind of potluck where I did most of the cooking. Most of the faces I recognized.

For years we'd forgiven Keith's nosy-neighbor surveillance because we thought he liked being around us. In hindsight, the conversations with our supplied *friends* had been leading, probing, if friendly interrogations coerced by booze and similar world views. But I'd come to realize these people's jobs told them to like what we liked. I'd fallen for it. I could never turn away a potential friend. Mother had done that to me, I realized—made me seek the acceptance of the others. But she wasn't entirely at fault. The attention padded my ego, and I ate it up. Jesus, we'd even had couples vacations with some of these people. Platonic, thankfully. Yuck, the thought made me want a decontamination scrub down.

I looked around the room at empty glasses. People could damn well refill themselves, I thought and sat at a table with Becca's friends to pick at the cheese and crackers. Affectionately, I called Becca's friends the boob jobs. They were the women I couldn't avoid inviting to my dinner parties, as to invite Becca meant the silicone squad came too. While I'd never really connected with Becca, she had been my *friend* by default, the wife supplied by Keith, the constant in his equation.

"So, Aline," Becca brought me into their conversation, changing the topic from babysitters, "how's work been treating you." Her hair coiled tight atop her head, I noticed, not a strand out of place, and it wasn't even salon day.

"Well, Becca, FDA won't return my calls, and I'm working on a vaccine study that appears to have some corruption going on around it."

Walt, whom I'd met a couple times, long-distance dated a friend of Becca's. He joined our table, and I continued to vent about the study and its issues. The boob jobs had begun to stare into their wine glasses with boredom.

"Never take an understudied drug or an under-tested vaccine. Never. Promise me," I pointed to the women at the table, who responded with perplexed expressions. Actually, even the vaccines they claimed to have vigorously tested had become suspect, in my opinion.

"I could look into that for you," Walt offered, "if you give me a little more information." His date, Becca's friend, elbowed him under the table. Gossip amongst the boob jobs was that Walt concealed a cocaine problem alongside a wife and kids in the country. As far as I could tell, Walt was not one of Keith's supplied personnel, but it didn't make him a better person.

With scorn in my voice, I said, "I don't deal in insider information."

Walt stood and shouted, so everyone at the party could hear, "I make money for my clients going both ways, up or down." His boob job tugged at his shirt sleeve to sit, but he backed a step away from the table. "You're an idealist," he said, pointing at me with an accusing finger as if it was a dirty word. "If you're serious about addressing the moral dilemmas in that study, getting to the money is the most effective way." He stalked off to sell his services to the other guests.

Walt had a point, I thought. Becca's friends resumed their discussion, this time about jogging strollers. When I couldn't take any more kid talk, I left the table and sought out Walt, whom I found smoking in the back yard. I gave him the names of the pharmaceutical companies contracted by the government to manufacture the vaccine (public information). Then I told him what I knew about the vaccine, which didn't amount to a lot.

Ends and means. While I didn't stand to make a cent off of his insider trading, I'd have bet that's what he intended to do with the information. I hoped people would leave soon. Before the party was over, I excused myself to heave my hypocrisy into the toilet. My lips trembled as I smiled at the guests on my way out. If anyone stopped me, I'd start crying. With my head down, I walked through my bedroom to my private master bathroom. I opened the door and startled to find a man in there. A new face, one I didn't recognize.

"Oh, so sorry. God, I should have knocked," I stammered and averted my eyes until I realized what he was doing. The man wasn't using the toilet. He stood in front of my medicine cabinet with his phone held up to one of my vitamin supplement bottles. Click. He'd taken a picture of it.

"Wait. What are you doing? I don't take painkillers if that's what you're looking for." But I didn't think that's what he was after. Why take pictures of my vitamins?

He hastily returned the bottle and closed the cabinet door, smoothed his shirt, and patted his pockets, feigning as if he'd forgotten or lost something. He added, in an offhanded manner, "Oh, headache. Do you have any Acetaminophen?"

"No," I said in a dull tone. I stood blocking the doorway and felt anger heat my face while I waited for an additional explanation, but none came.

"I'm done here," he said, and I stepped to the side.

The audacity, I thought, opening my cupboard door and emptying the bottle he'd held into the sink. The cellulose casing on a few of the pills looked like it had been damaged, and a dusting of free powder coated the others. I reached under the sink, grabbed the waste bin, and emptied the entire contents of the cabinet, including the toothpaste, into the trash. How to explain this to Jeff, I wondered.

"Aline? Walt here," Walt said. His voice sounded nervous, but lack of confidence was unusual for the egocentric VP of Stock Analysis at JJ Morland Banking Group. Walt had the Wall Street connections I needed, so I told myself I wasn't putting ends before means.

"Oh, good to hear from you. Hold on; let me get to a private phone." Afraid someone would walk into my office or hear through the wall, I transferred the call to the conference room and trotted in, locking the door behind me. "OK, I can speak now without being overheard."

"I looked into it, and I'm afraid I have bad news and worse news." He paused a moment. "Take me off speakerphone," he said.

I complied readily. "OK, you're off."

"Which do you want first, bad or worse?"

I gulped. "Bad?"

"You're blacklisted at the FDA."

"What? Is that for real?" Unbelievable. I never imagined they had a blacklist, let alone that I'd get blacklisted for doing my job.

"It's very real. They will never answer a call from you again. If I were you, I wouldn't call them again. It will only make things worse."

"Do they even do that? I mean, I've never heard of that."

"Well, you're not the only one blacklisted, but you're the only one I've ever met. You must have really pissed them off." He spoke in fast clips. Time was money to him; I'd heard him say as much at my party.

"OK … so, what's worse than that?" A government agency blacklisting an ethics analyst was unconscionable enough.

"I can't speak to you ever again."

That wasn't a tremendous loss for me, I thought, shrugging and stifling a laugh. "And, why is that?"

"I have been … *warned*," he said, pausing with dramatic effect, "that if I continue to pursue your claims regarding these vaccines, I will lose all of my contacts—the FDA and the pharma contacts. They'll shut me out. I need those contacts to make money for my clients."

The seriousness of his tone and the fact that he could suffer for getting involved—then it hit me like bird shit to the forehead: How was I supposed to do my job without talking to FDA?

"So, what does this mean?" I asked. The ramifications spun faster than I could keep up.

"That should be answer enough, Aline. These people can ruin your life, my life. Take care of yourself, your safety, I mean. You won't see me ever again, and do not call me, please, *ever*."

"Walt, thanks for your honesty, at least." Ironic, I thought, that he, of all people, had been the most honest with me.

"Stay idealistic, Aline. The world needs more idealists."

The dial tone sounded, and I hung up the receiver.

Head down on the conference room table, my thoughts reeled. I felt like a telemarketer, repeatedly rejected with "never call me again." Threats to my safety? Had it really come to that?

A few days later, the gossips were all atwitter because Walt had broken up with Becca's friend. He had wasted no time, I gathered, and dumped her the very day he had spoken to me on the phone. Walt made sure he'd never have contact with me again, not even through mutual acquaintances.

CHAPTER 17

DAY 3, 2020 CONTINUED, FOUR AND FOURSCORE

can't figure this thing out—this button, here. Ahem," an old man's voice sounded over the loudspeaker. Scott and I paused in the hall on our way to inspect the south building from a new position.

"I'm on? Can you hear me?" the old man asked the one-way speaker. "Class is now in session, folks. Something fishy is going on here. Show of hands, how many of you tested positive?" he asked. "I can't see you, but I bet every single one of you tested positive. I asked around. Ask yourself how no one here ended up here by scores alone," he said, referring to the Clinical Features Scoring System, "and why doesn't anyone look sick? I am four and fourscore years old. That's a math problem for you and a joke," he chuckled. "Get it—fourscore? Just kiddin'."

The words caused me to freeze as if they instilled programming or a way-point I recognized.

"The point is," he continued, "I'm old, got nothin' to lose. I'm tellin' you right now, I'll be God damned if I let those sorry-excuses-for-patriots hood-wink the rest of us. If you haven't got that vaccine yet—don't! I'm counting down the seconds until they come for me. If they take me, then you'll know." The microphone screeched, and a crash sounded. "They're here," he said with finality in his voice. "Don't you touch me, boy; I am a veteran!" The microphone muted with a click.

Scott's dark eyes bulged in their sockets.

"We don't have long," I said. "I don't know how that old guy got to the intercom, but security will confine our movements shortly."

"Right," Scott said. He turned, and we sprinted down the hall.

A decent runner, despite my short stature, my feet bore one of the most prominent evolutionary adaptations in the Chromotype 6. While I have flat feet, I carry more potential energy per step due to increased ranges of plantar and dorsiflexion in both my ankles and toes. Adrenaline and overdeveloped calf muscles created torque, allowing me to overtake Scott, who was less than half my age and a full foot taller. He has other features—different, I thought. For one, he was tall. Most of the Chromotype 15s were tall like him. But there was something else I couldn't identify, something on another chromosome. And his mutations were de novo (new); otherwise, his parents would be here too. Scott resembled the people in the photo he'd shown me. His mother appeared to be of possibly Japanese origin, and his father of European ancestry. Scott had his mother's plate-black hair, only his had a shaggy cut.

He rounded the end of the hall behind me, and without raising his voice, he commanded, "Stop."

I hit the polished-vinyl flooring on my side and slid five meters, just before reaching a bank of windows I'd been too distracted to notice. At times, I let myself slip so deep into thought, I risked harm from what I didn't notice. The extreme focus was a Chromotype 6 trait.

On all fours, Scott crawled toward me, short of breath. "If you look out this window, you can see through the entrance doors. There's a big room. Do you think that's where they'll take the people who got vaccinated today?"

I peeked my head over the edge of the window. A guard stood a few meters away. With his back to me, he shifted his feet over a manhole cover and clutched his rifle to his chest. After only a brief glimpse of the south building, I dropped to the ground.

"What?" he asked.

To quiet Scott, I placed my finger to my lips and pointed in the guard's direction.

Someone called from the south building, "Ronny, come help us with this." The guard's rifle made an action noise, and heavy boots stomped away. The sound of a door closed.

A few moments after the sounds stilled, I peeked again. Through squinting eyes, I found the doors Scott had described. Superior vision was not a feature of my type. Still, I could make out a distinct red X on one glass door. Beyond the glass doors, I saw men in military fatigues opening boxes in an auditorium. One man unfolded white-plastic rectangles and laid them on the floor in rows while another followed, unzipping the rectangles.

"Body bags." I slumped with my back against the wall. Dry and tight, my throat fought down vomit. I'd expected evidence of death, but the vindication still shocked.

"Think you know a way out?" I asked.

"I don't know. Maybe. It's just an idea," Scott said.

"Well, cross your fingers then. We leave tonight," I said with authority. For some reason, this kid listened to me when others didn't. I hoped not to make him regret it. He believed I was in charge, ensured of success. "Let's go back now."

We crawled clear of the windows and ran back toward the emergency exit where we'd started. I grabbed the belongings I'd stashed earlier, and then Scott and I put our ears to the door to see if the hall beyond was clear. With an affirmative nod, he pushed the door open.

I stepped into the hall—clear. We walked toward the gym, forcing ourselves not to rush.

"Anyone caught in restricted areas will be sent to isolation," said the maternal voice over the intercom, causing me to startle.

They'd send the old man to the south building to die with the others, I thought. Heart racing, I looked over my shoulder with paranoia.

"It is important that you remain calm and follow instructions," the voice continued. "For your protection and to control the spread of disease, stay in authorized areas."

"Such a joke," I said to Scott, metering my speed but not my pulse. "If they were worried about disease spread, we wouldn't be here. This building doesn't even have negative pressure ventilation." Airborne pathogens were free to travel the whole building; they'd never planned to treat patients here, but I knew that.

"Ventilation," he said and clenched his fist; "that's it! Escape through the ventilation ducts."

"I'm not seeing how that gets us past the perimeter," I said with a gentle voice, so as not to discourage ideas.

"Oh, yeah," he huffed. "Well, my other idea was to find a basement and go out the sewer, but I haven't found a basement. Maybe there is no basement." He gazed into the distance, appearing to consider options. "Why tonight? We need more time to come up with a plan."

"It has to be tonight. The reason they asked for volunteers first is that they don't have room to hold twelve hundred dead people at once in that auditorium. Once they move the first round of bodies into the trucks, they will come for everyone left in this building."

"Oh." Head bowed, he exhaled and stopped walking.

I hadn't meant to scare him but to instill a sense of urgency. "You know," I said, reconsidering his sewer plan, "Your drain idea has merit. That guard was standing on a storm drain."

Scott raised his head for a moment, then lowered it again. "But he was standing guard on it."

"Well, what if he doesn't guard that side of the building all the time?" I suggested, trying to sound hopeful.

"But that hallway will be restricted."

"But, Scott, smartypants, you disabled the alarm—but they don't know that—so they won't think the hallway needs a guard."

"Maybe," he said, and his head ticked up again. "So, we'd just wait there for the guard to leave the storm drain cover? There is a door at the end of those windows, but I didn't look to see if it had an alarm."

"Can you disable it?"

"Ya, but it takes time. If I set it off—game over."

"No pressure," I said, patting him on the back in encouragement. But it was our only chance.

"But the minute we go out the door, they'll see us from the auditorium. There're portable stadium lights all around the place; it's bright."

"True. I'd still like to try."

"I'm not sure." He shook his head, no.

"Why?" I threw my hands up in frustration. Why'd he change his mind now?

Shouts came from the direction of the cafeteria as we reached the gym entrance. People filed in to claim cots for the night.

Voice lowered, he leaned in toward me and said, "I know we don't have a choice. I'm just not sure it will work. We should wait and come up with a better plan."

Time for my trump card. I lied, a white lie but still a lie. "But you said they put me in charge, right? So, it must be the right plan." Lying and manipulating scared teenagers went completely against my moral code, yet I needed Scott's help, and truthfully, I didn't want to do it alone.

"Aline, what if I fuck it up?" He closed his eyes and leaned against the wall.

With astonishment, I concluded he feared failure more than death. I hadn't been his age for a long time, an age of uncertainty and low self-esteem. Since high school, I'd failed plenty, but how could I give him false assurance—tell him that failure was OK when, in reality, failure meant death?

"I've failed before," I said, "and people died, some injured for life." It was true. When I worked, I couldn't convince people to listen or to do the right thing. But it didn't stop there. Failure to stop that database, failure to recognize it for what it was (a method to identify us), had led us here—to this quarantine—to this genocide. I had failed repeatedly and spectacularly.

He raised his brows.

"That's right—the one *they* put in charge is a proven failure. I tried my best, but it wasn't good enough. And you know what? I'm sad, but I'm not holding it against myself. The only thing we can do, Scott, the only thing we can ever do, is do our best and keep trying."

His mouth twisted, and tears welled in his eyes. As if to prevent the tears from falling, he tipped his head back.

"If we fail," I said, tugging his shirt sleeve to get his attention, "*we* fail. It's not on you. It's not on me. Just do your best. Got it?"

An undecided expression crossed his face.

"OK," I said, ignoring his skepticism, "go gather what you need to disable that alarm. We'll meet back in the cafeteria at dinner. I need to go find a tool for the manhole cover."

It was his choice, I told myself. As I watched him walk into the gym, I wondered if he'd show up. I wasn't staying another night—I meant it. I left to find my pry bar.

In the cafeteria, people stood with their arms crossed around a man who addressed the crowd, "They said we should remain calm. If the old man was right, and we aren't sick, then we can wait it out here. If you don't want to wait it out, go get the vaccine. It's simple. There are two choices."

"But why won't they let us talk to our families?" a woman asked from the back of the crowd. People shook their heads in agreement with the woman, and conversations erupted.

To calm the dissent, the man addressing the crowd made a lowering gesture with his hands. When the noise died back, he said, "Maybe they are trying to prevent the spread of misinformation." Half accepted his answer, the others nodded their heads and began to quiet, uncrossing their arms.

It ate me from within to say nothing. The old man on the intercom had given his life to convince them, but if they would not listen, then whatever happened was on them.

Another dissenter broke the calm. "They won't even send someone in to unplug the toilets. If we try to wait it out, as you suggest, there may be no working toilets within a couple days."

The apparent leader responded. "They probably don't realize the toilets are plugged. Let's make a list of things we need and leave it for them here in the cafeteria before they close. When they come to change the food, they'll find our list."

Once again, the people appeared pacified with the rational approach. Nods of agreement bobbed in the sea of heads. A woman with a notepad and pen stood next to the leader and began writing requests. I recognized her as the yoga/meditation leader. A doer and organizer, she seemed sold on the rational approach, waiting things out. But I didn't have time to try and convince her.

"Phones, we want our phones back. We want to talk to our families," a young woman shouted.

Yoga woman scribbled the request on the notepad and shook her head in affirmation.

"I need diapers," a woman shouted over her screaming infant.

"And tampons," shouted another, and others shouted agreement.

"My meds are almost out," shouted a man over the women.

"One at a time, people. Form a line," the leader directed. "We'll have to prioritize the list after. The requests affecting the health and safety of the most people will be first on the list."

"You all better prioritize my meds because if my Dr. Jekyll comes out, it will jeopardize the safety of *the most people*," the man out of meds insisted, with mockery in his voice. He huffed and paced and then left the cafeteria, turning over a chair on his way out.

I suspected he was schizophrenic. The gene for dysbindin lies on Chromosome 6. A mutation downregulating dysbindin leads to schizophrenia, while an extra annealed copy upregulating the gene leads to increased intelligence. Chance had favored me with the upregulated gene. It was only chance that he had the genotype leading to a serious mental illness, while I had the beneficial upregulated version. An unfortunate error in gene-editing processes, he'd done nothing to deserve his condition.

"I'll need volunteers to collect the full garbage cans and bring them in here, so they can be cleared out," the leader instructed.

With the crowd facing the leader, I grabbed a dining chair and moved quickly toward the locker rooms. The Pacific Islander family, whom I assumed had left to get vaccinated, sat at their table and eyed me. Their attention almost caused me to drop the chair. I avoided eye contact and worked my way out of their view.

With the chair, BOB, and my blanket, my arms were full, and I waddled. I removed my tweezers from BOB and left my belongings just beyond the cafeteria. I'd not need those things after tonight anyway, I thought. "Bye, BOB." I blew him a kiss.

In the locker room, I turned the hand driers on for cover noise and took the chair into a bathroom stall. Placing the chair upside down on the toilet, I used the tweezers and worked on unscrewing the steel legs. I'd removed three screws from two brackets on one pair of legs, but I stripped the fourth screw and couldn't pull it free. The crude tool made my fingers ache, but I persisted, unscrewing brackets on the second leg. With one bracket free of screws, the leg wobbled. I started on the other, dropping the bracket on the floor with an unnatural clank. The dryer turned off at that moment, and I held my breath, listening. Nothing. The second bracket came free. I draped the U-shaped legs over my shoulders, grabbed the chair off the toilet, trying to corral the half-attached set of legs, and exited the stall.

The concrete-block-shaped, Pacific Islander woman stood one meter in front of me as if she'd been waiting for me to come out of the stall.

"What are you doing?" she asked.

"Nothing," I said, scooting around her to place the broken chair in a corner.

"I don't think so." Sidestepping, she positioned herself to block my way again.

I pointed to the intercom. "Shsh!" Then I pointed to the dryers and waited for her to approve my movement. With a grudging glare, she nodded, and I walked over to turn a dryer on.

She followed me to the same place I'd talked to Robin, between the lockers.

"They listen?" she asked.

I turned to face her and shrugged. "No idea."

With my shirt fisted in her hand, she said, "We're going with you."

"What are you talking about?" I squirmed under her grip and wondered how she'd leaped to escape theory from my disassembly of a chair leg.

"My boy, he's not smart, but he's never wrong about people, and he says you're leaving."

I'd wanted to approach them as potential allies before, but were they manageable? "Look," I responded, pulling her hand off my shirt, "anyone who tries to leave here will probably get killed."

"My son says we're going with you."

"I am not a tour guide, lady."

Her hand struck out to slap me, but I bent back and avoided the strike.

"You can't bully me." I stood my ground, but she stepped closer.

"If you don't take us, I will turn you in." Nostrils flaring, she placed her shiny face a hair width away from my own.

"To who?" I laughed and stepped back. "There's no one to turn me in to." Unable to approach guards, the officials had not given us a way to communicate with them.

"Take us, or I'll tell everyone."

She had me there. I couldn't take everyone, not on a clandestine escape, but did I even want this family? Why were they so hostile? I didn't need hostile forces. Our plan involved quietly sneaking around without being seen. Opposed to deception, but without a choice, I concluded Scott and I would decide if we'd take the family after we fine-tuned our plan.

"I'm not promising anything."

"My son says he knows you. Says we are going with you."

"I'm sure I've never met you."

"Not me. Just my son—up there," she said, pointing skyward.

Oh shit, another one.

"You're Aline, right?"

They knew my name! A knot formed in my stomach. I'm not in charge of this, I thought, fighting the growing reality. At least I didn't have to convince them. If Scott bailed, the family was backup. There were six of them, though, a lot of responsibility. And they were big, not an attribute for sneaking about undetected.

"OK. When the time comes, you do what I say. Remain extremely quiet— quiet walking, no talking, no children nonsense—I mean it," I said, shaking a finger at her.

Firm as a monolith, she stood unintimidated. Still, I had reservations.

How could she make six kids be quiet … and two huge parents tiptoeing around like ballerinas? Well, I do my best, I told myself.

"You come meet our family now."

"Are you asking me?" I asked sarcastically.

"No. I am Emma," she said as if her name alone explained why she gave orders.

"OK, then." I opened a locker, pulled myself up by the top shelf, and slid the disassembled chair leg on top, out of view. It would cause suspicion, walking with it around my neck.

Hands on her hips, Emma followed or, rather, herded me to the cafeteria.

CHAPTER 18

2009 TERRORIST

Three hours in, the ethics committee meeting dragged on so long, I had to take multiple pee breaks. I listened patiently, awaiting my opportunity to hand the committee members the agenda addendum I'd created for the review of the vaccine study. The letter explained what information was missing and why it was important. As soon as they were finished reviewing the other studies on the agenda, I'd hand it to them. But for now, I twiddled my thumbs while they discussed the naturopathic studies on the agenda.

An acupuncturist, conducting an acupuncture study, had accidentally used the same needles on two different patients. I was pleased I hadn't been assigned that study.

"But this isn't supposed to be possible," one of the committee members said. "Don't the needles come in single-use packages, and don't they open a new set for each patient."

My coworker floundered. "We'll have to ask them for more clarification," she said. She should have asked them for that information before the meeting, I thought.

Karla looked to me. It was my turn. "I assume you all read this?" I asked the committee rhetorically. I knew they hadn't. They preferred to have the staff explain it to them. "The physician proposing this study on our HMO's patients is not an employee of the HMO. So, that's strike one. I don't believe he should be allowed to conduct research on our patients unless we have some clear understanding of who will be responsible if they sue us." He should find his own patients, I thought, but I had to appear to remain unbiased. "Strike two is that he has not received Federal Drug Agency (FDA) clearance to study this dietary supplement as a drug in these diabetic patients."

Karla stopped me there. "Dietary supplements don't require FDA oversight."

"They do, actually, if you intend to use the supplements to treat a disease. This physician intends to take our diabetic patients off their insulin and give them this dietary supplement instead, and then see what happens."

Some of the committee members gasped. "I'm sure it's not as drastic as that," Karla said, diminishing my portrayal of the study. "This doctor is a well-respected colleague of the Director's. I can call the Director in here if you'd like to hear from him?" she offered. It was against the rules to have other physicians pressuring committee members, but Karla had broken the rule a few times.

"I'm almost afraid to ask," the committee chair said to me, cutting Karla off, "but what is the third strike?"

With a flat affect, I said, "There have been no prior studies establishing a safe dose for the dietary supplement. The doctor has chosen to study, what looks to be, three times the recommended dose, and we don't know what the side effects are."

Karla started squirming. "It's just a dietary supplement. You don't really think they're going to overdose on it, do you?"

"I have no idea," I said. "You can overdose on iron, or vitamin D3, or A, or K. Why not this—this—" I finally pointed to the page where the supplement was listed. I couldn't remember what it was called as I'd never heard of it before reading the proposal.

Karla stopped the committee from making a motion to disapprove the study. "We'll have the physician make some clarifications, and we'll bring this study back to you when it's in better shape." She'd have to change the committee members for the rereview—assign new members who wouldn't remember what I'd said at this meeting. Karla and her assistant nodded at one another. And I would be removed from the study, I thought.

The chair called the H1N1 vaccine study next on the agenda.

I introduced the study and let the committee fawn over the principal investigator's qualifications and the hefty budget before starting in on them. I handed them the letter addendum and offered a break if they needed time to read it.

"Why don't you summarize it for us?" the chair asked.

"The application is incomplete," I said. "We have no verification that this study received a protocol number; we have no preclinical study information, no chemistry or manufacturing information."

Karla crunched her plastic water bottle and then took a long, loud pull from it. I stopped talking until she was done.

She placed my letter under her agenda and said, "These are purely administrative concerns that should not prevent the committee from approving the study. Aline can have these documentation issues handled before the study starts."

I glowered at her. The committee was supposed to read and consider the missing information before approving the study, but they didn't realize it. Can't ask if you don't know what to ask. "Well, I can't fix the consent form for them," I said with my eyes trained on Karla. "They need to state who is paying for adverse events, and they haven't disclosed that the antigen originated from pigs. I can think of two religious groups who might take offense to not being told they were injected with pork product without being told."

Karla shut off the recording device and said, "The researcher would prefer not to drive people away with scare tactics in the consent form."

One of the physicians commented, "Sometimes, what people don't know won't hurt them." A stunned silence ensued. As the sole representative of the Jewish ethnic faith on the committee, everyone's eyes turned to the man in the kippah sitting in the corner chair, looking like he'd rather crawl under the table. He cleared his throat and said with a crack in his voice, "I wish to abstain from the vote." The secretary scribbled down his abstention.

"I think we're getting off track here." Karla broke the silence, "We're on a timeline. Universities and healthcare institutes all over the country have already approved this study. We can hammer out the kinks along the way.

Administrative issues only; I assure you." She smoothed her hand over her stack of papers for effect and reached to turn the recorder back on. Just before she turned it on, she hesitated and looked at me. "I think we can handle it from here, Aline." She snipped each word. "Why don't you take the afternoon off? We'll talk later." Then she pushed the recorder button and waited.

My face felt hot from embarrassment. She'd dismissed me like a child! I stood and looked at the committee members for support, for any of them to come to my defense, but they all sat in recorded silence with their eyes to their papers. Spineless!

Karla resumed while I gathered my papers. She said, "The CID alters the regular seasonal influenza vaccine every year before flu season, and nobody reviews that, so reviewing this H1N1 flu vaccine in detail isn't really necessary. It's a formality."

Rather than a genetically engineered vaccine for an entirely new influenza virus, she'd described it as though the new H1N1 vaccine was merely a slightly altered version of what people already got every year. Like a Poodle was only a slightly altered version of a Great Dane. Both were dogs. One came with poo bags and the other with a bucket and shovel. Her characterization strayed far from the truth. My eyes pulsed with exasperated steam as I left the room.

Though my heart hadn't been in it, I harassed the barista and then took my small latte on a walk. When I'd walked a kilometer, I stopped to rest in a dirty park. While I waited for—I don't know what, rain, I guess—I watched nicotine-addicted pigeons peck cigarette butts and chewed gum. Then I walked back and took the elevator to the wrong floor. Then I took the stairs to the right floor. Avoiding contact with coworkers, I collected my purse and keys and went home.

There were times I couldn't remember driving home, I realized, when I found myself there already and pouring a hot bath as if hot water could wash out that kind of dirt. Luckily I hadn't hit a pedestrian, I thought; it must have been the caffeine.

First thing in the morning, I fired up the PC at work and checked the database for the vote on the vaccine study. After I left the meeting yesterday, the committee approved the H1N1 vaccine study without requiring any changes, or so the database indicated.

On my way in this morning, Karla had asked me to come to her office at 11:00 a.m. She never called me into her office. It was usually the other way around—I'd seek her out when things weren't right. But before I left yesterday's meeting, she promised we'd have a discussion. I hadn't been looking forward to it.

I knocked at her open door. "You ready for me?" I asked with the meekest tone I could muster.

"Yes, have a seat."

This might be it, I thought; I might actually get fired this time. I sat at the table, which she had cleared for the occasion, and clasped my hands in my lap as though my grandmother was standing behind me ready to whap me on the head for poor posture. I wasn't afraid of being fired, but I wasn't looking forward to the perception of being fired as if I'd done something to deserve it.

"Well, I don't know how to say this," she began, "so I'll just come right out with it." She kept her eyes on the papers before her. "Did you threaten anyone here or on the phone?"

I sat in silence, trying to comprehend her words. "Are you kidding?" I finally asked while squinting a lone skeptical eye at her.

She returned the silence for a moment. "The CDOD claims that you '*harassed them on the phone and disrupted our principal investigator.*'" She traced the verbatim words with her finger. Her face turned up then, but she closed her eyes, apparently not wanting to look at me.

"What?" I sneered in disbelief. My mind raced, but I tried to recall the conversation. "I called them and asked them for documents I needed. I asked the principal investigator, and then I called that rude General at the CDOD. No, I did not harass anyone. I was doing my job. I am very professional, I can assure you."

Intense anger welled in my gut. Last year, pharmaceutical companies harassed some of my colleagues for publishing unflattering drug safety data. It was a hazard of the job. My work involved money, egos, and telling people no—people who felt very entitled, physicians who had always been told yes, and apparently generals now too. I preferred communicating by email, so I could prove that my communications happened and happened professionally, but I didn't have an email address for the General. The principal investigator, our physician, hadn't responded until I'd gone to his office to ask for the documents in person. It was my word against one physician and one general.

"Well, I believe you, but the CDOD has ordered us to fire you."

"OK." I sat back in my chair. She did not respond as if she awaited my resignation. "I wasn't aware that I worked for CDOD." Then it occurred to me, the reason they might have smeared me. "Is this because I said they had to pay for adverse events? I told you they'd try to stick it to us. It's their vaccine; they should pay." Last night's committee meeting couldn't have mattered to them; the committee approved their study.

"No," she said. "They've agreed adverse events will be covered under the Vaccine Injury Compensation Fund set up by the government."

"Really!" I clapped my hands. "Hope you got that in writing. That's a good one. I'll believe it when I see it." The fund didn't cover adverse events from investigational vaccines, and it didn't cover anything that took more than a year to diagnose. Nice trick; no one pays. "So ... do you want me to go clean out my desk?" I gave her a sideways stare. What did she expect?

"No," she said. Her tone denoted displeasure. "The Director has decided not to fire you. *He* thinks you're smart," she said the last in a contrary tone. Karla had hired me because she thought no one would listen to me. Had the Director intervened in my firing, I wondered, because he'd figured out that Karla had tried to ambush him with the MMR/autism study.

"Sooo ...?" I asked.

"In addition to firing you, CDOD has ordered us to change our door codes, hire a security officer, and limit elevator access to our offices. They sent this letter." She pushed the letter toward me. "You're named there," she pointed to my name in the letter.

My heart pounded. My eyes kept rereading the first sentence.

Today's earring hoops were plastic, and they clacked distractingly when she moved her head. She smoothed her skirt under the table but lost patience. "They've called you an anti-vaccine terrorist." She snapped the letter back.

"Terrorist?" I gulped, and my arms felt like rubber. "That's a little heavy-handed, don't you think?"

She smiled the smile of someone with something up her sleeve. "Well, the Director," she started, "has decided to defend you."

He must have negotiated something out of it, or he wouldn't defend me, I thought.

"That being said," she continued, "I ban you from speaking to the principal investigator. You are not to ask him any questions. All questions will come to me first. And I am removing you from further review of his studies."

"The physician doesn't seriously think I'm a threat, does he?" I curled my eyebrows in consternation. "Actually, you know what? Never mind. I'm OK with it. I want nothing to do with these studies anyway. They're poorly designed, and they'll be trouble down the road."

"You are lucky, Aline. If the Director hadn't stood up for you, you would be in big trouble right now." Without saying it, she implied she would not have stood up for me. "When the CDOD names you a terrorist in writing … that is no small thing."

The air left my lungs, and Karla bore a smug, victorious grin. Now I needed my employers instead of them needing me. I needed them to defend me. But why had the Director defended me? What had he negotiated for himself? Had Karla and he specially selected me as the scapegoat?

"We will be changing your job description," Karla said. "You will no longer review new clinical trials. But, don't worry, we have something much better for you. You can review the annual reports for the minimal-risk studies."

She'd just removed my teeth. Without the power to help patients, what was the point in even keeping the job? Annual reviews were a formality; once the interventions were complete, opportunities to undo harm or prevent risks were gone.

"And," she continued, "if you would like to transfer to another department, every effort will be made to accommodate your move."

"I do not wish to transfer to another department, thank you." I'd never be able to defend myself from another department. I had to maintain access to our departmental files.

"Fine." Her voice clipped, and her lips closed tightly.

"Fine," I said, parroting her. The Director thought I was so smart that I'd just been rewarded with a demotion and offered a transfer. I stood to leave and shot her a smile that held a grudge on my way out. At that very moment, I wanted more than ever to urinate in the hall on my way out the door for good. Fucking corporate whores, I thought.

Pajama-pants-payroll lady peeked around her cube from her rolling office chair. I stuck my tongue out at her, and her legs wheeled her lard butt back to her monitor. I *wanted* them to brand me the urinator terrorist but restrained my anger and went home early with a full bladder. Salaried employees are allowed to keep their own hours, I fumed.

I logged into work from home and then spent hours copying emails and printing reams of documents in my defense. If I printed that many documents at work, someone would have noticed and asked what I was working on.

The dog placed his head in my lap and eyed me with black eyes that gave off an expression of perpetual apology. We'd never named him, simply called him: The dog or just Dog. A lady had abandoned him with us at Green Lake Park. She'd asked us to hold him for just a moment while she ran into a store across the street, but she never returned. Never tagged or chipped, he was our medium-sized, black dog of unknown breed, age, or origin. Our dog, anonymous.

"You were meant to be with us, Dog," I said to him and scratched behind his ear. I thought he understood. His devotion warmed my heart. All was not lost, I told myself; I had love.

Jeff walked in the door around 6 p.m. and found me in the office buried in stacks of paper. "What's going on? Everything OK?" he asked.

"They shut me down at work. I told you they were up to no good, but I didn't expect this."

"Did you get fired?" he asked, cocking his head and wrinkling his brows.

"No. They demoted me, but Karla didn't mention a pay decrease."

He whistled like a ballplayer, between his fingers. "Right on! Less work for equal pay." He stuck his hand out for a high five.

"Jeff, it's important, my work. Now, I'm just a paper pusher." I slumped and started crying.

"Don't worry, love. You're smarter than anyone. You can get a job anywhere. I'm sure the pharma will take you back." Jeff tried to comfort me, but my emotions rolled downhill.

"I would rather die than go back to work for those butt sniffers." I was trying not to swear as a resolution of sorts, something I'd tried in the past, but it hadn't stuck.

"Here." He stepped forward and took the papers from the printer tray. I pointed to a pile. He stacked them on top of the pile, squaring the edges, then he closed my laptop and pulled me out of my chair by the shoulders. "You need a hug."

"I need a hug," I cried into his abdomen, throwing my arms around his waist. He stood more than a foot taller than me.

"There's more," I said, pinching my nose to keep it from running on his shirt.

"What else?" He rubbed his hand up and down my back.

"The CDOD sent a letter calling me a terrorist."

"Who?" His hand stopped mid-back.

"The Central Division of Defense sent Karla and the Director, and— actually I don't know who all got the letter—but they sent a letter and—" I sank back into the chair.

"What do you mean? Why would they do that?" A skeptical look crossed his face.

"I told you about those studies. The CDOD is pushing some vaccine studies through without testing them first. They're saying it's for preventing bioterrorism or something. Anyway, I called them out on it. I did my job and asked for the documentation they were supposed to have already given us. Well, they got mad and wrote a letter to my work telling them to fire me and change the door codes. They called me an anti-vaccine terrorist. Me!"

He laughed and patted my shoulder. "Maybe you should bring your vaccine records to work." We'd both had more vaccines than I had fingers and toes. We'd traveled twice around the world.

"I know! Of all people. Seriously. Can't they look that shit up? Crap up," I corrected myself in haste. "We have travel documents with vaccines listed that we used to get into Africa, and where else? Oh, I can't remember."

"Yeah, that's right. We had to show proof of vaccination a couple times. Was it yellow fever and Japanese encephalitis?"

"Yeah!"

"Yeah!" he repeated. Now we were ready to form a mob of two. "Well, Aline, I don't understand, but I'm sure it will blow over. It's just too ridiculous."

"Ridiculous or not, they still demoted me."

"Well, maybe that will blow over too," he said, making a good effort at hopeful.

"I kind of don't think so. Karla offered to transfer me to another department."

"She wouldn't?"

"I said I won't transfer. Jeff, I want to quit, but I think I'd better wait and see what happens with this. I think they're going to scapegoat me. If I can just keep access to some of the files a little longer, I can document my defense."

"Well, whatever you think is right. I support your decision one hundred percent." He put my face between his hands.

"I need a hug," I repeated and squeezed his middle again. This was one of those times, I felt I didn't deserve Jeff. How many husbands would be so supportive, I wondered. "I don't feel like cooking," I said, stopping my nose from running with my finger. "Can we go out to dinner?"

"Sure. Greek or Vietnamese?" He offered our usual go-to's.

"How about that new taco place in Queen Anne?" I'd need to have a serious discussion with him about changing our routines. I hadn't told Jeff about my discussion with Wall Street Walt. Walt said those people could ruin my life, and I believed him. Pharmaceutical-hired thugs had already threatened my coworker's family; threats were cheaper than buying cooperation. CDOD could do worse. First things first, I thought, I had to blow my nose and wash my hands.

CHAPTER 19

2009 SALT AND LIGHT

You are the salt of the earth … (Matthew 5:13)
You are the light of the world. (Matthew 5:14)
By what way is the light distributed, or the east
wind scattered on the earth? (Job 38:24)

(World English Bible) Public Domain

Journal of Aline Orr: The answer to Hermes Trismegistus' riddle is: salt and light. I would have written the riddle this way: Uranus contributed the seed, and Gaia the nourishing womb. As the Sun and Moon rise above, so the Earth remains below. Birthed from the foam of the sea, the Sun and Wind rise together in the East to bring the Dawn. Venus the sublime.

The alchemical symbol for Salt is a circle with a line through it—the sun or moon bisected by the ocean's horizon. From beyond Uranus, a comet from the Kuyper Belt crashed into Gaia's Earth creating water (seed and womb). The water pulled salts from the prima materia that was the early volcanic Earth to create the oceans. Venus is said to have been born from sea foam and taken up on the wind, which describes the alchemical process of sublimation.

hoped this would be over soon. I had to go to work in the morning, I thought, as I placed a salt crystal on my kitchen counter in front of a night light plugged into the counter outlet. Then I stood by the sink to wait. It had been my mother's crystal. She'd found it on a dig at an ancient sea cave in Utah.

From a corner deep in my subconscious, I drew on that other knowing personality, the one who knew what was happening. That other me had intuitively directed me to prepare for another test—a judgment—on this day, one month after my first encounter.

After my first encounter with the hooded being, I had a vague recollection he'd come back to give me lessons in levitation. I couldn't recall discussing these lessons with him, but nonetheless, I expected him.

In that first encounter, the hooded being ordered me not to return to his cave location, but one night earlier this week, I'd found myself exactly there. I'd arrived out-of-body, in a dream state. Without conscious control over my out-of-body experiences, I simply appeared places. In search of the guide, I had called out for him in the cave, but my own voice had echoed back to me from the black depths. It told me the cave was a place of sacrifice. A pyramidal pile of skulls lay stacked in a neat pile to my right. Unlike my first experience when I had ruled my fear, the second experience left me filled to the brim with it as if I had inhaled it into my lungs. The fear flicked at my consciousness, causing me to return to the safety of my body asleep in bed. That was last week.

Now a different hooded being appeared opposite me on the other side of the kitchen. He stood contained within an iridescent bubble of plasma, snaking with thin streams of electric energy. Cloaked within a hooded cape, he looked identical to my original guide; he even carried the same staff. My instincts told me he was not my guide, but I played the charade.

Telepathically, he said, "It's time for your lessons," emphasizing the last word.

I took what he'd said to mean both lessons in levitation and punishment. The ironic double meaning contributed to the evidence that this was not my original guide. My first guide had not appreciated irony or sarcasm in any form.

"Resist the force of my field and levitate toward me," he instructed.

I cocked my head down and forward. With clenched fists, my arms stiffened at my sides as I concentrated on resisting the force of gravity. Next, my legs stiffened, daring the floor to drop away. With my toes scraping the floor, I floated my body in his direction. The opposing force of his plasma bubble was like the dragging force I'd felt in the rainbow light stream and when I'd dematerialized through the wall of my bedroom, like walking against an ocean wave chest-deep. Inching forward, I fought being bowled over by the wave of resistance. Out of intuition or my other self's privately hatched plan, I stopped short of the light emanating through my salt crystal.

"You *are* special," he said. My other guide had said the same thing, which I dismissed as flattery meant to influence me. I was certain now, this was not my guide, due to the way he'd said the words, as though my actions had just confirmed what he might have been told about me. He continued, "You should not have come," he admonished.

I stiffened in confusion. He'd told me to come. So, should I have disobeyed? I seemed to have difficulty understanding the meaning of their telepathic communications, interpreting what they said in so many ways. Was that my fault, or had the hooded guides meant to be vague? I suspected he meant I should not have been capable of resisting his field, but perhaps he meant I should not have disobeyed the other night when I had entered their cave realm uninvited. My other self took over and told him, "Now you come towards me."

Within his circular field, he floated forward towards me. I thought about the salt crystal I'd placed and wondered why, exactly, I had placed it there as if I'd had prior knowledge of an intended effect. He approached the light from the salt crystal, seemingly unaware. I wondered if I'd placed a weapon the second his bubble field touched the light emanating from the crystal between our paths.

His bubble stopped and turned opaque with light, and then his arm flung up to protect his eyes. The field recoiled from the light. Telepathic anger hit me. "You should not have come," he said, "and now you will pay." Before I could react, he pointed his staff at me and shot me with a condensed ball of electric energy. The energy blasted into my chest. I flew across the kitchen and slammed into the kitchen cabinets. As electric pain rippled through my body, my other self laughed with wickedness and knowing. Although the laugh had come out of my mouth, I didn't own it, and I instantly resented it. Had my other self experienced the pain of the blast too, or was my other self more than happy for me to suffer the consequences of actions I had not knowingly endorsed?

The hooded being's bubble disappeared. Had I hurt him? A short-lived pang of guilt hit me until I recalled he'd come to punish me for something over which I had no control. Had that other part of my consciousness, the one who'd planned this ambush, experienced guilt too? Somehow, I doubted it.

I crawled back to bed and climbed in next to Jeff and the dog, who both snored in unison, sound asleep. My heart beat so hard, drumming in my ears, I thought it would wake them. My mind raced uncontrollably, reliving every moment of the experience, searching for explanations, but formulating more questions than answers.

For years after my child-mother had told me all time was simultaneous, I'd read rudimentary lessons in time and quantum physics, meager knowledge I drew upon now. Unlike my first meeting, this guide appeared in a bubble. Was the bubble a void? Was a void a vacuum? Did a void contain antimatter? Did the void exert a repulsive force? Like charges repel, mass energy interacts with gravity. Did we share the same spin? Does spin depend only upon the plane of observation? Were we the same mass? Were we entangled? Entanglement is nothing more than understanding that all time is simultaneous; therefore, all mass, matter, antimatter, and gravity are simultaneous as well. I exist in all states simultaneously.

If I was matter and he was antimatter, I should not have been repulsed. Instead, we should have attracted one another, and our waves should have canceled each other. Annihilation. But I felt the repulsive force of his void, and I resisted it. The force of my forward movement was greater than his repulsive force. How had I created that force? I'd been floating in the air, with only my tippy toes dragging on the floor. What force resisted my forward force? Then there was the unaccounted force of gravity.

Had I moved in a plane out of phase with his void? Right hook. I had approached him through the light that passed through the salt crystal—light I believed to be polarized. Seeing double. Perhaps I'd split into two when passing through the light. Had he thought the other me was the real me? But why had I been able to approach him? Why had my mass not impeded my way? Presumably, the other me had no mass. Was I supposed to understand this, I wondered.

The mind racing questions turned instead to the burning pain in my hands and feet. Punishment. Stimulus-response. Electric shocks. Mouse on a hot pad. If my heart regained a normal rhythm, I wouldn't be going anywhere, invited or not, anytime soon. I'd have to call in sick to work.

CHAPTER 20

DAY 3, 2020 CONTINUED, FAMILY

Kids," Emma said in the cafeteria. They poked each other and ignored her. "KIDS," she repeated in a commanding tone. They stopped harassing each other and sat straight-backed to attention. "That's better." She waited a moment to ensure their attention spans held and then introduced me. "This is Aline. She will help us."

"Ahem," I stopped her before she attracted too much attention, "I think we should discuss this somewhere more private."

"In a minute." She proceeded to name the girl children by age. "Malia is the oldest, then Moa and Sarah."

With sheepish grins, each child waved at me.

"And then our special boy, Kimo. It's Kimo's birthday next week. He'll be ten."

"Kimo. Kimo is like Dad." Kimo clapped his hands in his father's direction. Kimo must have been the one I'd met before, I thought.

"I'm James," the father said, "like my son." James gave me a welcoming smile and reached for my hand. His hand engulfed my own. "Only, I will not be ten next week," he added.

I surprised myself by recalling my honeymoon trip to Hawaii. The Wiki Wiki bus driver had explained to Jeff and me the translation of his name, Kimo to James, and that Wiki Wiki meant fast.

James had snapped at an old man earlier. Perhaps he'd simply released some of the stress everyone in quarantine felt. I'd formed an opinion of their family based upon that interchange, but my opinion softened with James' pride at sharing a name with his autistic son.

Sarah, the youngest girl, asked, "Are you a Menehune?"

The family laughed at a private joke that I didn't understand.

"It's the Hawaiian version of a fairy," Emma said. "Kimo, you're a Menehune, too, aren't you?"

"Kimo and Aline are Menehune," Kimo said. He got up from the table, stood beside me, and held my hand.

"Wow, he likes you!" Emma said. She cupped her hand and said only to me, "He doesn't like to be touched."

"We fairies have to stick together," I joked, winking at young Kimo, who still held my hand.

"Can you read people's minds like Kimo?" Moa asked, picking up the empty bowl in front of her and placing it on her head as if it blocked mind reading. Cheerful laughs circled the table.

"No, I'm afraid not. I wish. You have no need to wear bowls around me." My only *powers*, if one could call them powers, had proved useless or unreliable. I could astral project and view past lives and glimpses of the future, but only during sleep or deep meditation. When I encountered the foreseen future moment in real life, it gave me great anxiety. My rational mind told me, irrationally, that because I'd seen a future moment, it must be important, that it had come as a warning or omen. But so far, I'd only arrived to experience insignificant moments, like walking into a house I'd never been in and recognizing hand-made-kitchen tiles I'd dreamed of before. Not very useful unless you're an interior designer.

True, I'd seen many of my past lives, but the past lives had not informed me how to live this one, and I usually only witnessed the unpleasant moment of death from any past life, hardly a superpower. For instance, in my last life, I died in Vietnam. Had that made me a pacifist this time around? The time before that, I'd been hit by an old motor car while trying to fish a letter I'd dropped down the storm drain. A pointless death. Before that, a missionary nun who died of a heart attack alone in a foreign land. And before that, a Native American who died from a snakebite. I'd been a merchant who froze to death in the snow carrying goods on yaks between mountainous towns, a woman accused of witchcraft drowned in a lake, and an Armenian who watched helplessly as his children were slaughtered in front of him before the knife was turned on him. Did these lives inform this life? Perhaps, but mostly they made me want to be done living lives.

I tried not to let this endearing family get into my heart. Emma had been so bullyish, but here with her children and husband, I saw her behavior as the way she got what she wanted in a family of strong characters. She was clearly a caring mother. Worry for the lives of their children must stress Emma and James to a level I could never comprehend, at least not in this life.

"So, did you all test positive?" I asked. I hadn't noticed many complete families in quarantine.

James responded, "Just Kimo, but the family came together. We stick together, right Buddy?"

"Right Dad."

"Aline is good," Kimo said, trying to pull me to the table.

I patted his hand but resisted sitting down. Good isn't enough, I thought; I'd been good my whole life and still unable to affect an outcome. The tremendous weight of responsibility made my shoulders ache. We could die trying to escape.

"Look, I'll do my best," I said, "but I guarantee nothing. I require complete cooperation from all of you." I eyed each of the children and then whispered to Emma, "Let's regroup at dinner time. We'll go over the plan then. The cafeteria closes soon for the meal change. I still have some things to do." Round up Scott first, I thought. "Don't tell anyone, got it?"

"Can we do anything to help?" Emma asked.

"No." I opted not to tell her we'd leave tonight. "On second thought, behave normally. Do not pack. OK?" If they started packing, it would draw attention. Others would want to join us. I couldn't be responsible for any more people's lives.

"We'll lie low," she said, under her breath.

Emma turned to instruct her children, and I left to piece together the remaining parts of an incoherent plan. Everyone dies in the end. I thought of the English Lit professor's books and reminded myself that I was here in the flesh, not in a story. If the events of my life were predetermined or at least partially determined, I'd eventually be expected to take charge of situations more perilous than this.

CHAPTER 21

2009 ALBEDO-OHR

*... To him who overcomes, to him I will give of the hidden
manna, and I will give him a white stone, and on the stone a new
name written, which no one knows but he who receives it.*

(REVELATION 2:17 WORLD ENGLISH BIBLE) PUBLIC DOMAIN

My bedside light was on, but I hadn't turned it on. The light woke me,
and my eyes opened.

"Rest Vedra," said a woman in a white, high-collared gown.

"That's not my name." I came in and out of consciousness. My hands and
feet burned as if submerged in boiling water, and a whimper escaped me. I'd
slept in fits and starts since last week when the hooded being in the bubble
void shot me with an energy ball. My toenail had fallen off, and the toe fes-
tered, red with the beginnings of gangrene where I presumed the electrical
charge had exited my body. Worse, I hadn't traveled out-of-body since the
event. The shot had done something to me, prevented me from astral trav-
eling, and prevented me from returning to the caves where the hooded people dwelled. Punishment, he'd said.

My hand grasped the bed sheets next to me for Jeff. He was there, a
mountain of comfort, rising and falling with warm, living breaths. Relieved,
I reached to turn off the bedside lamp and was taken aback to find the

woman in white still there. She sang a lulling tune in a foreign language. "Aurore," she sang. I interpreted it as Aurore, but it could have been ohr ohr, or, oror. The other lyrics, I didn't understand, but Aurore, repeated with each chorus. As she sang, she held a white, quartz-like crystal flat in her hand and passed it over my body from top to bottom in slow repetitions.

"Aurore," she sang a final verse. My eyelids opened and closed, fighting sleep. I forced myself upright to get a closer look at the comforting angelic being who now stood near my feet. Before I could discern her face, she repeated, "Rest, Vedra." Why does she keep calling me Vedra? I wondered.

Another figure appeared in the room, but I couldn't see it. I only knew it was there because it spoke to the woman in white. "Why can't we just take her?" the second being asked. "Because she doesn't understand," the woman in white said. In the next second, I lost consciousness.

When I regained consciousness, I found myself in a classroom surrounded by other students. I did not know how much time had elapsed since I'd encountered the woman next to my bed or how I'd arrived in the classroom. To test if I was present in the flesh, I pinched the top of my hand, but no sensation of pain answered the question.

Formulas materialized in the air in a steady stream before the students. Though no instructor taught the class, we all understood we were to memorize the formulas. But I became distracted by the space; the entire space was white and lacked substance. Above, below, and to the sides—all white. No floor resisted beneath my feet, and the white space overhead supported no structure.

Pay attention, I admonished myself, renewing my focus with serious intent. Partial definitions of variables entered my head, and I scrambled to keep up with the speed of instruction. As if in a trance, the other students watched unmoving and with a higher level of focus than I was capable of maintaining. Anxiety crept into my subconscious as I worried over the consequences of not remembering the formulas. The student to my right showed no signs of difficulty with concentration or comprehension of the material. He stared with a blank expression, eyes tracking back and forth as the mathematics continued at breakneck speed.

I scanned the writing for anything I might latch onto and found an equation with three variables written larger than the others. Emphasized variables. T to the minus 1 equals H times e, plus or minus other de-emphasized (though likely terminally important) variables. The three variables, I could remember, and I gave them a pneumonic: THe Equation.

Equations and functions progressed to the point that I lost track, so I dismissed myself from the classroom. I left the all-white, sensory-deprived learning environment and found Jeff awaiting me on a pebble beach. Finding Jeff on the beach, picking polished agates from the sea pebbles, confused me because I thought he had been sound asleep next to me in bed. Had he attended the class too, I wondered. I'd never seen Jeff when I traveled astrally. Why was he here, I wondered; he didn't have my genetic anomalies. Not that I didn't appreciate his presence, but it reminded me of when my mother had appeared before me in child form. That experience had made me question whether it had been someone else using Mother's image. I observed Jeff for signs he might betray his true identity, but he looked, acted, and sounded like Jeff.

He sat next to me on the beach, and together we discussed the meaning of what we'd been shown. We had experienced something of dire importance; of that much, I was certain. The math had been so difficult that I fretted whether I was up to the task. Perhaps the experience was meant for my other self—my other consciousness—the one called Vedra?

Jeff and I continued our serious discussion until the tide advanced and wet our feet. The water was cool and relieved the burns I'd sustained from the guide having zapped me with an energy ball. I still couldn't actively recall discussing specifics with Jeff, but a countersink weighed my spine. I had the feeling one has when a parent dies, and you can't comprehend the rest of life without them—not sadness precisely, as life is impermanent, but uncertainty for the future and fear of having to brave it alone. The experience ended, and I slept while my brain worked overtime, encoding equations into stored memory for later use.

In the morning, Jeff and I woke beside each other and then drank coffee and read the news. The routine propelled the façade of normalcy, but apprehension from the experience the night before tainted my morning. Meanwhile, Jeff went about his routine as if nothing had happened. Had he really been there?

I didn't ask him if he recalled any of it. I knew better. He'd think I was crazy. Instead, I searched the internet for THe equation, trying to recall the meaning of the variables or find a similar equation. Every search topic resulted in time spent wading through irrelevant topics and hunting for Easter egg equations. Space weather, gravity, electron flux, and relativity—no topics contained THe equation or anything resembling it. Perhaps my mind had fabricated the white angel and the classroom, but why, then, had the experience left me with a feeling of impending doom?

CHAPTER 22

DAY 3, 2020 CONTINUED, DAY OF DEPARTURE

found Scott in the hall near the gym. He milled about with an uncertain expression.

"Were you able to get your tools together?" I attempted to sound reassuring rather than too hopeful or demanding.

"I think so," he said. He sounded hesitant. "I still think we should wait until tomorrow, so I can work on disarming that door before we leave."

"It would be *ideal*, Scott." I put my hand on his shoulder. "There's a difference. Don't worry."

"No pressure, right?" he asked, his tone sarcastic.

"Well, actually … we have some tourists coming along for our adventure."

"No." He smacked his palm to his forehead and scrunched his face. "But what if I can't do it? I mean, this probably isn't going to work."

"We just do our best. Remember?"

"You mean we just do our *ideal* best. That's what you said a second ago."

With my palms together, I put some sweet syrup in my voice and begged. "OK, yes. Do your *ideal* best, *please*."

"How many?" he asked. We walked together toward the cafeteria for dinner.

"Six."

He halted mid-stride and looked to the ceiling with an air of disapproval. "You're shitting me?" He sounded uncomfortable using swear words. I bit my lip; I had no right to correct foul language.

"Hey," I said, "I didn't have a choice. Like you, one of them had already met me and decided I am in charge."

A group of the quarantined made their way to dinner in animated conversation or debate; I couldn't make out which. A few made eye contact as they approached, and I nudged Scott to continue on to the cafeteria to prevent them from engaging us as they passed.

"Come on, Scott. We'll go meet those tourists now," I said.

He dragged his feet, feigning exhaustion.

"Hey, maybe you already know him, like you knew me," I said.

"Ya? Who?"

"The autistic kid with the Hawaiian family."

"Hmm. I'm not sure."

"And he has three sisters. One of whom looks about your age."

"I didn't notice," he said, brushing his hair out of his eyes and straightening his posture a fraction.

"Really? She's, like one of only a handful of other girls here your age ... and she's pretty."

He didn't respond. I detected an almost eye roll. "I don't want to do this," he said and stopped mid-stride again.

"Just come meet them."

"What's the point? We're going to die anyway." He slumped against the wall.

"Well, if we're going to die anyway, why don't we go talk to some people and help each other try to feel better about it?"

"Stop pushing me," he huffed. His fists formed tight knots at his sides. "This is not my responsibility; it's yours!"

I let the disappointment show on my face. "You're right, Scott. I'm sorry. I'm leaning on you a little too much. You're not ready for this. None of us are." I waited for him to process what I'd said. "I'm still going to try, with or without your help on the alarm. And I'm going to go talk to those people because I like them. I don't owe them anything, and they don't owe me anything. I just don't want to be alone right now. Do you?" It wasn't entirely true. I didn't owe them anything, but I had committed to them.

"God!" He slammed clenched fists into the wall behind him.

A woman near the cafeteria entrance looked his direction. With a maternal look of concern on her face, she started toward us. I recognized her as the yoga woman who had helped the consoler-in-chief guy compile a list of requests, or grievances, depending on your perspective, for our detainers. I didn't want to get tangled up with her. She didn't strike me as a rule-breaker; rather, she seemed the type to probe your feelings until you surrendered from fatigue. How does that make you feel? I could almost hear her ask. She rubbed me wrong.

"I'm going, Scott. That woman is coming to talk to you." I nodded in the woman's direction and then stiffened. "Please, don't tell her our plans. If you want to join us tonight, meet at 11 p.m. in the bathrooms closest to the hall door you disabled. Take only what you need …" I had to pause a moment. The latter words triggered a flashback to the ant being, but I finished the thought awkwardly. "… to disable the door near the storm drain. Leave the bathrooms at 11:05." I motioned my hand in an ordered, chopping motion, and he nodded, affirming comprehension. "If you're there, great. If not, good luck to you." I turned to go and then reconsidered. If he decided not to come, he'd die here with the others. So, I gave him a brief hug, and he patted me on the back as the yoga woman closed in to console him. "Oh, and no talking in the bathrooms."

I looked at the floor as I passed her—my teeth ground with guilt for those I'd planned to leave behind. I'd devalued them in a way, and it made me a hypocrite.

Someday, I may regret not being more like yoga woman, an organizer, a doer, a woman who doled out concern. Someday, I'd ask myself, what would yoga woman do? Yoga woman would remain calm and compile a list of grievances, I thought, while I would continue to lead the vulnerable on the path of most resistance. My fingernails had dug into my palms, I realized, and I grimaced at the red marks I'd left. I was the kind of woman who harassed underpaid baristas for my own amusement, went into fights with my hands tied, and led death marches to nowhere. Ugh.

With a deep breath, I settled my tensions and entered the cafeteria. The overflowing, unemptied garbage cans remained, I noted; the letter to our keepers apparently having had no effect. My eyes searched the room until I found my conspirators' table. The jovial Pacific Islanders acted as if they had not a worry in the world—except Emma. Emma wore a wistful expression, but her eyes focused in the distance as if she searched for a fragment from the past that could be pasted over the foreseeable future.

Concerned, I plopped down in the chair next to her and tapped her on the shoulder. "How we doing?"

"What?" She appeared to shake herself free from her thoughts and entered the present. "Aline." She patted my hand. "You're here, good."

"You OK? We still on?" I asked; perhaps she'd reconsidered. Scott had cold feet, so I couldn't expect less of her.

"Yes. I have something important to ask you." She grabbed my hands between hers and looked me in the eyes. "If something happens to James or me …" The sentence ended in a gulp.

"I'll do my best, Emma," I said, unable to say anything more reassuring. "I'll do my best."

"If something happens to us …" she started again. "I mean if we get separated," she said, seemingly unable to put into words the fact that any of us could be killed, not just separated, "will you take them to Hopi, Arizona?"

"What?" I squeezed and patted her hand nervously and wondered if she was losing her marbles from the stress.

"Their godparents live there. Their godparents will care for them." She gave her children a wistful glance.

"Hopi? As in, the Native American Tribe?" I asked, curious how a family from Hawaii might have even met Hopi people, let alone make them godparents to their children.

"Yes. If you just get them there, they will be taken care of. Promise me if something happens to us."

"Emma, I told you, I'll do my best. I told you; I can't make any promises. Arizona is a long way from here. If we get out of here, my first priority will be to get us to safety. Anywhere … do you understand?" I hadn't thought that far in advance. Could we make it to Arizona? We have no car.

"Just promise," she took my hands in her own once again.

"Emma, why did you bring them if they're not positive?" It was something I'd wanted to ask earlier but thought it might be construed as insensitive. The whole family had come to quarantine, but only Kimo was positive. One of them had said that they stuck together.

"We came for Kimo," she said and looked away from me. Her expression changed to a look of discomfort, and I wondered if my question had caught her off guard. Perhaps she'd regretted the decision, I thought. Suddenly, I felt bad for asking, as if she should have chosen the other children, the greater number, over Kimo. There I go again, I thought, turning myself into a hypocrite.

"Hopi?" she asked again.

My face relaxed, and I asked myself, what would yoga woman do? "Yes, of course," I answered, consoling on autopilot. Arizona was as good as anyplace, I thought. A *goal* was better than no plan.

Emma's daughter Moa sat next to her. Moa had picked up on the serious tone of the conversation and stood to give her sitting mother a hug from behind. Emma started to cry.

"Stop that right now, Emma," I said. "We need to stay strong and focus." I had no concern her crying would give us away to the others, many cried in response to our circumstances, but I was dismayed. If Emma kept crying, I'd lose it, not from emotional weakness, but from lack of sleep and high cortisol. Moa started crying, then Kimo next to her, and finally Sarah. "Stop it! Stop it!" I commanded and covered my eyes, but crying proved more contagious than VHF.

James and Malia had yet to join in the crying when we were abruptly interrupted by a blaring fire alarm. The family's faces bore expressions of startled confusion until the entire table reached a consensus, and we burst into laughter. The unexpected distraction caused joy for only a few seconds until the sprinkler system initiated, spraying copious amounts of water on the dinner crowd, who now groaned and slipped their way to the doors. I grabbed at the family's arms and shirts to corral them before they could get away.

"Wait," I pled, "this is it, now's the time. The plan—start it now." The kids looked to their parents to interpret what I meant. "Move slowly. Do not attract attention," I said, trying to raise my voice enough to be heard over the sprinklers and the exodus of people. "I will meet you at the bathrooms shortly." I spoke for Emma's ears only, "I have to go get my pry bar for the manhole cover."

She nodded and herded her dripping family out of the cafeteria.

A crush of people migrated to the gymnasium to retrieve wet belongings, and I pushed through them in the opposite direction, jabbing my elbows. When I reached the locker rooms, I shimmied myself up the locker where I'd stored my makeshift pry bar and let it fall to the floor with a clang. Fortunately, the sound of the sprinklers drowned out my noise. I dropped to the floor and draped the pry bar over my shoulders. Perhaps I should have checked the bathrooms first, I thought, just as I heard the stall door slam shut.

I spun to face the noise.

Rivulets of water dripped from yoga woman's light brown hair as she struggled to tuck her wet shirt into her compression pants. I froze, like a hunted rabbit, with the chair-leg pry bar around my neck.

"What are you doing?" she asked accusingly. She stopped trying to tuck her shirt into her pants.

My mouth hung open without an answer. Then the intercom beeped. "This is a false alarm," said the same woman from the previous announcement. "There is no need to panic. Please proceed in an orderly fashion to the front of the building for a headcount."

"See you out front," I said to yoga woman and waved goodbye.

She yelled after me, "Wait, you can't leave. I'll turn you in."

I sped up and pretended not to hear her. "I just need to grab my things from the gym. See you out front!" I yelled back at her, hoping I had misdirected her.

We had to move fast, I thought. No one issues consolation prizes to the dead.

I jostled against the crowd of people now headed to the front of the building for headcount. Dubious glances lashed at me from those I passed, but I ignored them. To no one in particular, I said, "I left my purse in the gym," as the statement might hide the fact that I carried metal chair legs around my neck.

A plaid-shirted man at the back of the push of bodies tried to force eye contact with me. Still pretending to collect my belongings, I hunched and scurried into the gym to hide. Just inside the gym door, I waited and hoped the man had lost interest. After what seemed minutes, I peeked around the door frame and saw four plaid-shirted backs moving away in the crowd. Two of the men had strikingly similar hair, height, and build. Had he worn blue plaid or red? I couldn't remember. Well, it must be one of the two, I thought, the other two men wore red plaid, and one of them had no hair. People love their plaid, I thought; it functioned as camouflage in herds of Northwesterners. With the man a safe distance away, I left the shelter of the gym and proceeded to the bathrooms to meet the others.

With efficient strides, I reached the women's room and entered. One … two … three additional people milling about with my posse of Hawaiian girls and Emma. I nearly swore in shock. None of them spoke to one another, and I prayed the extra people were there to use the restroom before joining the headcount at the front of the building.

To wait them out, I entered an empty stall. The floor was wet from the overflowed toilet. I became anxious after peering under the door and seeing too many legs still at the sinks. I came out of the bathroom and shot Emma a puzzled look.

"Aline," she clasped her hands together in front of her and turned sad eyes on me that made me shrink. "I couldn't," she said. "They have children. The children, Aline."

I closed my eyes and swayed a bit. The fire alarm still blared, although the sprinklers had stopped spraying. I counted three women and one boy child. "How many?" I asked Emma over the alarm.

"These three ladies, this boy, one husband, and another boy in the other bathroom," Emma said.

The women approached me with their palms up, stuttering explanations of their situations.

"Stop!" I hissed. "Did she tell you the rules?"

The three women nodded and backed away.

"No talking in here!" I snapped, waving my hands at them to turn away from me. "Look busy," I said and shot a glare at Emma. I walked up to the sink basin next to Emma and said through gritted teeth, "Are we ready then? Nobody else is going to jack-in-the-box out of the toilet, right?"

She shook her head, no.

I made a round'em up motion with my finger in the air, and everyone lined up behind me. I approached the bathroom door to leave and pushed.

The door pushed back against me. I stepped back to make room, and yoga woman entered the doorway.

"There you are," she said. Her voice was tacky and made me want a shower. She took count of the others lined up behind me. I shot them a warning look over my shoulder not to say a word, but they each bore guilty-caught expressions on their faces. She paced the length of them, looking them up and down.

"What is it you want?" I asked.

"I think I will accompany you."

"We don't require an escort."

"I'm not asking."

"Where is it you think we're going?"

"You tell me?" She stopped in front of me with her hands on her hips.

"We're not going to the headcount. Go ahead and turn us in. You run up there now. Run along." I scissored my fingers at her.

"You can't leave. You'll infect everyone out there." She pointed in the direction of town.

Did she want to go with us or not? I wondered, shaking my head in confusion. "I don't have time for this. Get out of my way." I shouldered her to the side, and she backed a step away. The others followed me into the hall, and she trailed them.

With every passing second, our plan unfurled at the corners. "Come on out, guys," I called tersely into the men's room. By calling them out early, I had disregarded the plan. The men stumbled into the hall with confused and wary expressions. Scott appeared with the other men. Relief that I'd won him over took some of the weight off my shoulders.

With her hands on her hips, yoga woman said, "You can't leave. You all need to go to the front now, or I'll turn you in."

One blue and one red plaid shirt approached from behind the boys and men.

"You two," yoga woman said to the plaid-shirted men, who I now recognized were twins, "these people are trying to escape. Please stay with them while I go get the authorities."

One of the twins said, "Escape?" They shot each other wry grins and appeared to nod in agreement. "Sounds like a plan to me." They both removed their belts, and I cringed. "Well, don't just stand there," the speaking twin said, "help me tie her up."

James, the Hawaiian father, pincered his enormous hands around the biceps of yoga woman and pushed her into the women's bathroom.

"Scott," yoga woman yelled, kicking her legs on the doorjamb to the bathroom, "get help!"

Had he led her here? I glanced at Scott to assess whether I'd mistaken his intent to join the escape. But he followed James into the bathroom without hesitation, and the twins followed close behind. Our numbers had swollen to unmanageable levels, but I would do my best, I continued telling myself.

Kimo clung to Emma, and the girls wrung at their wet shirts and hair. The new women hugged their startled children.

Emma nodded toward Scott. "Who's he?" she asked.

I felt the accusation in her question. I had additions as well. "I couldn't tell you because he hadn't decided."

Kimo tugged at Emma's dress. "Scott is good."

"OK, Kimo, if you say so," Emma said.

The men emerged from the women's room. One of the twins spoke, "She won't hold for long. If we're going somewhere, let's git."

I waved for Scott to join me in leading the group. Except for Kimo, who refused to budge, the rest of us moved towards the exit doors. Emma stood with Kimo in the hall, trying to coax him, but he sat on the floor. "Not enough people," Kimo said. His arms crossed in defiance.

With irritation, I interrupted to see if I could impress the urgent nature of our predicament. "Time to go."

"Not enough people," Kimo repeated. Emma tried to take his arm to bring him to his feet, but he jerked it away.

"There're already more than we can handle, Kimo. We have to go now, or we'll lose our chance," I said.

"No. Get more people."

"Kimo, I can't convince them," I said exasperated. "I tried to convince some. They'll just turn us in, then none of us will escape."

"Not true." He pushed his wide lips out in a pout.

"You know someone who wants to come, then?" I asked.

"I can tell who."

Emma interjected, "It's true; he can read minds. Well, sort of. He might be able to find more people."

"That's great, but we don't have time. Now or never, people." I turned and started to go. The others huddled patiently outside the bathroom doors. Their faces, faces that would soon perish, were it not for this one chance to survive, looked to me for leadership. Assailed with guilt, I shrugged in defeat. "Fine. Who wants to go with Kimo to find people who *might* come with us, try to convince them in mere moments while the guards do a headcount, and get back here without getting caught yourselves?"

Most looked at their feet or messed with wet clothing. A couple retied shoelaces.

"No volunteers?" I snapped.

One of the new women stepped forward. "I'll go with him."

Her wife/partner pulled her arm back. "No. Julie, we need you."

"Think of Joe, Kera," Julie said. She gave her partner, Kera, a level gaze and patted the boy on the head. Not exactly the goodbye of a distraught mother, I thought. Maybe the women were sisters.

Too young to know what was going on, the tow-headed boy, Joe, did not fuss. Kera, one of the boy's two mothers, pulled on Julie, trying to keep her there.

"You and Joe leave," Julie instructed her. "I'll catch up." Then she approached Kimo and Emma.

Emma said to her, "Julie, I'll go with Kimo. He's my son. You go be with your family."

Julie responded, "Emma, I am a political consultant; it's my job to convince people."

"Emma," I said, "I need you and James to take care of your girls. We have too many children and not enough adults. I need adults."

"But he's just a boy," Emma said, pulling Kimo up from the floor. "He's my boy."

"And, he'll return to us." I placed my hand on her arm, gently encouraging her to release him. In a tone that said, you're getting what you asked for, I said, "He's the only one who can do this. *You* wanted to save more … well, so does he."

"Kimo?" Emma looked at her son as if they shared a private bandwidth.

"I go with Julie, Mom." He threw his arms around Emma's waist, ran and gave a group hug to his father and siblings, then returned to stand beside Julie.

"Come back with whoever you can," I said. "Go through those doors." I pointed to the double doors. "Turn right at the end of the corridor. Go out the door at the end of that hall and down the manhole. I guarantee nothing. We won't wait for you."

Julie nodded and walked at a stiff pace next to Kimo as they left towards the front of the building to try to recruit more people to escape.

"We won't wait," I repeated after them.

James took Emma's hand and led her back to their girls. "He's not afraid, Emma. He'll be OK."

"The rest of you follow me," I said.

We entered the first set of doors and proceeded down the hall. The fire alarm blared on, so the door alarms didn't matter. Wait, I thought, as a realization hit me. My head jerked to find Scott. Disarming the alarms didn't matter! My mind played catch up with the events. When the alarm initially sounded in the cafeteria, I'd known from instinct that we had to go that moment. Scott had known too, or he wouldn't be here.

"Scott, the alarms don't matter." I shot him an insiders' glance, and he grinned. He no longer had to fear failure as lives did not rely upon his disabling of the alarms.

"Did you trigger the fire alarm?" I asked, astounded I hadn't thought of it before.

"No, I thought you did." He stopped and held his hand up for the others to stop behind us before we reached the bank of windows.

We looked at each other and then at the windows with apprehension. There could be guards on the other side of the windows, this time more than one. My mind raced. Was someone else trying to escape too? Had *they* set off the fire alarm? Was there actually a fire? No, the intercom said it was a false alarm. Why a headcount, then?

I held my finger to my lips to ensure the others stayed quiet and approached the windows alone. Edging against the wall, I peeked my head around the first metal window frame. My eyes went straight to the manhole cover first. For reassurance, I gripped my hand to the chair-leg pry bar. No guards stood over the manhole. My sights turned to the trucks. They were in the same places they'd been before, ramps down and ready to load. No guards at the trucks either. Black smoke billowed from the opposite side of the building. The guards would be on that side of the building … fighting an actual fire.

My eyes scanned the glass auditorium door, which had only an X earlier in the day. The door now bore a word that froze my heart. In what appeared to be finger-painted blood, the word "genocide" dripped vertically down the door and through the X.

My hand stifled the scream that threatened to escape my mouth, and with weak knees I sank to the floor. A warning written by Red Robin, a warning meant for me. I'd been right. The vaccine had killed them all. Robin must have started the fire and set the alarm to warn us, or to give us a chance, or to mutiny, or … I don't know, but it was an opportunity, a thin chance. I snapped my gaping mouth shut and dug my fingernails into the palm of my hands with resolve. I motioned for the others to follow me in a crawl below the windows.

We reached the door at the end of the hall, where I instructed them to form a line. "James and I will go out the door and remove the manhole cover. When we've removed it, one of us will hold the door open and send you out one by one. Children first. Got it?"

Everyone nodded, all fifteen of them. They efficiently re-ordered the line to place the children up front. The new toddler, Joe, stood in front of Malia, the oldest girl, who draped her arms over his shoulders from behind. The calm toddler looked at me with intense blue eyes, the same color as my own, raising the skin on my neck in goose flesh.

"No talking," I instructed. Despite the alarm noise, I aimed to attract zero attention. "And no wiggling." I pointed to the girls, and they straightened.

Armed with my chair leg and his brute strength, James and I pushed the door open to tackle the manhole cover.

CHAPTER 23

2009 NEXUS 12

Journal of Aline Orr: The distance from here to there is both vast and insignificant. It boils down to a simple matter of astrophysics, a simple equation, a not so simple ability to be the equation, to work it and come out the other side. The equation is $1/T = H*e$, or T to the minus one equals H times e. I call it THe equation, as in the way out, the back door. Goodbye, bastards.

After a rough couple of weeks at work, getting blacklisted, labeled a terrorist, and demoted, I dragged with mental and emotional fatigue. I had found myself going to bed earlier and earlier, almost as soon as I got home from work. I chalked it up to the weather turning cold, but the truth was I'd begun to lose faith in work, in humanity, in a lot of things. My dreams held the most hope for me now. In dreams, I found purpose. In the dream world, I had things to figure out. I'd met an angel who called me Vedra, and I'd learned an important equation. If I dreamt more, perhaps I'd learn more, I thought, so I crashed into bed at 8:09 p.m. and pulled the goose-feather comforter snug around my body.

Jeff and the dog joined me, but I knew it was too early for Jeff to sleep. He'd stay awake reading for a couple hours first. I nestled into his arm, and he kissed my forehead. The dog got his kisses in too, and before I knew it, I was sound asleep, searching for someplace far from the troubles of reality, a place where each night presented new things to learn and research.

My consciousness entered a room reminiscent of Swiss, ski-resort gondolas. A room meant for transport. A meter-height, gray furry creature directed me to secure my head into a transparent round helmet, one of many attached to a conveyor track overhead. The creature had golden eyes to either side of its mouth, which arched over the top of what might be its head, if one could call it a head. It had no chin, only a continuous broad neck, extending between the eyes and up to the arched mouth. Two small breathing holes dotted the back side of where its head should be, fogging the back of his helmet. He reminded me of an otter, but I couldn't say why exactly, except his fur, and the skin beneath his fur, moved with the fluidity of an otter.

I followed his lead, slipping into the harness and then placing a helmet over my own head and tightening a gasket around my neck. His hairless hands bore stubby and creased, two-jointed but agile fingers, as he helped me secure my helmet. His hands didn't hide or twist in my active memory, I noted with amusement. Finally, hands I could discern and recall.

Our now weightless bodies floated side by side below the helmets along the tracks. I asked, "Where are we going?"

"Nexus 12. Don't you remember?"

I didn't remember. I must have arrived in my split-consciousness state, as Vedra. I didn't even know what a Nexus was, but before I could ask, our helmeted bodies jettisoned off the gondola track. Where we were, I couldn't say, as neither of us wore pressurized suits, except for the helmets, but I thought of it as space. We approached a void or vast area of darkness much darker than the surrounding space. Without warning, a thundering male voice rang in my head like a gong. "PRIMA FACIE!!!" the voice announced in Latin. Then a female voice (in contrast to the first male voice) emanated from the void. "I am Bab," it said in humble greeting.

Who is Bab, I wondered. I searched the blackness for the otter being but found myself alone and drifting toward the void as if it pulled me to it. Nexus 12, he'd called it.

My other self's out-of-body activities left me worried. Did we share a soul, Vedra and I? Was my other self, jeopardizing my soul? The increasing awareness that my consciousness lived a life outside my waking life caused me to return to my sleeping body.

Of late, I'd noticed my out-of-body (out-of-consciousness) experiences had declined in duration. The moment I'd become aware I wasn't dreaming, but in the middle of some other existence, I'd lose conscious awareness and return to my sleeping body. I couldn't maintain the link.

With a deep inhalation, my body re-inflated next to Jeff, who now slept and snored a soft whoosh in, Hzshhh out, whoosh in, like waves lapping a pebbled shore. It reminded me of our time in Galaxidi, Greece—pebbles, pines, laurel, octopodi, azure sea waters, and the procession to the center of the ancient world. I should have gone *there* in my dreams. Jeff was probably there, dreaming of vacation, I thought, jealous of his slumberific snoozing. I turned to the side. The clock glared 3:22 a.m., the time I often found myself awake. The rest of the night, I watched the clock count to dawn while my mind scrambled to make meaning of the Nexus 12 experience.

Through the fuzz-brained grog of sleep deprivation, I rolled out of bed at our usual time and made the coffee on autopilot. Jeff read the news, and I searched the internet for Bab, which I discovered meant gateway. Ancient Egyptians had placed Babs as paired obelisks flanking the entry gates to cities. The obelisks functioned as gateways, or Babs, not only to city entrances but also as gateways to the afterlife. Paris' Luxor obelisk is considered, by some, a chariot upon which the Bennu bird, a Phoenix-like creature, resurrects and takes flight. The Luxor's twin obelisk resides in Egypt. When together, they were considered a gate. Reading of resurrection made me hope Vedra operated only on her own behalf regarding any afterlife dealings. There wasn't much I could do about it, either way.

My attention turned to researching the meaning of Nexus 12, starting with the tedious process of reading through every page containing the keyword nexus. A cold swig of coffee convinced me to give up searching. I'd read one more page, I told myself, when on page thirty-three I stumbled across THe equation or something very similar to it. I didn't understand a good sixty percent of the article about the cosmic web but was engaged enough to have read that far with determination.

Since the invisible instructor had taught me THe equation, I'd read with obsession countless articles explaining the theories of Dirac, Fermi, Faraday, Planck, Einstein, Bell, Bohr, Schrodinger, Hilbert, Hesse, Hamilton, Hubble, and others, but none of their formulas revived a complete memory of what I'd seen written in the air … until Nexus 12 and the cosmic web. Did such coincidences exist, I wondered? Could I have simply stumbled upon a possible meaning of THe equation while searching for the meaning of a nexus?

If I applied the information from the article to my experience, THe equation represented how *they* get here, or how we get there, or both. The article explained that the cosmic web and the connection points between, nexus points, may well offer gateways to other dimensions.

Terrified the article would blip away from my screen forever, I ran to our office and crammed the printer full of paper. At any moment, I expected the words: Unauthorized Access to appear on the screen as if I'd stumbled upon classified documents or that I'd lose my answer, never to find it again. Print! Print!

"What's so exciting, Aline?" Jeff asked.

"I'm just trying to print this article. I just need to print this," I said through clenched teeth.

"I see," he said. Jeff was well accustomed to my online research discoveries. For clues I thought life-altering, he yawned.

I stood in front of the printer, tapping the lid while waiting for the lengthy article to print. "God. Mother Fucker!" I screamed.

"Do you need help?" Jeff was also used to my sailor's mouth.

"No. It's just out of ink."

"Uh-huh," he said without budging from the couch. He supported my endeavors in his own way.

I responded to technology mishaps in this way with some periodicity. Once, when my phone was hacked and turning itself on to take pictures of me, I'd thrown it out the car window. It flew over the guardrail, off the bridge, and landed to sink into the murky depths of the river that flowed beneath. "Die! Die! Die," I'd yelled out the window. I'd killed it, the indestructible yellow jacket. Jeff had stopped the car and stared at me wide-eyed until he appeared to realize that I was as sane as I'd ever be and that he'd married me in this condition. He turned his face back to the road and drove on without a word.

I fussed around with a new ink cartridge and resumed the print job. Half printed sheets ejected from the feeder, and an error message appeared on the display: Incompatible Printer Cartridge.

"You whores don't even know your own product when it's inserted into your filthy receptacle!"

From the couch in the sunroom, Jeff asked, "Would you like another cup of coffee, dear?" His voice was doting and tolerant at the same time.

"Yes, dear." I was sure I'd disturbed his news reading with my tirade. "Sorry for swearing, honey," I added over my shoulder, and then I opened the contraption to re-insert the printer cartridge repeatedly, despite the same error message. Finally, the error message disappeared for no good reason, and I resumed the print job from page fifteen. The ink faded again on page thirty, so I reprinted the last ten pages multiple times, cobbling together the parts I needed.

The equation section, page thirty-three, came out semi-legible on one of the printed sheets. For good measure, I shook page thirty-three in the air. I didn't need the references. I had it. I had found the answer. It was real and in my hand.

Disordered, half-printed papers in hand, I fell onto the couch next to Jeff, beaming from ear to ear. He handed me my coffee and asked, "Would you like to hear your horoscope?"

"My horoscope?" I scrunched my nose. Jeff didn't believe in superstitious happenings. I knew he had no interest in my quest for the elusive equation, so I agreed. "Sure, let's hear it." I took a swig of coffee.

His eyes trained on me over his reading glasses. "Your horoscope says: Mercury is retrograde. Expect technical difficulties."

I choked on a laugh so hard that the coffee came out my nose and splattered my faded-ink papers. Then we both laughed ourselves to tears. The dog, disgusted by our antics, dragged his four-legged self from the room with a grunt, sending Jeff and me into continued rounds of laughter.

CHAPTER 24

DAY 3, 2020 CONTINUED, ARIADNE'S MAZE

Only James had strength enough to lift the solid cast iron manhole cover, and it hadn't been easy for him. Another man had to apply leverage with my chair-leg pry bar, as I didn't have enough body weight to lift the cover. The cover had barely inched up enough for James to get his fingers under the edge before the pry bar bent into a useless piece of scrap metal, but they removed the cover. After the children and the others descended, only Emma, James, and I remained. Kimo and Julie had not yet returned with additional escapees. If they didn't return, I doubted Emma would leave with us, which meant the rest of us were as good as caught.

Before I could voice the thought, Emma said, "I'm waiting for Kimo."

"OK. Your turn." I motioned to James.

"No, Aline, you go. Emma and I will wait for Kimo and Julie."

"What if they don't come? One of you needs to go with your girls. Besides, those people down there have a better chance with you." I said to James.

James' expression brightened, and he motioned to the windows. I turned to look. Our argument about who went next evaporated. A beaming Kimo led what appeared to be fifteen additional people and Julie, all lined up at the door. No time to arrange them by speed, or age, or need. James dropped his shoulders into a hug around Emma and Kimo. All three wore expressions of relief on their faces. I opened the door and hurried Emma and Kimo to the manhole first.

"You're next, Aline," James ordered me down the hole. "I go last. I'll try to put the cover back as best I can."

"Good thinking." A minute ago, I'd been urging him to go first, but he was right. The longer it took our pursuers to discover how we'd escaped, the better chance we'd have to evade them. I left Julie to hold the door open, and then I stepped onto the first rung of the iron ladder into the manhole.

Before I'd descended completely, my peripheral vision caught a flash of movement from the south building behind the genocide-marked window. "Go to ground!" I ordered Julie to instruct the people inside the windows. She closed the door. James stood frozen outside. "Come on, hurry. Come here." I said to him.

He went for the manhole cover, but I stopped him. "Forget it. Just get down here." He started down the ladder behind me and stopped with his chest still above the hole. "Come on," I said. "Move it." He didn't respond. Was there a guard above? Why wasn't he moving? I turned to the group lined up and waiting in the tunnel. "Move quickly. Don't wait. Go as fast as you can. Follow this storm drain all the way out to the Sound. Emma, you're in charge."

"James," Emma said, looking at her husband's legs stopped on the ladder.

"Shush. Go. We'll catch up," I urged, shooing her to leave. She directed the others to place a hand on the shoulder of the person in front of them, and they moved into the abyss with only the sound of their feet splashing through standing water on the tunnel's floor.

Was James caught? Perhaps he'd frozen to avoid drawing attention. I tugged at his shoe. His toes pointed toes to the floor. What did that mean? I tugged again. Sucking his abdomen in and out, he took gasping breaths and twisted his trunk on the stairs. Too big to fit in the manhole, he was wedged like a cork in a bottle, his torso, shoulders, or both, impeding clearance.

I remained silent, waiting for James to speak first, not knowing if the movement I'd seen in the building had materialized into guards outside the building. The longer James stayed silent, unease spread through my veins, chilling me from inside out and freezing my feet in place.

"Go. I'm stuck, and I can see guards." He hissed through a small gap in the manhole created by the arc of his ribs. "We'll make it. I have an idea. Just get going."

My stomach sank. Leave him? What would I tell Emma? And what did James plan to do with the other escapees in tow? If the guards caught him stuck there, I reasoned, at least they couldn't follow us—the way was blocked. There had to be something I could do.

"Aline?"

"Yes?"

"You're still there. Go!"

"OK."

A few seconds passed. I waited. Although the alarms had turned silent in the building we'd just come out of, the South building on fire in the distance still blared.

"Aline?"

I didn't answer. Hot tears warmed my eyelids.

"Take care of my family," he said.

A rectangle of light emanated from a drain hole cut in the curb, and I climbed up a rebar ladder to assess the scene. The drain hole afforded a narrow field of view but allowed me to see a guard's boots at the south building across the grass area. The boots faced away from our position. The guard opened a door at the foot of the truck ramp and ascended, dragging a bagged body.

Through the curb cut, I heard a click-swoosh—the door where I'd ordered Julie and the others to wait. The guard had almost reached the top of the loading ramp and stopped at the noise. Hunched over the bagged body he dragged, his head turned our direction. Then the door where Julie and the others waited slammed shut with a metal clank.

The guard pulled the body bag the last meter into the back of the truck and then jumped off the truck bed. Handgun drawn and aimed, he ran our direction. "Hands in the air," I heard the guard yell.

James had told me to leave, to save myself, but I hung there paralyzed. There had to be a way to salvage this.

James and the guard were out of my view, behind my curb cutout where the manhole entered the sidewalk. Although I couldn't see them, their voices and sounds were within range. "Out of the hole," the guard ordered. Was he talking to me? Had he seen me descend the hole? I remained frozen, hanging from the curb cutout.

"I'm stuck," James said, from his stuck position in the manhole. "Give me a hand," he told the guard. His voice sounded hollow, carrying through the drain.

"Only you?" the guard asked. "Anyone else in there?"

"Only me," James lied.

Unless the guard came down the manhole, I remained out of the field of view. Without backup, I doubted he'd search further. I prayed the others behind the door stayed put. Somehow, they had escaped discovery despite having caused James to be caught.

"Will you give me a hand out of here? I can't breathe," James said to the guard.

A sickening crack emanated from their direction.

My chest pounded. I dropped to the floor with a splash and returned to the manhole, expecting military boots to descend and arrest me, but I stood helpless and lame. After some shuffling noises overhead, the manhole cover slid into place.

I let out an audible sigh of relief, then covered my mouth. It had to have been James; the guard wouldn't have covered the manhole. What had James planned for the others? Why hadn't he sent them down the drain before covering it? Yelling at him would only arouse other guards within earshot.

The door where the others waited clicked again, and James' voice said, "Follow me."

I rushed back to the curb cut and climbed back up the rebar to peer out. Wearing the guard's cap and a camouflage fatigue shirt over one arm, James led the rest of the escapees to the truck ramp. He was so bulky, the guard's shirt fit over only one of his arms.

"Up the ramp and into the truck." I heard James order the others. They did so in obedience and silence, to my surprise. James then entered the building below the ramp. What was he doing? Why risk going in? I wanted to leave, but I had to see them escape first. The back of my neck sweat, and I found myself holding my breath.

Under a heaping arm full of empty body bags, James exited the building and entered the back of the truck. At that moment, I understood he planned to have them hide in the body bags.

James vaulted off the truck bed, pushed the ramp up into the truck, and closed the gate. He strode around front and leaped into the cab. The ignition started! The keys must have been left in the truck. The truck rolled slowly toward the stadium lights and barbed wire perimeter. When it had disappeared from view, I descended the rebar to the floor of the tunnel—no time to wait. The guard above may wake up, or the other guards may discover the missing truck.

It was dark, smelled of mold, and water soaked through my shoes, but I sloshed into the black hole using the wall as my guide, like Ariadne in the maze.

Thumping blades of a helicopter echoed in the tunnel. I prayed James and the others passed the perimeter. By splitting up, he had given those of us in the drain a better chance, but at what cost, I wondered, as a sick realization hit me—that cracking noise I'd heard. To protect his wife and children, James must have killed the guard. He wouldn't risk the guard reporting our escape. I hoped the guards would remain ignorant of our escape, at least until they'd completed the headcount.

CHAPTER 25

2009 THE CONSTRUCT

I needed time to decipher the Nexus 12 dream and the discovery of my equation, so I resigned to save them for a later entry. Pen poised to strike, I stared at my journal's blank page. Too afraid someone might discover and read my journal, I wrote of my experiences from a circumspect, nuanced approach. Without putting to ink the dismissible, I danced around phenomenal accounts of my dreams. It was a challenging exercise, hiding in plain sight.

> *Journal of Aline Orr:* A man enters a room; he is within the room. The room does not recognize the man; the room is the room. Yet his body is part of the room. The man recognizes the space that his body occupies within the room. The man controls the space his body occupies; he controls that part of the room which he occupies. He can occupy every part of the room; therefore, he is the room. You are the man; you control the space you occupy within the room; therefore, you are the room. Your room has no walls; it is infinite; you are infinite.
>
> A thought is created; the thought exists in your consciousness. Your consciousness does not exist in the thought. The thought is consciousness. The thought rules your consciousness. You are the creator and the ruler of consciousness. You are immortal.

You create a thought; the thought enters your consciousness. Your consciousness does not enter the thought. The thought manifests. Your Self created the thought; your Self created the manifestation. If you release the Self, you are left only with consciousness. Only consciousness can become infinite and immortal.

The Buddhists have this thing called Sankhara. It describes the way in which our actions, thoughts, sensations, etc., combine to construct conditions that set in motion our reincarnation existences over and over again. The very conditions we create to perceive our environment, propel our future reincarnated existence(s) in this system or the next.

I liken Sankhara to open and closed quantum systems. Placing measurements or descriptions upon a quantum system means placing measurements on the systems' environment, which results in a combined system. System plus environment = combined system. Then one must go about measuring and describing the combined system, which necessarily requires describing the environment of the combined system. System builds upon system, each with new environments—Hilbert Space. Ultimately, the Buddhists say these systems, these lives, these environments, these constructs, and conditions, come into and out of being. They undergo coherence and dissipation. They are transient, impermanent as a flock of starlings, a school of fish, or a box of mice.

The Hindus describe enlightenment as Moksha. As far as I can discern, it is the same as the Nirvana Buddhists describe. There is a difference, though I think it all ends up boiling down to the same sauce. The Hindus describe an understanding of the self that leads to becoming one with all, while the Buddhists describe releasing the self to cease existence to become one with the infinite. The result of either Moksha or Nirvana is to end the cycle of rebirth.

Mother warned me not to go to the grayscale world because it was a trap, a box. I think it may be a holding place for those awaiting reincarnation. They have died, they will die, they are dead, and their paths are fixed. Their eyes were black and blind.

I put my pen down for a moment and recalled the grayscale world. In ignorance, the inhabitants of the grayscale world moved as if driven or propelled toward the inevitable future of their minds' creations. Through the black blindness, they witnessed a future incarnation that they created there in the grayscale world. Compulsion or attachment led them to create and describe their new cage. It's only natural. If unable to describe the environment in terms familiar, we'd all refuse to name it reality. If I'd continued to visit the grayscale world, or if I'd encountered my spirit there, my path would have been fixed too. And it would have been my own fault. It's a trick.

There are no shortcuts. I supposed if one needed to be reborn, if one missed a critical life lesson, then it was written, and rebirth was inevitable.

I sketched a calendar in my journal and marked the days and times I intended to meditate on releasing attachment to this world, to the self, and to the construct. First, I'd commit to completely emptying my mind for fifteen minutes a day, then I'd work my way up to expanding that emptiness, that nothingness, and apply it to my whole existence.

After I finished writing, I put the journal to the side. What happens to this life if my system, my construct, is deconstructed? Will no one remember me? Why do I care if I am remembered? Attachment.

Nirvana would have to wait. My thoughts were interrupted when the ever-vigilant dog started barking with uncharacteristic ferocity. No squirrel could set him off this way. Thump, thump, thump, thump. A throbbing noise drowned the barking, and I got up to investigate. Shoving the dog to the side with my leg, I looked out the window to find the lawn and shrubs blown flat from the force of two black helicopters that hovered above. Blown dirt and leaves pecked at the window, causing the dog to renew his vocal assault.

Jeff joined me by the window, and we viewed the scene unfolding over our house with amazed entertainment. It would be the talk of the neighborhood for years. "What do you think they're doing," I asked, "looking for a criminal?"

"Those are military helicopters. I don't think they're after a shoplifter," he said, leaning forward to get a better look. The Magnolia neighborhood had little crime and none of the type that warranted helicopter chases.

"Well, I hope they leave soon. The dog's apoplectic." I hooked my hand in the dog's collar and dragged him from the window. He resisted with such vigor that when my hand released his collar, black tufts of hair remained between my fingers.

"Must be somebody important in town. Maybe they're escorting a ship out in the Sound, or Airforce One, or something." Jeff stood and watched the helicopters with rapt attention, and I comforted the dog in the living room until they left.

"Well, that was some excitement," he said when they flew away. "They stayed long enough, I thought they'd come down for lunch."

I chuckled uneasily. Even if they were stationed above our yard waiting on someone else, I felt slightly trampled upon. The dog panted, and his tail thwapped the floor nervously. For both our comfort, I sat next to him and stroked his ribs. "It's over, Dog. It's OK."

Jeff's phone rang. It was Keith. Jeff pointed to his phone and mouthed that Keith was coming over. I nodded, stood, and hunted for my jacket, so I could take a long walk with my journal. The timing of Keith's call told me the helicopters had been intentional, but not why.

CHAPTER 26

DAY 3, 2020 CONTINUED, THE MAZE

In the storm drain, I caught up to the group faster than expected. Together, their pace lumbered. As the last to have left the manhole, I encountered Emma first and touched her shoulder lightly so as not to startle her.

"It's me. Aline."

"James?" she choked.

"No …. A guard showed up. The others couldn't come down the manhole. James escaped with them on the surface. They left in a cargo truck." I wasn't actually certain they'd escaped and didn't want to give her false hope but didn't know what else to say.

She stopped as the girls ahead of her tripped and cried out.

"Shush. Someone might hear us through the curb cuts." I pointed up to a light emanating from the tunnel about twenty meters ahead. But pointing was useless; the tunnel was dark enough, no one could see me pointing.

"Sorry," a girl said. I recognized Malia's voice.

"Shush! Keep walking."

We inched forward, wary of tripping in the dark. Each person placed one hand on the shoulder of the person in front of them. My hand barely reached Emma's shoulder ahead of me. If she hadn't been shuffling her feet, she would have kicked me in the shins. I was so close. As it was, if she slowed, I'd run into her.

"They almost caught him, Emma," I explained in a whisper. "He left in the truck to save us." Technically, the guard *had* caught James, but I'd reserve that part for later. No need to add to Emma's anxiety. Her shoulder sunk under my hand. I couldn't tell if it was a sigh of relief, extreme disappointment, or both.

My free hand slid along the wall for support, and I felt myself turn a corner. "Stop," I whispered and tugged at Emma's shoulder. "Tell the one in front of you to pass it to the person in front of them, and so on. Everyone stop."

She whispered, "Stop," to the next person. The people train continued to move jerkily until the first person in line stopped.

"I think we just made a turn," I said. "I'm going to check. Wait here."

I left them blind and in silence and backtracked along the same wall to the hard edge of a corner. From there, I stretched a step diagonally but did not find an opposite wall. Dread filled my stomach. If I left the wall we'd been following, what were the chances I'd find it again? With my spine lined up against the corner, I walked a straight line, measuring and counting my steps along the way. At fifteen paces, I worried. What was this large cavern?

An uneasy feeling settled into my tailbone, challenging each step forward into the unknown, open space. My fingers groped air until I finally hit a moist wall. I took a few thin breaths and prepared to continue the search. Searching three steps to each side, I found nothing.

Perhaps it was an intersection, I thought, and expanded the search to each side, counting steps to either side of my starting point until I found another corner and stopped to orient. From the school, we had set out in the storm drain heading west towards the Sound but had turned to the north on accident. This tunnel is west, I decided and then counted my strides back to the opposite wall across the opening. If I got lost now, I couldn't chance calling out to the others—someone above might hear. The others, down tunnel, wouldn't hear me from this far away, anyway.

A few stumbles and a deep spot later, I found my original corner and trailed my right hand along the wall. The prospect of losing the others and navigating the maze alone caused trepidation, that, and the silence stretching ahead—all silence, except for my feet sloshing water. I should be there already, I thought; it was taking longer than it should have. Was I lost? I stopped and hugged myself both for reassurance and to ward off the damp chill. A few more steps, I committed, as I considered the risk of yelling ahead or turning around to find another tunnel.

A few more steps again, I told myself before giving up, when with a start, I bumped into Emma's back. I almost collapsed with relief. Whether I'd wanted them or not, I suddenly felt grateful for the others, grateful I wasn't alone.

"We have to go back," I said. "This tunnel goes north, and we need to go west. Whisper ahead. We're turning around to take another tunnel. I'll lead." Whoever had been at the head of the line hadn't even realized we'd rounded a corner. I waited for Emma's hand to touch my shoulder and then a few moments more for the message to reach the end of the line. I inched forward a few steps, and our people train departed, but the progress was short-lived.

"Ouch!" An accented female voice cried. Momentum halted with a jerk on my shoulder. It sounded like one of Emma's girls. Emma confirmed by releasing my shoulder to go to her daughter. Broken ranks! The people train disintegrated in the dark. Figures shuffled, and the sounds of feet splashing water obscured their locations. I had to control the situation fast.

Desperate, I barked an order. "Everyone, stop and place your back against the wall." Separation meant failure. "And stop talking."

"You don't have to be a dictator," a voice accused. It sounded like the woman with the toddler, Joe. Her name was Kera, I recalled.

"We need to keep quiet for all our sakes. I'm coming to count you all, so we know how many of us there are. Stay still." We should have taken a count first, but the group had left the manhole before me. Feeling my way down the line, I grabbed both of each person's hands to make sure I didn't double count anyone. We'd had sixteen, including me, when we left the bathrooms. We'd lost James and Julie. But Kimo was with us somewhere—there. I found him next on the wall.

I tried to touch both of Kimo's hands, but he yelled, "No!" and swatted at me. He didn't like to be touched, I remembered, for future reference. Then I found the twins, Emma and the girls. Scott, I noted, had found his way to Malia, the only other girl his age.

"Is she OK?" I asked Emma.

"Sarah hurt her leg," Emma said. "She got it stuck in the branches of that vault back there. It's cut." Each curb cut was surrounded by a cement vault that had sunken areas, catchments for branches, and mud before the tunnel continued.

"Is it bleeding heavily?" I prepared to remove a sock to tie it off.

"I can't see it," she said to me.

"Can you walk, Sarah?" Though thin, the girl was tall and too big to carry.

"It hurts—it's stinging," she said.

Far from sterile, I balked at putting my hands on her leg, but I needed to determine the severity of her injury. Who was I kidding, I thought; her injury had already stewed in storm-drain water.

I reached to palpate around the wound. "Sarah, I'm going to check it. Put my hand where your leg got hurt, and try not to cry out." I placed my hand in hers, and she directed it to a quarter-sized tear in her jeans. I pulled the stretchy jeans up her calf and prodded the shin gently. She squeaked.

"There?"

"Yes." She tugged her leg away, and I grabbed it back. I wasn't done.

I felt no additional warmth, which meant it wasn't gushing blood, but the skin was pierced. A distinct knot had formed at the site, and the skin was rough under my fingers. "I hope you've had your Tetanus shot, young lady."

"She's current," Emma said.

"Sarah, can you walk?" I asked.

She limped forward two steps and replied with trepidation, "Yes."

"Emma, I think it will be fine. It's a gash, not a lot of blood, as far as I can tell. There's a knot forming at the wound. It will leave a gnarly bruise and abrasion. And it will hurt for a while."

"OK," she said, "off we go, then." To Sarah, Emma said, "Good girl. Strong. Head up."

I resumed my counting activities. We had to be missing a few. I counted eleven, including myself. There had been a family outside the bathrooms, a mother, father, and another little boy. We were missing three. I asked Emma,

"What happened to that other family with the little boy? Not Julie's boy, Joe, but the other one?"

"Before you caught up with us, they went a different way. They said we'd be safer split up."

"Why did you let them go?" I asked, smacking my head in the dark. Better for who? Pressure built in my head like a steam cooker. Which other way had they gone? What if they went west, ahead of us and then got caught? We'd walk into a trap.

"What?" Emma said. "You think I could force them to stay with us? Besides, maybe they're right. They might be better off without us."

"What's that supposed to mean?" I regretted the defensive tone, but the words had left my mouth, no retrieving them now.

"We're slow, Aline. With James, we'd have a better chance, but we don't even know where we're going. What's the plan when we get to the Sound?"

We whispered, but our conversation was audible, almost amplified by the tunnel. Suddenly, I didn't feel in charge of anything. Maybe I had been barking orders like a dictator, but I didn't notice anyone else stepping up to lead.

"Sarah, hun," I called ahead to her, "you come upfront with me. We all go your speed. OK?"

"Mmhmm," she replied and hobbled to my side.

"Emma, why don't you and Kimo take the middle with Joe and that other lady," I said.

"That other lady is Kera," Kera announced herself in a biting tone.

I didn't respond. Fewer words meant less noise. Did she blame me for getting separated from her partner, Julie? It had been Kimo's idea to rescue more people, not mine. And Julie had made her own decisions.

"You guys, you brothers," I said.

The twins responded in unison, "Gatlin and Gowen."

Only their mother could tell them apart, I thought. "Can you bring up the rear?" The twins would stick together, and I wanted adults at the end of the line.

"Sure, thing," one of them responded. They made their way to Scott and Malia at the end.

"OK, we're returning to silence now. Heading out to the Sound. Do not separate from the group. Anyone separated increases the risk we all get caught." I sounded like that woman on the intercom, I thought, disgusted with myself.

I moved my way to the front with Sarah hobbling at my shoulder. We engaged the train, rolling back to the bend and the intersection where we'd find the correct tunnel out to the Sound. Emma was right; I didn't have a plan. But one thing was certain; if that other family got caught, they'd turn us in. We had to get out of the storm drains.

Despite the fight-or-flight pressure, we limped our way back to the west tunnel. Sarah walked timidly after having fallen in a hole and gouging her leg on branches. Her pain and limp weren't fake. She didn't complain or whine, for which I was grateful. If the wound didn't get infected, it would be a miracle. I, too, walked forward with more apprehension. First in line meant first to fall into any unseen holes. No one from behind pushed us to go faster, I noticed.

We crossed the intersection I'd found earlier and entered the tunnel that headed west toward the Sound. After what felt like thousands of meters, my hand discerned a change in the wall texture. The tunnel had narrowed considerably, and the sound of water crashed ahead. The Sound, I thought. It had to be the tide lapping on the drain exit. I tripped on the edge of a submerged step, my hands catching my fall on the sides of the tunnel.

I stopped and raised my voice to counter the noise from the waves ahead. "There's a step up, and the tunnel narrows. Pass it back," I told Sarah to warn the others. Sarah repeated the information, and I moved ahead in the tunnel to make room for the others. As I inched forward, rough ridges in the wall scratched my fingers—rusted metal. We must be in a giant metal pipe, I thought. My head banged against a hard object, and I stopped to rub the fresh lump on my forehead.

"Stop," I told Sarah, and she passed it back.

"I have to separate from you to feel what's ahead for a second."

"OK."

"Wait there, I'll be right back." I took her hand off my shoulder and patted it for reassurance, and then my hands went for the spot I'd bashed on my forehead. The pipe tunnel narrowed again. I entered the new pipe hunching. A meter more and the pipe forked, forming a Y, where I thought I saw light to the right.

I returned to Sarah. "The tunnel narrows and splits. Hunch down. Take the right-hand path."

Sarah passed the instruction back, and I hoped people understood. We didn't need more bruises. Allowing time for the message to reach the other end, I stepped forward with extreme hesitation. Following me, Sarah groped the metal sidewalls. I had turned to give her a hand, but she had turned to give the person behind her a hand. Pride filled my chest. We'd been able to lead each other blind through an impossible system.

The ridged pipe had grown slippery with kelp or algae, but my shoes gripped on a few rough objects, barnacles, or rust, which I appreciated, so long as they didn't cut me. I inched toward the Y. The dim light at the end of the right tunnel had disappeared, but I moved that way anyway.

A roar surged through the tube. Before I had time to react, an icy wall of seawater met our people train, and we toppled to our knees, choking and wet. Those behind me swore and gasped for air.

Kera's voice screamed, "Joe! I can't hold him."

"I got him," Emma said. Joe started crying. "You're OK, Joe. We're just having a little swim, is all. You hang on tight now. I'll carry you." Joe choked more, but his crying stopped. Emma was good with kids, I thought; kids never believed me. They thought I was a kid myself.

"Mommy's right here, Joe." Kera comforted him.

I passed instruction back. "We may have to swim our way out. Push through the waves. They aren't strong, but it will be work to get out."

Fortunately, the tide was low, and the wave action did not fill the entire drain pipe. The pipe's slope further impeded incoming tidal water.

Emma had Joe; her hands were full. "Gowen or Gatlin, can one of you help Kimo?"

"On it," one of them replied.

Next time, I'd say Gowen's name, I thought. Time to learn them apart.

"Kimo swims good," Kimo said. I hoped it was true.

I inched forward, and another gush of water soaked me up to my stooped chest, but I stayed standing. "Wave," I called behind me. "Rush forward after it passes."

I rushed forward, hoping to gain ground before the next wave made its way into the tube. I gained and lost with each wave, as did the others. They'd have less wave action at the back end, so it seemed unlikely they'd get separated. A surge left only a headspace to breathe, and I hoped we didn't have much further to go. My eyes adjusted to dim light ahead, and I lunged forward.

Just as another wave hit the opening, I reached the light and held my breath. I clawed at the sides of the ridged metal tube, trying not to lose ground. My arms flailed forward, and my knuckles scraped painfully along a metal bar. In a lull between waves, the water subsided, and I pushed my head up for air.

A metal grate of bars blocked the opening. I grabbed them furiously, wrenching inward. Tears of fatigue warmed my eyes, but another cold dousing of gritty-ocean water washed them away. Salt given, salt taken. I gasped, blowing air out in a fury, and wrenched on the bars again.

"It's blocked," I yelled backward.

"I'm coming forward," a voice said. Gowen or Gatlin, I thought, the indistinguishable twins.

"Scuse me." He squeezed around the others through the tight tube, up to the front.

"Lemme try," he said. From lack of air, his voice sounded pinched. I could hear the heavy breaths of the others. The cold pressed our lungs and our energy.

"Happily." I slipped my way back towards Sarah.

Another wave. He waited for it to pass, then with the water rushing back out the tube, he pushed the grate outward, and it moved, attached at the top by a hinge.

"It's a one-way grate. It opens out. Heavy." He grunted and dropped it with a clank.

"Can you hold it open?" I asked with skepticism. The manhole cover had been heavy; this might be heavier.

"If they go out on their bellies when the water is rushing out … maybe."

"Is it safe?"

"Nope," he said, matter-of-factly. "But I'll do my best."

At that, I smiled and shrugged. "It's all we can do."

"That or go back," he added with sarcasm.

"Not a chance."

"That's what I thought."

"Right. So, Kera, you're first. Come on up," I said, looking out the grate, wondering what hazards lie on the other side.

"Why me?" she asked.

"You're small, and we need an adult out there to help the kids when they come through." If the grate proved too heavy, smaller people had a better chance of getting through.

The other twin joined us at the front, and I backed away to make room. The two of them had to stand parallel to fit side by side, but together they'd have the strength to push the grate open.

"Kera, I'm Gowen," said the one on the left, who had come up first. I took note. "Gatlin and I will push this forward when the water flows out, and that's when you go out fast on your belly. Got it?"

"Got it. Don't drop that grate on me, please," Kera said. "Emma?" she called behind, her voice strident.

"I have Joe," Emma said.

Kera's voice turned to a quaver. "Joe, honey, you swim to Momma like we did at the pool—remember?"

Emma provided motherly encouragements to the toddler, but he hadn't seemed to need them. Tough little bugger, I thought.

The water receded, and Gowen ordered Kera, "Lay down. Now!"

Kera laid flat on the bottom of the tube, water rushing out, creating a fountain over her body. Gowen and Gatlin yelled, "One, two, three. Now!"

They pushed the grate with their shoulders, and Kera sluiced forward on her belly between them.

She stopped moving, grate poised inches above her neck.

I ran forward and shoved her feet with all my might, and she dislodged from the rough tube, ejecting into the Sound.

With a loud clank, the twins dropped the grate. Silence. No one spoke or even let out a breath.

"I'm clear," Kera's voice said from the other side, echoing through the drain. Amplified cheers erupted within the tube.

I gritted my teeth against the next wave. Waves and grates, you just try to stop us; we are escaping this trap. We *will* beat this maze.

CHAPTER 27

2009 MILAB

So, let's revisit the class you talked about last time," my *friend* Keith said from across an interrogation table. He had been my friend, anyway, until now. As for Becca, I considered her "friendship" an act, a performance of marital duty. She knew the monster she'd married and had even helped him. God, their kids would grow up to be psychopaths. I thought I'd known Keith once, the Keith who had saved my life years ago, but I'd been gullible to think a National Intelligence bigwig wanted to be friends with me and my husband. Not unlike corporate politicians, bureaucrats like Keith were only interested in people who helped them climb ladders. To Keith, *I* was an assignment, a longitudinal asset, a stone to step on, and a stone to step from.

My vision blurred as I tried to focus on Keith's face. "I told you, I can't remember anything. Why are you doing this? You know they wipe our memories. Same as you." By now, I had concluded that it wasn't that my memories had been wiped after my experiences with the otherworldly, but that a different me held the memories—my other consciousness. But I hadn't told Keith about Vedra.

He had given me an injection of an experimental hallucinogen, a truth-serum drug called BZ. As part of my ethics education, I'd read about BZ and the studies performed on soldiers. In fact, the man who'd created the drug had given a guest lecture to my class. Why he wasn't in jail, I'd never know.

The drug didn't work the way they thought it did, at least not on my chromotype. They thought it worked as a truth serum, but what it really did was create an altered state of consciousness that allowed people like me to travel out-of-body, or, in my case, to remember some of my other self's activities. This was Keith's go-to drug cocktail: BZ truth serum first, followed by the memory wipe drug.

"You only have to remember *enough*," he said. "You'll stay here until you do. We've prepared a cozy cell for you. There's a hole in the corner for shitting in and a steel bench for sleeping." He leaned forward on flexed biceps.

Military meathead, I thought. "You know I don't fear you." I mimicked him, leaning my petite torso forward, clenching my jaw, and flexing my comparatively puny arm muscles over the tabletop like a show wrestler. I'd have fallen off the stool, but they'd chained my right hand to the table. I grabbed the chain to steady myself. "How about some more of that BZ shit? Let's get this party ON!"

He straightened. "I can arrange that," he said and motioned to another soldier to bring him a syringe from a nearby table. "Or, you tell us something useful, and you can have the antidote and go home."

He lied. What he offered, and what he'd given me on other occasions, *was* a memory-wiping-experimental drug created by a D.C. university under a Central Division of Defense (CDOD) grant. It was not an antidote, and it hadn't been very effective on me. The last time he'd given it to me, I went home, slept it off for a few days, and then recovered the memories over the next few days after that. If I hadn't obtained complete recall, I'd recovered enough to remember who Keith really was and not to trust him. My Chromosome 6, P450 mutation, and the Chromosome 16 metallothionein mutation, made me resistant to many drugs, a plus in this situation. Keith hadn't done his homework. His files contained the details of my mutations. The BZ he'd given me had an effect, but not as strong as if it had been given to someone without my mutations; I exaggerated my drugged movements for his benefit.

He lifted the syringe of BZ. A guard came to my side and held my arm down on the table.

"OK, OK." I feigned compliance.

"I'm waiting."

I stared down the guard until he released my arm, and then I glared at Keith. "They gave me an equation, Keith. I don't know what it's for. But I'm sure you and those fuckers," I waved at the mirrored glass window behind him, "... can find some inappropriate application for it."

"Cut the sanctimonious crap, Aline. My job is to protect people, not aliens."

"I've told you, they aren't aliens. God, do you listen at all, or do you just enjoy hearing yourself say stupid shit? What did you say your IQ was again?"

The *friends* Keith had supplied, the ones who came to my house parties, the astrophysicist, the physicians, the physicist *(spies all)* had made a point to tell me their IQs like it mattered to me. Keith had obviously lied. Egos. They'd missed the point entirely. My mutations included some for higher intelligence, larger brain capacity, longer head, cervical rib adaptations to accommodate the weight of a larger head, and stretchy tissues to allow the birth of offspring with larger heads and to allow upward movement of the brain within the skull during space travel. But in the scheme of evolution, my actual IQ didn't matter at this juncture. The spies, the people like Keith, had convinced themselves their clade of people were superior. The big, strong men with inflated egos and inflated IQs made sure I knew *they* owned a birthright to inherit the earth, not my kind, and not *aliens*. Territorialists. I wondered what other measurements they'd inflated and nearly blurted to Keith that my dick was bigger than his but thought better of it and held my tongue.

"So, the equation?" He snapped his finger at a guard who handed him a pen and pad of paper.

"T to the minus one equals H times e."

"Uh-huh." He made a revolution with his hand, indicating for me to continue.

I stared at him without expression.

"And what does that mean, Aline?"

"That's some IQ you have, Keith."

A sneer tinged his voice. "Just define the variables, and we'll do the rest," he said.

I chuckled. His posture straightened. Uncontrollable laughter burst from me, and I pointed at him with my handcuffed hand.

"You'll do the rest! Ha!" Tears and peals of choked laughter streamed from me.

"We can do this all night." He leaned back in his chair.

"Sorry, sorry … ahem." I attempted to control myself but repeated, "You'll do the rest!" I laughed even harder this time. My amusement wasn't fake. "You all think you're dealing with aliens and contaminated humans. You can't see the benefits of our mutations. You're killing your only chance of survival, but … you'll do the rest!"

"She's wasting my time," he said to the two-way mirror behind him. He picked up the syringe of BZ again.

I held my hand up. "No. OK, wait. OK."

"You ready now? Cuz I am," he said, pushing a drop of BZ through the needle.

I nodded and leaned my elbows on the table. I did want to go home, eventually. "So it's how they get here. It's an equation for how they get here. It has to do with our geomagnetic field and E, you know Einstein's E," I said, with condescension, as if he might not comprehend $E=mc^2$. It was partially true, THe equation was the equation for how they got here, but I didn't remember what the variables were. T could be Tidal field, Tensor, or Inverse Time. E, a vector, energy, or eigenvalue. And H represented Hilbert Space, the Hessian, the Hamiltonian, or Planck's constant. For all I knew, the whole thing could be an inverse variation of a Compton wavelength formula. From the class, I remembered this small piece of a very long mathematical proof but nothing else. My gut told me THe equation involved the cosmic web. It was more an equation for how to get anywhere—at least, I thought it was—but it didn't involve our geomagnetic field. That was a red herring I'd created for Keith. I'd been duped by these government stooges enough not to trust they had anything close to good intentions for using the information I gave them. So, I fought the truth serum and withheld details.

"And ...?"

"That's all they told me, Keith. I'm sure you can figure out the rest. The variables are easily defined in a textbook." It should keep them busy for a while anyway, I mused. "So, how's it feel to be protecting humans ... ahem ... I mean working for corporate interests? Which defense contractor is behind that glass salivating over the rights to develop technologies?" I nodded in the direction of the opaque glass window behind him.

"Their interests are our interests. I work for the government; they work for us."

"Keep telling yourself that, if it makes you feel in control. But you've got it ass-backwards. You work for them, and their interests are their interests, not the interests of the people. They could give a shit about you, Keith. If you get in the way of their money, you'll find out as fast as I did .... You are disposable."

"You might be disposable too, Aline. I'd watch it if I were you. You're not the only one the aliens have contacted." He stood, pulled his shirt straight, and marched out of the room, irritation evident on his face.

It was true, what he'd said, that I wasn't the only one. I didn't know any others, but I knew they existed. After all, I'd sat in a class full of them. But it didn't mean the others could remember any better than I had, and I was pretty sure Keith hadn't spent years grooming other assets, as he seemed to spend all his free time sticking his nose in Jeff and my business.

Despite Keith's assertion that they'd keep me there until they had the information they wanted, the guard injected me with the mind-wiping agent and returned me to my bed next to my sedated husband.

I woke in bed the next morning, next to Jeff. The same as always, we took our coffee in the sunroom and read the news. Jeff complained of a headache, and I thought, *welcome to my world*. A few days later, I remembered most of the interrogation. Still, I invited Keith, Becca, and their friends over for a backyard party.

At our last party, I'd caught one of Keith's spies in my private bathroom taking pictures of the vitamins in my cabinet. I asked Keith not to invite the man to this party. He was after drugs, I'd told Keith, though I'd found the man had tampered with my vitamins. What would they have given me? A tracking device or something to induce contact experiences? It didn't matter; I'd preserved the charade. After the interrogation, Keith believed his mind-wiping drugs worked on me, and I tolerated his people observing me like an animal in its native environs.

CHAPTER 28

DAY 3, 2020 CONTINUED, A HERMIT LIGHTS THE WAY

D on't send Joe yet," Kera yelled through the grate into the tube where the rest of us waited. Emma had already made her way to the front with Joe and Kimo. "There are rocks," Kera said, between waves. "The children will need help climbing the bulkhead."

I turned to Emma. "The girls and Scott can help the little ones up the bulkhead. I need you to attend Kimo." Emma clutched Joe and Kimo.

Then I had an idea. "Wait." I turned back to Emma. "Kimo and I should go at the same time. We're both small and can fit together, then I can help him until you come out."

"Kimo," she asked, "can you go with Aline?"

"Kimo swims good," he said.

"She has to touch you. You have to let her help you?"

He didn't respond.

Shivering sapped my patience. I was desperate to escape the drain. "Kimo, it will be OK. Let's go. We gotta get out of here. Kimo?" I plead. My brain fogged with the beginnings of hypothermia. The smallest of us will grow the coldest. I have to get out, I thought, as my heart beat weak and rapid.

Emma nudged him forward, and I patted him on the shoulder.

"Kimo, it's just like a slip and slide, buddy. We gotta lay down on our bellies and shove off into the water. Do you understand?"

"Kimo swims good," he said.

"Good, then. Do what Gatlin says. OK?"

I stood next to Kimo and took his hand, which he pulled away. Emma stood behind him, ready to coach. The wave came. We struggled to keep our footing, and then the retreating tide rushed into our backs.

As the water receded to less than a foot deep, Gatlin said, "Lay down. Now!" He and Gowen put their shoulders into the grate.

I dropped to the ground. Kimo remained standing next to me. I reached up to pull him down, and Emma pushed his shoulders.

"No!" Kimo yelled and flailed his arms. He hit me on the head, but I stayed focused on the grate. I put my arm around his waist and the grate opened.

"Now!" the brothers yelled.

I shoved against the ridges of the tube, pushing against the barnacles with my feet. Although my arm gripped Kimo's waist, I managed only a short distance forward. He had gone limp as a lead fishing weight. My head and torso were out of the grate, but his head and torso lagged. I grabbed the back of his shirt at the neck and yanked. Emma shoved his feet from behind, and we flew out the grate together, splashing into a rough-water surge and rocks. My spine scraped a boulder, and I wound my fist in Kimo's shirt. With fury, I kicked my legs to swim us away. The metal grate came down with a crash, and I looked back to see Kimo's feet just clear.

My knee and ankle scraped a boulder as I bobbed with Kimo in the surf, so I pulled us even farther offshore to save my legs from the rocks. He choked and spat. I got behind him and put my arm over his chest, attempting to float his head above water.

"No!" Kimo said in a panic, arms flailing.

His elbow cracked into my nose, and warm, metallic blood ran into my mouth. Fighting for consciousness, I held his shirt as he continued to flail. He was much stronger than I could have anticipated, and I felt my grasp falter. He turned and pushed me under by my shoulders to keep his own head above water.

My lungs threatened to collapse as I kicked to reach the surface. In Kimo's parallel fight to breathe, he pushed me under once more. I hadn't caught a breath before he submerged me. My hand released his shirt, and I resigned that one or both of us would drown if I continued to restrain him.

Kera jumped from the bulkhead between us and pushed us apart. Still gasping, I swam away from Kimo. Kera gripped Kimo from behind just as I had tried. He must have tired himself out flailing, I thought, because the fight left him, and he stilled under her arm. Slick hair reflected moonlight from their heads, bobbing in the waves. A sort of battlefield peace came over me, the kind where you realize nobody won, but you're happy it's over.

A few hundred meters down the bulkhead, lights from a harbor provided faint illumination. The waves pushed me shoreward, where I scraped my knees and ankles once again on the rocks. The last wave crested higher, launching me up to a boulder that allowed me to gain a foothold. I took two frigid breaths and then scrambled up the bulkhead. At the top, I collapsed in a spluttering heap.

Emma came through the drain grate, relieved Kera of Kimo, and then assisted him up the bulkhead. The disturbingly calm toddler, Joe, came next, followed by the girls and Scott. Unable to help, I laid flat on my back above the bulkhead, paralyzed by cold and pain.

Emma jumped off the bulkhead and back into the Sound like a professional swimmer, returning to the grate to assist the twins in getting themselves out. I spit nose blood from my mouth. At this moment, I did not feel so evolved. Their size had saved us, Emma's and the twins'. Their size, strength, and leverage had allowed them to push the grate open while I was almost drowned by Kimo.

Kera plopped in a wet mass next to me and placed her shivering toddler between her legs.

If we all died right now, I thought, with little emotion, we'd have nothing to show for it.

"Thank you, Kera … for helping with Kimo."

"We're not friends. I didn't do it for you." She turned away from me, Joe still between her legs.

"It's true. I don't know any of you. Not really." Yet, each of us had some connection, genetic or otherwise, or we wouldn't be here together. But she was right. We didn't owe each other anything. "I didn't ask Julie to go," I added under my breath, but I didn't want her to respond.

"No, but you sure had no trouble leaving her." Her tone held accusation. "You may have gotten her killed," she hissed, covering Joe's ears to protect him from the truth.

She had me there, but I didn't have the energy to bear her guilt trip. Our survival required miracles, but I wouldn't give up yet. From my back, the stars twinkled in agreement as if they listened.

With blank emotion, I watched the others stumble their way up the bulkhead, shivering and choking, and I wondered which of them had the grit to keep going. This segment of our journey might have been the easiest.

"Anyone know how to sail?" I slurred and tripped as I stood. My breathing had slowed. Hypothermia gained on me. Soon I'd become irrational. Diagnosing didn't help. We needed to move fast.

"I can sail," Scott said.

"I can paddle an outrigger," Emma said. Her girls chortled through chattering teeth, huddled behind her. A quiet option, but much too slow.

"I don't think we should do it at night, though," Scott added, referring to sailing.

Sailboat rigging clanged in the harbor not far ahead. I hoped motorboats moored there but would accept any boat. "Let's get to that harbor. We need to keep moving," I said.

"Joe is tired and cold," Kera said. "We should find shelter."

"We can shelter and get warm on a boat," I said.

"There you go, all dictator again," Kera said.

I rolled my eyes. She didn't like me; that much was obvious. I wasn't trying to decide for everyone; I was trying to survive. It wasn't my job to soothe her insecurities. "It's time to go," I said and started in the direction of the harbor.

The others grumbled and stumbled to their feet. We looked like zombies, I thought, stooped and disheveled, dripping wet and foot-dragging—except for Emma. She stood like a monolith, solid, reliable, and unshakeable.

Gatlin walked up to Kera. "I'll carry your boy." He extended a hand to help her up from the ground.

Teamwork! Good. Survive. Great!

Without further injury, we tripped our way along the bulkhead to the harbor's asphalt-parking lot. Sarah still limped from her leg wound, but her speed had improved. With Gatlin carrying Joe, we moved faster than in the tunnels.

The lot was empty of cars, but every slip in the harbor moored a boat. Buoys squeaked, rubbing the dock in time with the waves.

Scott approached the dock's entrance gate and tried to open it. "It's locked," he said. A flickering lantern and barbed wire topped the gate. Impassable. A sign on the gate read: No admittance after 8 p.m.

"Let's go around," I said. "We can climb onto the dock from the water." Grumbles followed. No one held enthusiasm for re-entering the water, but we couldn't access the dock any other way. The bulkhead wasn't steep below the dock ramp, but it was fenced. I started off to find a break in the fence.

The others followed, except for Scott. He called out to me, "Go ahead. I'm going to check something first."

Too tired to respond, I trudged on, resigned to get back in the water.

We found the last section of fence and formed a chain of adults to help the children down the bulkhead. Emma's girls stood at the water's edge, and Kera and Joe had made it halfway when Scott came running towards us.

"Get down!" I told the others. Everyone fell to their knees or lower.

Scott approached excitedly. I looked beyond him to the lot but didn't see any activity.

"What is it?" I whispered loudly. "Is someone there?"

He stood at the fence conspicuously, moving with excited jerks of his arms.

"I have keys!" he exclaimed, grinning and jangling the keys above his head in celebration. "The harbormaster's shack is over there. I broke in. I got keys to the gate and a boat!"

Gowen shook his fist in the air. "Right on, Scott!"

I hoped Scott's parents wouldn't be too disappointed that we'd encouraged their son into burglary. He'd disabled the door alarm at the school. Now he'd stolen the keys to the harbor *and* a boat. Still, I couldn't hold back my excitement that we didn't have to get back in the frigid water.

I ordered the others back up to the parking lot, and we approached the gate once more. Scott slid the key into the lock. Click. The gate's hinges groaned from rust, a relieving sound mimicked by the twins.

"The pegboard said the boat's called Argo Navis," Scott said, descending the ramp.

"OK," I said, "Let's split up and find it, but, everyone, be quiet. There might be someone living aboard one of these boats. We can't get caught now." If someone lived aboard, they'd have to be deaf, I thought, as we'd forgone operating quietly. The gate had been locked, I reassured myself; no one would be inside.

Each of us searched sections of slips. It only took a few minutes. Without yelling, Gowen and Gatlin jumped and waved their arms to catch our attention at the farthest end of the dock. We filed our way among the boardwalks to a slip closest to the harbor channel.

"This is it?" Scott asked, tossing the keys back and forth in his hand, eyeing them as if he'd grabbed the wrong keys.

"What? This tugboat?" I asked, then I saw the name painted in faded letters on the cabin. The Argo Navis was a thick black tugboat with a cramped pilot cabin. No one seemed to care or notice that fitting us all in the cabin would be like one of those circus clown challenges where they all try to fit in a phone booth. Ten pounds of shit in a five-pound sack, Jeff would have said ... if he was here. Each person jumped aboard, eager to get warm and get going.

"Were there no other keys?" I asked, trying not to sound ungrateful. At least he'd found keys. If I'd been in charge, we'd be in the water again.

"Nope, just these and the gate keys. Sorry." He shrugged.

I hopped over the tire bumpers after the others. Our feet sounded like distant drums on the painted metal deck. Scott unlocked the cabin door and entered. When he put the key in the ignition, it beeped loud enough to wake the dead.

"What's wrong?" I asked and jumped back.

"Nothing. Boats always beep like that when you put the key in." He searched and found the lights, then searched for the heater. The others waited just outside the door. "Someone, go untie the ropes from the cleats, but keep one loop around it, so we stay docked until I figure this out."

Scott delegated well. Emma and Malia had experience handling boats, and they skipped off to follow his instructions. Kera vigorously rubbed Joe, whose baby lips had turned blue to match his eyes. He stood unmoving as she attempted to massage warmth into his limbs. Then she cupped his hands and blew warming breaths on them. I felt as the toddler, numb and unable to think. He must be a Chromotype 6, like me. We were meant for warmer temperatures.

"I found a tarp," Gatlin said, "Let's tent the back of the cabin."

Excellent idea, I thought, still unable to move. I shuffled around aimlessly. We'd be warm in the tent once Scott got the heat going.

The twins found a rope, spare tires, and a toolbox they used to weigh the edges of the tarp, forming a lean-to, surrounding the cabin door.

"I think the heat's on," Scott said, holding his hands up to a vent under the dash.

I put my hands where he indicated. "Can't feel anything," I said, noting my purple-tinged fingertips.

"It's battery operated. It just needs to get going."

Malia and Emma ducked under the tarp.

"It's warm!" Malia said and huddled with her sisters and Kimo.

It's warm? I smacked my cheek. Nothing.

"We're tied off with a slip knot," Emma said to Scott, who nodded.

Gowen, Gatlin, Scott, and Joe squished into the cabin. Joe was the coldest, so they put him directly next to the heater vent while they tried to figure out how the controls worked. The rest of us huddled under the tarp just outside the door. Through the crowd in the cabin, I stared at the controls, but my mind was blank. It may as well have been an airplane or a tractor; I hadn't the first clue.

My throat burned from choking on seawater, or bile, or both, an acute sensation. My toes ... I couldn't feel them to tell if they burned.

The engine turned over twice and then backfired, causing everyone to duck at the unseen threat. Great incognito! I smacked my forehead. Maybe we should set off flares next.

"Oops," Scott said. "I can do this. Just give me a minute."

He turned the ignition again, and the engine rumbled to life, vibrating the entire vessel. Diesel exhaust seeped into our tent. I gagged and then ducked my head out of the tarp for a few gulps of air.

Scott said, "Emma, go pull the ropes and give us a shove off the dock."

She scooted around me through the flap in the tarp. Again, I stuck my head back through the flap for air.

Lights appeared up the hill from the parking lot, but I didn't comprehend them at first. Lights! "Cut the cabin lights!" I yelled to Scott through chattering teeth. "Someone's coming."

He turned off the cabin lights and cut the engine, and the noise reduced to only waves, buoys, and rigging. Headlights from a car rounded the lot, followed by another car and three vans. Everyone froze in place. I thought I'd stopped breathing, but steam rose from my mouth. Were we caught? How had they found us?

The vehicles rounded the lot and parked facing the exit. Did I hear helicopters in the distance, or did my mind trick me, an auditory hallucination? As the cold crept back into our tarped shelter, I realized the heat *had* been on. Irritably, I reacquainted with the cold and almost started crying. Did I care if we got caught and killed, I wondered; would it be worth it to be warm again, even a temporary warm?

Emma let out a squeal from outside the tarp.

"Shush!" I said, irritated that my thoughts had been interrupted. I had almost accepted death as inevitable.

"It's James!" Her voice trembled.

I looked to the lot. The unmistakable hulking figure of her husband, James, exited a van and walked toward the docks. He was looking for us! Emma ran on the slick dock, up to the lot. The girls exploded out of the tarp and followed. I cringed and prayed they wouldn't slip.

Behind me, Kimo sat rocking and fidgeting with a rope end, unaware his father had arrived. I wasn't irritated James was here; in fact, I was ecstatic. What irritated me was our group's lack of discipline and inability to creep around without causing a commotion, or burglary, or murder, or tying people up against their will. None of it was their fault; we'd done what made sense at the moment. Resigned, I turned and said, "Kimo, go with your sisters. Your father's here."

Kimo dropped the rope end and burst out of the tarp flaps like they'd announced his name at the stadium. First, he ran the wrong way, then he turned to find the path out. With his fists bunched and his shoulders up near his ears, he made his way, last in line, to his family reunion.

Kera collected Joe from the cabin and pulled him up into her arms, preparing to leave the boat. Julie must be with James, I thought. The twins and Scott stepped out of the cabin with terrified expressions. They hadn't heard Emma tell us it was James.

"James has come with vans and cars," I informed them under the tarp. "It may be the better option for us."

"It will be warmer, anyway," Scott said, dropping the tension from his posture.

"Good job getting us this far, Scott," I said. Scott deserved credit for finding the keys and figuring out how to operate the boat. But with James' return, a fraction of the pressure had been taken off everyone's shoulders.

Kera and Joe waited outside the tarp. "Guys?" she called to us.

We exited and found the back half of the boat had come loose from the dock with no one manning the ropes. Only the bow remained tied. A jump from the front of the boat to the dock looked impossible, especially with Joe.

"Shit." I stomped my foot.

"I can jump it," Gowen said. "Then throw me the line, and we'll bring her back in."

Waves chopped. I gave a dubious glance at the see-sawing front end of the tug and the slippery dock beyond. If he misjudged the distance, he risked slipping upon landing or cracking his head on the boat.

Gowen wasted no time scurrying around the cabin to the front bumper. He bent and grabbed a buoy for support. When a wave troughed, the stern dipped low, and he stepped on the bumper and leaped to the dock. One foot landed squarely on the doc, and the other landed behind him. I winced. He squatted on the one planted leg. His hand snatched for the rope and cleat as his other leg dipped into the water. The boat lurched and the bumper cracked on the dock.

"Oh god," I said, going rigid. Had the boat just crushed his leg?

"I'm OK!" he yelled and rolled away from the edge of the dock. The boat had just missed him.

Nauseous, I slumped, bracing my hands on my knees.

"The cleat's come loose, though. It won't hold," Gowen said, springing to his feet. He placed himself in front of the next cleat.

Scott and Gatlin took turns throwing Gowen rope ends, but they all landed short of the dock. Kera found an emergency oar affixed to the cabin and attempted in vain to create a use for it. After multiple unsuccessful attempts to secure the boat, Scott threw a rope that landed wide of Gowen. Half landed in the water, and the other half snaked on the dock toward the water, weighted by carabiners. Gowen ran to the rope's disappearing end. With only inches remaining, he lunged, stomping the rope end with his slopping wet boot.

"Did he get it?" I asked no one in particular and covered my mouth.

He stood and held the rope over his head. "Got it!" He pulled the motor end of the boat around to the dock.

"Can we get off yet?" I asked impatiently. I'd realized something about myself tonight—more than the other significant events that had taken place over the last few hours—I was not cut out for boating!

Scott ran to the front of the boat and leaped over the edge, as Gowen had, only Scott landed on the dock with sure-footed grace. Scott immediately secured the front rope to a metal loop instead of the loose cleat it had been attached to.

James walked up behind the men. "What's taking so long?"

Gatlin helped Kera and Joe off the boat. Then I jumped to the dock, a much easier task with the boat securely tied off.

Gowen jumped back on the boat with his brother. Scott looked at me, then at the twins with an unsaid question.

"Maybe we should take the boat," Gowen said. "Split up. It would be safer if the group weren't so large."

He had a point, but I interjected with my previous concern. "If you get caught, they'll force you to give us up. All of us or none of us, I say."

Gowen said, with a diplomatic tone, "We don't know where you're going. We can't give you up."

"You can tell them which of us escaped and by what kinds of cars." I waved my arm in frustration at the lot.

"Or," he offered, sounding a little edgy about having to debate, "we can misdirect them. Tell them there were only four of you, and you went north or any direction you tell us to tell them."

Gowen didn't understand, I realized. Those people had ways of extracting information.

The sound of a helicopter approached from an unseen distance. We looked in random directions attempting to get a location on the sound.

Scott said, "I'm not going with any of you."

"What?" I said, incredulous. I understood Scott's meaning, but the others probably took it to mean Scott thought he'd do better without us, that, or that he acted as a willful teen.

James cut the argument short. "Time to go. Now!"

He was right. Sink or swim. I ran with James up the dock. Scott followed. Gowen and Gatlin remained at the boat, discussing their options. They had a point too. With the lights and engine off, they could float in the Sound for hours undetected, hidden by the black water, in a black tug boat. Even if the Argo Navis was big, she might be the only one of us able to creep around undetected in the dark if she didn't run ashore or into another boat.

"Scott," I said to him over my shoulder as we approached the gate, "you can't go to your parents' house. It's the first place they'll look for you. Then you'll be right back to square one. They'll send you straight back to quarantine, where you'll die. They might even send your parents there for good measure."

He looked at the ground as the gate creaked open.

Julie stood next to a sedan, holding a door open for Joe and Kera to pile into the car.

James got in one van with his brood. Scott squeezed into the back seat of Julie's car with Joe and a couple of the second group of escapees, but his face said he did so grudgingly. I stood peering into the packed cars for an available spot, waiting for someone to pick me, like a kid lining up for baseball team selections on a playground. But no one opened a door and said, "Aline, why don't you ride with us?" Why would they, I thought. Kera had made clear her opinion of me. Did the others view me in the same light?

I turned to see if the boat was still docked, but Gowen and Gatlin startled me.

"Is there room for us?" Gatlin called out.

James opened his door and barked at the three of us. "Get in the van now! Or, by God, I will leave without you."

The back doors of the van sprung open from within, and Emma stood there with her hand held out to me. "You slow girl!"

They'd waited for me. I grabbed her hand, relieved someone wanted me. I was a hypocrite. I hadn't wanted them, but here she was, welcoming me to flee with her family. I choked from tight lungs, and tears stung my cheeks. Get it together, Aline, I told myself.

Gowen and Gatlin hopped into the van. Gowen sat in the luggage space behind the last row of seats. I sat next to Kimo and Emma.

James jammed on the gas and roared the engine, leading the vehicles out of the lot. I shrugged to myself. Being big and loud had advantages too, I thought. It worked for the Argo Navis.

CHAPTER 29

DAY 4, 2020 RUNNING SWORDS

Orange streetlights streaked reflections across the van's tinted windows. "Where are we going?" asked a woman in the front seat next to James. She was one of the new escapees. I tried to place her from the quarantine center.

"East. Can you just direct us to head east?" James asked her. He squinted every few seconds in the rearview mirror and gripped the steering wheel at arm's length as he redlined the engine. I glanced out the rear window and made out a sedan and headlights. It resembled the car Julie, Kera, and Scott rode in, but the cars had indistinguishable attributes. They all looked like rentals, or cop cars, or personnel carriers. I wondered how they had come by so many vehicles, but it wasn't an appropriate time to ask.

"And pick the least visible way." James touched his finger to the roof of the cab. "We don't want to attract birds."

"Up here at this next light, make a right," said the new woman. She leaned forward and looked up through the windshield for helicopters. "That should avoid downtown, so we can get to the freeway."

"We won't be taking the freeway," James said.

"Right ... birds," she said. "Still, take a right at that light. It's coming up." When James did not slow to take the corner, she turned to him with surprise evident on her face. I heard his blinker clicking to warn the caravan behind us. The van squealed around the corner, its tail end skidding into the opposite lane. He righted the vehicle and pressed hard on the gas. I turned my head again. The sedan took the corner with more grace but had to accelerate to catch us.

Still transfixed in a state of cold numbness, I had trouble keeping up with events and lost the desire to try. Instead, I tried to relax and think of anything but escape and pursuit. I drove like a grandmother, I thought to myself while bracing my arm against the door. It worked for me. I'd never gotten a ticket. I'm square like that, though. Not a rule breaker—not I. Why was I such a conformist on things like speed limits and following laws, tangible things, while on other subjects, I strayed so far outside the confines of reality, outside of accepted norms of behavior, that I risked floating away in a bubble? My fellow escapees' level of urgency and the desire to survive was understandable, but this speeding felt needlessly reckless and attracted attention. In my thought bubble, I suddenly felt alone as if society had abandoned me. Burst your bubble, Aline, I told myself. None of us are acceptable, or we wouldn't be fleeing for our lives.

In the cafeteria, Emma had talked about going to Hopi, Arizona. But now? We'd never make it that far. James was too busy speeding to ask. Besides, distractions at this speed risked our lives. It didn't matter which direction we fled as long as it was away from quarantine. My mind resumed its rambling cascade, and I realized I hadn't slept for days. Not really. Who could sleep in a gymnasium with a thousand people and all their worries to keep them tossing on their cots?

I pressed my feet on the floor, and water squished out the sides of my running shoes. At least they looked cleaner, I thought. Before our swim in the Sound, my shoes had appeared as if they'd been subjected to more than a few dirt mile runs. Damp clothes clung to my skin, but I drifted off to sleep and didn't wake when our vehicle careened about corners. The urgent and worried minds of my fellows no longer penetrated my bubble.

"Get up!" Emma said, waking me from a full sleep.

"Where are we?" I rubbed bright sunlight from my eyes. The van bumped to a stop in a gravel runaway truck ramp down the side of the highway embankment.

Emma unlatched Kimo's seatbelt and opened the side of the van. The kids poured out. Gowen and Gatlin jumped out the back of the van. James and the new lady were nowhere in sight.

My bladder hurt. When was the last time I peed? Maybe they all had to pee too.

Gatlin stuck his head in the car, "Come on, little lady, time to get moving." He held his hand out like a gentleman. He wore a silver cowboy belt buckle, I'd noted, and now he'd called me little lady. I'd assumed they were typical millennials, wearing their plaid-flannel shirts and an Oregon brand of work boots, but they could have been from Eastern Oregon where there were still a few real cowboys. Washingtonians had more tattoos and wore boots that could double as work boots or evening boots suitable for S&M bars.

My head pounded, so I stretched my neck. "How long have I been asleep?" I unbuckled my seatbelt. People fled the other vehicles and ran into the nearby brush.

"Doesn't matter. Time to go!" He grabbed my arm and pulled me out of the van.

I stumbled. "Jeez." So urgent, these people. I deserved this, I thought. I'd pushed them through the tunnels; now they pushed me. "Have they found us?"

"Not yet, but they can't be far. You've become a celebrity overnight." Gatlin pushed a Big Sagebrush to the side. "After you, your highness," he chuckled.

"Your highness has to pee," I said with a smirk.

"No time for that. It'll have to wait. James says we need to be long gone from these cars before someone finds them." He broke a branch off the shrub and wiped our dusty footprints. The others had formed a line and trotted down an animal trail. Emma corralled the stragglers at the rear of the line.

"What did you mean? Celebrity?" I increased my speed to rejoin the others.

"I'll catch up to you in a minute." Without answering, he took a shoe-lace out of his boot and cut it in half on a rock. Then he tied one branch of sage to his ankle, so it dragged on the ground, sweeping our tracks. From the other ankle, he dragged a switch of rabbitbrush. "I'm bringing up the rear," he called ahead.

Every step forced me to squeeze in my urine. By now, I imagined it back-ing up into my kidneys and hobbled faster, but the group pulled farther away until a small rise in the trail allowed me to take advantage and sprint down-hill. Less than fifty meters ahead of me, Emma and Kimo climbed another rise with awkward steps. They had fallen behind the others.

Gatlin caught up to me. Without a lace, his boot threatened to fall off with each step.

"You'll get a blister. Cut that other lace in half and share it with that boot?" I struggled to speak through labored breaths. I wasn't out of shape but exhausted.

"I'll stop in a mile or so. They won't look beyond that if they notice at all."

"Downhill!" I sprinted again and clenched my bladder, closing half the distance to Emma and Kimo. "So, are you going to explain that celebrity thing, or should I start acting like one?" It was a poor attempt at humor.

"Oh, yeah. We got to listen to the news while you were sleeping, and guess what?"

"That's what I'm asking! What?"

"Well, your husband made a pineapple upside-down cake. He says he can prove you don't have the virus. He says they should release of all the quaran-tined people or at least have everyone independently retested."

I stopped short and bent at the waist. Jeff had done it; he'd saved the extra blood sample the doctor had left on our dining room table. Who had he gotten to test it?

"Ooh," I cried out.

"Are you OK?"

"No, I have to pee."

"Well, go in that bush over there." He pointed to a defoliated shrub that looked as if the deer favored it with vigor.

Modesty was a virtue I held some other time, I thought, waddling up to the bush. "Turn around," I ordered him. Not waiting to see if he had turned, I dropped my drawers and squatted. Nothing came at first. Unbelievable. I pushed harder.

"They're picketing outside the detention center," he called over his shoulder. "People's families are there demanding retests. They want to see you released! I mean, can you believe it? What are they going to do when they cannot produce one, Aline Orr, outside that detention center?"

What would they do indeed? Finally, a high-pressure volume jetted out into the sand, splattering my pants and running rivulets into the back of my shoes. I knew what they'd do … they'd stop at nothing to catch me, to catch us. Jeff was in danger. Poor Jeff, I thought as I peed the longest duration pee of my life and choked back tears. Tears plus pee, too much body fluid at once, I thought. Jeff didn't deserve to be married to my drama. I waddled with my pants down in an undignified manner, searching for something without thorns to wipe away my drips. Your highness indeed. I slapped at my privates with a frond of rabbitbrush and called it good. Pants up, time to go. The urgency resumed.

I sprinted up the trail past Gatlin. "Where are we?" The desert vegetation didn't match the Pacific Northwest green we'd come from. I turned my gaze skyward. Symmetrically dispersed meringue-cookie clouds ornamented the blue expanse.

"Somewhere in Utah. I forget the last town we passed. James says there's a through trail here, nobody uses … goes all the way to Mexico."

"Mexico?"

"I don't know. Just going with it. Not like I have someplace better to go. Do you?"

"No," I admitted. He stuck close behind me, pushing me faster. "We can't go to our families. We'd just get them dragged to detention, to their deaths. Jeff doesn't know we escaped; goons will be coming for us." The CDOD, the CID, or some government agency, one of them would be coming for us.

"We put that together from the radio after there was no mention of escapees."

We caught up to Emma and Kimo. Gatlin patted Kimo on the back as he passed him. "Good goin', man. Keep it up."

Emma winced, but Kimo didn't seem to mind Gatlin's touch this time.

"I'll go check in with James and Pen," Gatlin said. "Emma, you got the rear, 'til I get back."

"Tell my husband, I love him," she said to his back. He waved in the affirmative.

"I haven't had a word with him since the docks," Emma said to me.

Pen must be the lady who directed James in the van, I thought. She must have been from the area and knew the roads. If we'd had phones, we could have mapped our way.

"How long did I sleep?"

"Overnight. We drove for at least fourteen hours. Only stopped for gas. One of the escapees—forgot his name already—he had a wad of cash in his underwear. Good thing, or we wouldn't be here."

No wonder I had to pee, I thought. My head still pounded from lack of water. "Where did James get all the vehicles?"

"He said they found a shuttle business there in Everett with a red X on it. It had an owner's apartment upstairs. The man was probably in detention with us," she paused. We both knew that meant he was likely dead. "Anyway, it wasn't hard to get into the building and get the keys."

If the man were dead, he'd want us to have them, I thought. "Are we going to make it, Emma?" I asked, my tone dubious. Emma knew what her family was capable of, and I thought she'd be the most likely to level with me. I compared myself to her family. They were my measuring-up sticks. If they could do it, so could I. Before today, I'd thought of myself as the measuring stick. But at this moment, I questioned my resolve to deal with whatever came next. Confrontation beckoned sometime in our future. We'd be forced to confront them, our captors, and their agenda, sooner or later.

"We'll make it," she said, though her tone was unconvincing. "James will make sure we make it," she added.

Did she question her own strength? Why else put the responsibility on James? "So, is it Hopi or Mexico?" I asked.

"It's still Hopi. We haven't told the others yet. It's better they don't know."

We lagged behind the rest of the group. I observed Kimo pumping his arms, but they didn't propel his legs any faster. It couldn't be helped; he was a Chromotype 1. Speed and agility were not indicative of his type. His mutations led to his psychic ability via increased numbers of cells in the choroid plexus and right parahippocampal gyrus activity. I had yet to observe if he'd acquired pain and hunger resistance from any number of the Chromosome 1 genes. The FAAH gene, perhaps. We shared the same youthful appearance, but his age-related mutations were on Chromosome 1 and involved lamins, while mine were on 16. Since the escape, I felt we were one-for-all and all-for-one. That was Kimo's doing. None of that value add came from his chromotype; it came from him. Because of him, others had escaped. If I'd been in charge, I'd have left them.

"Kimo." We slowed to a walk-jog for a time to catch our breath. "I'm sorry. You were right. You got those other people out. I was wrong to want to leave them." Shame forced my eyes to the trail.

He stopped and grabbed my hand. "It's OK, Aline. Aline is still good, Aline."

"That means a lot," I blinked back tears, "coming from a hero." I threw Emma an appreciative grin. In turn, she gazed at Kimo, not with pride but with something else. She knew what kind of person he was … better than us all. I wiped my face with my sleeve.

"How did you and Julie do it? How'd you convince them to come?" I was both curious and jealous, as I hadn't been effective at convincing anyone of anything. Somehow Julie and Kimo had convinced a respectable number to leave with us from among the mass in front of the building, awaiting headcounts.

Kimo explained in his way, throwing a lot of hand gestures. "I tell Julie which people. She tells them they have a phone call inside from their family." He slapped his hands together, as if dusting them off, easy work. "They go inside, and we tell them we're escaping."

"Easy as that?" I shook my head in disbelief. "They fell for that and left with you?"

"I hear it in their head, the ones who want to leave."

He was psychic, that much he'd proven. They made quick work of something that I was incapable of accomplishing, no matter how much time or effort. Convincing people of anything was a skill I desired.

"I hope the others will forgive me," I said. "I haven't even met them yet, but I would have left them at quarantine to die."

"All right, now. That's enough of that. We're all making mistakes. Quit blaming yourself," Emma interrupted, then nudged us to move. "We're falling behind. I know James; if we slow them down too much, he'll turn into a drill sergeant."

"Left, right, left," Kimo said, taking lunging steps.

I lunged to match his march. "That's good, actually. Hey, let's sing a song." My head pounded, but I needed motivation. I needed a rhythm, a constant.

CHAPTER 30

DAY 4, 2020 CONTINUED, COMMUNAL

James held back the group to allow the slower people to catch up. We trickled in, one by one, and two by two, circling around him as we arrived. When everyone had arrived, he addressed us. "The others are down that ravine making camp." He pointed in the direction of an enormous cliff.

I thought he was joking and chuckled under my breath.

"We're going down there?" asked a woman. I'd met her a few hours before. Had she told me her name was Sandra? A musician. She'd led the group in song, becoming our pacer, our campfire leader, and our hymnal all at once. The songs distracted us from our pursuers.

"It's not as bad as it looks," James assured her. "I will help you."

I gulped. A cliff. James called it a ravine as if there was no steep drop. If the others had descended, it must be passable, I told myself.

Kimo stomped his foot. "I'm hungry."

That answered the HTR1D or OPRD1 gene question, I thought to myself; he does feel hunger. Stop diagnosing people, I told myself. Still, I wondered if he had reduced pain perception as I shifted on aching feet.

"We're all hungry, son." James patted Kimo on the shoulder, then continued with his plan. "So … I'll take small groups down the ravine a few at a time. The rest of you look for things we can eat while you wait up here."

One man scratched his forehead. "Like weeds?" he asked.

I tried to remember his name. I'd met him on the trail. It began with an A-A-Arthur. Art. He said he liked roller skating, I recalled, not botany or camping. I'd wanted to ask his ancestry, but I was afraid he'd misinterpret it. I didn't want to make him feel like he didn't fit in. Everyone here had experienced the isolation that came from being different. From his lanky build, I guessed he held the same gene as Scott, a Marfan-like gene on Chromosome 15. He was African American or perhaps of Haitian or Jamaican ancestry. His dark skin reflected the sun like a mirror. Whether the others identified with each other, most of us carried the genes and our ancestries mattered little. The chromotypes were equally distributed irrespective of race or nationality.

"Don't worry," I said, "I can identify some plants that are edible." One of my hobbies, foraging, I'd learned after the experience when *they* showed me the world on fire and mass death. It caused me to take interest in surviving off the land. Although, even as a child, I had taken great interest in the natural world, plants, and practical applications of common things found in nature. There wasn't a plethora of growth here in the desert, but I'd find plants with nutrients and calories. My balance wavered. So thirsty, I thought, licking my burned lips.

"And, there's water at the base of the ravine," James added. I looked at him askance, as if he'd read my mind. Did he have the Chromosome 1 genes too? At quarantine he'd said, only Kimo had tested positive from his family. I shook myself free from wondering over things that didn't matter. Here we all were, together, with or without genes from aliens. My mind drifted back to water. Water had to be on everyone's minds.

"I want water, Dad," said Kimo.

James ignored him. "So, if it's OK with you, I will take my son and wife first?" James asked the group. He winked at Emma.

The group gave amicable assents and gathered in my direction. Emma needed a break. She'd been limping, and the heat had swelled her ankles. James took his son, wife, and Art, and led the three down the ravine.

"So, you know those yellow flowers we saw on the trail that looked like small sunflowers?" I asked the group.

Affirmative nods.

"Well … they're sunflowers."

"I didn't see any sunflower seeds in them," Sandra said.

"They're in there. They're just tiny. We can eat the whole flower. And my favorite: we can eat the roots."

Surprised expressions crossed their faces, causing me to beam like a vindicated schoolteacher. More important than sharing my knowledge, I felt needed. It had been a long time since I'd been needed. After what I called my "period of disillusionment" when I'd quit work, I'd abandoned the assumption that people were good at their cores. I'd become a cynic. I was coming to realize I'd blamed others for my predicament, but the truth was I had been harboring resentments because I felt pushed out of the tribe of humanity, no longer needed, abandoned.

"We've got to hurry," I said. "It'll be dark soon. Follow me." I back tracked the trail until I found a sunflower plant and unceremoniously denuded it of flower heads, which I tied up in the front of my shirt. Then I ripped the plant from the sandy soil, shook the roots clean, and tore the roots from the stems, also placing them in my shirt. The others followed suit. "Stick to the trail," I called after them, "We can't have you getting lost." We'd never find enough to eat for today, but it didn't matter; a curious vitality filled me with optimism. Tomorrow, we'd collect as we walked.

Sandra approached to me. "I have a plastic bag. You want me to carry them?" She pointed to my overflowing shirt.

"Sure, that would be great." I pulled the roots and flowers out of my shirt, and she pulled the bag out of her back pocket. Before handing it over, she removed a few photos from the bag and placed them back in her back pocket. Displacing her family photos from the protective bag caused me a foreboding guilt, but I handed over the roots and flowers. "Save that bag. You'll want to tie it off over a leafy plant, so you can catch some condensation. It's the cleanest water."

"Good idea." She held the bag up, appearing to assign it a newfound appreciation, and then went off to search for sunflowers.

I scanned the trailside plant life for anything edible. A yucca. I plucked the milky flowers from the cactus. "All cactus flowers are edible!" I hollered at anyone in earshot.

None of this would taste good, I thought as I filled my shirt with flowers. It would be bitter as hell, but it had nutrients and calories—fuel. I passed a few young men who were busy laughing and throwing plant parts at each other. Not the flowers, I noticed. I tried to remember their names. All K sounds, I recalled, Caleb, Kyle, and Cameron, but which faces applied to the names?

A star shaped white flower and ominous spade-shaped leaves led me to a nightshade growing in the sand next to the trail. I tried to pull it up, but the stems snapped at the soil. After baking in the sun, the soil was hard. Digging up roots would be easier in the morning when the pores of the earth opened to release moisture, but I didn't have until morning so I dug around the plant with a rock and tugged again, releasing the tubers from the soil. A Four Corners Potato. Good find. I held the tubers up and marveled, then shook the sandy soil loose. I didn't think they grew this far south, but, then, I didn't know how far south we'd come. Rust colored stone lined the "ravine" as James had called it—sandstone. It marked our entrance to serious desert territory.

I came upon a scraggly pine and pinched pitch between two weed leaves. Pitch made a good antibiotic and fire starter. I wrenched on a few thin branches and pulled them free, damaging the tree bark. The pith was edible and had vitamin C. Patting the damaged spots, I thanked the tree and wished for it to heal. Pine cones littered the straw under the tree. My shirt was full, but pine nuts held great fuel, protein, and calories.

"Can you help me gather these pinecones?" I asked a teenager. "What's your name?"

"Kyra." She bent to collect the cones in her shirt.

"Are your parents here?"

"No, just my brothers." She rolled her eyes and pointed toward the boys I'd seen rough housing. "Our parents ..." she started to say, but didn't finish the thought. "I don't know. They got the vaccine. They wanted us to wait to see if it was safe first."

Smart, I thought, but now their kids were orphans. I patted her on the shoulder. If they had the genes, her parents were dead. "We'll get through this together, Kyra."

She shook her head and pinched her lips.

"What about these?" Scott ran up to me with a hand full of berries.

I sniffed at them, the pungent odor unmistakable. "I'm afraid Rocky Mountain Juniper berries will give you a stomach ache."

He dropped the berries and shrugged his shoulders in a deflated manner.

"It was a good idea," I said in a conciliatory tone. "They are kind of edible, but I wouldn't recommend them raw." We'd probably all get stomach aches anyway, I thought. "Kyra's shirt is full. You wanna help her?" Scott blushed. "Not with her shirt, but the pine cones, goofball." I'd said the last for his ears only, but his eyes widened, and he took a step back.

"Uh … I'll go help Gatlin." He thumbed over his shoulder to where Gatlin crouched, setting a snare with the remaining bits of his shoelaces.

"So shy." I laughed but was sorry I'd scared him off.

Despite blistered feet and thirst, the group's unusually high spirits boosted me, and I longed for the feelings of collaboration and community to last. This was how people should be with one another.

Sandra approached Kyra and me. "How about these?" She held a prickly pear pad and its red fruit gingerly by the tip of a thorn.

"Hell, yes!" I said. "It might be difficult to get the thorns out without a knife, but they taste great. Actually, you can roll the pear part around in the dirt. That should get the little ones, but the big needles on the pad …. You could try to dig them out with a sharp branch end?" I suggested.

Sandra set about finding a suitable tool. It might not be worth the effort, picking thorns, but at least she tried, I thought.

James returned and prepared to lead another group. I loaded the second group with the food we'd collected, making room to collect more.

"What do we do with these?" James asked, surveying our collection of wild foods.

"Set the pine cones on the fire until they open a bit, then pull the pinion nuts out, and the sunflower roots, and these," I handed over the tubers.

"Wet them and cook them a short time in the coals. You can eat the white yucca flowers raw."

I glanced over my shoulder. Sandra was still working on the cactus.

"We'll have more when you get back," I said.

James hesitated. "I didn't want to have a fire." He leaned over and inspected the wild foods in the shirt of a boy I'd loaded like a pack animal. James scratched his chin in consideration and looked up at the sky. "It may get cold tonight … so we'll risk it. Throw us some wood over the ledge. See that tree, there." He bent and pointed. "Do it there, so you don't drop logs on our heads."

"Got it." I said. "Wood." We didn't have a saw.

I gathered Gatlin and Scott and asked for their help to find wood.

Gatlin asked, "How big?"

"I don't know. Something we can burn. We dump it over the ledge at that tree, over there."

"Then let's go look there," he suggested.

Reasonable, I thought. I would have wasted energy lugging wood around. About ten meters from the ledge, we found a twisted stump of dead juniper on the ground.

Gatlin said, "This will work. Good and dry." He and Scott rolled it toward the ledge.

"Wait!" I stopped them just shy of the edge and approached the log. "Don't handle dead wood when we get farther south. There will be scorpions for sure." And snakes and bees and all manner of biting, poisonous creatures I kept to myself. "Let me check the wood for a second." I pulled bits of decaying wood apart on the surface, scouring for tracks, and then palmed a sharp rock and dug a little deeper. "There, see." I pointed with pride at the grub I'd uncovered.

"A worm?" Scott asked with disbelief in his tone.

"A grub," I corrected. "That's full of protein." I tried to sound enthusiastic; though, I'd never tried one. But it was true; they were full of protein. The ousted bug squirmed in revolt at being evicted from its home. Its coppery, mandibled head looked like a pain inflictor, but the jaws were meant for chewing wood. "I think we just eat the body." At least, I couldn't bring myself to crunch its head. The body, an articulated sac of pus, held little appeal but was less intimidating than the mandibles. "Well, let's gather him up and find his relatives."

"Aline, you have a way with words, don't you?" Gatlin said. He glanced over his shoulder to check his snare.

"Well, this is here, now, right in front of us, and we don't even have to cook it."

"You're right; I know it. Just … ugh." He made a gagging noise, rolled his eyes back in his head, and wiggled like a preacher had put hands on him.

"Come on. It won't be that bad."

"You go first," offered Scott.

"When we get to the bottom … rock, paper, scissors," I said.

"You're on!" Scott said with uncharacteristic excitement.

We depopulated the log of ten whole grubs before yelling a warning over the ledge and pushing the log over. Then we returned to the others to measure the harvest. Sandra had removed most of the thorns from one pad and had started on another.

James returned and directed the rest of us to descend the ravine. "It's getting dark," he said. "Everyone, follow me." Scott, Gatlin, Sandra, me, Kyra and her brothers went with a few adults in the last group.

We stumbled along close together. The grubs' constant writhing in my shirt distracted me, and I tripped, nearly dropping them and causing Gatlin to run into my back.

"Sorry," I said. "The grubs made me do it."

"Don't think you're gonna get out of eating one of those grubs, lady. It was your idea."

"Grubs?" asked James over his shoulder.

"Aline found some worms in the log and thinks we're going to eat them." Gatlin winked at James.

James said with a serious expression, "You will if you know what's good for you." He exhaled and stopped. "They aren't that bad. I ate them when I was a Marine."

"I thought they gave you guys MREs?" Gatlin asked.

"I was a sniper. I had my gun and my camo. If the target didn't show, I pissed myself laying in the dirt, and ate what was in front of me. Grubs, if I was lucky."

The group fell silent. *Thanks for your service* just didn't fit the occasion. That I ever thought I was in charge disconcerted me. James had been in charge from the start. A man of stature and convincibility. Stop feeling sorry for yourself, Aline, I told myself. These people had listened to me. They'd been respectful and caring; I reminded myself that not everyone in the world was like Keith or those jerks I'd worked for.

We walked on in silence. James helped us over the slick, steep parts and lowered us chain-wise down a gravel slope. By the time we reached the camp, we were covered in dust. I imagined the others had received dustings too. Except by the firelight, it had now grown too dark to see the dust on their clothes.

"Aline," Kimo called me to the fire. "Come eat a flower!" In the palm of his hand, he held a singed object that had once been a sunflower.

"Yes, please!" I said to Kimo. "I'd like that." I grinned with appreciation and collapsed on the ground close to the fire with my hand still clutching the grubs in my shirt. I was sure I'd squashed the pus out of a few of them, but I still had them.

Scott and Gatlin walked up behind me. Scott said, "After flowers, it's time for rock, paper, scissors."

I groaned in good humor, half regretting I'd ever agreed to it, but the entertainment value made it worthwhile.

"But things have changed since we escaped," Pen said with frustration.

Art backed her up, "Aline's husband says everyone should get retested. If we turn ourselves in, we can get tested and prove them wrong."

James and I shot each other dubious glances over the fire. Someone had brought up the suggestion that we turn ourselves in for retesting. By now, everyone realized they didn't have hemorrhagic fever.

"You all saw the body bags," James said. "You escaped in them. But what you didn't see were the bodies. Those bags were meant for you too."

"What are you talking about?" Art asked. "The body bags were for the infected who died."

"They killed the first group," James said. "I saw them in the South Building."

Art waved a dismissive hand at James.

"Why did you want to escape, Art?" I asked him. "Why didn't you go get the vaccine with the first group if you thought it was safe?" Kimo had to have read Art's mind. Art had wanted to escape, but perhaps he had other reasons, I thought.

Kyra's youngest brother cried out, "They're not dead!"

Kyra turned to comfort him and said, "I think they're right, Caleb." She bent to embrace him.

"I'm so sorry," I said to Kyra. My heart sank. It was a cruel way to find out your parents were dead. These children didn't deserve this, I fumed to myself and took a step to comfort them, but Emma got there first. She was a mother, a comforter, and I left her to the job. Kyra's other brothers Kyle and Cameron stomped off, leaving the group. Then Art left too. Maybe Art knew the truth, I thought—he just didn't want to believe it.

"I want to accept what you said as true," Sandra said, "part of me does, but I don't understand why. Why are they doing this? What have we done wrong?"

"It's genocide," I gulped, unsure of myself. Should I even try to explain it to them?

The others glanced at each other with curiosity and raised brows.

"What about Art and Miguel over there?" Gowen asked. Miguel was another of the new group, the ones who'd escaped quarantine with James. Art and Miguel were both of different ethnicities. "Doesn't make sense. We're all different."

It was true. We were different. We didn't even have the same mutations, a lot of us. "Not ethnic cleansing … *genocide*."

I allowed a moment for the words to sink in and then continued, "We all have something in common that they don't like."

"What, for Christ sakes!" Sandra said.

"We have genes that come from *them*." I pointed to the sky. It was one thing to convince people we were mutants being killed by our fellow man; it was another to then say we had alien DNA and expect them to believe it. The group was silent. How many of them had any recollection that they'd been abducted? If they recalled aliens, they might accept my genetic claims.

"So. Why do they care," Miguel asked with a Spanish accent, "if some alien experimented on me? This has been going on for a long time. This is not new. My people have known about aliens for hundreds of years."

"It's a security threat. Think about it," James said, "some alien force they can't control, coming and going as they please, tampering with our genes."

"That and other insecurities. Our mutations mean we are more evolved," I explained, "That scares them—that we might survive, and they might not."

A young woman I hadn't met slumped against a tree. Someone walked up to her to comfort her, and she flinched, a post-traumatic response.

"It may seem like there's no one we can trust," I said. "Our own people just tried to kill us, and the aliens have changed us without our consent. But the point is, we can trust each other." I hoped we could trust each other, anyway.

"Aline tells the truth," Kimo said.

"Thanks, Kimo." At least I didn't have to convince the mind reader.

Scott pulled his phone out of his pocket, inspected it as if it was a foreign object, and then threw it in the fire.

"You had a phone this whole time? You little shit." One of the men from the new group stomped his way to Scott, chest puffed.

"It's broken," Scott stepped back from the man.

"But you had it this whole time and didn't say anything! God dammit— we might have been able to call for help." He reached for Scott to grab him by the shirt.

"Dude," I said, stepping between them. "We swam through the storm drains and in the ocean. Trust me; it's broken. No phone can survive that. *We* almost didn't survive." His group had escaped in the truck. Apparently, he hadn't noticed our sopping wet group at the docks. "Back off." I pushed him, but not before James had him by the arm and dragged him away from the fire.

The man took a disciplinary lecture from James. I saw him nod in comprehension, or agreement, or both. Then he walked over to Scott and apologized. Discomforted, everyone averted their gazes to let it be between the two of them, but the fire circle was small. There was no privacy.

Art returned to the fireside. "Look," he said, shifting on his feet. "I don't believe in aliens. Fine, the government tried to kill us. They've tried to kill the black man with injections before. But the point is, I have no doubt none of us are sick. And you're right about one other thing … that vaccine probably killed those people. But that's as far as I'm willing to go with it. Right there. No aliens," he said, and he made a neck-slicing motion with his hand. "They could have picked us at random—none of us mean shit to them. They could have … they could have …" He slumped to the ground and sobbed. "That's what it's like to be black. Your life is worth shit to them."

The value of a life was an idea I'd wrangled with at work. It depended upon whom you asked. Not worth much to the pharmaceutical companies. The government worked for the pharmaceutical companies. Some government employee got a new pharmaceutical dream job and a bonus if they got the government to sign a contract with the pharmaceutical company. Whether it was to supply strategic stockpiles, supply the armed forces, supply a pandemic, or just to get the drug covered by Medicare, contracts were career gold. Deaths or disabling adverse reactions cost the value of government Joe's pharma bonus. Likewise, the value of our lives to the medical profession was weighed against the greater good. If it was good for most, then it was worth it for some of us to die.

"Do you know what he's talking about?" Gatlin whispered to me.

"The government funded research in African American men with syphilis."

"Is that bad?"

"That wasn't the bad part. The bad part was that they didn't tell any of the men that there was a cure. They didn't give them the treatment. They just let them stay sick or die. It went on for years."

"Holy shit." He bowed his head and backed away from the fire with a mixed look of contemplation and disbelief on his face.

"Art has a point," I said. I did know what it was like to be different. I did know what it was like to be dismissed. And I definitely knew what it was like to be devalued. "We need to be valuable to each other. That's what matters now, not whether you believe in genocide or aliens. Because I don't hear anyone denying that the government wants us dead. We need each other." They'd want us even more dead after our escape, and after Jeff stirring the pot, I thought.

"I don't think that's what Art meant, Aline," said Sandra. She didn't sound confrontational but challenged my view nonetheless. She continued, "I think we need to be valuable to each other, not to simply save our skins, but because we actually care about each other as people."

"I care," I said and caught the eye of each person around the fire. She was right. I came off harsh because I was pragmatic to a fault. "You may not believe me, but our government still does experiments on civilians, on military, on anyone they have power over—anyone who's disposable. Make no mistake, in their "us versus them" world, we are them. Our government sprayed San Francisco with bacteria from airplanes that killed a ton of people. They wanted to test it as a bioweapon. The hospitals collect the data for them. Even in the last ten years, they funded research on an experimental measles vaccine without telling people it was experimental." I nodded to Art. "That one was especially for African American and Latino Infants. Then there was that doctor who made his own herpes vaccine and gave it to people in hotel rooms. No consent, no animal tests first. The one where they gave babies oxygen to measure how many went blind or died. And that one in Portland, I think it was, where they gave people in ambulances synthetic blood. They didn't ask their permission because they only gave it to unconscious people. That killed more than a few. All this happened recently. Seriously, people, not everyone has your best interest at heart." It was to be expected, I thought. Our society holds physicians on a pedestal. If you tell people they can do no wrong, they go ahead and do whatever they goddamn please.

People started shuffling in a restless manner. I let it go. I wasn't trying to beat it into them, but it filled me with rage. Suddenly, I flashed back to my guide asking me what I willed. If I could answer that now, I'd say: "Expose the government and make them repent ... ON THEIR KNEES."

Sandra said, "Well, I don't care if they do kill me tonight; my feet hurt. Let's save our sad skins tomorrow. Go to sleep." She curled up in the dirt by the fire and rested her head on her arm.

A few nervous laughs rang out, and ghoulish expressions, highlighted by the firelight, faded into the darkness. Within moments most had picked a spot to sleep for the night. James and Emma had gone after the boys, and the twins comforted the girl by the tree. The guy that had acted aggressively toward Scott kept an ashamed distance from the group. Everyone accounted for.

We'd made it this far. I tried to clear my mind of the intense conversation as I lay on my back, observing the immense Milky Way. I hadn't seen it this intense since I camped in the Australian Outback with Jeff years ago. For the first time since the escape, I allowed myself to worry for Jeff, and quiet tears streamed into my ears. Jeff had worked so hard to save us, to let the truth liberate us. I had been so naïve once. They'd get to Jeff in a million ways he'd never anticipate. The easiest route would be through me.

We woke on the hard earth after a night of sleep that occurred only because of extreme exhaustion. Campfire smoke filled my nose and burned my adenoids. I rolled away from the smoke onto my other stiff shoulder and rubbed crust from my eyes. Sandra removed her plastic bag off the branches of a tree down the way. Scott had inched closer to Malia, I noticed. Kyra and her brothers laid facing one another in pairs. James and Emma had woken early and now returned to the camp with hands full of leaves. James woke his girls, "Time to get up, chickens. Take the leaves and go bathe in the water." Kimo let out a "Cock-a-doodle-doo." The others grumbled as they woke from the noise.

The water source amounted to two large puddles, both ferrous brown from iron leached free of the sandstone. We had designated one puddle for drinking, the cleaner-looking one, and the other puddle for cleaning. Yesterday, I drank the gritty *clean* fluid; it scratched my parched throat. Today, I'd do the same and be grateful for the hydration.

"Washcloths, anyone?" Emma asked the group, offering the extra leaves she'd collected.

"Ohhh! What I wouldn't do for a real washcloth and a shower," Kera said. Her hair looked like it hadn't appreciated the last two days of sun on top of salted Puget Sound water. She took a few of Emma's leaves and flashed a gesture of gratitude.

Running my fingers through my own hair, I wondered how it could be both sticky and crisp at the same time. "Coffee!!!" I blurted. The adults groaned. No coffee, not even a poor chicory weed substitute, welcomed our future. Maybe I'd get lucky and find a Mormon Tea plant; the plant contained natural stimulants. I stood up and smacked the dust out of my clothes.

Gatlin and Scott approached. "You've forgotten something, Aline," Gatlin said, wearing a mischievous grin.

"Oh really?" Cream and sugar, I thought to myself.

"The grubs," Scott said, cocking his head.

Last night, I put the grubs to bed on a piece of wood. People ate everything else we'd collected, but after the tense conversation, I didn't bring up the grubs again.

Scott presented the firewood from behind his back. "They're right here." He pointed to where the grubs had tunneled the beginnings of a new shelter.

I squinted, pretending I couldn't see the grubs writhing in search of coverage, safety. "Rock, paper, scissors then," I said, defeated. "Winner or loser eats?"

"Loser eats," Scott said.

"Confident, are we?" I smirked.

Gatlin and I played first. His scissors beat my paper. "Loser! Loser," he cried, circling the camp like a clown and making an L with his fingers on his forehead.

"Gloater." I rolled my eyes, then faced Scott, who studied my face for a tell. I resonated with paper, and I was a creature of habit. At the count of three, we placed our bets. He splayed his scissor fingers. "Blood and oil," I swore and stomped my foot.

"It's all yours." Scott pushed the log forward.

"OK, OK. I'm eating a grub." I picked tentatively at the end of the log and pinched a grub by the tail. I sighed in relief as its head ripped off, leaving only the pus sack of a body. To eat that coppery-bemandibled head would have given me nightmares for life. I sighed. Despite its headless state, the yellow body curled into a tight circle. "Wait, wait. Maybe someone else is hungry? I just couldn't if any of you are hungry?" I took a few steps to the teens, and they shrieked and ran in scattered directions. A crowd formed with amused expressions.

Kyra turned and covered her face.

"Bottoms up!" I grinned before throwing my head back and dropping the dangling thing into my mouth from an outstretched arm.

Art bent at the waist and pretended to gag. Making disgusted noises, the onlookers exclaimed *"yuck" and "gross."* I chewed with exaggerated motions, not allowing my face to display emotion. The initial gush of fluid popping forth from between my teeth had little flavor. The texture, on the other hand …. I masticated.

"Well?" Julie asked. Kera held Joe up so he could see. Pen stood at their side.

"Well … it tastes like chicken. I think I'll have another."

Groans ensued, and people turned their heads the other way, unable to watch. I reached for the log and pulled another grub. This grub didn't do me the service of getting its head stuck; I had to decapitate it first. I dropped it in my mouth the same as before and tried not to picture it. The grub was protein, and I needed food. I told myself it was chicken as I chomped. For a moment, I thought I tasted chicken if I pictured drumsticks and lots of barbeque sauce.

Cameron stepped forward. He ate three grubs, one by one, spitting and fighting, but he ate them. Then his brothers accepted the challenge and ate what remained. We'd find more—wood rots.

CHAPTER 31

2009 SEARCHING FOR PROOF

Alienated as I was, my office felt increasingly confined. I sat at my desk,
wondering if the entire research center received the mass email. Enough
of my coworkers knew it was about me, I suspected. Too many had avoided
eye contact in the elevator. The receptionist hid in the supply closet and pretended not to hear me when I said hello this morning.

Without naming me, the email stated the Central Division of Defense
(CDOD) had identified an anti-vaccine terrorist and that all employees
should prepare to receive new door codes and key cards. The email didn't
mention a security guard as Karla had. HR had revoked my access to patient
records and copied the entirety of my emails since the beginning of my
employment. With the keycard and door code changes, they'd be alerted if I
worked late. I sniffed for justice but wouldn't reach for such lofty goals now.
No. Now I wanted vindication; I wanted to prove them guilty.

A response bleeped into my now monitored email inbox, distracting me
from plotting revenge. It was from a friend I'd emailed a few hours before
in an attempt to dig up more dirt on the autism study conflicts of interest. I shouldn't be giving Karla more ammunition to call me an anti-vaxx
terrorist, I thought, but at least I could sleep at night if I did everything in
my power.

From: BSherman3@nihr.gov

Aline,

These are just a few of the research proposals we have received and not funded for various and legitimate reasons. I cannot give you a list of researchers who published autism studies or collected autism data within one year of receiving federal funding for a vaccine study (or studies). I know, I owe you. You saved my ass. I wouldn't have a job if it wasn't for you. But please don't ask me to jeopardize my job further by stirring up an unwarranted controversy.

You could try a Freedom of Information Act request, but I've heard they won't honor them for medical research studies, even if patient identifiers are excluded. Personally, I wouldn't waste my time. CDOD-funded studies and field operations are exempt, anyway. If that's what you were looking for, you won't get it.

As you can see below, there are a plethora of well-thought-out theories regarding the causes of autism spectrum disorders. And you are correct; few researchers are willing to jeopardize their careers to research a link to vaccines (I supplied a couple proposals below that were not awarded funds). You well know there is little chance the government would contradict itself or waste money by funding studies into such a connection when so many studies have already disproven a connection. Take my advice, and let it go.

Sincerely,
Bob Sherman, Ph.D.,
Director, Grants Management Program, NIHR

Attachments: Appendix A

I browsed the list. Interesting, but not what I'd asked for. I really wanted to know if the NIHR or CDOD had coerced any other researchers into collecting or publishing autism data in exchange for future funding on vaccine studies.

The Sound and the glass buildings reflected a blurred haze of gray drizzle outside my window—always gray and shades thereof. My office had a coveted view of the Space Needle; I was surprised Karla hadn't taken it away with my demotion. They could have it, I thought bitterly. Though white, the Space Needle didn't shine; it was no beacon. The lack of sunlight caused my blue eyes to dim and match the gray this time of year, and I wondered if I was going color blind or if maybe Seattle was the grayscale world.

My mind turned back to Bob. It hadn't been fair of me to ask Bob for the list, but I thought he might help me, to pay me back. He had run into regulatory troubles with one of his own studies a few years back, and I helped him defend himself. Bob had done nothing overtly wrong; he'd just been bad at documenting what he had done, not an uncommon occurrence in the sciences. But Bob got caught.

When I was still naïve, I preached that most research was conducted with ethical intent and that lapses usually resulted from a lack of proper documentation, as in Bob's case. Those instances, I'd advised our committee, should not result in harsh punishment, but instead heavy training.

Recent studies, however, had altered my opinions. More often, researchers and the government were looking for ways around regulations or ignoring them outright. Or, without the threat of substantive sanctions, they'd break the rules and ask for forgiveness, only to break them again. Children play the same games.

A knock sounded at my office door. An unfamiliar, tall brunette woman stood on the other side of the glass. "Come in." I motioned for her to enter.

"Hi," I said, as she walked through the door, and I pointed to the available chair. "How can I help you?"

She reached her hand out to introduce herself, "I'm Tammy. Karla sent me to sit in with you for training."

My hand dropped, and I felt my face sag. I shouldn't be surprised, I thought; Karla had made it very clear. She'd wanted to get rid of me and hadn't wasted time hiring my replacement.

"Sure thing," I said, forcing manners. "Tell me about yourself. What brings you to work here?"

"Well, Karla and my boss over at the U are friends. Karla called her and asked if she knew anyone who wanted a promotion to come work here."

"A promotion? So what did you do at the U?" I asked. The U, my alma mater, was what locals called Emerald City University.

"Same department, Ethics Review, but I only did the expedited reviews. Karla said she needed someone efficient." Tammy punctuated the last word with a crisp bite. That word, *efficient*, had come from Karla. For Karla, the corporate-speak word summed up what she expected of Tammy, which was everything I was not—*I* was not a rubber-stamp queen. Tammy continued, "Someone who can fast track a large volume of studies, and well, that's me." She beamed with pride.

"Wow, that's great!" I bit my cheek and changed the subject. "So, for now, I'm working on studies that don't qualify for expedited review, just clinical trials that require full committee review." Karla had demoted me to perform expedited reviews and promoted this expedited reviewer. Expedited reviews were reserved for less risky, less complicated, studies and small changes to existing studies.

"Yes, I'm looking forward to a change."

"Good, then. So what's your background? I mean, do you have more experience with preclinical studies, or did you work for pharma?"

"I have a Ph.D. in Literature."

I blinked twice without responding.

"It won't be a problem," she said. "It didn't stop me at the U. Besides, Karla said she can explain any of the science parts I don't understand."

She can, can she? "Alright, then," I said. I wouldn't take vengeance on Tammy, but I couldn't believe Karla had the nerve to assign me to train an inappropriately-qualified replacement.

This whole scenario—Karla not telling me she'd hired my replacement, making me train my replacement, and the "efficient" comment—felt orchestrated to entice me to quit, but I resolved not to let Karla bait me. "I'm working on reviewing adverse event notices on the FDA site—seeing if any of them apply to any of our studies and if they might represent new information that must be disclosed to our research subjects." I opened the screen

I'd been working from and pushed print. "So, this is our database of studies, and I search for the drug name like this." I showed her on my computer screen. "We have a hit." It seemed we reviewed a collaborative study with Veterans Affairs for an off-label use of the drug in question.

"So, Tammy, how would you go about determining if we need to tell our research patients about this possible side effect?" She should know this, I thought, but I'd test her before passing judgment.

She glanced from the Federal Drug Agency notice to the screen and said, "I don't think we did this at the U."

I could see why Karla liked her. Karla often used the *but–they–aren't–doing–it* argument. "You need to read the informed consent and see what the people were told might be the possible negative consequences of participating in the study. Did anyone get consent from the patients at the U?" I immediately felt ashamed for my sarcasm and didn't let her answer. Because our patients deserved it, I'd provide Tammy with adequate training. What she did with the training was up to her.

For the rest of the day, I trained Tammy until my energy stores had hemorrhaged. She must have told me *"they didn't do that at the U"* a hundred times. I worried I had little fight left in me but told myself the patients deserved what I had left to give.

When I got home from work, I leafed through bills on the counter. The annual mammogram invoice sat at the top of the pile. Expecting only a copay, as the employee health plan covered mammograms, I opened the invoice to find a bill for five hundred dollars and change.

I glanced at the clock. Twenty minutes until they closed. I pulled my cellphone out and dialed the number on the bill. The billing agent answered.

"Hi, there must be a mistake. I got a bill for a covered service. I'm an employee." I read the bill details to her, and she put me on hold.

"No mistake. It says here in the record that your previous mammogram records were not available, so they had to perform a diagnostic mammogram, and we do not cover diagnostic mammograms, only annual preventive mammograms. They have to have the previous records on file for comparison, or they do a diagnostic."

The mammogram I'd received was the same as it had been every year. "Why weren't my previous records available? They did the mammogram last year. They should be in the file."

"Let's see." She paused to read the notes. "A researcher, a Dr. Mignoret, has your mammograms. She is using them for a research study."

"Well, why didn't my doctor call her to get them back?"

"I can have your doctor call you tomorrow if you like."

"Yes, please." I hung up and tried not to seethe, but anger filled me to the brim. As an employee of the HMOs research unit, my health records were off-limits. Because I audit the researchers, I had specifically noted in my records that I did not want researchers digging through my medical information. Dr. Mignoret had no right to keep my mammograms.

Jeff walked in the door, wet and bedraggled. He shook the drips from his coat, hung it, and then walked over to give me a hug.

"You OK?" he asked.

"I am now." No use letting work ruin my evening. I'd deal with it tomorrow.

CHAPTER 32

DAY 5, 2020 FRATERNITY

For everyone will be salted with fire,
and every sacrifice will be seasoned with salt.

(MARK 9:49 WORLD ENGLISH BIBLE) PUBLIC DOMAIN

Gowen poked the fire and kicked sand onto it to put it out, while James rounded everyone up for a pep talk.

"We survived the night, but I will not lie to you, the trek ahead of us is tough," James said. He looked like he'd survived a lot better than the rest of us. His topknot was tidy, and his clothes didn't have grimy dirt marks all over them. Experience, I guessed. I'd washed the pee sprinkles from my pant legs at the designated water source but couldn't bring myself to wash the whole pants and wear them wet all day.

"Could it be harder than what we've already been through?" Kera asked. "We did swim through storm drains and nearly freeze to death the first night."

"Some of you had it harder than those of us who escaped in the truck." He looked people in the eye as if appraising their abilities. "Yes, it could get a lot tougher," he said, eyes settling on the young woman who'd been sitting by the tree. Last night she'd experienced a traumatic mental episode, but this morning she seemed alert and eager to take part.

"Is the hiking going to be about the same?" asked the man who had attacked Scott for having a phone. I'd since learned his name was Dan.

"More or less. But we'll be that much more tired, hungry, and sore. And if one of us gets injured ..." James trailed off.

"We might have to leave someone behind?" Kyra asked.

The poor girl had just lost her parents and now contemplated abandonment again. "I don't think we need to take things that far," I said, although I wondered if I was telling myself the whole truth or clinging to virtue.

"What will we do then," Sandra asked, "form a village on the side of the trail so we can stay together? I don't mean to be snippy, but we escaped to survive. Stopping won't help us survive."

"But how does *going* help us survive?" Julie asked. Joe squirmed in her arms, and she passed him off to Kera, who took him to the bathing waters. She hadn't had diapers for him since we escaped. If it wasn't for sunburn during the day and cold at night, the child could have gone without the pants. "Where are we going *to*?" Julie continued. "Not to contradict you, Sandra, but are we going to form a village at the *end* of the trail instead of the side of the trail?"

James and Emma hadn't shared their plan with everyone. They'd held it back as a precaution, or so I assumed. The captured couldn't reveal our final destination if they didn't know it. But perhaps the real reason was, there wasn't room for all of us in Hopi.

Emma looked at James, and he nodded. She said, "We're going to Hopi, Arizona. We have friends there. James' partner in the military."

"Are we going with you?" Gowen asked uncertainly.

"When we get there," James answered, "they won't turn us away, but they didn't invite us, and we bring trouble. It's not like I could warn them we were coming. But I think we'll be safe there. The government doesn't have jurisdiction on their lands."

"Hasn't stopped them in the past," Julie said. For a moment, I wasn't sure how she meant that statement.

"I haven't heard any good ideas, aside from turning ourselves in," Pen said.

I smacked my forehead. Did we have to revisit that again?

Miguel asked, "How do you know where you're going? What if we're already lost?" He cocked his head to the side and squinted.

Fair enough, I thought, avoiding the conversation on purpose. I didn't have answers.

"I've walked this trail," James said. "Well, not all of it, but I walked a good section of it with my military partner after we were discharged. Long story, but I've done part of this before. The trail isn't well marked, but we're on the trail. I recognize the landmarks."

The only sign of civilization had been yesterday. For a few kilometers, we'd warily followed a motorcycle track dried in the mud. When the track took off to the north, we left it behind, and with it, all signs of people.

"So, what *is* the plan if one of us gets hurt and can't go on?" Art asked, raising the issue James had left unsaid.

"That's not my decision to make," James said. He moved closer to Emma and put his arm around her.

"I won't leave anyone behind," I said, wanting to believe it of myself, wanting redemption. A lonely death was a curse. "I'll stay with anyone who can't go on."

Kera had returned with a clean Joe in her arms. She snapped, "But you'd been more than willing to leave Julie and the others behind to die. Why would we believe you?"

I shrunk. All the true and mean things sat on my shoulder, mocking me. I had been willing to leave others behind, and it hadn't been the first time. Despite having not even tried, I convinced myself the others were unpersuadable. Just like the pharmas and researchers who claimed there was no evidence but hadn't even looked, I'd deluded myself into believing what I wanted to believe. Convenient of me. Julie and Kimo deserved the credit for persuading the others to leave with us. I didn't bother to defend myself to Kera.

"I'll stay too," Kimo said.

I gave Kimo an appreciative glance which was lost on him. His autism hampered his ability to respond to others' emotional cues. Yet, he reads minds and has had my back more than once, I thought.

"Maybe the aliens will save us," offered Art, the unbeliever. He laughed alone at the jest.

Emma interrupted what had somehow morphed into another argument. "We'll decide when it happens. We need to get moving," she said with her hands on her hips.

Emma always got to the point. No reason to decide now. Abandonment would be decided at the time, by necessity. Leave now because the alternative was getting caught and killed.

Gatlin came down the ravine swinging a rabbit by its hind legs. He'd relaced his shoe with the one he'd used to make the snare the night before. "Dinner is served!" he called out.

"It's breakfast time," Caleb said. Kyle play punched his shoulder.

"Bring it along. Time to get moving," James said. "And collect what you can on the way today. So we have more food tonight." He directed the comment to me.

No easy task, I thought, looking at the grub juice on my shirt. We hadn't come with backpacks or tools. "I guess I'll start at the front then and work my way back," I said. Malia and her sisters were busy ribbing each other. I interrupted their play and said, "You girls ever eat crickets?" I was starting to remind myself of Uncle George.

They flapped their arms, ewwed, and looked to their parents for salvation. James and Emma ignored their pleas, taking to the trail. The others fell in line. Julie and Kera joined us at the front, which pleased me. Perhaps I'd use the chance to redeem myself. Malia carried Joe to give Kera a break.

"Where shall we begin," I asked myself. "Let's see, there are the Mormon Crickets. We'll find them at dusk when they're feeding, and acorns from the scrub oak, which are out of season, and … oh yes, rice grass. We can find that first!" I bounced ahead, excited to share my knowledge. Was this what my guide had meant? Was this how I was supposed to teach people to survive? My life must mean more than this. At least, I hoped it did.

We reached the top of the ravine and came upon a June Berry Tree. I jumped up and down at the site of it. "Wait, everyone. Stop here first."

James and Emma stopped short. Both of their expressions said, *what now.*

We'd just gotten started, and here I was, stopping everyone. "It will be easier to graze along the way, so we don't have to carry these." I pulled a handful of purplish berries from the ends of the branches and held the little rolling things out in my palm for inspection. "Mmm. They're ripe. Everyone," I invited them to come with a wave of my arm, "come have berries!"

The children ran to the shrubby tree and gathered around. The adults followed.

"Is it safe?" Pen asked.

"Safe as a Saskatoon!" I said. The others eyed me dubiously. "They're also called June Berries."

"Beats grubs and dried up dirty roots." Art reached for a branch and pulled a handful of the berries from its ends. "I'm in." He popped them in his mouth. Kyra and her brothers watched him wide-eyed in anticipation of his reaction.

Art hesitated as he chewed, then held up a purple palm and licked the juice clean. After Art, the others dove in with confidence. They didn't trust me; I'd eaten grubs. Garlands of purple-lipped smiles wreathed the tree, and within minutes we had cleared the tree like a flock of starlings. We were lucky the birds hadn't cleared it first.

We resumed our trek. Julie and Kera walked closer to me, and Malia and Sarah swung Joe by his arms between them. The teens were showing each other their purple tongues.

"So, be on the lookout for grass that looks like this," I said, splaying four fingers out straight.

Kyra crinkled her nose and crossed her brows.

"You'll know when you see it," I explained. "And you know what Ice Plant looks like at the beach?" I asked the group.

Sarah said, "Yes .... We're not at the beach."

"No. But there's a weed here that has that same kind of green, water-filled leaves, called pickleweed, and we can eat it. If you see it along the trail, let me know, and I'll come identify it before we eat it."

"Kimo," I said. He'd been quiet this morning.

"Ya," he snapped.

"Bad night's sleep?" Was he brooding or sleepy, I wondered.

He threw his arms down, slapping his hands at his sides, in an exaggerated motion, "The worst!"

I stifled my laugh with my hand. Julie started laughing too, and then it was contagious. Kera and the girls laughed the loudest.

"It's not funny." Kimo scowled.

"We're with you, Kimo," Kera said. "You just expressed exactly what we are all feeling."

"Oh," he said and raised his brows. "OK." He walked on, seeming satisfied with the explanation, but we continued giggling for some time.

I assigned Kimo to acorns. While not in season, he might get lucky. They were easy to identify, and he could carry them in his pockets. We'd process them into flour when we found water next.

I pulled the dull-gray, toothed leaves of Lamb's Quarter and showed Julie and Kera how to identify it by its leaf and mealy seeds, and they had recognized mustard weed from the yellow flowers and the pungent aroma.

"Don't forget to get the seeds off that Lamb's Quarter," I said. "We can sprout them later." If we find water again. It was hard to collect food predicate on the need for water, but what choice did we have?

"Malia and Sarah, you two will look for Dock."

"Oh no. We're not going back there," said Malia. The harbor experience had been traumatic.

"Very funny." I wagged my finger at her. "Dock, the plant. It has curly leaves, and it looks like a weed. You've seen it in your yard, almost guaranteed. Let me know if you find it."

I gave the kids the easy ones, plants without poisonous lookalikes.

Moa asked, "What about me? What can I find?" She shrugged her shoulders and turned up her palms.

"Do you know what a thistle looks like?"

She nodded, yes.

"Well, thistles are edible. If you find one, you come get me, and I'll help you pick it, so you don't prick your fingers."

"I will!" She bounced away on a mission.

The girls, with studious expressions, began inspecting every plant on the trail. Everyone had a job. The plants were comparatively abundant here, but the farther south we ventured, edible plant options might be as scarce as water.

"Hey, guys," I said, catching up to Gowen and Gatlin. I still had trouble distinguishing them apart unless I remembered which one wore blue plaid and which red.

It was Gatlin who responded. His cobbled-together shoe laces revealed his identity. "Hey there. Collecting your rabbit food, I see." He pointed to my pocket full of mustard greens.

"Yeah, that's me." I showed buck teeth at them and made a sucking sound. "Seriously, I'm so happy you can set a snare. It's not something I ever learned. More of a forager."

"Well, we grew up in desert almost like this. Pendleton." Gowen said as if it explained his snare-setting skills. Gowen wore blue, I noted.

"I knew it! So, are you guys real cowboys?" I asked, hoping they were bronc riders and lived for danger.

"Sheep boys," Gatlin answered.

"Haven't heard of that," I said, wrinkling my brows.

"Shepherds? We tend sheep … for the wool?" He paused and looked at me with a curious expression on his face. "Haven't you heard of the woolen mills?"

"Oh, God! I'm getting dumber." My ears grew hot. "Or, is it more dumb?"

"It's dumb and dumber, I think," Gowen said.

"Glad we cleared that up." I rolled my eyes in good humor. "So, I'm making the rounds, teaching rabbit food collection. You guys know Cottonwood trees?"

"Yep. Got one on the farm back home," Gatlin said.

"Good. So, as we get farther south, we'll see more of them. You can find water under the base of the trees if you dig down a foot or so. And look out for Russian Olives—they grow near waterways."

"I did not know that," Gatlin said. "Did you, Gowen?"

"Surely not," Gowen replied. "That might have come in handy a time or two. How do you know all that stuff, anyway?"

"It's a bit of a hobby since I was a kid. When *they*," I pointed up to the sky, "showed me the scenes of destruction, I started focusing on identifying edible and medicinal plants. I studied edible plants of the West Coast, Rocky Mountains, and the Desert Southwest." I had an abnormally efficient memory; that helped too. Identifying plants in a book and doing it in the field are two different things. When I was learning, I'd spent a lot of time hiking and photographing plants up close, then comparing the photos to the descriptions in my books at home. I'd also learned the lookalike poisonous imposters and how to prepare many of the plants to reduce oxalic acid, tannins, saponins, and other bitter or indigestible features. Jeff probably thought I was crazy, especially when I made him taste test weeds. I'd even selected our vacations based upon growing seasons. My lungs felt sandpapered at the thought of Jeff, so I fell silent for some time.

Gowen broke the silence. "*They*," he pointed up like I had, "showed us that shit too. Pardon my French. The fiery scenes. What do you make of it? I mean, why show us the whole planet blowing up and not this—this VHF virus charade? I mean, if we don't survive this, what's the point of it, anyway?"

"Maybe they didn't know this would happen. Or maybe because the pandemic isn't real." Real. What is real, I thought. Maybe they showed us because they wanted us to make it real, think it into being.

"But our own people tried to kill us? They might have mentioned it." Gatlin said. "If that isn't a threat, I don't know what is."

"An experiment?" I offered. "The aliens just wanted to get our reactions. See if we'd be afraid." I recalled feeling tested and observed. Stimulus-response. "Even if they'd warned us, we'd still be here, and our government still would have tried to kill us. So, what if they only show us stuff we can do something about?"

"Naw," said Gatlin, "I agree they're experimenting on us. Ever notice how they're the ones asking all the questions but won't answer a single one? Not even, *where ya from*. We're guinea pigs to them." He kicked a clod of dirt hard off the path ahead. It exploded at the base of a twisted juniper, sending fragments of rock scattering and disturbing a few Mourning Doves from their hiding spots.

Ahead of us, the PTSD girl darted at the sound of the dirt explosion.

Gatlin called forward, "Sorry, Terra!" He said to us in a hushed voice, "Skittish, isn't she?" The three of us watched her for a moment to make sure she'd recovered.

"Our own people treat us as guinea pigs too," I said, responding to Gatlin's earlier comment. "We do to each other what's been done to us." I'd learned this long ago. Life cycles repeat, behaviors repeat, everything is arranged so we learn not to judge one another until we realize we cause each other's pain.

"Isn't it supposed to be the other way around? Do unto others as you would have done unto you?" asked Gowen, nodding and clearly proud of himself. "I went to Sundee school." He tapped his chest.

I didn't mention the phrase had been used by other religions more than a thousand years before Christ. "Yes, that is what it's *supposed* to be, but not what seems to actually happen. Doesn't it seem more like the person who traumatizes you had something similar done to them once, and they're just taking that pain out on you?"

Gowen looked up, appearing to contemplate what I'd said.

I continued, "Life has a way of turning us all into hypocrites. Sometimes you don't have to look hard to see it." My feet moved forward one after another, but my mind wandered to thoughts of my own hypocrisy. My pickles. I'd done research on animals because I thought the benefits to mankind made it worthwhile. Yet, here I sat in judgment of those who experimented on mankind, for whatever reasons. I'm sure they meant well. So had I.

Forgive them, for they know not what they do, I recalled from the bible. As a syncretist, I'd take wisdom from any source that presented itself to me; but I wasn't married to one religion, as Mother had been. My experiences with *them* had caused me to take another look at "religion" and the general meaning of life, but many questions remained.

Right now, I longed for connection with people, for belonging, to fill a hole in my heart, so I focused on what people had in common. "And, Gowen, for the record, I went to Sundee school too ... until they kicked me out!"

"Kicked you out? What?" asked Gatlin. "You trouble causer! What'd you do?"

"I fell asleep," I said, raising my chin.

"So you didn't go to Sunday school after all," Gatlin teased.

"I'd read the material before school, actually." I pursed my lips and glared.

"Of course you did. You little nerd bucket!" He tussled my hair.

"Guilty." We chuckled and kept our pace. I didn't have brothers, but if I imagined brothers, I'd want them to be like Gowen and Gatlin. They were too young to be my brothers, but I smiled at the thought of adopted brothers, and happy tears formed at the corners of my eyes. I could like people again, I told myself. I might trust people again and believe they intend to be just and honest. I'd found these people, and I had one odd thing in common with them: most of us must have experienced the same life-altering event, setting us apart from our fellow man, and in a curious route, bringing us together.

"Wonder how many miles we've walked," Gowen said.

"If I knew, my feet would hurt more." I tuned out as the brothers calculated miles per hour and hours per day.

Sandra's song carried on the sage dusted breeze, a lilting melody that lifted my feet and my spirits.

CHAPTER 33

DAY 5, 2020 CONTINUED, WATCHERS AND DRAGONS

By dusk, the trail had become uneven and difficult to see, so we stopped to make camp. Emma organized the collection of the foodstuffs gathered throughout the day, and I put people to work instructing them how to prepare the foods. James led a small group to gather firewood. Sandra removed her shoes to rub her feet and swollen right ankle. Unless she'd twisted the ankle, I recognized right-side swelling as a potential heart problem.

Once I'd finished instructing on food preparation, I hobbled my way over to Sandra. "You alright?" I asked, removing my tennies and peeling sweaty socks from my toes. I started to rub my feet too, but it didn't ease the blood blister or the busted toenail. What I craved were clean socks and underwear, better shoes, toothpaste, a hairbrush …

"Yeah, I'll be fine." She pulled her pant leg down to hide the swollen ankle.

"I think you and I are the oldest of the group. Maybe Miguel, too," I said. "Look at those kids," I grunted and nodded at the teens who were playing football with an abandoned wasps' nest. "It hardly phases them."

An uncaught Hail Mary resulted in a shower of disintegrated wasp-nest-confetti. The would-be quarterback yelled, "Sprung!" and treated us to a primal dance and guttural hoots. I wondered if "sprung" was slang.

"You? Old?" Sandra sneered in disbelief. "You can't be over 28."

"I get that a lot. I'm 45."

"No way." She shook her head but continued to rub an angry bunion. "Now I think I don't like you," she humphed. "I'm fifty." She pulled the sides of her cheeks taut. "Where are your wrinkles, girl?"

It wasn't just my short height, but big eyes, and fair skin that added to the illusion of youth. For better or worse, I wasn't sure I aged the same rate as most people. Grandmother's FOXC2 gene is associated with longevity, but Grandmother had looked her age when she died. A few in our family had aged over one hundred years and many into their nineties, but none broke world records.

Most of the time, my youthful appearance and gender meant people didn't take me seriously. I'd never grown accustomed to it and often overcompensated in my attempts to show leadership, using my intelligence and reminding myself and others of my accomplishments. On more than one occasion, this had the undesired consequence of being judged a bossy, egotistical snob.

"I may not have wrinkles, but I'd trade to be able to sing like you," I said, clutching a hand to my chest. "You have the voice of an angel."

"Thank you. I worked hard at it." She flitted a smile and looked away as if avoiding something.

Maybe she avoided the idea she might not be singing much longer if we didn't survive. Maybe she avoided thinking about home, people she loved, or regrets. "How long have you been a musician?" I asked.

"As long as I can remember, really. My parents were bluegrass musicians. Dad played banjo, and Mom sang and played the tambourine. I grew up with it."

"You are special." The words stuck in my throat. I hadn't intended to use *their* words, the aliens, that is. I swallowed and rephrased, "You have the power to change the way people feel and think, just by making music. And you can draw people together. A good musician is a magician."

"That is thoughtful of you to say!"

"Well, it makes a difference, especially while we walk. With pacing, with stress, with our attitudes. I'm so happy you escaped with us."

"I'm fortunate to be here with you too. I just hope I don't slow everyone down too much."

"We all make contributions, even if we have needs too. We'll get through it together."

"Unless you all ditch me on the side of the trail." She smirked. "At this rate …"

"Nah," I said, touching her arm, "just keep going. You always have more left in you than you think." I knew from experience.

"I'll try." Her voice cracked. "But sometimes, I don't know why. What kind of life can we have after this, anyway? Will they ever stop trying to kill us? Eventually, they'll catch us; we can't run forever."

I shared Sandra's reservations, but on top of them, I included disillusionment and shame over my ill-prepared plans, leading these people to god knew what.

Before I could offer encouragement, James raised a startled voice at the edge of the camp. "Everyone, get down!" He motioned his arms to the ground and shuffled, torso bent, to the edge of the brush. In unison, we dropped. A few kids curled into balls and covered their heads as if for an earthquake drill. Others hid in a bush. I laid flat, unintentionally blocking the walkway.

James peered over the shrubs, squinting his eyes into the distance. "I saw a flash, like light reflecting off something. Binoculars, maybe." He sounded out of breath.

"A hunter?" Kera asked. Joe squirmed and escaped her grasp. He toddled his way away from the group. "Grab him," Kera ordered, to no one in particular.

He was closest to me, so I reached for his arm to stop him. "Hey, little man," I said. When Kera saw I was the one to grab Joe, she sat up with a startled expression. Julie pushed her back down. "We're all pretending to sleep," I said. "It's a game. Can you pretend to sleep with me?"

"No!" Joe yelled. I had him by the arm, but he pulled and stomped his feet.

"But, it's a game." I spoke in a hushed tone, attempting to calm his tantrum. "We're pretending, Joe, because we're hiding from a dragon. He's on the mountain, over there." I pointed to James, who searched the mountain with his hand over his brows. Joe's gaze followed my finger, and he stood on his tiptoes to see what James was looking at. "If the dragon finds us, we won't win the treasure. Don't you want the treasure?"

Joe clasped his hands over his pants zipper and crossed his feet. "If you go to sleep, you can win your own King crown." I raised the inflection of my voice. "With jewels and a magic cape," I added, for enticement.

He laid next to me on his back and raised his legs up in the air. Then he slammed his feet down on the trail and snorted like an animal through his nose. I didn't bother to stop his movements. He'd complied enough, I thought.

James kept his eyes trained to the hillside. As a group, we watched him for a sign he'd identified what he'd seen. Still as a statue, he leaned over one bent knee. After some time observing, he shuffled closer to the rest of us. "No fire tonight," he said but kept his eyes on the hillside.

There went dinner plans. My stomach clenched. We'd grazed along the way, but much of what we'd collected would benefit from some level of cooking.

The few men who'd been out collecting firewood returned to the camp. James met them before they could make much noise. They dropped their wood in a pile and got on the ground with the rest of us.

James took Julie with him to investigate what he'd seen and ordered the rest of us to stay on the ground until they returned. I couldn't be the only one wondering *if* he'd return. Dread filled me. After this painful journey, if they'd found us … all for what?

Joe stood and made a run for it; his little hand slipped from my grasp. Wet urine marked the front of his pants. I shuffled over to him and hugged him to the ground as if play wrestling. He laughed for a second, then started crying—poor kid. For the first time since we'd escaped, he'd tried to tell us, tried not to wet himself, and I had stopped him. No diapers, no water, and days in the heat; he must have hellacious diaper rash. It made me want to cry. I held my breath as if my breathing somehow added to the noise of Joe's crying. Hopefully, whoever watched us was out of earshot. A cry could be mistaken for a hundred things. Quail, I thought, coyotes, and … my list stopped, distracted by my grumbling stomach and the thought of poached Quail eggs.

I brushed my hand over Joe's forehead and pushed his white-blonde hair back from his brow over and over in a frantic attempt to calm him. It had calmed me when I was a child. After a few seconds, his sobs turned to short gasps for air, and then he fell asleep, still whimpering and gasping as he slept. With a real sense of accomplishment, I sat up and looked into Joe's peaceful face and smiled. But the peace didn't last long.

Kera stomped my direction, making no attempt to conceal herself. She took Joe's arm in her hand, pulled him to his feet, and into a possessive embrace. He instantly began crying again. With Joe in her arms, Kera seethed, "He's not yours!" Then she marched him back to where she had been sitting.

It didn't need explanation. The shocked stares of the others told me I'd interpreted correctly and that some of them already knew this secret. I didn't know why it had been done or how it had been done. Beyond the similar hair and eye color, somehow I knew, a good portion of Joe's genes had come from me. If I thought it would help, I'd tell Kera that I agreed with her; Joe wasn't mine. But it wouldn't help. What had been done to us couldn't be undone. We all lived with the insecurity that came with unknown origins. We had to question our identities.

CHAPTER 34

2009 DISCLOSURE RATIONALE - THE WANTING

Journal of Aline Orr: Beware the one who assigns value to the sacrifices of others.

Once again, I found myself restrained before Keith. My head pounded, and my vision blurred. I wanted to rub my temples and feel for injuries, but the chained cuffs extended only to the edge of the table, not to my face. With both chair and table bolted to the floor, my intimidating four-foot-eight body (142 cm) sat in the chair of defiance, a prescribed safe distance from the table.

"We don't need your vigilantism. We don't need you," Keith said, the usual contempt present in his voice.

I bothered him. I liked that about myself.

"What are you talking about?" I asked. I couldn't remember any of the conversations we'd had before this moment. I couldn't even remember being brought here.

"I mean your wasted efforts to derail the pandemic vaccine program. It isn't even about that, and you know it."

"I do?" What did I know? My senses blurred as I searched my memory for context. The room spun, and figures split into doubles. What did he want from me?

"Wake her up a little—she's not tracking," Keith said to a goon at his side, who turned my arm up and injected into the crook.

Within seconds, my heart raced, and my face burned. Adrenaline—it wouldn't make me remember.

"You ready?" Keith asked.

"Sure, Quiche. I'm ready." I had no clue what came next but couldn't resist calling him Quiche.

He looked at me expectantly.

I shrugged.

"OK. You just had to know, so I'm going to lay it out straight. You," he pointed a finger at me and traced it up and down, "are not more evolved. In fact, you're a mistake."

I squinted, trying to see if he was real. Had I told him I had alien DNA? Wait, he knew that already. Confusion gripped my forehead.

"We did it to you, Aline. And all of them."

All of whom, I wondered.

"We created your lineage in the 1930s. We selected your family because the U.S. Military's Dr. Stanford lived next door to your great-grandparents' family and because your grandmother was a genius, as was her maternal aunt. We determined it was heritable. Your grandmother and her siblings were given the alien genes in their Tetanus vaccines. One of her siblings got Marfan's from the transgenes affecting Chromosome 15 genes. And your grandmother acquired her FoxC2 mutation on Chromosome 16, which messed up the rest of you. Talk about way off target."

I sat unmoving, in disbelief. I'd memorized my family's history and had concluded the aliens had done it to us.

His eyes rolled to the ceiling. "Nobody, and I mean nobody, wanted the subjects to start looking like the aliens. But that Marfan's look and your short body type …. What can I say? Oops." He shrugged and then went on while scanning the papers. "Let's see here. Their generation attended Dwight School in San Francisco, which was a grooming school for selective service.

Is this sounding familiar, Aline?" He paused briefly. "Let me know when you understand."

I looked away.

"Right," he said curtly. "Dr. Stanford followed their IQs throughout their youths. Unfortunately, there was no change. Next generation." He opened the next file folder. "Dr. Dwight, an asset, delivered each of your grandmother's children. Dr. Dwight's brother ran the Dwight School." He nodded as if to indicate to himself the duplicate name was not in error.

"Dr. Dwight enrolled your grandmother in the first RH compatibility study at Berkeley and followed your mother and her siblings throughout their youths. The RH compatibility study was supposed to tell us how the mother's genetic modifications affected the immune system and if the mother's immune system would attack the fetus. From this study, we discovered your grandmother's FOXC2 Chromosome 16 mutation had some crossover effect on Chromosome 6 in the region coding for the immune system. And, just adjacent to the immune system genes, the TNXB gene and dysbindin gene, which gave rise to your generation's defects after a few hiccups.

"Each of your grandmother's siblings had one child with Asperger's—one a savant. Next generation. A select few in your mother's generation were given alien DNA in their Measles vaccines. That was the 60s—Wild West sort of thing. The gene for dysbindin was one of the genes they'd found in common with a particular alien species. They had hoped to upregulate the dysbindin gene to increase intelligence. But instead of upregulating it, the mutations caused the gene to become ineffective, which led to schizophrenia in two from that generation." He thumbed distractedly through the records on those subjects, my tragically impacted relatives. "That generation didn't amount to much," he said nonchalantly.

I stuck my chin out, but he was right. Despite the few with genius IQs, no one in my family had made life-altering or world-changing discoveries. Convinced aliens had contacted me and chosen me because I was more evolved; perhaps the truth was I'd let my ego get the best of me. My head hung in humiliation. My guide had told me I was special. Someone had shared THe equation with me. Why, if I wasn't smart enough to use it?

"Yours wasn't the only family, obviously. And we have a few problems on our hands, autism, chronic fatigue syndrome, and that HOX gene issue. Can't have you all running around looking like *them*. Nobody wants that," he repeated as if the real problem was that humans might start looking like aliens and not the debilitating issues his experiments had caused in so many people.

"How do *you* even know what a HOX gene is?" I asked. "You're no geneticist."

"Community college." He paused, and I couldn't tell if he was serious. "Look, Aline, I know what I need to know to get my job done. Satisfied?"

I sighed but sensed there were problems he wasn't willing to share. My focus drifted a moment as I observed the men in the room. Identical builds and heights, they wore the same haircuts atop block-shaped heads. I could swear I often saw Keith on street corners and in grocery stores. They enjoyed looking like clones, these military types. Quiche everywhere. Quiche on aisle three. Quiche in line at the post office.

Keith snapped his fingers at me, and I flinched. Pay attention, I told myself; I need to remember this information.

"There were two test groups," he said. "The civilian groups from the 60s and the later groups that got MMR as part of their military service. We were aiming for somatic cells in the soldiers, same goal—smarter, and it worked on those soldiers. They were smarter, the ones that didn't end up with chronic fatigue, Gulf War Syndrome, you name it. The autism issue took a while to discover and even longer to determine the cause. That MMR vaccine used an added recombinant retrovirus to deliver the alien DNA."

"That was dumb." I rolled my eyes. Recombinant retroviruses are a special type of virus that can enter germline cells (sperm and egg) and alter chromosomes. They'd aimed to make the soldiers smarter by introducing genes that only affected the soldier's own genes, but additional unintended alterations ended up being passed on to their offspring. I shuddered to think of potential mitochondrial mutations he hadn't even mentioned yet.

"Well, they didn't know then what they know now. Autism wasn't the only issue, as you can imagine. We weren't trying to cause an endogenous, germline retrovirus." He stopped and glanced at my face. I nodded. I didn't need an explanation, but I was surprised he understood viral genes had integrated themselves into people's genomes. He added blithely, "That's what caused all the cases of post-viral syndrome, chronic fatigue. But more importantly, the mutations are becoming fixed in the population."

The consequences were real. Fixed mutations would not self-repair. "Genetic instability." I shook my head in disbelief.

"The end of mankind." His voice held an air of finality.

Perhaps not the end, I cogitated in a grasping attempt to find the stitch of silver lining. Possibly a new species, depending on—

"But, we're trying to fix it, Aline, and I'd personally appreciate it if you'd stop interfering."

"Fix it? You fouled the evolution of mankind overnight."

"We've been at this a lot longer than you realize."

Nature had been at it even longer, I thought. Even though Keith had proven his character time and again, his arrogance astounded me.

"Have you heard of the Genome Security Division?" he asked.

I hesitated. "Yes." I almost didn't want to know their subterfuge.

"It's a Security Research Agency program."

Of course it is, I thought. Just what we need, defense intelligence sticking crude fingers in human evolution.

"They find and figure out how to remove unwanted or accidental genes from the population." He spoke excitedly, as if the clandestine government entity would canvas the community in an ice cream truck. "We formed the Genome Security Division thinking someone would do it to us—you know, a foreign country creates a deleterious gene editing bioweapon, and how would we know until it's too late? Anyway, they've figured it all out," he said, implying there was no longer a need to worry. "The GSD has a gene therapy in the pipeline that will replace the engineered genes and return us to baseline. They're collaborating with industry."

Genome Security Division—a black-op program to gene edit Americans without their knowledge? Oh, my pickles. I was a pickle. I'd pollute the wild types. Keith's voice faded with my reflections, but I snapped back to attention. "No doubt another retrovirus." I rolled my eyes. It was the only way to transduce the germline cells—to make the changes heritable, lasting for generations. Why did the government think they could control this? They had proven the technology surpassed their abilities. I let out a pent-up breath.

"Actually, no. We're going to try perfluoro-chemicals and transfect DNA into cells by aerosol. If it works, the edits can be inhaled, and no one will even know."

More chemicals, I thought. I'd heard of the chemicals, PFOAs. They'd been found in high concentrations on military bases and in groundwater, and scientists had discovered the chemicals in sperm. They claimed the chemicals' uses as a fire retardant foam constituted an irreplaceable and necessary pollutant. From what he'd just said, they'd tested it on troops already. Bile came up my throat.

"You see," Keith blathered with confidence, "we know who has the alien DNA—who has the problem genes that can be passed on. That's why we created the infant heel stick, so we could find out how many there are in the public health records. We can find the fuck-ups born since the 70s. Prevent it from spreading. Remediation."

He thought I was a fuck-up. Now I did understand. With pursed lips, I held my tongue back.

"And that genome database. Even your ethics committee approved it." He seemed to await my response.

By associating me with his plans, he sought to cast blame from himself, and I took the bait again. So focused on the vaccine studies, I questioned whether I'd done enough to stop them from harvesting our patients' genetic information for their national database. I'd done my best. No one else had done more. A dreadful defeated dirge danced all the way down to my limp feet.

"We're working our way through it," he said, "but it's tedious. There are too many to go door to door." He wound his hand in a come-along gesture, "Are you with me?"

"You can call it remediation, but I call it eugenics," I said, and then I recalled the notice from our lawyers and the patient they identified from the genetic database—the prostate cancer patient. A matter of national security, they'd said. They'd hunted him down through the genetic database. And the Wellness Program at work had collected genetic markers on employees! I reeled in my seat at the breadth of the resources they'd amassed. The government juggernaut put employers and public health agencies to work compiling data for them. And the best part—the government hadn't spent a dime on Wellness Programs or the collection of samples from patients for genotyping. The government was capable of efficiency, after all.

"There's my girl. Aline, so predictable, moralistic," he clapped. "It's more like taking care of an invasive weed problem." He extended his arms at length and gave a sidelong pucker-lipped grimace as if to put distance between himself and a smelly mother-in-law coming in for a kiss. "Or, those invasive Chinese zebra mussels. They shouldn't be here."

He meant to be offensive. This monster had saved my life once and was my husband's closest friend. I struggled to keep a flat affect and not respond to his taunts, but I burst. "You can't be better at evolution than nature. You must realize you weren't successful at putting genes in people, so what makes you think you can fix them without harming them or screwing things up more? And just how do you plan on stopping the private companies from continuing to deliver gene edits or transgenes in their vaccines? They're going to choose which genes, Keith, not you."

"You're wrong, Aline. We have them by the balls. They can't get federal funding to develop gene editing, and FDA won't allow them to do it. Only the Security Research Agency is allowed to create the edits and transgenes."

"You work for them," I reminded him and stopped myself. I wasn't supposed to remember our previous conversations. Months ago, I'd informed him he wasn't on the right side. He didn't catch that the mind wipe hadn't worked on me—at least his face didn't show that he'd caught it. "That won't stop them, you big dummy. It's not expensive to create the genes, and they have the technology. They're the ones with the upper hand, Keith."

His confident posture told me he believed his own words. He believed the rules, that had proven so easy to break, would keep the pharmaceutical companies in check.

I diverted, "Look, they have their own money, Keith. And they don't have to get FDA approval if the transgenes are not intended to treat a disease. You should know that." I certainly knew their tricks. "FDA regulates therapies intended to treat diseases. Not all transgenes are therapeutic, and if they're anything like what you've already done, they aren't meant to *treat* anything, are they? Or, they might just claim the genetic material is in there accidentally. They've done it before—accidental contaminants, mouse viruses, bug viruses." Come to think of it, I suddenly wondered if swine virus contaminants had made their way into a vaccine or two. "No one will know unless they independently sequence the final product. Right now, you take their word for it, don't you?"

He snapped his fingers behind his head at someone behind the glass. I hoped I hadn't just helped them figure out more loopholes. Nobody reads the actual regulations. Nobody but lawyers. Why read? They did what they wanted, anyway.

"What kind of people will you create," I sneered, "you and the pharmas, *who supposedly* work for you?" I sweated from the adrenaline. "Will you create soldiers who feel no fear, hunger, pain, need no sleep?" Or people like me, I wondered silently, people with adaptations for living in space or on other planets. If I was an error, why had my guide told me to reproduce? Perhaps Keith fed me misinformation. Or, perhaps the government hadn't identified the utility of my mutations as beneficial to living in space or under other planetary conditions. I turned my head and eyed him with suspicion.

"The current program is remediation only." He placed his arms over his papers and curled his fingers around the stack.

"You work for the pharmas," I repeated. "Your soldiers are their soldiers."

"You're missing the point entirely," he said with an exasperated edge in his voice.

"Have I now?" I mocked his previous come-along hand motion with both cuffed hands. "So, enlighten me."

"You're the one who wants to stop autism, right?" He was referring to my role at the HMO questioning the autism studies.

"I wanted safe products. I wanted to keep the research ethical," I said, clarifying my intentions. "I wanted the government to preserve the public trust by telling the truth." My empathy for the plight of those unwittingly damaged and dismissed had grown since discovering the deceptions. I wouldn't let Keith put words in my mouth. I had started that fight because it was my job, not to crusade for an autism cure. "There's a place for everyone." I stopped and shook my head. He'd never understand. "Our differences are a gift, can't you see? You can't predict changing circumstances. Differences are all mankind has to survive what may come. Warming, atmospheric pressure changes, living in different environments …."

"They're off-target effects … not *differences.*" Spittle formed on his lips. "Mistakes," he added, sounding like the government stooge he was. He folded his arms and leaned back. As if his chair was meant for a child, his shoulders overreached the back of the chair by a good eight inches on both sides.

My feet dangled from my chair, my toes barely able to touch the floor. "You could kill them—you are killing them." I gave him a pointed look in the eye. "And me too." A crack in my voice split the last words, and I looked away.

"Don't be dramatic. You're still here." A look of disappointment crossed his face.

I *was* still here. Their gene edits hadn't worked on me for some reason. Or, had they? Perhaps, I had mutations they didn't know about.

"Some will die," Keith said, interrupting my thoughts. "True. Not all. They might have died from their mutations anyway," he hesitated, then beat his perspective in with a hammer. "The only way to stop it is to stop the genes from spreading to the offspring. You know that, Aline. Unless you think forced sterilizations will go over any better."

He had a point. Targeted sterilizations couldn't be performed discreetly. The government had sterilized autistics in the past. The action had caused an uproar. Keith avoided using the terms murder or euthanasia; I noticed he referred to what he was doing in a detached manner as "stopping off-target effects." His types clung to their language, their ways of describing things to hide the truth and shift blame. It made them feel powerful. I screamed inside. But part of me realized his disclosure, this unnecessary conversation, wasn't for my benefit. Keith had provided me with a rationalization. Did he think I would champion his rationale, and if so, to whom? How had he become convinced I'd ever agree to his schemes?

"What I don't understand is: Why have a vaccine at all?" I asked. "You guys manufactured the H1N1 virus—this pandemic scenario—so why not just have the virus deliver the gene edits?"

"The virus did deliver the gene edits. The vaccine is the mop-up crew. Anyone who didn't get the virus gets the vaccine. That way, we have maximum coverage."

Create a pandemic. Scare them into getting the vaccine, I thought. They needed public buy-in. That's why they were so angry I'd questioned its safety. I pulled my hands towards my head to rub the tension from my temples, but the chain stopped them short. Part of me was at work—still fighting to prove them wrong.

"How did you get that past FDA?" I asked. He'd just said the vaccine had gene edits, while he'd previously said FDA banned gene editing. He didn't answer. He didn't have to. I remembered the email from Bob Sherman.

"… Field Tests," I said, coming to the realization on my own. Field tests do not require FDA approval. The General had been adamant that he didn't need FDA approval. The government runs military field tests—experiments—on the general population. Emergency use—bioterrorism act—all covers. These regulatory screens served dual purposes: a. The laws were complicated and dissuaded investigation and comprehension by the public; and b. Their language propagandized an urgent need, instilling fear to promote apathetic compliance.

Keith didn't acknowledge field testing. I was certain he preferred to name it something that sounded supportive of his goals.

"We control distribution of the final vaccine product," he said. "We keep the sequence and what materials we need in a classified, private databank. It's in Switzerland, so it can't be subpoenaed." He added the last defensively as if I might call a lawyer after our meeting. At one time, I might have. He had not responded when I pointed out that the pharmas could add edits, and they wouldn't be found unless someone sequenced the final product independently. They'd covered that loose end. By controlling final distribution, they prevented anyone else from validating the product purity. Only his people knew what was in the final vaccines.

He said, "I can see from your expression that you finally understand."

"Yes," I said. My voice sounded defeated. These people were unbeatable. That's what I understood. I had met numerous wealthy individuals at parties who railed on over cocktails about all the ways they'd duped the IRS, finding loopholes to avoid taxes. It was sport to them. This was no different. They hunt for means to beat the system, bend the rules to meet their ends.

"I've told you what you wanted. Now, I'll need you to do your part," he said in a paternal tone.

I gulped a startled response down my dry throat. Had I promised to do something for him that I couldn't recall? Oh no. My heart sank. Vedra. I felt my eyes widen. I hadn't told him about Vedra, but maybe he'd encountered her in place of my consciousness, during one of my interrogations. What incentive did she have to deal with Keith? Did Vedra understand the risks this posed to me? To humanity?

"We need more information on THe equation." He said it as if I worked for him. "Come on, Aline. Make the sacrifice worth something."

Why would I tell him anything, I wondered, if he was going to remediate me, anyway? Besides, it wasn't as if I could call up an out-of-body experience to connect to alien intelligence at will …. Could Vedra? My vision swam, and I swayed in my chair. Did Vedra control me? Was she inside me, just sitting in my subconscious listening, spying? I looked over my shoulder, half expecting she'd be corporeal and standing there behind me.

All I had wanted was a confession, truth from the horse's mouth. But why? Was it worth it to have only received vindication? Suddenly, I wondered if I'd compromised my ideals. I thought of the employees who began careers thinking they worked to help others but ended up enabling oppression. Was I a hypocrite? What had I traded for a truth no one else would hear?

"You will get the information you promised us, and you will stop interfering with the remediation program," he said. His tone implied a threat.

Sight disappeared behind my eyelids. Before I could respond to Keith, I lost consciousness.

Cross-legged and straight-backed, I sat in the center of the blue paisley living room rug. I hate this rug, I thought as I tried to live up to my own promise to release myself from the trappings of this existence. The paisley held me back, I reasoned. "Argh!" I kicked my feet out of their knot abruptly, startling the sleeping dog, who released a surprised fart.

Last night, I'd seen Keith. I didn't have full recall of what he'd told me, except that it had been one of those *bad news and worse news* scenarios. Now, I struggled to meditate and blamed it on everything but the truth. The real hold-up was that I'd come to discover I'm a hypocrite. I'd sold out for vindication and vendetta. That's why I couldn't let go of this construct, because I'd sat in judgment of everyone who'd done me wrong, who'd done others wrong, everyone not on my side. But the mutable truth was, I might have done the same had I been in their positions. I harbored resentments and couldn't forgive others for being fallible, and, therefore, I couldn't forgive myself. A fine trap I'd woven for myself. And I was willing to put others in harm's way before putting myself in harm's way, even though I expected more of people—the layers of deflagration built upon themselves, fed distraction, fed destruction.

"I will do my meditation," I humphed and beat my fists on the ground. My jacket hung on a hook by the door. I snatched it, tearing the hook loose and leaving a sprinkling of white plaster powder on the floor. The door slammed behind me as I jammed my arms into the coat sleeves and lay down on the lawn in the front yard. I should have gone to the backyard, I thought, but this lawn was closer to my coat. It had rained recently. Water soaked my socks and seeped through my pants at my tailbone, but I squeezed my eyes shut and focused with extreme intent. Clear the mind, feel the emptiness, I told myself.

When my heart and breaths slowed, I embraced nothingness. But my body was still there. I could feel it and wanted to reject it.

I tried to merge with the creator as I had once long ago when attempting to heal a friend. My eyes opened, and I let them stare at the sky for so long I lost color vision—fatigued retinal receptors. Do over. Release all fear ... release thought ... approach with an open heart. The center of my head pulsed with a pleasing thrum, and I latched onto the sensation. The golden-white light that was and was not appeared far from my grasp. What is my will? The question seemed to come from another existence, but I willed it, and I was there at the edge of the source of all creation. Except there was no edge, I realized. The space within and without. The Source has no border. It is. I am. I am the Source. The Source is all. Vibration racked my body, and I felt bits of myself disintegrate into pixelated confetti. And then there was no me; I was a surge, a bolt of lightning.

"Whatchya doin', Aline?"

Startled, my eyes popped open to the familiar voice. I blinked twice.

Jeff stood over me; both legs straddled my body in the grass. "You look like you're about to spontaneously combust."

"I'm *trying* to meditate, Jeff."

"Meditation looks uncomfortable. Not at all peaceful. You should see yourself," he said, sounding self-satisfied.

"I assure you; it's very peaceful. Now go away. Or, better yet ... why don't you lay down here and meditate with me?" I patted the grass next to me.

"Well, I guess because I don't want to spontaneously combust."

"It's too wet for combustion," I said, wiping my hands down my coat. Then I held a hand out for him to pull me up. When Jeff wanted attention, he wouldn't relent.

Pulling me to my feet, he said, "Actually, I'll try combustion with you, but not out here where the neighbors can see." He shook his fist at the neighbor standing in his front window. "No free porn today, Fred." The neighbor pumped his fist back at Jeff.

It could wait, to release the self, attachment … Jeff. Just like he had carried me years ago when we married, Jeff patted his back, and I hopped up for my piggy back ride over the threshold. I heeled his butt cheeks and yelled, "Yehaw! Faster, number seven."

CHAPTER 35

DAY 5, 2020 CONTINUED, SYZYGY

James and Julie had been gone for what seemed hours, investigating the potential sighting of hunters James had spotted on the mountain. While awaiting their return, those of the remaining group, who could sleep, slept. When I wasn't dozing, I noticed Kimo watching me from across the trail where he shared shade with his sister Malia.

I drifted off into the dream world to find myself standing over my sleeping body in the desert. Only, in the dream a storm raged and the others were nowhere in sight. Horizontal rain bulleted my cheeks, and fingers of lightning stretched overhead, wide as the hand of God. Crack. A swarthy, loin-clothed man appeared in the flash of light. Ghost or apparition? Dead people once lived, I told myself—release all fear.

A black-tarry substance painted the hollows of the man's eyes, making them appear ovoid and much larger than the glint their centers betrayed. Crudely cut, sun-bleached curls framed his moon-shaped face and broad, shining nose. Not much taller than me, lanky limbs belied his height. There was something familiar about his posture, I thought. One arm hung straight and rigid at his side, and his shoulders hunched. Kimo or an incarnation of Kimo.

He waved an invitation for me to follow him. I left my body on the ground, somewhat unsure it would be there upon my return. The next moment, I stood on a mountain-side waiting as the tawny man made cere-monial preparations. A lull in the storm allowed a clearing in the clouds to expose the Milky Way. He pointed to the stars and moved his arms in an elliptical pattern, which I understood to mean the transit of our solar sys-tem about the galaxy. Next, he pointed to a naturally exposed slab of smooth black stone on the ground and made the same elliptical motion with his hand. No words were exchanged between us but weak telepathic commu-nications. So, hand language sufficed.

He placed dry leaves about the perimeter of the stone and then picked up a staff. Pole straight, the staff had few adornments, except for a couple feathers loosely tied to the top. Twining laces secured a leather sack filled with rocks to the bottom of the pole. It clacked with the sound of the rocks rubbing in the sack.

He motioned for me to lay on the stone slab, which I did, completely trusting as I had always been. It had gotten me in trouble before, but once again, for better or worse, I opened my heart to new experiences. The disin-carnate man walked the elliptical circuit about my body, chanting unintel-ligible words and pounding the rock-filled sack at the end of the pole onto the edge of stone slab. After a couple laps, the leather sack had begun to wear through, and sparks shot out with each smack of his pole. Flint, I supposed. As the sparks came, thunder and lightning matched each crack of the pole. The chanting became more labored and frenzied with each of his circuits.

My perspective alternated. Vedra stood over me. I could see her standing there, but I could also see through her eyes, watching me on the stone. The two perspectives finally merged, and we lay there on the stone slab together as one person. I had no thoughts of fear during this process. It was not a stranger I'd merged with; it was Vedra. Our physical bodies may be worlds apart, but our ethereal bodies were merged there on the stone as a moment or place, or a moment in a place.

The leaves about the ellipse caught fire, ignited by the sparks from the flint. They burned weak as kindling, releasing an acrid smoke. Lightning struck in synchronicity with the pole. Vedra and I writhed as if snakes hatched from our bodies. This *hatching* contained pain but not unbearable pain. Trepidation crept into my consciousness when I realized I'd lost deliberate control of my spirit body. I couldn't leave, stop the ceremony, or separate from Vedra, so I tried not to struggle.

An enormous serpent sat partially coiled at our feet. The man stopped his circuit and motioned his pole at the erect snake and then to us on the ground, and once again at the snake. As with Vedra, I saw through the snake's eyes, then through my eyes shared with Vedra, and back through the snake's eyes again. A swamp-green cloud of smoke left our ethereal bodies in a gratifying exhalation, as if we'd released some plan, some intention, from our beings. We each viewed through the eyes of the snake once more. The rain poured down on our stilled, ethereal bodies, and we watched our now combined body decay as if in time-lapse. The raindrops tore and pummeled at our dead flesh until the soil had consumed all that we once were, and only a single skeleton remained as evidence of a life passed.

CHAPTER 36

DAY 5, 2020 CONTINUED, INITIATE

I'd had the most intense dream earlier. One of Kimo's past incarnations presided over a ceremony in which Vedra and I had merged. At least, that's what I thought happened in the ceremony. I looked for Kimo, but the night was dark and moonless, and he had moved closer to his mother.

No one had eaten, but none of us complained. James and Julie had yet to return. Everyone was grateful we weren't still hiking, but Emma was beyond herself with worry. In hushed tones, she had spoken with Gowen and Gatlin about forming a search party, but they noted that starting a search in the dark didn't make sense. If James and Julie had gotten lost in the dark, a search party would get lost too. Gowen reassured Emma that James would find us in the morning. We'd committed to waiting, and that's what we did.

I sat awake for the next hour until underfoot sounds, crunching dry leaves and pebbles, neared the camp. I held my breath, unable to distinguish the noise of James and Julie returning from the hunters they'd gone after. No sounds came from our people that I could discern. The last I checked, they all slept. We were caught, or we weren't, I thought; no sense in fretting about it. But my heart pounded. No running now ... it was dark.

Faded forms morphed in the shadows. Was it an animal? It had to be our people, I willed; it had to be. A cramp formed in the hand I had clenched about a stone. No lights. That was a good sign. Our people didn't have flashlights but, then, neither did animals. I listened for animal grunts or snorts. The rustling grew closer.

A circumstance I now regretted, I had chosen to lay at the edge of our camp, away from the others and closest to where the leaves now rustled. Proximity to an eventuality made no difference. I'd be eaten first, captured first, or second, or third, or twelfth. An outcome existed. Still, I couldn't help myself but worry. Had I seen a glint of green eyes? Stop. You have no fear, I told myself, but I continued to grip the stone. With a deep, steady breath, I stood, and faced the direction of the noise. My eyes perceived only dark, ill-defined forms in a still darker night.

Something jolted into my back, throwing me to the ground palms first. I dropped my stone just as snarling teeth penetrated my shoulder. A tooth scraped along my scapula until resting deep in muscle. The weight of the lion pressed the air from my lungs and stifled my scream. Its claws released my hips for a second. My free hand groped for another rock but came back with only sand. I twisted. Flesh tore, resulting in a new rush of pain in my shoulder, but I gained freedom from its jaws. Placing one arm protectively over my neck, I threw my fist of sand at the lion's eyes, but it only growled and pinned me between its legs. Green eyes glinted as it moved to poise its fangs over my abdomen. I lashed at the glowing targets with pointed fingers, eliciting an angry, but still determined, snarl.

Feet shuffled about me, and suddenly a tree branch crashed over the beast's back with a loud crack. The lion spun and swiped with extended claws at the new threat. Screams filled my ears, and panicked legs darted in every direction. A hand took mine and dragged me by the arm through the dirt, away from the attack.

Stars.

A warm, moist sensation spread down my neck and back, causing my shirt to cling.

Lost consciousness.

No longer aware of my body, bleeding out in the desert, I stood behind Keith and viewed myself sitting across from him at the interrogation table. Was I there now? Or, did I view myself in the past or the future? I tried to remember how I saw these things. Let's see, if this were the future, my consciousness would hover behind my body. But I observed my corporeal self, sitting at the table. Was I drugged? My eyes were wide, blue, and unblinking. He'd drugged me every time.

This had to be the present or the past. What did he say to me? I tapped my ears as if I could turn on hearing. In repeat of my experience with Mother years ago, here I viewed an unidentified place in time, unable to discern the words. Keith's voice came into my brain, sharp and louder than he was speaking. My astral self reoriented to stand next to the table between Keith and my corporeal self. The air smelled damp, of freshly poured cement and sweat tinged with fear. Or was it the memory of a scent? Who's afraid?

"When you see this symbol." He held before my unblinking eyes a picture of an obelisk with a Ferris wheel behind it. He replaced the picture with one of an obelisk capped with a gold pyramidion. Beneath the gold, one face of the pyramidion bore a symbol. I didn't recognize it, a zigzag with a bar through it. Wait. Zeus. A symbol for Zeus. Why was a symbol of Zeus hidden on top of an Egyptian pyramid? That can't be right. The other three faces of the pyramidion were beyond my view. They'd have provided context and clues.

"And when you hear this phrase," he continued, "Karnak in the news."

Karnak in Egypt? It was where the obelisk had come from. I remembered now. Paris. The Luxor. I'd seen this obelisk in person once with Jeff. Had Keith stolen this memory from me? Not possible, I thought, as I'd had no prior memory of the symbol.

How to tell; was this now or then? I didn't remember this experience, indicating it occurred in the past. But I wasn't home, so Keith hadn't taken me away for interrogation in the night. Or had he? He'd only ever taken me from my home. But that meant he had knowledge of where I was, in the desert with the other escapees. Or was I with him, being interrogated? Was the desert now, or was this interrogation now?

"I am Bab," he said.

At his words, my astral self flew back from where I stood and crashed into the wall. I recognized the phrase. It was something someone else said … to Vedra … at the Nexus. Was that Vedra sitting there in a trance or me?

Sitting at the table, my corporeal body snapped out of its hypnotic state, blinked, and then looked around the room in confusion as if it hadn't heard the conversation with Keith.

"All right, Aline. You've done well for tonight. Time to go home," Keith said, with signature paternalism. He stood and gestured for the man in the lab coat to inject me with the memory-wiping drug.

My astral self mouthed the words on mute, "But what have you programmed me to do?" Aline stood from the table and was escorted away by an officer.

My astral self slammed into my shivering body, sleeping in the dirt. I sat up, gasped for air, and my hand flew to my shoulder wound, where I felt someone else's hand applying pressure. Crusted blood pulled the skin taught on my neck. Pain is present. The pain assured my mind that I was real and present.

Miguel sat watch over me. It was his hand attending my wound. "Thank you." I eked out. Delirium threatened.

"Sleep, chica."

I fell back to the ground, but my thoughts raced. What had Keith done to me, and why remember it now? I had just witnessed a memory in the astral body, I decided. I'd traveled to my past. It's not that I had never experienced reliving memories in a dream state, but I understood they were memories because, well … I remembered them. I had never witnessed a memory from an astral body state, except past life memories. I had to have traveled there astrally to witness it, allowing this body in this time to remember the experience. Had Vedra directed me to that experience? Did she want me to remember the interrogation?

Keith had programmed me hypnotically; that much was clear. But why? He hadn't interrogated me for some time, that I remembered. I couldn't still be of use to Keith, or our government wouldn't have tried to kill us. Maybe I'd already completed my programmed task—my payment. Why remember this now when I could die of blood loss or a blood clot at any moment.

Light has no mass, I thought. The thought came unbidden. As if Vedra still spoke to me, I remembered her directing me to place the salt crystal in front of the light, and I understood as if she'd explained it to me and I'd just now remembered. A massless third-plane observer, Vedra's consciousness, determined the direction and helicity of one object. Vedra had canceled the void of the hooded entity, sending him away, and causing him permanent harm, if he became incompatible with his native environment. She'd changed the way he moved through my space-time by observing him from her massless third-plane state. And Vedra had to have guided me to the classroom to learn THe equation. I had given credit to the hooded guides, but the teacher of THe equation had been formless.

"Sorry," a man's voice grunted, having tripped over my foot. "Didn't mean to wake you."

"James?" I asked. All concentration ended.

"James?" Emma repeated and ran to greet him. "There's been an accident."

"I'll be fine," I said. "Talk later."

James addressed the others, who were all wide awake, but he couldn't see that in the dark. "Sorry to wake you all up. Everything is OK. Go back to sleep. We'll talk in the morning."

Few slept after the mountain lion attack. James had given us little information on the other threat. I hated to sleep with unanswered questions rolling around in my brain. I wanted details. Jeff used to do that. He'd say: let's talk about it in the morning as if the unidentified *it* was something to look forward to. Jeff must have enjoyed taunting me. I fingered my wedding ring, wishing I was in bed next to him, sleepless and tortured by the promise of irritating discussions in the morning.

Julie took a spot on the ground near Kera, and James picked his way through people to his kids.

Sleep was impossible. After assuring Miguel that I'd survive to see morning, I thanked and dismissed him to get some rest. Then I took over applying pressure to my wound while contemplating mortality until dawn. The Mourning Doves cooed just before the first bits of light filtered into camp. I watched my compatriots, some of whom eyed me with worry. But I worried more for them. Was I a danger to them—programmed? Did Keith know the future? Had he foreseen our escape? Had he let us escape?

It didn't take prescience to know this was coming—this whole fake pandemic they'd used to capture the genetic mutants. Keith claimed he'd tried to fix the government's bad gene edits with the last pandemic-vaccine campaign, but it hadn't worked. Had I told him we'd escape? No. Our escape remained uncertain. My orientation to time had become muddled. Perhaps the injury had caused me delirium, but I didn't think I'd lost that much blood.

Kyra and her brothers stirred, and I watched them with guilt. Had I put them at the mercy of Keith's plans against their wills? I hugged my knees to my chest and rocked. The safest thing to do would be to leave them all. Gowen and Gatlin, my newly adopted brothers, stirred. Gatlin rubbed the sleep out of his eyes and looked for me as if to make sure I was still alive. I'd been staring at him and looked away.

Scott slept not far away. Poor kid—alone. I'd stopped him from returning to his parents. He would have been happier with his parents, but I thought he'd be safer with us. A jab of pain seared my shoulder to remind me both of the danger I'd put us all in and my questionable judgment.

James stood and stretched. He jostled the shoulders of his kids, and Emma startled awake as if a threat loomed. I had encouraged them to escape. The family had trusted me. Kimo thought I was good, trustworthy. He didn't know I was a mole, a plant, contaminated, an unwitting traitor. He'd always had my back.

Soon, we would leave camp. James wouldn't chance us being caught or discovered if we hadn't already been. If I was going to leave them, now would be the best time to go. I was injured, a burden. I had to choose now. Perhaps if I stayed behind and lit a fire, a distraction to provide them time to escape our pursuers? But why did the pursuers watch us? Why not come off that mountain and arrest us all? That they weren't interested in us, lent credence to the hunter theory. I got up and stumbled my way to James and Emma, stopping along the way to regain balance from dizziness.

"Can I talk to you guys?" I wrung my hands.

"You should lay down, Aline," Emma said, using her motherly persuasions.

"In private?" I started to turn my head toward the others, but the pain prevented the motion. Some stirred and woke from the noises of those already awake.

"Kids," James said, "the three of us are going to scout the trail ahead. Stay here and tell everyone to keep out of sight."

"Right, Dad," said Malia. She shot me an uncertain look.

Before I followed James and Emma, I gave a glance at the others. If I stayed behind, I would never see them again. Shame filled me. I deserve to die alone, I thought. This whole cockamamie escape plan had been my idea. But James will salvage it. He will lead them out of here, I reassured myself. James had an actual plan and a safe place to go.

"You should sit." Emma's voice held concern. She reached to remove a strand of hair from my eye. Her hand hesitated, and my fingers went to my cheek.

"Ouch. I didn't know it got me on the face too." I probed my cheek tentatively. "Just a bruise there?"

"It's a real shiner," Emma said and raised her brows, but her eyes went to my neck.

I stood stiff and determined. "What did you find last night? Was it hunters?" I asked James.

"Not sure," James said. "We got pretty close without being detected. We saw two large vehicles. Trucks like the ones we'd escaped in, and a flatbed. Didn't look like hunters. But there were only a few men. It doesn't add up. What would they be hunting with those trucks? King Kong? Also, there's a rail line over that ridge. It's possible they're doing something with the rail line, something they don't want anyone to see if they're military. Bottom line though, if they were after us, they would have come for us already."

"That's what I thought." I paused, considering my next words. I was used to people dismissing me. I reminded myself that their son Kimo had been abducted and that they believed. "I ... I ..."

"What is it, Aline?" Emma asked.

"I think I should stay behind, just in case." Words eluded me.

"In case of what?" James asked.

Emma grabbed his forearm. "Your injuries?"

"No. I'll survive." The reassurance rang false, even to my own ears. I wasn't sure how long I could deal with the pain without rest. My collarbone throbbed, likely fractured by the lion's bite, but that kind of injury was rarely serious. Blood soaked my torn shirt. The tear revealed a fang puncture in my brachial plexus. While not deep enough to have nicked my lung, the wound had probably grazed an artery or major vein and had definitely damaged a nerve. Half my arm pulsed with a numb pain, and three fingers couldn't flex. I couldn't see my scapula, and I didn't want to. There were no major arteries back there, though, so I tried to ignore it. The injuries posed a clot risk more than anything. No new blood oozed, only clear exudate, and the puncture hole was cherry red, both good signs.

"It's hard to explain, but I had a ... memory." I drew the word out, unsure of how to explain an astral experience to them. "Last night ..." How to begin. I wouldn't tell them I'd seen one of Kimo's past incarnations. It didn't seem relevant, and I didn't want to lose credibility. "Uh. The military interrogates me after my *experiences*." I pointed up. Why did I avoid the words alien or abduction? "Anyway, I remembered one of those interrogations last night. They may have hypnotized me to do something, and I don't know what." I winced. "And, the point is, I might be dangerous to you all."

Emma sat on the ground and put her head in her hands. "But you'll be a danger to us if you don't stay with us. You know where we're going, Aline!"

The other escapees knew too at this point. Emma and James had told everyone around the fire. Anyone following us could guess by drawing a line south on a map and discovering the only inhabited places along our route, but it was still important to Emma that we all stayed together, it seemed.

"What should I do?" I asked as though I sought their approval. I had disappointed them. Fear of judgment and fear of abandonment lashed at my ego. Subconsciously, my good arm wrapped itself over my abdomen, holding my emotions together. "I'm sorry. I don't know what they did to me. I don't know what they want."

James started asking questions, the same questions I'd asked myself last night while sitting awake in the dark. "Why? They wouldn't have put us in quarantine and tried to kill us all, only to let us escape," he said.

Let us escape? The question stuck in my head, but I kept it to myself. "I agree. I haven't heard the trigger words yet, but I think I know what they are." Or did I? "Karnak in the news" was to be my wake phrase, along with the obelisk and the symbol. Together they were a trigger. I hadn't *seen* my trigger symbol yet, I realized, and I wasn't likely to out here in the Utah desert. "What if I'm chipped or have a tracking device? That girl, Robin—who wrote in blood on the door—said she'd had a chip in her neck." I clenched my hand and paced back and forth to distract from the pain.

James said, "You should stay with us. They've taken Kimo before too. If you're programmed or chipped, maybe they programmed or chipped all of you. They do that kind of stuff in the military."

Point taken. Of their family, only Kimo carried inherited mutations. James had likely received edits in a vaccine during his military service. But he didn't seem to realize he was one of us and the source of Kimo's mutations. In quarantine, hadn't he said that Kimo was the only one who'd tested positive in their family? Stop being suspicious, I told myself. You have to trust people sometimes.

"I won't pose a risk to you all," I said. "I just can't. I couldn't live with myself."

"We'll figure it out," he said. Worry wrinkles formed in the corner of his eyes as he gazed far into the distance.

"If I stay, I'll light a fire. It will throw them off and give you time to get away," I offered.

"You're going with us," he ordered, his tone final. "Now, as far as I can tell, Emma, the girls, and I aren't programmed or chipped. So, tell us your trigger word, and we'll try to stop you from doing whatever you're programmed to do."

James didn't rattle under stress, I thought with envy. "Good idea," I said. "It might be this symbol." I grabbed a stick and drew the pointed obelisk, then next to it, I drew the zig-zag symbol of Zeus in a triangle. "Or, it could be the words 'Karnak in the news.'" I stopped for a moment, concerned I might inadvertently trigger James.

"What does it mean?" Emma asked.

"Nothing," James said, unaffected by the words or symbols. "It's just something nobody else will ever say to her. And I don't think we'll be seeing those symbols." He put his hand on my arm. I flinched, and he pulled his hand back with an apologetic wince. "Aline, they want something. All we can do is resist, or give it to them."

"If it helps, I think the shut-off phrase is 'I am Bab,'" I told him, in case I became a homicidal maniac, and they needed to unplug me.

James and Emma repeated it to themselves.

My gaze traced my stick drawings in the dirt. I'd lost too many battles, I thought, and here I was smack in the middle of another unwinnable situation.

"We'll light the fire and leave it burning," James said. "That will give us time."

"What if it causes a brush fire? It could give us time or kill us." I ruminated out loud.

"It's the only distraction we have." He turned to walk back to camp.

"What if they don't know we're here? If we light a fire, we may as well shoot off a flare."

He stopped and turned back around. "If they aren't hunters, we'll see them again. It will prove they're waiting for us to do something."

Julie came up behind James. "Oh, sorry. Didn't mean to interrupt." She dragged Joe by the arm. "Just going to clean him up again." Her eyes shone hard on James as she edged by us on the trail. Then she stopped and bent to inspect my dirt drawing. "Art?" she asked me pointedly.

Emma or James were just as likely to have drawn it. I thought it curious that Julie had attributed the drawing to me. Joe got loose from Julie's grip and kicked dirt over my drawing. She grabbed him up in her arms and said something into his ear as she walked away. After a few paces, he stopped squirming. James shot Emma a troubled look as if he didn't want her to say anything.

We returned to camp, and I thought of the discussion along the way. I didn't want to be alone, but I was hesitant to put them in danger. Why would someone want to watch us, I wondered?

CHAPTER 37

2009 NARCOLEPSY

K arla, I'm on the privacy list. Dr. Mignoret can't dig through my medi-cal records." I explained to Karla what had happened with my mammo-grams. It violated patient rights, and I was a patient. Dr. Mignoret should at least receive a warning that she'd broken the rules, to my mind anyway.

"Well, we don't know that she dug through your records."

"Really? How did the billing lady pull her name from my chart, then?"

"Do you have proof?"

"If you hadn't rescinded my access to patient records, I'd have proof."

"I'll have someone look into it, Aline, but I'm sure it was a simple mistake."

"Mistakes shouldn't cost me five hundred dollars."

"Sounds like a billing issue."

Infuriated, I stormed out of her office. I'll be damned if I pay one red cent for that mammogram, I swore under my breath. They'd drive me to hire a lawyer yet. I took the stairs to the tenth floor, to Dr. Mignoret's research office. She was an adjunct at Emerald City University, so the chances of find-ing her here were slim, but I stomped through the halls on a mission anyway.

The front desk receptionist tried to stop me, but before she could get the words out, I barked at her, "I work on the eighteenth floor. I don't need an appointment."

"But she's not in the office," the receptionist squeaked. "I was trying to tell you; she's giving a presentation." She pointed in the opposite direction. "Lecture room A-5. Can I leave her a message?"

"No! I'll find her in there."

"You don't intend to disturb her presentation … I hope?"

"No," I mewled, mocking her tone. "I'll wait until she's done. I won't have her slipping out the back door before I talk to her."

"I think I will take lunch now." She grabbed her lunchbox adorned in children's cartoons, clicked her computer off, and ran to the elevators.

Prudent, I thought as I marched my way to Lecture room A-5. I opened the door a fraction, crept in, and took a seat in the back row. The lights were off except for the projector.

"Welcome." Dr. Mignoret stopped her presentation to acknowledge me. "Better late than never."

"I wouldn't miss the opportunity. Please continue."

We were about the same age. I'd never had cause to dislike her or her research, but this was personal, and it had cost me money. Besides, researchers digging around in auditors' private records was a big no-no in my book. The patients didn't have the luxury of opting out of researchers digging through their records, but the Research Department had afforded that benefit to its employees. I couldn't be the only employee who didn't want my coworkers digging through records of my every sneeze and PAP smear. Some of my coworkers looked like they had venereal diseases. Mean, but true. And the HR lady looked like she harbored a nasal gnat farm. Something strange going on up her nose, for sure. Though probably not worth digging through her medical records to find out what.

"As you can see from this film," Dr. Mignoret continued, "identifying breast micro-calcifications as benign or precancerous is at least partly dependent upon the cluster pattern."

I shuffled in my seat, crossed and recrossed my legs. Part of me wanted to shout and confront her before her peers—not that they'd care that she dug through my records.

Dr. Mignoret's expression turned devious. "This next film is special." She changed the film on the projector. The profile of a breast mammogram filled the wall in black and white. "Rarely do we see such *density*." She stopped, and I felt her eyes on me in the back row. Or perhaps I imagined her attention. "This tissue is in the ninety-ninth percentile for breast density."

My physician had told me I had dense breast tissue. How rare could it be?

She continued, "As you can see, finding micro-calcifications in tissue this dense is nearly impossible." She circled an area that apparently held the calcifications, and I squinted to see. "Sometimes *density* impedes good research." My gaze drifted to the top of the screen where her marker now rested, pointing to a name—my name. My name and my breast, up on the wall for my coworkers to ogle. "But not if we expose it first." She paused and shot me a challenging grin.

No one pointed out that she'd failed to remove patient identifiers before sharing the private information, and I wasn't about to stand up and exclaim "that's my boob." She'd made her point, called me dense, and hinted a threat to *expose* me like a schoolyard bully.

I stood up to leave the lecture and slammed the door behind me. I had begun to suspect my coworkers targeted me for causing an inconvenience to the lucrative vaccine studies. Over the years, I'd kept audit and ethical findings private, sharing results only within our department and our committee, but the researchers talked, and Karla talked, and now they'd set against me. The Director wouldn't fire me, so others worked in concert to drive me out. Pack of hyenas. It's what happens to whistleblowers, or anti-vaccine terrorists, or other similarly labeled and stigmatized workers. It's what was happening to me.

The swine flu vaccine studies were in full swing. On numerous instances, Karla made a point to tell me how few adverse events had been reported. She said I'd worried for nothing and declared the vaccine safe. Of course, they hadn't analyzed data from medical records, as they were still giving it to millions of people, and it could take a year to collate the vaccine records into the medical records, but in Karla's world, it was safe. The only adverse events they could review, at this point, were ones that got collected immediately after the injection. A discredited anti-vaccine terrorist, who was I to question? I didn't have access to patient records or the clinical trials anymore, so neither validating safety reports nor auditing was possible. Tammy ruled clinical trials now, and Karla rubbed my face in it.

I still had occasion to review the Federal Drug Agency (FDA) website and came across new safety bulletins regarding the pandemic swine flu vaccine. It seemed one manufacturer's version of the vaccine was linked to autoimmune narcolepsy in Finnish children. In Seattle, pregnant research patients had received the same vaccine as the Finnish children. The law required us to notify our patients of the new safety information. I printed the flier to bring to the team meeting. The secretary took meeting minutes that Karla would later alter, but at least I'd have a few lame witnesses.

I reached for my printer to grab the flier copies. Through the glass, I saw the Human Resources lady standing outside my office door, motioning to me.

"Sure, come on in, Freda." I waved her in. "I wasn't doing anything anyway," I said under my breath. Before she opened the door, I added, "But keep your nasal gnats to yourself."

"Aline, I'm afraid there's been a complaint," Freda said.

"About?" I asked, trying to sound innocent. I was sure Dr. Mignoret must have complained that I'd disrupted her lecture.

"Your shirt."

Surprise didn't cover the range of emotions I felt cross my face. I almost laughed. "Someone without a sense of humor?" I wore a red t-shirt I'd had specially made. In white script across my back, it read: *Too Big To Fail.* I thought it was funny. To me, given my extra-small body, it meant: don't fail the little guys—we may outnumber you.

"It violates the dress code."

There's a dress code? My lips pursed, I sat silent for a moment, deciding whether to take offense. I was the only person on this floor who regularly wore business attire. True, since they'd removed my access to patient records and demoted me, I'd stopped taking work so seriously. But *in* all seriousness, Karla dressed as if she was on her way to Woodstock, but in colors appropriate for Santa's elves. The payroll lady tried to pass off flannel pajamas as clothes. And what about that stats guy who moonlighted in a band? Hair, strung thin, came down to his knees. He wore a thrift-store, maroon-velvet vest. Jesus. Velvet! Even the Director wore polo shirts and khaki trousers that hung below his gut, and he had money to afford a suit or at least a belt. It seemed the dress code didn't cover gut overages.

"So, do you want me to go home and change?" I asked.

"No. That won't be necessary. Just don't wear it again."

"Will do, Freda." I swiveled my chair to face my computer, but she didn't leave. I looked over my shoulder. "Was there something else?"

"No. That's all."

I resumed my computer work, but HR Freda remained seated, staring holes into my back. Did she want me to bring up Dr. Mignoret having stolen my mammograms? If she wanted me to broach the subject, I would not. Of course, the possibility existed that Freda was plain weird. That fit too.

"I have a team meeting," I said and locked my computer screen before standing up to go. "I'll just leave the door open. You go ahead and rest here as long as you like." With my FDA fliers and notepaper in hand, I patted her shoulder on my way out the door.

Including Tammy and Karla, I handed the printed fliers to the five people present from our ethics department.

"What's this?" Karla asked. Today's earrings resembled a nursery mobile, something meant to train infants to recognize primary colors and shapes—strung parts that spun just beyond grasp to prevent an infant from ripping them free of their taunting orbits and devouring them in a suffocating slather of saliva.

"New relevant information," I said and took the farthest seat so as not to temp myself.

She scanned the page. "I don't see how it's relevant. We haven't had any reports of narcolepsy, and none of our patients were children."

Across the table from me, Tammy bore a smug expression atop her recessed jaw while two other departmental staff squirmed in their seats. Karla had already seen this notice, I realized. Otherwise, she couldn't have known there were no reports of narcolepsy in our patients.

"That's good," I said. "I wonder, did the informed consent form say we'd notify patients of new relevant information that might affect their health or willingness to participate?" The statement was required; my question was rhetorical. Patients didn't have to have been specifically harmed for us to have to notify them of any new risk of harm, and all patients had received the consent form.

"I'll have a look," Karla said. "But that doesn't make this relevant."

"The patient population was pregnant women, if I recall."

"Yes, not children, and I've pointed out that we didn't have any reports of narcolepsy."

"So, someone has looked for narcolepsy for no reason in the infants born to those pregnant women?" I asked. "This notice just came out."

"I'm sure they have looked," she said, flipping through her notes as if moving on to the next topic.

I was sure they hadn't looked enough, but it didn't matter. If I knew Karla, she'd throw the notice in the trash at the end of our meeting.

"I wonder, how can they tell if an infant has narcolepsy?" I asked rhetorically. "And how long does it take to diagnose an infant with narcolepsy when the symptoms are excessive sleepiness or suddenly falling asleep?"

No one wanted to cross Karla except me, but the others still chuckled. I continued, "Are there any babies that don't suddenly fall asleep?"

"Well, there's no evidence the vaccine crosses the placenta or causes this narcolepsy condition in the unborn infants," Karla said.

How could she know if the vaccine did or didn't cross the placenta, I wondered to myself. "There is no evidence because we were the only trial site who studied that version of the vaccine in pregnant women. Our study would have the only evidence, if there is any, and you'd have to look for it to find it," I said, struggling to keep contempt from my voice.

Tammy interjected, "The FDA notice doesn't say anything about notifying patients."

"That's because CID has stated that nobody in the U.S. received this version of the vaccine as *treatment*. Which we know is not exactly the truth. Our patients received it, but for them, it was considered research, not *treatment*. We still have to notify our research patients." I pursed my lips shut.

Centers for Infectious Disease (CID) had played such ruses in the past. They were more than happy to say there was no evidence of various side effects, but then they'd leave out the itchy detail that there wasn't any evidence *because* no one had searched for it or studied it. If unflattering data reared its ugly head, CID, the National Institutes of Health and Research (NIHR), or the manufacturers would commission a study to show the data couldn't be reproduced. The contrarian researcher would withdraw the offending publication, tail between legs, or be denied future NIHR funding. After the dust-up, contrite contrarians, if they played their cards right, might have found themselves in the employ of the drug company, working on unrelated but well-funded research.

The current scenario wasn't much different. Tell everyone—nothing to see here—no one got that vaccine here—doesn't apply to us—nope. When our researcher finally published study results, the materials and methods section would conveniently leave out which version of the vaccine they gave to our pregnant participants or purposefully fail to state the trade name of the vaccine, an error of omission that buried the results for anyone keyword searching for journal articles. Nobody would notice; they'd assume each manufacturer had produced the same exact vaccine.

I knew why they went to such lengths to lie, CID, that is. They didn't want people filing claims to the Vaccine Injury Compensation Program. The government protects itself from lawsuits, just as our healthcare organization did. I took a calming exhale and reminded myself that I'd invaded Tammy's territory. This wasn't my job anymore.

"Thanks, Aline," Karla said. "I will pass this on to the principal investigator."

If at all, our researcher would look for adverse events in the medical records for only six months after birth because the other vaccine studies had only reviewed patient records for adverse events six months post-vaccination or less. Some studies had only reviewed patient records three months after the investigational vaccine was administered. It never mattered how many months or years symptoms took to develop or diagnose, or even how many months most people could wait for an appointment with their doctor; they'd only look for reported adverse events in the medical records the same amount of time post-vaccine.

They'd never find a narcoleptic baby in six months based on reported symptoms. No parent would bring a four-month-old in to the doctor and say, "Doctor, my baby is awake and then, for no reason, suddenly falls asleep. Is something wrong with her?" Testing was the only way to find narcolepsy in the infants, but it required calling the mothers and informing them of the possible narcolepsy side effect.

Based on her response, Karla had already had a discussion with our legal counsel. And if I knew her, she had preformulated leading questions to get the answers she wanted out of him. I could almost see the lawyer on the other end of her line. A man of stature, the fat fucker, surrounded by stacks of buried complaints to be forgotten. He'd shift in his leather office chair to avoid pressuring the hemorrhoids he'd earned. In his head, he'd acknowledge the probability we'd get our asses sued and rough-calculate the damages. And then he'd think to himself, why tell the mothers at all? If they never knew, there would never be a lawsuit. Even if a child were eventually diagnosed with narcolepsy eleven years later, they'd never link it back to this vaccine … this vaccine that CID has claimed no patients in the United States received. He'd keep his job but still have to sit on hemorrhoids. I stopped daydreaming as Tammy wrapped up briefing the group on the studies she'd been assigned.

"… so interesting and disgusting," she said. "They use a margarita blender to liquefy the donor poo and then inject it into the infected patient's rectum." Fecal Transplant was the latest treatment for antibiotic-resistant *C. difficile* and was still considered investigational. I hoped Tammy knew enough to ask the physicians to screen the donors like they would organ donors or at least blood donors.

"Do they use a turkey baster?" Karla asked, and the others laughed.

"I don't know, actually," Tammy said, tapping her cheek.

After our departmental meeting ended, I returned to my office. My email instantly dinged with a message from Karla. I opened it. My presence was no longer necessary at the departmental meetings, the email said, but Karla would be happy to meet with me one-on-one.

To avoid passing Karla's office, I took the long way around to the conference room. Occupied. Then on to the breast pumping closet, where I shut myself in, turned off the lights, and locked the door—deep breaths. I've done what I can. No one left to call. Can't call patients (don't have access to records), can't call Wall Street Walt, can't call FDA (blacklisted). Breathe. Let go, I told myself. Already tried a few journalists and a private attorney. Nobody wants to touch this because to do so will brand them, as they have branded me, labeled and stigmatized me ... anti-vaccine.

Noises emanated from outside. No one on this floor nursed an infant, I thought with irritation. Someone tried the handle. A knock sounded.

"Are you OK in there?" a man's voice asked.

That guy's definitely not nursing an infant, I thought. "I just pulled my back out," I lied, calling through the door. "Stretching it now. I'll be out in a minute."

"OK. I just saw the lights were off, and ..."

"Well, I'm not jerking off in here," I snapped. They could fire me for that, I thought, instantly regretting my choice of words. I held my breath, waiting for a response. Silence. "I'll be out in a minute."

Too upset to face anyone, I waited for the nosy person who had knocked to go away. Sometimes, this place was like a Homeowners Association, I thought. Not allowed to use the breast pumping closet unless I'm actually breast pumping. Definitely not allowed *in* the breast pumping closet unless the lights remained on. Note to self. I imagined a notice on the door tomorrow: *This space is for the exclusive use of persons requiring breast pumping. Anti-vaxxer terrorists will be shot for trespassing.*

I put my hand on my lower back, exited the sacred breast pumping space, and fake hobbled back to my desk. I should email Freda about going home sick for the rest of the day, I thought. She'd need to mark it down for payroll.

A new email dinged into the inbox, stalling my plan. Notice: Within one week, all eighteenth-floor employees will be required to receive the novel H1N1 pandemic vaccine to continue working, whether or not you interact with patients. Since patients receive treatment on the eighteenth floor, we will protect ourselves and our patients from the new pandemic threat by receiving the vaccine. Drop in to the eighteenth-floor clinic when your schedule allows for the free vaccination and Wellness Program genetic markers testing. Wellness Program surveys are available online. Complete yours today to receive a discount on your premium.

I shook my head in disbelief. They couldn't legally require the employees, or anyone for that matter, to get an investigational vaccine. And the Wellness Program nonsense went against that GINA law I lobbied to pass. Employers are not allowed to collect genetic information. I smacked my head.

Without knowing if they'd administer the questionable vaccine, I refused to get it at work. Besides, I no longer trusted my coworkers. I'd find a public health clinic offering a different manufacturer's version and stand in line for hours before I got it at work—no need to email HR. Instead of a sick day, I'd have an excused medical appointment. I allowed myself a coy smile as if I'd outwitted the opponent until I realized I'd only outwitted weird Freda, which was akin to outwitting the barista. Then I realized I wasn't sure I had outwitted the barista in the first place. We played a stupid game in which each of us dug our heels in and claimed victory. Anyway, I had bigger outwittings to perform in this circus. Time to focus; find a public health clinic.

CHAPTER 38

DAY 6, 2020 SHINTO KAMI

When we rejoined the camp, James relayed the plan to the group without explaining the hypnotic programming part. He put a few men to work building the decoy fire and explained we'd leave it behind to flush out our pursuers' intentions. Were they hunters or the government? We'd leave as soon as the fire was lit.

The danger of our situation hung in the air on unsaid words. Kera hugged Joe and finger-combed his hair. Art took his shirt off and whipped the dust out of it. Sandra sat with her back against a tree, and Scott walked off into the bushes with a scowl on his face. Kyra held Cameron's hand and kneeled before him, whispering encouragements or prayers in the tones of an older sister practicing maternal instincts. We'd come so far, I thought, but it felt like an ending, at least for me. How far could I get with this injury?

James and Miguel ringed the fire pit in a small wall of sand and rocks. One of the other men pulled loose branches from brush nearby to prevent sparks from spreading fire. Gowen and Gatlin took turns twisting a branch in kindling, trying to ignite a spark. I supplied the pitch I'd saved between leaves in my pocket. Some of the pitch had leaked and effectively glued my pants pocket together. With a wince, I applied one of the leaves to my wound as an antiseptic.

The fire ignited with the pitch. "Terpenoids," I said, giving the twins a knowing look.

"You're a noid. Noid bucket!" Gowen teased, and I choked back pride.

"Line up at the trailhead," said Emma, getting everyone ready and accounted for departure.

"I'll go find Scott," I said to Emma. He hadn't returned. The task of walking both heightened and distracted me from the pain.

I set off in the direction I'd seen Scott leave the camp. I presumed he'd gone to go relieve himself, but he'd taken too long.

Scott sat on a ledge overlooking an expansive valley of red-rock monoliths. I sat beside him and bit back a groan of pain. "They're waiting for us," I said.

He didn't budge. What went through his mind? Turmoil was plain on his face.

The morning sun illuminated the thorned pod of a Jimsun plant at the edge of the cliff. Both of our gazes turned in the direction of the sunrise. Venus glinted above the horizon. We watched a moment in silence but were startled when the seed pod burst open and flung its seeds over the cliff's edge.

"Sprung!" I borrowed the slang I'd heard the kids using.

Scott chuckled, but then his serious expression returned.

With a grunt, I stood and placed my toes near the edge to glance over the rim. How long would the seeds fly on the wind before finding a crag of sun-baked stone in which to germinate, only to wait in stasis until revived by spring rains? A divine, fresh wind drew up the face of the cliff and entered my lungs, causing tingles in my feet. The mother nightshade swayed proudly next to me. It devoted its perennial existence to creating seeds. Having received the light and the divine nourishing breath of the creator, the plant gave everything to the seed. Why? For the benefit of the creator. To perpetuate the infinite cycle, it disperses its progeny and starts a new beginning, a new creation, mirroring our own processes. Love is light and divine breath, the keys to the gateway of perpetuity.

Scott stood up next to me and looked over the rim as I did. Loneliness seeped from him, taking my breath away. For a moment, I thought he might jump. "Your parents are always with you. Here." I placed my hand on his heart.

He nodded but looked away.

My mind wandered to my loved one. Jeff, you're with me, right? I'd see Jeff again. I looked into the morning sun and let it fill my heart. He'd be with me in other lives. He'd always been with me.

"Time to go, kid. Destiny awaits."

"Right," he forced the word.

We walked back to camp in silence. When we arrived at camp, the fire flamed. James poked it a few more times with a stick. A plume of smoke rose, and he dropped the stick. With James in the lead, we broke camp to face an unknown future.

Except for the percussive sounds of feet on decomposed stone, crunch shsh, crunch shsh, which grated my nerves, we walked in tense silence. Every time we rounded a corner or a hill, James stopped our momentum to scout the area ahead. The downcast expressions of the others revealed what each of us understood; if the military were around the next corner or hill, we were as good as caught and as good as dead.

I tried to remain positive, telling myself our pursuers had fallen for our fire ruse back at the camp. But that ruse would deter them for only moments. At best, we were twenty minutes per mile away from camp. That put us about three miles, or four and a half kilometers, away. I wished Sandra would sing something to calm my nerves.

Art, the unbeliever, broke the silence first, "Maybe they're using you all as bait to catch an alien." He chuckled under his breath. Pen glared at him.

Some people made jokes to comfort themselves, and some used humor to mask the truth. The first night of our escape, Art talked about the abuses his people had endured; he was black. It made little sense for him to set himself apart by poking fun at our differences. Many of us believed in *aliens* or at least something different. Perhaps he denied the truth, or he thought he was the only sane person in our group.

"You all?" Terra, the traumatized girl, challenged Art. "You're one of us, Art. I saw you with the aliens."

"I told you, I don't believe that. You can ..."

She cut him off. "Stop, right now, or I'll remind you what they made you do."

The group kept pace. Terra stepped to the side to get an unrestricted view of Art, who walked a few persons ahead of her on the path.

Art did not respond.

"You remember, don't you?" She rolled her eyes and nodded her head as though she'd outed his secret.

"He might not remember, Terra," Julie said, in defense of Art. "The mind-wipe doesn't work the same on everyone."

"He knows what he did," Terra said to Julie behind her, without turning around or averting her eyes from burning holes in Art's back.

"They make you do things. You can't hold it against him," one of the other men said. It was the guy that paid for fueling the cars.

Miguel nodded agreement.

I stayed silent for fear I'd done something I couldn't remember. After last night, I was certain the military programmed me. Obviously, some of us withheld information out of fear or embarrassment. I didn't remember ever meeting any of my fellow escapees, yet Scott and Kimo recalled encountering me. Terra remembered a trauma. She'd seemed the most distant from the outset. Well, except Kera, but Kera thought I wanted her kid. Or did she remember something I'd done? Had I given her any other reason to hate me? I let myself fall to the back of the group by pretending to stop and retie my shoes.

Multifarious memories blipped through my mind. Coded, embedded, identified, and retrieved in disordered packets of information. Fifty-two pickup. Part of me wanted the complete picture. Another part of me wanted to hide from the truth, like Art. The things I couldn't remember would keep me up tonight.

"Somebody change the subject, please," Emma said from the head of the line, deflecting another quarrel. She pinched a cramp in her waist as she walked.

Two nights without sleep and hiking all day without water had not improved my ability to compensate for blood loss. My heart beat in a weak but frenzied rhythm, hypovolemia. More irritating, a fly had been hounding me for the last twenty minutes, attracted to my blood-soaked shirt. I swatted at it with little conviction. The corners of my mouth itched with crust, but my feet moved in automated motions, and I wondered if this was reality or the road to hell.

The group stopped, and people scattered to the bushes to relieve themselves. I hadn't peed since yesterday. Gatlin sauntered up to me as if he had not a care in the world. Such a positive attitude, I thought. I wished I could adopt his outlook, so I smiled back and swooned at the stab of pain in my shoulder.

"Any nerdy ideas on how we can find some water?" he asked.

"Sure, but we're not going to find it on this trail. We'd need to leave the trail and find some ravines. Look for those Russian Olives I told you about. They like water." I sat and contemplated whether to remove the pebbles from my shoe and decided it would take too much energy and cause too much pain.

James left his family to come check in with us. "We need water," he said, in a flat, matter-of-fact tone.

"You are a mind reader!" I joked.

"No. That's Kimo," he said, still serious. "And Kimo says, we need water."

"Mind reader," I repeated. "You've been on this trail. Is there anything ahead?" I squinted at him standing above. With the sun behind him, his face was a black hole, or maybe I was losing central vision.

"I don't think so. Not on the trail. If we leave the trail, we risk getting lost. Experts have gotten lost out here, and I am no expert."

That worried me. "We have to, James. Somebody is going to get heatstroke, eventually. I'm shocked it hasn't happened already." I verged on heatstroke but tried to remain a leader.

Gatlin said, "We can try to mark our way with broken branches and rocks?"

"Hansel and Gretel?" I asked dryly.

"Hey there, you have a better idea?"

"James, we're going to have to go west, closer to civilization. Closer to people," I said, looking at him for approval.

"Why?"

"Because in the desert, civilization happens where water is." I scratched my head where the fly landed and dragged a hand down my salt-crusted face. "If we go east, we're less likely to find water. As I recall, there's nothing between here and the Rockies."

"That sounds right. West it is." He turned and went to relay the plan to the group.

"Wait. James?" I stopped him.

He turned, fatigue apparent on his face. I'd thought him practically superman until now. Sandra and Emma looked worse for wear. Miguel sweat more than anyone I had ever seen, but he hadn't slowed. I'd stopped sweating; no water left in me. The young fared the best. The only signs of strain they showed were red cheeks.

"What if Art is right?" I asked. "What if they're using us as bait?" I hadn't considered the idea in-depth, but just now, it made me feel a little less culpable, as though I hadn't put us in danger. We'd done it to ourselves.

"Well, I guess it buys us time." He shrugged, as if it didn't matter to him one way or another what the military was up to. I supposed the attitude came from years of serving someone else's mission. "Don't call any aliens, and maybe we'll stay alive." He waited for me to respond. I sat with my mouth open.

As if I could call aliens at will, I thought. But James was right about one point. Our priority at this moment was survival, not strategy. Had they programmed me to lure an alien? The military wanted information on THe equation. I couldn't give them enough information. Did they use the escapees to attract an alien to capture?

Gatlin responded, "Can anybody here get those aliens to do what they want, anyway? Seems to me, we work for them."

There was that phrase again, the one I'd repeated to Keith multiple times. I felt so manipulated. I didn't know whom to trust. The military used us to get to the aliens; the aliens used us for some undetermined purpose. Maybe this was a test to see if we'd survive—test the survival genes they'd given us.

So far, our survival had relied on James' leadership the most. He had to have acquired genes from a vaccine during his time in the Marines. I suspected he had an increased IQ, and, if not his son's psychic ability, James had serious intuition. I couldn't believe Kimo's mutations were new to their line, even if James claimed that only Kimo had tested positive from their brood.

I could trust them, I reassured myself, eyeing our band of escapees. At least, I hoped I could. We all wanted to live. Besides, with or without a will to survive, I'd come to care for them. I didn't have children, but Scott had been alone, without a mother, and I'd connected with him in quarantine; he'd accepted my motherly advice. And Emma. At first, I'd thought her a bully, but she was a mama bear, willing to do anything to save her children. Kimo always had my back. And James, so stoic and steady. And Sandra, who shared more emotionally with us than a deep conversation just by using her voice. And my adopted brothers. If I never saw Jeff again, these people would have to be my family. Jeff. A lump of self-pity formed in my chest.

"I'll ask around," said James, "but from what I've seen, Kimo never invited the aliens to visit him. I assume it's the same for everyone else. They come on their terms."

I squinted my eyes and pursed my lips, reviewing my experiences in my head. The *aliens* had come to me. I hadn't sought them. The one time I'd sought them by trying to return to the underground caverns landed me painfully punished. My fingers burned with the memory of the energy ball. Once, I'd tried to telepathically contact the angelic woman in white, but as soon as I connected, my consciousness flitted out. How many contacts had Vedra performed in my place? If she knew what was good for her, she'd stay away.

James marched away with purpose, to inform the others of our new direction.

"I hope the canyons to the west aren't impassable," Gatlin said to me.

I hoped the same thing. I wouldn't make it, traversing a deep ravine only to find no water. With assurance I said, "Water cuts ravines into sedimentary rock, and we are surrounded by …" I waved my good arm wide as a panorama.

"… sandstone." He finished my sentence and snorted.

Perhaps we *had* relied a bit upon my survival skills, I thought. We each contributed in our own ways.

CHAPTER 39

2009 SUBJECT OF—SUBJECT TO

I arrived at my vaccine appointment early. No public health clinics had appointments available, but my Alma Mater would let me get it free at the university hospital, and they were testing a different version than the one associated with narcolepsy. Not that it meant it was any better. I had no way of knowing.

The front desk clerk, a surly woman of middle age, gruffly handed me a clipboard and pen. "Sign the marked areas and return this to me."

With great irritation, I signed the overly generic consent for research without the doctor present, which was against standard procedure. The unapproved vaccine was technically research, but this consent form lacked any mention of the vaccine at all. Because I had to get the vaccine to appease my work, I signed the form and returned the clipboard to the receptionist.

"You know, I have questions about this form."

"Save them for the doctor." She took my papers from the clipboard and left the room.

A medical assistant called me back and showed me to an exam room where I waited for the doctor. Considerable time elapsed, and I walked out to the front desk to see about rescheduling, but no one sat behind the desk or in the lobby. The med-tech seemed to have disappeared too.

I returned to my exam room, sat on the padded and papered table, and studied the colorectal anatomy diagrams that hung on the wall next to a framed Washington State medical license bearing the name of a Dr. Greenbladt. Just as I was about to give up waiting, an older male physician and a woman in scrubs walked into my exam room.

Without introducing himself, he reviewed my paperwork, folded the top page in half, and stuck it in his pocket. Odd, I thought.

"Well, Aline." His smile struck me as practiced, and he still had not introduced himself. I'd begun to worry, but it was just a vaccine.

"We're almost ready for your procedure."

I frowned. Procedure? I'd never heard a vaccine referred to as a procedure.

"I'll just have you lean back on the table, and the nurse here will take care of everything."

I'd never leaned back for a vaccine before, either. I looked at the nurse questioningly, but she went about preparing a tray with a butterfly needle and a vial. I'd never had a vaccine with a butterfly needle either.

She inserted the butterfly needle into the top of my hand.

"Wait. I'm just getting the swine flu vaccine so I can go to work. What are you doing?"

The nurse stopped and looked to the doctor to answer. He turned around and seemed to consider what to say and then, without answering my question, he told the nurse to "Proceed" and turned back around. She reached for the vial with an apologetic expression.

"No, you don't. What are you doing?"

"Doctor," the nurse said, "she does not consent; I cannot anesthetize her."

"She signed the form," he said.

"I'm here for a vaccine," I said and sat up. "That's what I made the appointment for—a vaccine. I did *not* sign a consent form that mentioned anesthesia. I think there's been a mistake."

The doctor approached my exam table and pushed me down flat by my shoulders.

"Nurse, continue."

"I am not allowed to anesthetize anyone without their consent," she said.

I started to breathe heavily. "I don't consent. What are you doing? I grabbed at his hands, but he pushed harder."

"Nurse," the doctor said, "I will see you fired if you don't complete this now!"

Her face twisted into a tormented expression, and she wouldn't meet my eye. I had begun to cry and struggle against the doctor's grasp on my shoulders. The nurse was quick and plunged the anesthetic into the butterfly line, sending pain into my wrist from the speed and pressure she'd injected it.

"That's it." The doctor's grip on my shoulders relaxed, and I went limp. "This is a teaching institution. How are the students supposed to learn if we don't have patients to teach them."

"What are you dooooiiiinnnggg?" My voice slurred in protest, but my consciousness faded.

The room spun, and sleep coaxed me back under. Wake up, I told myself. I fought the anesthesia and bolted upright on the exam table. A sheet fell to my waist, exposing my breasts. No gown. No underwear. An auditorium of empty chairs faced my exam table, which sat perched on an elevated stage. A row of privacy screens stood useless behind my exam table. Movement from the corner of the room caught my eye. There stood a young man in a white lab coat, jerking off over a plastic waste bin. A gag forced its way up my throat.

"Who are you? Where is the doctor?" I screamed, but it came out gurgled. Still too weak, I struggled to get off the exam table.

"You're awake." Startled, the man zipped his pants and ran towards me with his hands out as if to discourage me from getting up. Drug resistance genes on Chromosomes 6 and 16. These people didn't know my medical history. He obviously thought he'd have a lot longer alone with me unconscious on the table.

"Get away," I said and made an uncoordinated leap off the exam table. With a raucous clang, I crashed into the bedside metal tray.

"I'll go get the doctor," the resident said and ran from the room.

My hand flew to my genitalia where cold slime wet my fingertips. Tossed from the metal tray, lay a tube of lubricant on the floor next to me. I sighed relief. The wetness wasn't sperm but lubricant. I didn't think it was, anyway. I stood and retched, but nothing came out. On the other side of the table I noted a reel of cable.

Another lab-coated man came into the room from a door behind the privacy screens.

"Who are you? What did you do to me?" I snatched the sheet from the table and covered myself.

His eyebrows raised in surprise. "I am a resident with Dr. Greenbladt. You consented to this colonoscopy, teaching procedure."

"I consented to no such thing." I took in the room; the chairs faced my exam table, and there was that reel of cable next to the table. My folded clothes sat on a chair next to the table, along with my purse and coat. I edged toward my clothes, clutching the sheet to my chest and not turning my back on the doctor.

"I'm sorry if there was a misunderstanding. But your doctor made the appointment for you. I presume he explained the procedure to you."

"I was here for a vaccine. What doctor?"

"Let's see here." He held my chart and flipped through the pages. "We gave you the swine flu vaccine while you were under. No point in feeling the pain. And ... the doctor's name is not here, probably because research is not for treatment purposes. Hmm. A referral from your HMO. No name."

"Get out!" It didn't matter who did it. Most of the HMO physicians had privileges at multiple institutions—access to more patients and medical records that way. Keith's goons could have had a hand in it. Whoever had done this, had done it on purpose just like Mignoret had stolen and displayed my mammograms. Message received; they'd make sure I'd give in and quit.

He started to make apologies I didn't hear. "Get out!" I screamed again, and he turned and walked straight-backed out of the room.

I never dressed so fast in my entire life. One arm in my coat, and shoe-less, I ran from the lecture hall through the hospital lobby before they could do something else to me. Someone I worked with switched my vaccine appointment to this "teaching" colonoscopy in front of a class of students. I wondered which of them hand selected the student who watched me recover from anesthesia—the guy jerking off in the corner.

A young resident stopped me in the lobby. "Are you alright?" he asked, looking at my bare feet.

"Yes. Leaving now." I jammed my feet in my shoes, squashing the heel parts flat.

"Thank you so much for letting us learn from you. Dr. Greenbladt is a genius." He shook his head and looked up with idolatry in his eyes. "It was just great."

I swallowed and shook my head, no. This student had just stopped me and thanked me for having a colonoscopy against my will. My eyes darted between the other people in the lobby. Had they all seen me naked and assaulted? Another student walked by and waved hello. What was that supposed to mean? Had she seen me naked and compromised? My brain rattled with images of the student jerking off in the corner, and panic gripped me. I ran. Shoving the resident out of the way, I ran and ran, limping on shoes I hadn't secured to my feet. I ran, propelled by a familiar fear, a fear I hadn't felt since I was seven.

When I'd run out of breath, and blisters formed on my feet, I stopped and collapsed on a bus bench. A disheveled woman approached and asked for money. Unresponsive, I stared ahead numb and blank, and she left grumbling something about me having had a worse day.

Where had I parked? The contents of my purse looked like foreign objects; I could hardly remember the uses of the items, but I dug for keys. I needed keys. Orienting to my location, I realized the car was three campus blocks back in the direction of the hospital.

Somehow, I limped back to my car. I didn't recall looking for it, or finding it, or the drive home, for that matter. When I pulled up to my house, I parked cockeyed in the driveway and crushed a sprinkler head at the edge of the lawn. Once inside, I tried to remember if I put the car in park and decided I didn't care. I stripped out of my clothes, and got straight into the shower.

Once I'd steamed myself red, I stepped out of the shower and pulled my robe from the hook. The hook ripped out of the wall and clanked on the hexagonal floor tiles. Plaster powder floated down like snow, sugar coating the hook and the floor. I left the hook curled on the floor, a useless thing, lying in repose, white dirt thrown on a casket, and I went to bed. Tears poured until my eyes puffed shut, and I couldn't breathe through my nose.

Jeff rushed in, still in his coat. He sighed, sounding relieved to find me. "What's wrong?" he asked, but his voice held fear.

"I don't want to talk about it; I can't talk about it. I'm not going back to work. Ever."

"I don't understand. What's happened, Aline?"

"It doesn't matter. I just can't go back there."

"That's OK. I'm here for you."

"I know you are. You're always here for me."

Fully clothed, he got in bed behind me and scooped the covers around me, squeezing me to him in a secure embrace for hours until none of it mattered. I had Jeff.

My work couldn't get to me anymore, but the government could. As surely as Keith's diabolical and flawed plans would require another round to get every last mutant in their database, I knew one day this pandemic scenario, or something like it, would repeat. Like widows wearing black for a period of mourning, they'd wait until people finally forgot—the extinction of a conditioned response.

The money was too good; money bought cooperation. With government-issued liability waivers, there was only money to be made—money to researchers to administer the vaccines or drugs, money to healthcare organizations for access to their patients, and money to pharmaceutical companies to hastily create a vital drug or vaccine. The scheme grew its own economy, attracting the types who knew no one was watching, corporate psychopaths, government psychopaths, and prosocial physician psychopaths—a club of players in a system.

Silencing dissent, silencing me, was in the interests of all the players; too much rode on it.

CHAPTER 40

2010 TAKE COVER

Journal of Aline Orr: January 14, 2010. There was an article in the Free Press Review today. No surprise, but it seems the Vaccine Injury Compensation Program (VICP) is not accepting injury claims related to the pandemic H1N1 vaccines. Instead, they are referring people to a newly created program called the Countermeasures Injury Compensation Program (CICP). It seems the VICP doesn't cover injuries from investigational vaccines. I had warned Karla to get their promise to pay in writing, but I suspect they never made such a promise. The patient consent form fraudulently promised patients that costs of treatment for adverse events would be covered under the VICP. Some have already complained that the new CICPs claim requirements are too stringent, and the program is underfunded. To top that off, I discovered that the new program (CICP) will, likewise, not cover injuries to pregnant women or children due to any of the pandemic H1N1 vaccines unless the CID issues a statement advising pregnant women and children to receive the vaccines as a priority group. They have yet to issue such a statement. Their rules state that all injuries must be proven, documented, and diagnosed within one year. One year is an impossible limit to meet, especially if you don't know the risk association, to begin with, not to mention the time it takes to diagnose complicated issues (e.g., average eight years to diagnose some autoimmune diseases).

This revelation had to be the reason Karla and the lawyers refused inform our patients of the risk of narcolepsy to their children. The HMO lied to the patients, gave them false assurance that they'd be covered or compensated if something went wrong. That lie, willful negligence, meant the HMO was liable for the adverse events. I'm pleased to no longer be employed by criminals.

CHAPTER 41

2018 THE INTERIM

H ow'd it go?" Jeff asked the moment I walked in the door. Rather than face his expectations straight off, I should have gone for coffee to clear my head before coming home.

"I told them I retired early." We'd been discussing what I should tell people when I decided to finally re-enter the work world. It wasn't a paid job I'd applied for, but a volunteer position as an administrator at a free local health clinic. "I think they thought I was a trust-fund kid. That, or they think you're loaded."

"Nothing wrong with that. What they don't know won't hurt them," he said. He sounded like Karla, I thought, but that wasn't fair. I detested dishonesty, but I'd come to learn a little deception was necessary in my case. Nobody hires a whistleblower. Enough time had passed, that potential employers wouldn't be calling my previous employer for references. Besides, Karla had finally retired, leaving no immediate supervisor to replace her.

"Aren't you excited?" he asked. His expression was joyful with anticipation.

I dreaded it, actually. "I think it will be good to get out of the house," I said, another deception, but there was some truth in it. The job could do nothing to heal my mistrust of people or the cynical outlook I'd acquired, but I owed it to Jeff to get back to some semblance of normal.

During my "interview," I'd tried to pay attention to the woman interviewing me, but my focus trained on the poster behind her. For most of the interview, she did the talking, relieving me of having to lie. The inspirational poster behind her read: *If you want to help people, all you need to do is walk out your front door and find someone to help.*

The helpless were everywhere; it was true. People needed help with all kinds of things. They didn't have to be research subjects to need help. The old lady down the street had just lost her driver's license, I remembered. "Jeff, we should go see if Sharon needs us to pick up her groceries." Jeff, of course, had discovered the fact about her license. He met people every time he stepped out the door.

"Well, let's go knock on her door now. Ready for a walk, Dog?" Dog groaned himself up onto his arthritic legs, and I fetched his leash.

Jeff's cellphone rang, and we rolled our eyes at one another. Dog looked confused when Jeff left the room to talk to Keith. "In a minute, Dog," I told him, and he lay back down where he stood by the door. We had moved away from Keith, and for the most part, Keith had left me alone, but he still called Jeff more than a few times a week. With less than coincidental timing, he'd call just as we were walking out the door.

Keith had gotten all he could get from me. In the monitor-only stage, I was no longer of serious interest. That I could recall, I stopped having experiences; whether that was from a change in my mental state or because of the vaccine, who could say? For all I knew, the periodic solar minimum might have quelled my experiences, but I wasn't about to ask Keith. Still, I had a sinking dread that Keith's National Intelligence people would be back at some point to make good on whatever it was I'd promised Keith or to perform the final vaccine mop-up operation, as he'd referred to it. I hadn't expected to live to the year 2018, but then Keith's was a long-game operation.

While Jeff was on the phone, I snuck into my office and flipped through my folio of pressed plants. I had resumed my childhood hobby of collecting and identifying plants, but my focus had changed to wild edibles and medicinals. A deceptive alien had once told me that I'd teach people to survive. The plants had something to do with survival, I reasoned, but the truth was, I didn't really know what the alien had meant. It didn't matter. I enjoyed my plants, and Jeff approved of the hobby. It gave us reasons to travel and, more importantly, to reconnect.

I eyed my desk with hunger but resisted the temptation. Jeff did not approve of my other hobby, the one requiring three computers and late nights. The endless search for the grail, he'd called it. With contractual privacy protections in place, I'd spent a lot of money paying a discrete company to sequence my genome and create a rather cumbersome database from which to search it. And, from their preserved locks of hair, I'd even had Mother and Grandmother sequenced. I had to know what they'd done to us. My discoveries led me to believe that Keith had either held back or that our other, seemingly innocuous, mutations had far greater importance than he knew. That meant some of our mutations had not come from the government's gene-editing programs.

Jeff worried and called it "obsessive behavior" when he'd find me slumped over the three computers, one for each of our genomes, mine, Mother's, and Grandmother's. He said I needed to get out of the house. For at least two years, I'd searched late into the night for SNPs and sequence anomalies indicating shifts, deletions, duplications, or possible translocations. When I wanted to spend more money on blood tests to confirm some of my suspicions and pay a pathologist to conduct cell structure studies, Jeff drew the line. "Aline, you do not have your own lab or your own funding, and we cannot afford to fund hobby research." He was right, of course. I'd wanted to tell him my work was important, but the truth was, it was only important to me. And since I had never told Jeff I carried alien genes, he didn't think it healthy that I pursued the cause of my "rare connective tissue disease" with such fervor.

In public datasets, I'd found startling groups of mutations similar to my own. More startling were their prevalence in the population. I'd identified a few *chromotypes*, I called them, people with whom key mutations (mostly classified as connective tissue diseases) were found on a specific chromosome. The significance of this correlation was that each chromotype had unique neuronal migration patterns. When they developed in the womb (embryonic development), for some chromotypes, neurons would end up clustered together. For others, the neurons ended up in the wrong spot. The point was, the neurons didn't necessarily lose function in their clusters or wrong locations—sometimes, they endowed those individuals with enhanced neuronal activity in those areas of the brain. These developmental anomalies formed the stuff of evolution.

It was all theory, of course, but my theory pointed to the notion that our government couldn't have inserted all of the transgenes. Maybe they were responsible for a few of the mutations, but not all of them. I couldn't say for certain if Keith's people were responsible for inserting genes other than those involved with intelligence. Keith knew many of my mutations, but I'd found still others I suspected he knew nothing about. They were all buried in the plethora of As, Cs, Ts, and Gs that comprised my family in the terabyte graveyard of my database.

It was time to give up the hunt; it was getting in the way, my fixation. I took the journal of my findings and reverently placed the external hard drives—copies of the three genomes—on top. I'd self-censored the journals, knowing only Jeff would read them someday. No point in bringing up the alien bit. If he ever read the journal, he'd probably figure it out, anyway.

A few years ago, legislation passed allowing federally funded research to be subject to Freedom of Information Act (FOIA) requests, so the drive also contained pre-filled forms with details on the vaccines and studies I knew about. The information requests would likely be denied, but at least someone would know where to look if someone decided to look. Keith's group had since reassigned the gene-editing vaccines to a new agency, Gene Drive Division (GDD), but GDD was not subject to FOIA requests.

Finished with his call, Jeff walked in just then and gave me a disapproving look when he saw me standing by the computers.

"You'll need these one day to prove me right," I'd told him and handed him the hard drives and the journal.

A look of pity crossed his face, a look he'd repeated more often lately as if I'd lost my marbles, and I was the only one who didn't know it. Of course, I never told him about aliens or our *friend* Keith. If I had, Jeff might have locked me up. I'd started to wonder if he'd ever believed me about the job

I quit and the whistleblowing, the blacklisting, or that they'd conspired to intimidate me into quitting. That was almost ten years ago. None of it mattered anymore. Someday, Jeff would know the truth, like it or not.

"Just keep them somewhere safe, please."

"I will." He set them back on the desk for later. "Ready for that walk?"

"Ready," I said.

"Good. After we stop at Sharon's, let's do the full loop. A real long one, all the way around the park." Dog walked in behind Jeff. Dog's tail wagged with enthusiasm, but I wondered if he could handle the long circuit. I trotted to the kitchen for his canine arthritis medication.

"What did Keith want?" I called behind me as Jeff put on his coat.

"You know Keith."

I did. Keith wanted our itinerary. Jeff didn't mind his nosy friend keeping tabs on us; it must have made him feel wanted. I had come to ignore Keith, especially since I hadn't seen him from across an interrogation table for some time.

On our way by neighbor-Sharon's house, I asked Jeff, "How about a trip to Arizona next? I think it's almost the season to harvest Saguaro fruit."

"Sounds prickly."

"They use a pole with a cross on the end to pry red fruits off the top of the cactus. I might need your help with that." Even with a long pole, I was probably too short to reach for cactus fruits successfully.

"The things I do for love," he said, raising a brow at me.

Jeff did love me, I thought. I tried not to forget it and batted my eyelashes at him.

CHAPTER 42

DAY 6, 2020 RUBEDO

We had been walking for hours trying to reach water when I started at the sight of a man standing in a clearing to the side of the trail. The vision caused me to feel faint and jump off the trail as if startled by a rattlesnake.

"What is it?" Sandra asked. She stopped the others behind her and searched the area for threats.

My hand at my throat, I fell mute. The man was the magician from the other night—Kimo's previous incarnation. Standing in the sunlight, plain as day, he waved to me to follow him. Then he turned, staff in hand, and walked into a boulder as though it wasn't there. I didn't dare ask Sandra if she could see him too for fear she'd think me crazy. Instead, I looked for Kimo. Just ahead of Emma, Kimo lumbered along the trail. He had just shared a moment in time with an incarnation.

"Well?" Sandra asked, irritation evident on her face.

"Sorry. I thought I saw something. But you know … I need a break."

"Already?" she asked. We'd stopped for a break a few miles back.

James left the others not far ahead and approached us to find out why we had stopped.

"James, I need to stop and think," I said. He smacked his forehead. It seemed even his patience had limits.

"But the river is less than a mile away," he said, pointing to a line of vegetation bisecting sandstone in the distance.

Emma sat with her head between her knees. Kyra had retched twice in the last hour. I'd felt her skin, hot and dry. Heatstroke stalked us all. Stay positive, I told myself; dehydration makes your brain work better; you have to want to survive. But the efficacy of positive thinking had waned.

During today's journey, a few ideas had fermented within our group. While Art refused to admit he believed in aliens, the rest of us agreed with his theory. The government had *let* us escape quarantine to lure an alien they intended to capture. If we were bait, then Keith and his people weren't far away. They were determined to get what they wanted, whether information on THe equation or more alien DNA for their genetic programs. Who could say? One conclusion rounded on me repeatedly: when Keith and his people got what they wanted, they'd have no use for us. He'd referred to us as fuck-ups, mistakes, and off-target effects.

But it was the secondary fermentation taking place in my dehydrated brain sac that brewed a realization to overflow: I am Vedra.

This realization and the vision of the magician had made me stop in my tracks. An overwhelming compulsion to meditate overtook me. I had to clear my head. Vedra and I shared some part of existence, a connection of space or time. Maybe it was entanglement, or something like entanglement, that caused our fates to be tied to one another, with Vedra acting as my counterpart on another timeline or dimension. Understanding why didn't matter. What mattered was that I finally understood that what happened to me also affected her in some way and vice versa. Otherwise, why had she bothered to show me memories of Keith implanting hypnotic triggers?

I stumbled away from the others in the direction I'd seen the magician and darted frantically in search of a clear level spot to sit and meditate. If I connected my consciousness to Vedra's, perhaps she could show me how to get out of this mess. Keith had programmed me to perform some unknown act. Vedra made sure I'd seen the programming, but what was I supposed to do about it? Neither trigger words nor symbols had appeared yet, and I still wasn't certain which phrases were the triggers. Karnak in the news, the symbols, or I am Bab, they all amounted to gibberish.

I plopped down on my butt next to a creosote bush and reassessed my encounters with Vedra.

Vedra had interfered with my interactions with the hooded entity. The guide, I'd called him. She'd directed me to place the salt crystal in front of a light. I had no prior knowledge of such mechanics. Vedra had antagonized the hooded entity, and it had shot me. Why had she put me in harm's way? Oh, dummy—of course—so I'd understand they were dangerous. Better than I knew myself, Vedra knew me, knew I suffered from misplaced trust. I should have trusted her above all. But of all the paranormal entities I'd encountered, I trusted Vedra the least. How could I have been so stupid?

When merged with my consciousness, Vedra had told the insectoids that humans deserved to die after they'd shown me scenes of destruction. I'd been aghast at the heartless response, as had the insectoids. But in startling them, she'd prevented them from controlling me, manipulating me. By telling them I didn't care about the outcome, they'd abandoned trying to make me perform to an outcome of their choosing.

Gowen and Gatlin waded through the brush toward me, I assumed to convince me that we needed to keep moving.

"Go!" I yelled at them. "I'll catch up. You don't understand; I have to do this now. I have to contact her. Find the way out." I have to warn Vedra, I thought. Keith would try to capture her if she appeared here physically, if being physically here was even possible.

Gowen and Gatlin narrowed concerned eyes on me. "Is she delirious?" Gowen asked Gatlin.

"I'm not delirious," I said, although I wasn't certain it was true. I could be in shock from the injury to my shoulder, loss of blood, heatstroke, or dehydration. My eyes went to the wound, and I shuddered, but I couldn't feel it much anymore. The memory of the lion's fangs hurt more than the injury. "I can't explain it. Just go. I mean it; I need total silence. I don't even know if I can do this. Be quiet, for the love of God!"

They returned to where James and the others waited, arms motioning in my direction. Glares of irritation shot my way.

I closed my eyes, took even breaths, and tuned out. Sunlight warmed the space between my eyes. My brain glowed inside the space; I could sense it. I opened, receptive to connecting with Vedra.

To my astonishment, my consciousness found her. Overwhelmed by questions, I almost lost the connection. In the past, Vedra had communicated with me—in a fashion. However, aside from the classroom, Vedra's communications consisted of me seeing, through her eyes, a point in time of her choosing, which is what I now experienced. A scene appeared through Vedra's eyes.

"They better not find out who you are," a bald woman of short stature said to Vedra. The woman sat in a chair with her back to Vedra. She wore a long-sleeved, white empire dress devoid of ornamentation, with a high-scoop collar.

I sensed Vedra considered the bald woman as her mother, as well as her leader like a ruler or a Queen. *I'm her daughter*, Vedra thought, and I received her thought. She admired the woman, but I sensed fear mixed with respect. Vedra had to obey her.

"You risk everything," the woman said.

Vedra said, "They will continue to influence our future if I don't help her."

She meant me. She needed to help me. I understood.

Vedra thought of the hooded entities, and I understood through her thoughts. She confirmed that the hooded beings had come for me in order to control her. The hooded beings hadn't tried to kill me, as Keith had, but still, they sought control. Vedra thought the hooded beings and my government each wanted to control and shape futures.

"I've told you before," said Vedra's mother. "They can't control you, even through her. If you would just meet her plane at the Nexus, you can choose a new path."

"But that outcome is not what I want," Vedra said.

"Let go of your ego, Daughter. Stop trying to control the outcome. Doing so lets them use you as a pawn."

The emotions Vedra experienced as a result of her mother's response rocked my body sitting in the dirt. Her embarrassment stung.

Vedra's mother faced an opalescent wall of brilliant colors. The wall performed a function for her, but I didn't understand its purpose. She still hadn't turned to acknowledge Vedra, and I felt the rejection through Vedra—abandonment. Then I understood. If Vedra met me at my plane, as her mother had advised, she'd never see her mother again. Yet, with the prospect of never seeing Vedra again, her mother seemed detached, uncaring. Why did Vedra show me this? What did it mean for me? I couldn't ask her to sacrifice her relationship with her mother for my benefit.

"Clinging to this time, wanting, your attachment to this existence, I find it appalling, Vedra," her mother said. "This is not how I raised you."

Vedra's head dropped. Through her eyes, I viewed the metal floor until tears of disappointment filled her vision. She longed for a motherly connection. She wanted a hug goodbye but knew her mother wouldn't offer. Vedra steeled herself and thought, *not from that frigid woman.*

"Fine!" Vedra snapped. "May we never meet again."

"Perhaps you will experience my role next time, and you will come to understand my decisions. That is all I can hope for you." She raised a hand to dismiss Vedra, still refusing to look at her.

She's such a hypocrite, Vedra thought. *She wouldn't give up her authority, her rule, but I'm supposed to give up everything.* "But I'm not doing this again," Vedra hissed.

Déjà vu hit me with those words. I'd said them once—that I didn't want to live lives again.

"Goodbye, Mother," Vedra said, approaching her mother's back with determined strides. I gasped, startled that Vedra might intend to harm her mother. Then my consciousness re-entered my battered body in the sand and pain returned.

CHAPTER 43

KETER 2020 BLESSED ARE THE MICE

The little one will become a thousand,
and the small one a strong nation.

(Isaiah 60:22 World English Bible) Public Domain

Julie's feet crunched the soil, and the sound of leaves brushed her clothes, snapping me out of my connection with Vedra.

"What?" I yelled in exasperation. "You're messing it up. I'm trying to get us out of this."

"Aline, I'm going to need you to come with the rest of us," Julie said with authority.

"Why?" I asked, challenging her. "I told James I'd catch up. I'll meet you there."

"We have your husband, Aline. I need you all to stay together."

I didn't budge. Jeff? My mind raced as I sat shaking my head in disbelief.

"I work with Keith," she said.

"What have you done with Jeff?" I jumped up to attack her.

She fended me off with an outstretched arm. "He's safe, as long as you cooperate. You know what you're supposed to do. You agreed to this."

"I did?" I backed away from her. Confusion and mistrust roiled my thoughts.

"You did." She made a simmer down motion with her hand.

No. I didn't believe her. If I held one certainty, I'd never trust Keith. Never.

"Jeff has the evidence to prove you're liars and murderers," I said, narrowing my eyes at her. "He has my blood sample proving I don't have VHF. He'll tell the media what I know. What you've been doing to people." To save me, Jeff would have done anything. A lump formed in my throat.

"As I said, Aline, we have Jeff, and he's agreed to cooperate. There is no sample. We destroyed it along with the results." She paused, letting it sink in.

"I don't believe you."

"Jeff shouldn't have used an NIHR-funded lab. If he'd gone private, maybe, but he used government labs. We didn't even have to mess with a warrant—too easy."

Bob Sherman, I thought, clenching my fists. He was our only friend with access to a lab and the ability to run the test. Poor Bob, sacrificed to my fruitless cause. He'd tried to resist, but in the end, Jeff had dragged him into my drama.

"Why did you bring your wife and son with you?" I asked. The only things adding up were questions.

"Kera and Joe are not my family. That was a cover. Kera is doing what she agreed to do, to gain their freedom. *She* knows how to honor a deal, Aline."

Had Kera and Joe gone ahead towards the river? I scanned the area for them but saw only James and Emma in a heated argument with Kimo. Scott and Sandra milled about with some of the others farther down the trail. What commitments had Julie forced onto Kera? It had to be more than just posing as Julie's wife for this escape charade.

Julie pulled an emergency locator beacon out from under her shirt and pushed the button. "This will signal Keith's team to come get us."

"But, Kimo read your mind. I don't understand? You're a mole?"

"Kimo knows who I am. He trusts you. That's all he needed. He's doing his part too. He's cooperating because he's going to get something out of this. Well, and because I let him bring the others. It should have been a smaller group, but we figured a larger lure couldn't hurt. Why not?"

I wanted her to stop talking, but I still had questions. "So, what is it I'm supposed to do, then?" My feet and neck moved like rubber, and I swayed in place.

"Contact, Aline. We need one of them so we can use your equation."

Everyone wanted to control the outcome, I thought. But Julie didn't understand. THe equation had come from Vedra, not the hooded entities. And I didn't know how to communicate with Vedra that way. She showed me events; she didn't take phone requests. I never told Keith about Vedra, so Julie must think it came from the hooded entities. Even if I possessed the ability to contact the hooded entities at will, they had nothing to do with THe equation. Keith had Jeff. The thought made me desperate, so I played along and said, "So … why don't we return to the others and see if we can make contact?" I motioned for her to shut off the beacon, attempting to coerce my way out of capture.

"No. It's over now. If they were coming for you, they would have done so already. We put you in danger, threatened your lives. A shame, really," she said. She shook her head, but her expression showed no remorse. "It has not attracted a response."

A pang of sadness hit me as I recalled the memory of Robin and those killed in the quarantine center. The aliens know this future already, I thought, but I wouldn't tell Julie. Did it mean we'd survive? Vedra's mother had advised her to stop trying to control the outcome. Perhaps I should take her advice too. Perhaps Vedra had allowed me to witness that moment to teach me something. Stop clinging to this existence, her mother had said.

Somehow, I knew I needed to meet Vedra at the Nexus, but how?

"Time to go, Aline. If you will follow me."

I ignored Julie as my mind grasped blindly for a solution. Frantically, I tried to recall the class and THe equation. I'd learned how to get to the Nexus but hadn't understood it—not smart enough. I smacked my head. Nexus 12—I'd been there. I had to remember how to travel there.

Julie approached me and took my arm.

I jerked my arm from her grasp and stepped backwards.

"Run!" I screamed past Julie to the rest of the group, who still waited fifty meters away. "Julie is a mole! Run! Run!"

"The tactical team will be along shortly, Aline. It won't do them any good to run." She shrugged. "Now, they'll just get hurt."

"Hurt? You're going to kill them anyway." At the trail, I could see the others' heads over the brush, scrambling in confusion. Scott looked in my direction with fear on his face. "Run!" I yelled again. If any of them got away, perhaps they'd survive.

James' angry voice rounded on his kids. From an unseen distance, the sound of helicopters thumped faintly. It didn't mean they were close, I thought. Sound could carry a great distance over sandstone. I wondered if Keith flew in one of the approaching helicopters. Would he observe me one last time as if I was an animal, less than human, running like a mouse from a hawk? Would Jeff be with him? Would he force Jeff to watch my humiliation? In another life, I'd watched helplessly as my loved ones were murdered. Perhaps it was Jeff's turn to watch. No! I could stop this; I had only to remember how.

"You were briefed on the risks and agreed to this. We need more control over who, what, and when these contacts occur." Julie's voice turned into a whine. "We can't have them communicating with civilians without our permission."

"I agreed, Julie? I was in handcuffs and drugged—under duress. You people keep coming up with a million reasons to justify murder. One minute you just want to capture an alien, so you can use THe equation, for God knows what purpose. The next minute you want to kill us, so we don't represent a security risk for you? Keep talking if it makes you feel better. I can tell you don't hear what you're saying."

Just then Kimo came up behind Julie. "I go with Aline."

"No, Kimo. Go with your family. They need you more," I said. He'd always had my back, and I'd dragged them all into this.

"Prima Facie," Kimo said the words as if Latin came naturally to him. The words had been given to us by Vedra. His hands bunched into fists at his sides, and he suddenly appeared heavier and immovable as a boulder.

Julie looked at him, stunned. "Those aren't the words," she snapped. "Stay out of it."

But they were the words, I realized. Vedra had imprinted those words into my subconscious as a trigger to save me from Keith's programming. Vedra paired me with Kimo in the class where I learned of THe equation. He'd been one of the students, but I couldn't remember until now. Kimo released the information with the trigger words, Prima Facie. It meant first face or on the surface.

My vision blurred until Kimo's face focused. As if my brain retrieved it from an encrypted storage file, the information from the class became available to me. The discussion I'd had with the hooded entity about molecules and chiral handedness applied, but he hadn't given me the whole story. He saw the Jimson flower differently because he could see elliptically polarized light, while humans cannot see anything but linearly polarized or non-polarized light. It was part of what I'd been taught in the class that I now remembered.

Vedra had even demonstrated it to me in my kitchen once. Vedra's consciousness had determined the direction and helicity of an object, a controlled outcome. Vedra canceled the void of the hooded entity, sending him away permanently. She'd changed the way he moved through my space-time by observing him from her massless third plane state. Vedra's mother had advised her to do the same to me, I now understood, only at a Nexus, not in my kitchen. But Vedra had disobeyed her mother.

The lessons from the invisible class poured back into my brain. It took two beings on each side—a double combination lock. When Vedra showed me the argument with her mother— Vedra hadn't approached her mother to harm her, as I'd thought—she'd approached her mother to force her to the Nexus. If Kimo and I had met Vedra alone at the Nexus, Vedra could choose a new plane of existence, and one of us, Kimo or I, would likely be destroyed in the same way the hooded entity had been. But if two pairs met, the four planes would become unentangled. A disassembling Penrose diagram flitted into my stream of thought—freedom.

I flashed back to my childhood jump rope games. Two long, crisscrossed ropes made a giant cross; a person held one of each of the four ends. Each person made a wave with their ends of the rope—transverse waves. The waves met at the center and stilled, canceling each other. But in the case with Vedra, if four planes of existence met at a Nexus (like the jump rope segments), we would become disconnected from one another at the cross point, the Nexus.

Still, it was more complicated than that. The waves we traveled through time and space moved something like elliptically polarized light instead of crossed jump ropes. I may never be able to see it with my eyes, but I finally understood.

"Go away." Julie gestured at Kimo to leave the clearing where I sat. After I'd yelled at them, the others had dispersed into the brush. "James?" Julie called after James to come retrieve Kimo.

I tried not to acknowledge that Julie had just ordered James until I saw James approach us. Face downcast, averting his gaze, James walked with what appeared to be a staggering effort.

When he reached us, he said, "Kimo, Son, it's time to go."

"I go with Aline," Kimo responded.

"We did all of this for you, Son."

"Lies, Dad," Kimo said, pointing to his forehead and indicating he had mind-read the truth.

"Please. You'll be whole again. Your mother and I want you whole. Don't make me force you." James' words hinted at a tentative threat, a threat he might not back up with action.

"What's he talking about, Kimo?" I asked.

"They want to *fix* me." Kimo's face screwed up into an angry knot. "But they won't fix Dad." He turned his attention to James. "Will they, Dad? You didn't lie to Aline, so I could be fixed. You lie, or they'll kill you too."

James staggered as if Kimo had slapped him.

At first, I thought Kimo meant they'd sterilize him. But he had read my mind, of course.

Kimo said, "They don't want an autistic son," referring to his parents. "Julie said she would fix me. But I am good, Aline. Like you are good." His voice pleaded for me to understand.

I looked to Julie for confirmation, but she controlled her reaction and stood rigid. I said to her, "You left out the part about you being responsible for Kimo's condition." Suspending judgment, I looked at James and felt only disbelief that I'd been duped again by being too trusting. I couldn't understand what it must be like to have an autistic son or what I might be willing to do to fix it. But James was perhaps as naïve as I had once been if he believed the government would fix Kimo.

Julie threw her hands up in defense.

James looked at me with accusation in his eyes. "You said the aliens did this to Kimo, Aline. Changing your story now?"

"It was alien DNA, but Kimo likely got his alien genes from a vaccine they gave *you* during your military service."

"Aline tells the truth, Dad."

James, hands-on-hips, looked to Julie to refute my claim, but to her credit, she didn't deny it. Without apology, she said, "Your country made you smarter. There were side effects we couldn't have foreseen, but we stand behind our service members, and we're ready to correct our errors. You get to go home, and Kimo will be fixed, just as we promised."

Though short like me, Kimo's Chromotype 1 mustered unusual strength in a thick form. With a fire-eating glare, Kimo bent his head and snarled, "I don't want to be fixed."

"Son, we can still salvage this. If you don't want to be fixed, that's fine, but we should all leave together, otherwise they will kill us."

"I go with Aline."

"Why?" James' voice went thin as if about to cry. If he forced Kimo, he'd likely never be forgiven, but could he let Kimo decide for himself when staying with me meant certain death?

Julie slinked to the side in an attempt to withdraw from the argument.

"Dad, I can't do what I'm supposed to do if I go with you. I know you love me; you have to let me go."

Julie asked, "What are you supposed to do, Kimo?" She sounded hopeful like she thought there might still be a chance he could conjure an alien.

Kimo rounded on her, pumping his fists in frustration. "I can stop you." He spat at Julie, and she gasped with an indignant look on her face.

Appearing to have accepted the inevitable or simply tired of arguing,

James approached his son and turned him away from Julie. "I'm proud of you, Son, just the way you are." He embraced Kimo in a long, tight hug. Kimo did not resist until the thumping helicopters lowered to hover over some of the others who had fled into the brush.

A few hundred meters away, I thought I could make out Scott and Sandra's heads above the brush. Emma and the girls were now out of sight farther down the trail. Without turning for a last look, James ran to the trail to rejoin the rest of his family.

"The deal is off, James," Julie yelled at James' back.

"I don't think they programmed Kimo to do that, Julie," I said, grinning with satisfaction while she wiped Kimo's spit from her face.

"What? What are you talking about?" She backed away from Kimo, who faced her again like an angry bull ready to charge.

"Karnak in the news," she said in my direction, without taking her eyes from Kimo. "Karnak in the news," she repeated, sounding desperate. When neither of us responded, she hurriedly pulled a paper from her pocket and held it at arm's length in my direction. The paper bearing the obelisk's pyramidion and the symbol Keith had shown me, trembled in her hand.

My vision blurred, but I walked to her outstretched hand and snatched the paper. Unaffected, I held the paper up close to my widened eyes. Then I met Julie's eyes, and my hand crumbled the paper into a ball and chucked it over my shoulder.

Julie licked her lips. Recognition that the triggers hadn't worked crossed her face, and she winced.

With a voice thin from fatigue, I said, "I am Bab." I taunted her with the shut-off words I wasn't supposed to know, the words Vedra made sure I'd learned.

Julie gulped for air and started to say something but stopped.

"That's right, Julie. Your mind games won't work on us." I wavered on my feet.

Julie straightened to look beyond where we stood for the backup she'd called. "You hear those helicopters?" she asked, pointing to the black specks in the distance. "They'll be here any minute. What's your end game here, Aline? They have a million ways to subdue you."

"They're good at that," I said, pursing my lips and remembering how they'd drugged me and cuffed me to a table. "My end game, Julie? Watch and learn."

"Kimo, we're going to Nexus 12. Ready, partner?" I asked.

"Ready." He held his fists out for a fist bump. "Wait, Aline." Confused, he dropped his fists as shook his head.

"This is ridiculous," Julie said. "I don't have time for this." Less than a kilometer away, military men repelled from helicopters. "We'll be back for you," she said and then turned and waded her way through the brush in the direction of the helicopters.

"Aline, wait!" Kimo interrupted. "Not twelve. Not twelve," he said and clapped his hands on the final, not twelve. "Twelve is the other one. Not with me."

"Why not twelve?" It was the only Nexus I'd visited. Where else could it be? Did he mean twelve was the Nexus where Vedra picked one path? How did he know that? I'd left the class early.

"Do the math, Aline." He nodded his head, appearing to agree with himself.

"The math?" I said, incredulous. "I can't do that math. It's way beyond me. Where do we go, Kimo?" Couldn't we have done this before I was almost dead from heatstroke and blood loss, I wondered? Why had Kimo waited so long to trigger me? Why now?

Having read my mind, he said, "*Now,* is the time," as if that explained everything. He shook me by my injured shoulder, and the pain roiled, blurring my vision. I panted and sat on the ground, too tired to go on. "Be the equation, remember?"

Kimo sat next to me. "Aline. The numbers. The next ones. The guy said the numbers on the speaker. REMEMBER?" His hands fanned in encouragement.

What numbers? I accessed my lesson, but I'd never learned a solution to the formula.

"The guy they killed. The guy," he repeated, sounding frustrated.

"The veteran on the intercom in quarantine?"

"That guy—that guy. The numbers!" He flapped his hands in an attempt to make me comprehend.

"He said he was four and fourscore years old." I tried to remember what a score was from Abraham Lincoln. "So, twenty times four, plus four, is eighty-four. Is that it—Nexus 84?"

"No. No. No. Just the numbers." Frustration amplified on his face.

"Forty-four?" Random guesses were far from doing the math. Still, at the time the veteran had used the phrase, it impressed me as meaningful or imprinted. He'd made a joke out of the clinical features scoring system and used it as part of his age. Maybe forty-four was the answer. Perhaps the veteran had been in our class too. Maybe *being the equation* meant willing it— all we had to do was pick a solution and believe it as a kind of observer effect.

"Forty-four. Yes. That one, Aline." Kimo let out a relieved sigh. Somewhere inside him, there was a way to relate to him, I thought, watching his frustration to convey meaning. He could read my mind, but I had a hard time even guessing what he meant.

"OK, let's do it!" I crossed my legs.

The helicopter noise and concomitant pressure of impending capture made it difficult to focus. It could all go terribly wrong. In fact, I half expected failure. But I took Vedra's mother's advice and tried to unbind myself from the desire to control an outcome. I had nothing to lose. Release all fear, I told myself.

Kimo sat, and we faced each other. "Do we hold hands? Or how does this work?" I asked, holding my hands out to him but expecting he'd resist.

"OK." With a shrug, he surprised me and grabbed my hands. He closed his eyes, and I followed his lead.

I felt him in my head. How had he done that? It wasn't foreign or uncomfortable. It was sharing a consciousness like I'd experienced with Vedra. I'd never understand this, but it didn't matter; we just needed it to work.

"Stop thinking, Aline," he said out loud.

"Sorry."

I remembered Vedra having approached the dark void, and the voice that responded to her had said, "I am Bab." But that was at Nexus 12.

"I am Bab," I repeated, trying to share the memory and experience with Kimo. Maybe he'd know how to use it.

My forehead tingled, and his consciousness mingled with mine. A golden circle appeared in my mind. I recognized this circle from my childhood when I fell from the tree. Steps led to a dais, and a faintly-lit inverted triangle appeared within the golden circle, but this time no creature of Saturn awaited on the dais. With my consciousness now paired to Kimo's, we walked up the steps and peered over the edge into a vast expanse.

From this vantage point, I realized the triangle was much larger than I thought. It was an octahedron, an eight-sided diamond that reminded me of the symbol from the obelisk Keith had used, only twice over. Two pyramidions; one pointed up and one down. Mother said there would be diamonds. In the dark, the eight fire-lit surfaces of the diamond appeared vague but just visible from the precipice. Symbols engraved each of the surfaces, but I could only make out the symbol on the surface closest to me. I'd seen it before, a chiral symbol if you viewed it from two sides. My gaze ascended, and a tinge of fear crept into my brain, fear I'd lose something to the expanse. I'd lose identity.

"Release fear," Kimo repeated my mantra to me.

"To the vessel comes the fire," a familiar female voice said—the voice of Bab.

"Is this death?" I asked Bab.

"All existence is creation," she answered.

A shiver traced up my spine. I suspected that meant, yes, you are dead or dying, but I tried to put it out of my mind. I eagerly looked to identify the remaining symbols; four symbols repeated top and bottom, but as I searched, they blurred.

"The name of God is not available to you, little one," the voice said. Though not malevolent, the voice conveyed power, and I trembled.

"Why?" I thought. I hadn't meant to question, to be disrespectful, but my thoughts were available, not private.

"What do you hope to accomplish with this name? Power? Control?" Bab asked.

"None of that." But, then I realized I didn't know what the name did or why I wanted it so desperately. Did possessing the name give one power? Keith would want that name, but I had hidden it from him.

Wait! I knew the name; I remembered it as if it was stitched into my being at the beginning of time. Air, Earth, Fire, and Water, the name spoken on the breath of the four winds, written in stone by fire, and consumed in the waters of life and resurrection. Stop. I told myself. I'm not entitled to use the name. "Stop trying to control the outcome," I said out loud. I didn't want to live forever. I didn't want to be reborn. "I surrender."

"Then you shall be free," Bab said.

Kimo's consciousness was still with me. We jumped from the edge of the dais and spiraled as birds on a helical draft into a promise, a covenant.

Flash. Time stopped. There is no time.

Upon reaching the apex of the pyramidion, a thousand rays of scintillating white light emanated like a burst star. Prismatic rainbows flickered in and out of view, riding each beam of light. Infinity, I recalled, resided in the rainbow-ribbon of light. I'd been unable to integrate into it before.

There were no boundaries, walls, or direction. No up, no down. Yet, I had the sensation of free-falling. The body we shared had no physical form. It was male and female, child and mother, the fire and the vessel.

With my mind, I searched the expanse and found Vedra. Opposite each other, we circled a clear orb. We spun until four faces flickered as if wrung free from a palindrome. Vedra's mother was with her, and Kimo circled at my side.

I had only ever seen through Vedra's eyes and had expected her to resemble me, but she looked unrelated, I marveled. Like her mother, Vedra had an ovoid-shaped, bald head, glowing bluish-white skin, and dark blue eyes like mine. Her mother's face flashed, and the round head morphed into the image of my mother. All time was simultaneous, I recalled my mother telling me when she'd appeared to me in child form. At the time, I wondered if the child was my mother, but I now understood. Vedra's mother and my mother had perceived existence through the same points in time. The Now.

Vedra and her mother had argued before meeting us here, and Vedra had brought her mother to this Nexus against her will. Yet, they appeared resolved as though none of the resentments they'd harbored mattered anymore. Awareness rippled through my remaining fibers of being. Things I had wanted and situations I had fought for at once became irrelevant. There's no going back, I thought. Release all fear; release attachment.

"Kimo," I communicated telepathically, "are you connected to these two, like I am? Are their fates and yours linked, as mine?"

Kimo's voice entered my head and said, "I go with Aline." Without explanation, I understood that we are all connected if we want to be—if we can comprehend connection—a conservation principle. There wasn't anything creepy about it. Kimo hadn't replaced Jeff. Jeff belonged to this life, and we'd shared other lives. Kimo and I had circumnavigated one another through many lives as well. Vedra had paired me with others who were able to perform this trick of consciousness, this travel without time. A dual combination lock, I couldn't have opened the door on my own.

Remorse swept over me—remorse for underestimating Kimo, for seeing him as an impaired, autistic kid, limited, as if he hadn't once been my sister, mother, husband, or friend in another life. He'd probably been overlooked and dismissed as insignificant his entire life, as had I ... as we do to each other. Yet were he not here with me now, we couldn't end the construct. We couldn't teach you how to survive what's to come.

"What's next?" I asked.

Kimo's consciousness controlled my incorporeal hand, and I took hold of one of the thousand rays of light and bent it until it crossed the helical path we'd traveled to enter this place. We sent the thousandth ray back to where we'd come from, to our previous existence—a gift of mercy.

Vedra and her mother reached forward to touch the orb, and Kimo and I followed. A synesthetic experience greeted us, enveloping us in a most melodious chorus of angelic voices, swirling in the form of golden, glittering smoke.

Had I always been able to do this, I wondered? I suppose I had. It was born into me. Did they give it to me genetically, or was everyone capable of the achievement? It no longer mattered. This was why they'd called me special. Not because I had genes that confer survival traits, as I'd let my ego believe, but because I used my consciousness to create my future and your future, free of attachment, free of wanting. One can choose from many paths, live them all, or one, or none, or repeat them over and over. Without fear of death or rebirth, the constraints of physical existence are no longer required of me.

For those who died, for those I can't save, for the people who kill each other, it already happened, it happens, it will continue to happen. Because you suffer, I suffer. We suffer together. If evil exists, it exists because each of us contributes to the conditions that nourish evil's ability to exist. We define the environment, the parameters of operation.

Flash. I am at once, all time. I choose your path, I steal your choice, and I am your liberator. We are creation. Forgive us.

I've taught you how to escape, my pickles. Now I will sing.

> *Journal of Aline Orr:* Time does not move; it is all that is, was, and will be. Our consciousness exists in positions in relation to time; it doesn't move through time. It picks a spot from which to observe, and then we cling to that spot of existence as though that moment in time and our consciousness's experience of that moment are reality. Space does not move. We create space. Our mind creates space as a coalescing of parts—a closed system in which to operate—a trap. We devise a box in planes of existence—time and space—and then we place our consciousness in the box and tape it shut—a trap set to prevent our own escape. As if we prefer imprisonment inside the box of our own making, confoundingly, the very freedom that awaits outside the box causes us to shudder in fear.

Vedra and I could have collapsed the wave, but we changed our minds. Selfish of us. Mother warned me I'd get stuck on a path if I'd observed my entangled self in the grayscale world. I would have been stuck in that existence, an existence created from a state of blindness. The observed path is the chosen path. Observation is singular. Now I control my path. No longer pawns in the hand of fate, Vedra and I chose freedom. Four waves intersect, two in each plane, entangled pairs of equal mass and energy. The waves disconnect. Disconnected, they become un-entangled from time and space. This is the Now. The Now does not move. The Now is eternal. All time is simultaneous.

The anchorman spoke in a monotone. "Decontamination of the nation's quarantine detention centers is underway. None of those who contracted VHF survived. All succumbed to the disease, alone, away from family and friends. God rest their souls." He turned his talking notes over and continued in an upbeat voice. "Equities markets have rallied after containment of VHF and a lower than expected death toll."

The anchorman spoke in a monotone. "Decontamination of the nation's quarantine detention centers is underway. Those who survived returned home to their families over the last week, but without knowledge of what happened to them. All survivors experienced amnesia as a side effect of VHF. Those who perished have been cremated, and their remains are being returned to families this week. God rest their souls."

The anchorman spoke in a monotone. "A small group of VHF positive patients escaped the federal quarantine detention center in Everett, WA yesterday, before officials caught and returned them to quarantine. Authorities have stated the escapees did not make contact with anyone or spread the disease before their capture and that the event does not represent a risk to the public."

The anchorman spoke in a monotone. "The husband of one of the quarantined VHF patients, claiming to have proof that his wife did not have VHF when she was first detained, has admitted to authorities that he fabricated the story in an attempt to have his wife released. The authorities have dispersed protesters outside of quarantine centers nationwide."

The anchorman spoke in a monotone. "Terror in the streets of Everett, Washington tonight, as a group of VHF positive patients escaped federal quarantine to run screaming through the streets claiming that they were never sick and that the government was trying to kill them. Authorities have captured all of the escapees and have stated the breach poses no threat to the public. CID would like to assure the public that those in quarantine are receiving the highest level of care by experts in the fields of virology and immunology. Though few are expected to survive, all are being kept comfortable with every attention to meeting their needs."

CHAPTER 44

2020 THE PURPOSE, THE MEANING, THE SHARING, THE PATH

Journal of Aline Orr: To forgive anything, one must realize that people do the best they can with what they are given. If they have been harmed, they may harm others. In this way, we are meant to share suffering. The cycle is disrupted by giving love and light and showing them another way. Give light to the seed.

Science and spirituality intersect. It is, of course, more difficult to explain spirituality in terms of science, but it is possible when we gain enough knowledge. Every religion, philosophy, and esoteric practice provides the solution—every one. We can find it in all of them or one of them or find it for ourselves. The answers are available to anyone open to finding them. Find wisdom in everything.

Thought creates. As the hooded guide and Saturn figure both predicted, I came to understand creation through nature. The three-thousand-year-old butterfly dream made me realize that I create by perceiving existence—the observer. But I also came to understand that I created existence in order to cling to it out of fear. True liberation comes from destroying the self—destroying the desire to create a reality in which "I" exists. Release the Self.

I understand the purpose of this existence, my purpose. 11:22:33:44.

11: Discover your purpose.

22: Put this discovery into everyday practice.

33: Teach others to discover their purposes and to put them into practice. Teach by example. Teach by doing. We are here to help each other.

44: Fulfillment. Release all fear. Want nothing. Let go of the Self. Surrender and achieve liberation from your prison construct. Infinity 8.

AFTERWORD

Having previously worked for many years in medical research ethics (a.k.a. IRB), I understand a few of the reasons why the public has lost trust in pharmaceutical companies, medicine, research, and our United States government. In 2017, I started writing *Sing the Mice* to provide an entertaining venue to explore these ideas. I am not anti-vaccine. I received a Tetanus booster while writing this book, and I have received more vaccines for work and travel than anyone I know. When my priority group is called, I will likely get a Corona Virus vaccine because I want to participate in solving the problems we currently face. I cannot comment on the research or safety of the new pandemic vaccines because I am not privy to that information. I do believe corporate interests and conflicts of interest in the drug development process, the ethical review of the COVID vaccines and research as a whole, should be subject to greater transparency requirements, additional oversight, and a very serious independent audit.

ABOUT THE AUTHOR

J. Daneway resides in Tucson with her husband and their blind dog-baby. A syncretist and a dabbler in the esoteric arts, she spends her free time researching, reading, writing, crocheting, cooking, and walking circles in the desert. Although university educated in the sciences, she will not tout almae matres until she has learned to forgive them, an act easier said than done. *Sing the Mice* is her first published novel.

If you enjoyed this book, please take a few moments to write a review. Please also visit www.jdaneway.com for the author's blog and for updates on future books.

www.ingramcontent.com/pod-product-compliance
Lightning Source LLC
Chambersburg PA
CBHW031545240626
47153CB00002B/385